GATEWOOD

A HISTORICAL NOVEL

TALES FROM THE LIFE AND TIMES OF LIEUTENANT CHARLES B. GATEWOOD

Do your duty in all things. You cannot do more, you should never do less.

Robert E. Lee

In every battle there comes a time when both sides consider themselves beaten, then he who continues the attack wins.

Ulysses S. Grant

HAL SHEARON MCBRIDE, JR.

OTHER BOOKS BY THE AUTHOR

To Bear Witness: A Memoir (2009)
Who Be Dragons: A Historical Novel (2010)
Billie and the Boys: A Memoir (2011)

Published by Virtualbookworm Publishing
ISBN 978-1-62137-533-3 (softcover)
ISBN 978-1-62137-534-0 (Ebook)
Library of Congress Control Number: 2014910888

McBride, Hal (1937-)
Gatewood: Tales from the Life and Times of Lieutenant Charles B. Gatewood
1. Charles Gatewood; 2. Georgia McCullough Gatewood; 3.Geronimo; 4. William Alchesay; 5.Thomas Cruse; 6. Walter Reed; 7. Dorsey M. McPherson; 8. Fort Apache; 9. Fort Wingate; 10. Fort Verde; 11. Apache scouts; 12. Verde River Valley; 13. Nelson A. Miles; 14.Geronimo's surrender 1886; 15. George Wratten; 16. Ida DeLand McPherson; 17. John Magruder; 18. Apache Wars; 19. Nana; 20. Naiche

FOR

Billie Jean
And the scent of pines through an open window
following an evening rain.

ACKNOWLEDGEMENTS

Apaches Days and Beyond: A Memoir by Thomas Cruse

Lt. Charles Gatewood and his Apache Wars Memoir – edited and with additional text by Louis Kraft

Geronimo: His Own Life Story taken down and edited by S. M. Barrett

CONTENTS

CHARLES B. GATEWOOD

An honorable man, often to his own detriment, chooses to walk the principled path. At times his rigid adherence to his personal moral and ethical codes will inconvenience those who so actively pursue their own self-interest. An honorable man may become a great aggravation to the personally ambitious.

ONE

ROUTE TO THE TERRITORIES

THE COACH CAREENED ALONG a route that likely begun as a game trail. The path slowly widened through years of varying uses by humans and other animals, before evolving into a crude roadbed formed by the compacting of the abrasive sandy soil. Sand and wheels carved the underlying stone into ever deepening ruts. It was now an erratic path interrupted by exposed and unyielding rock formations, seeming to the passenger to be at least boulder sized as iron rimmed wheels jarred their way over the road. The coach bounced and careened along this path that promised to lead from the railroad in Trinidad, Colorado, to Santa Fe, New Mexico.

As the stage jerked and jolted, passing from rut to rock, Gatewood became increasingly grateful that he and his traveling companions had been able to put together adequate funds to bribe the Trinidad stage agent into providing them with a larger coach. An aggressive outbreak of small pox in the Mexican section provided additional motivation for a prompt departure from Trinidad.

Regardless, the expenditure of a precious dollar apiece seemed wise as a revolving iron-rimmed wheel made a bone jarring descent into a rut at an angle that tossed the rider against the passenger seated next to them.

Nine passengers were aboard, inside four abreast on the plank bench seats on each side of the coach and one trekker on top facing the elements with the driver. The fact that the driver

1

would on occasion share a swig of a locally distilled whiskey which he kept beneath his seat in a sizable pottery jug gave the unfortunate traveler brief moments of respite from the elements.

January travel in northeastern New Mexico was cold. The snow-chilled air rushed downhill from the Sangre de Cristo Mountains that lay to the west of the stage route, propelling a brisk, steady, cold north wind.

It was this insidious chill that seemed to have prevented many of his traveling companions from bathing since the previous summer. He sat next to the window, having not yet lost his Virginia sensitivity to the fragrance emitted by the unwashed human body. He would regularly crack open the leather flap covering the small window-like opening, allowing breaths of cold fresh air into the coach.

"Shut da' God-damned 'monia hole!" The tone of the voice made the displeasure of the speaker obvious.

Gatewood seized a final gulp of fresh air, then complied with what he accepted as a rational request from an under-washed and under-dressed gentleman seated in the midst of the opposite bench. A more seasoned traveler, warmly wrapped under a throw of tanned elk hide, chuckled.

Dark came but it did not bring sleep.

Gatewood's thoughts ebbed before flowing back to Virginia. The stage swayed and seemed to be floating before slamming back into the uneven rocky surface. He smiled, rather laughing at himself.

He remembered his exhilaration when the envelope appeared on the parlor table. Despite his anticipation to know the content, he carefully sliced the envelope open and slid out the papers, his first posting orders since his graduation from West Point some five months earlier.

"Camp Apache, Arizona Territory, The Department of Arizona," though scarcely audible, he formed each word. He spoke the words just loud enough that only he could hear them, yet loud enough they careened about his mind. It was the posting he desired, it was the only place the United States Military was involved in active conflict, the only chance for glory and promotion.

When talking to his fellow cadets beside the Hudson River, such ambitions seemed not only appropriate but all a graduate of the United States Military Academy, Class of 1877, could hope to obtain.

Especially, a graduate from a southern military family who as a boy had seen his father choose to fight with the Confederacy. He had watched a merciless war and a callous Reconstruction through the eyes of a boy. He believed he understood the consequences of losing a war.

Although he was not lost, this modest and quiet Virginian, a twenty-four year old Second Lieutenant, was searching.

He again picked up the envelope he had just laid on the table, glancing at the formal address on the envelope, Second Lieutenant Charles Bare Gatewood. Seeing his new title written on official government stationary provoked a sense of personal pride.

"Second Lieutenant Charles Bare Gatewood, Sixth Cavalry," again spoken but not uttered aloud.

A New Mexico sized boulder jarred him back inside the coach. The pitch dark of the New Mexico night suppressed his urge to check the time on his genuine silver Elgin pocket watch, a graduation gift from his family, but he judged it several hours before daybreak, about twenty-four hours since they had left Trinidad.

He wished he had pocketed a couple more of the johnnycakes offered following a bite of supper at an early evening stop for a change of horses.

The stock tender had strongly suggested it.

"Not a wonder ya goddamn horse dung bony. 'spect', ya'll stay such," a sage observation from a man accustomed to judging the durability of horses by the muscle on their bones.

"Lotta rocks 'tween here and Santie Fe soldier boy," he muttered and released a large spew of tobacco juice toward a small lizard that scurried across his path. He walked to the corral feeling he could talk more sense to the exhausted horses that had just been left in his care.

The coach slid sideways in the sand, his stomach growled and Gatewood made a mental note. In the future when offered creditable local knowledge, he would give it ample consideration.

Georgia. Georgia McCullough, fantasies of her flooded his mind providing nature's opium for increasingly sore bones. He had found her repetitively intruding into his thoughts from the moment he laid eyes on her. He tried to close off the image, believing he could not allow himself to linger long upon Georgie, not now.

Her father, a judge of substantial Virginia lineage, had left no doubt that he had better things than a soldier, West Point graduate or not, in mind for his beautiful daughter. However, Georgie was possessed of the independent temperament of her Irish ancestors. That this statuesque, fair skinned beauty might choose to think otherwise gave a considerable dash of optimism to the tall bone-slender newly commissioned Second Lieutenant.

No doubt about it, Gatewood was smitten.

Another collision between the iron-rimmed wooden wheels and the uneven roadway sent a shock through the coach that every passenger felt to their teeth. Gatewood re-positioned himself. His father's repetitive directive, "Stand up straight!" brought him to stiffen his back into a most upright sitting position.

Shortly after sunrise, the coach arrived at another way station. Most of the men rushed to find a spot to relieve their strained bladders before making their way into the station. It took less than a glance to know the country had changed. The landscape now comprised of buttes and other forms of residual hills and mountains. Erosion had textured the most uneven of landscapes.

There were smallish green trees, really by Virginia standards little more than large bushes, dotting the otherwise barren sandy rocky soil. Gatewood had thought it curious that while they had splashed through several tiny trickles of water, there had been no running water of adequate size to rightfully make claim to being called a stream forded since late the previous afternoon. To the west, there were mountains with slopes that appeared to be green.

He took a deep breath, almost a sigh, and then noted the brilliant blue of the sky. He inhaled even deeper. He liked this cold mountain air that seemed to somehow cleanse his lungs.

Gatewood gauged this terrain to be an inhospitable land characterized by a barren and irregular landscape. The atlases he scoured in Virginia had been deceiving. The mountains were understated while rivers were little more than shallow streams. The erosion pattern did suggest torrents of water had passed at some time or another.

He begin to move toward the table and benches under a lean-to shelter attached to the log way station. There were mashed beans and some type of local flat flour bread being served and there was hot coffee. The beans and flour bread provided necessary sustenance. The coffee was hot and very much to his liking.

Thirty-eight hours after it left Trinidad, the Southern Overland coach pulled to a stop in front of the Santa Fe station. The sun belied the afternoon temperature. There was a considerable chill to the January air. Gatewood tried to disguise the substantial discomfort he felt in his knees and spine, until he realized all his traveling companions were also the worse for wear following their grinding descent. He stretched.

The buildings of Santa Fe seemed a collection of mud huts, some larger than others. Santa Fe was definitely not St. Louis.

He found the bed in the inn to be pleasing. He considered that a bed of thorns could have been pleasing after his trip in the Southern Overland stage, a coach stopping only to change horses. All passenger necessities were addressed at these times.

The unhurried pace of Santa Fe was restorative. Despite his impressions of the architecture, it was a pleasingly diverse place. Much communication was in Spanish and despite considerable Latin and some basic Spanish in his educational background, the sounds were unfamiliar. The city was filled with teamsters and traders, lawyers and members of the Territorial Legislature, so the spoken English was neither consistent nor classical.

Lounging in the hotel lobby, he listened to the conversations among the salesman, the politicians and other such entrepreneurs and shysters. Opinions of a new appointed governor, upcoming elections and the recent range war in Lincoln County seemed of more interest to the local population than was any concern about remnants of the Apache conflicts that sporadically raged in the more rugged southwestern reaches of the Territory.

Santa Fe judged itself to be civilized.

By the time the supply train fully loaded and manned, departed for Fort Wingate, Gatewood was again ready to resume his journey, comfortable that he would arrive at his first posting in a timely fashion.

The eleven wagons, each pulled by six mules, edged their way down from the pines of Santa Fe into the high desert of central New Mexico. The view of the terrain from horseback was far superior to the occasional glimpses he had obtained from the stage as it had ricocheted down the path from Trinidad to Santa Fe.

Most evenings there was fresh meat obtained by a proficient hunter, an odd little scruff of a man whose shoulder length hair just seemed to appear from under his flat crowned, wide brimmed hat, would seem to simply vanish before anyone knew it and just as oddly reappear beside the chuck wagon, visiting with the cook, with no one taking note of his approach. Only the fresh meat over which the cook labored gave testimony to the fact the man had really left the group. The game, mostly venison or a desert bird that the Mexican cook enjoyed preparing was whipped into a rather tasty meal. Fried bread that was used with the stews or sprinkled with a bit of sugar along with the beans was a stable of each meal. Judging by the reception the meals received from the drivers, they consider the cuisine to be excellent, a luxury insisted upon by the contract drivers.

While logic dictated the man had an actual name, his traveling companions simply called him Tazma. After both inquiry and observation, he accepted that the name was a shortened version of the Spanish word for ghost. Based upon his comings and goings, the man often seemed to be just that, a ghost, a figment of the imagination.

Only beginning to adjust to the liberal dose of what he labeled Mexican peppers, Gatewood took more than his share of fry bread in an attempt to extinguish the biting aftertaste of these peppers. At any rate, the food was far superior to that provided by the stage line that had carried him to Santa Fe.

As he stepped from the fire to tear off an additional share of fry bread at the cook's wagon, the cook kicked a tarantula away. The size and number of these spiders had surprised Gatewood.

Tazma noted the soldier's uneasiness and said, "Bite won't kill ya, butcha'll wish youse dead 'fore the hurtin' stops"

The cook's English was weedy, but his sage message was clear with the intent of assisting, "Sleep in your boots."

A grin broke the hunter's whiskey colored face. Realizing that his stained and rotting teeth had peeked shown behind the smile, he squeezed his lips back into place.

The night sounds, while foreign, were intriguing. An animal prowling in the night made a gritty rustling far different than the sound made in even crunchy dry grass. The vast openness of the landscape made judging the distance to the origin of the sound a new challenge. The night howls of coyotes and wolves seemed to descend from the pine covered mountains to the north although a daylight view of the distant mountains would bring such conclusions into question.

Gatewood was taken by the clarity of the stars when viewed through the cold night air of the high desert winter. The lengthy visibility of the "shooting stars" left him in wonder.

Few of the variety of animal tracks that dotted the sand around the campsite were familiar. One morning Tazma, having noted Gatewood's curiosity, explained the difference between the sign left by a "rattler and a sidewinder." Then, while Gatewood thought he was still talking to the man, he turned to find the hunter gone, gone as if he had melted into the sand. For the first time Gatewood looked to the sand for tracks and realized it was the sound of his own voice that concealed the departure. Moving in sand could make little sound, moving on stone even less.

That evening Tazma picked up the conversation as if he had never departed. "Snake's nothing. Ya don't wanta find a nasty damn lizard the color of the sand and child of Satan. Bite will squeeze the air from ya, dead," Tazma paused, straighten his hat back on his head and mused, "Ah, boy, ya gonna be chasin' ole Victorio all over the desert floor. Yawl see one of them lizards about time ya figurer out ole Vic is chasin' ya." Covering his mouth with the back of his wrist, he chuckled at his own wit.

Gatewood bristled at being called boy. He gave no indication he had been rankled by the word. No Virginian was called boy. But he was coming to grasp this was not Virginia.

7

He was gone. As the name suggested, Tazma was something of a phantom, a self-constructed apparition who vanished as the whim struck him.

The newly ordained Lieutenant contemplated the moody landscape. Over the remaining days, he watched Tazma, seeking the slightest insight to understanding his skills. His labors left him puzzled but with an increasing notion this land obscured its secrets with its subtlety.

Fort Wingate, 1879

TWO

FORT WINGATE

THERE WAS NOTHING SUBTLE ABOUT Fort Wingate in the early winter of 1878. It was a collection of buildings that protruded from the high desert floor like an ill-placed wart. A wart composed of wood and stone growing into a U-shape around the parade ground. The lumber hauled in from the pine forest some thirty miles away. Little quarrying was required to retrieve the stones, they were more harvested from the surrounding terrain. The open side of the U faced into the flatter ground to the south while a line of rusty tan colored bluffs, much of the face seemed to be a sheer vertical rise of unbroken stone lay to the north and rose some five hundred feet from the floor. These seemingly perpendicular bluffs were occasionally interrupted by what appeared to be layers treacherously loose rock.

Gatewood had seen a scorched and scarred South after the war, barren but holding forth the clear promise that leaves and limbs would return to the trees. Crops if planted would again grow and flourish. Fort Wingate gave no such suggestion. There was no hint that anything green had ever sprouted from its sand. The flag flying above the command office and the sounds on the parade ground gave the hints of the familiar, suggesting a hospitable edge had been craved onto an otherwise unforgiving landscape. Then it struck him, it was his concept of civilization this place so vehemently resisted. He smiled.

Second Lieutenant Charles Bare Gatewood reported. He was assigned quarters. Then, he looked for Tazma. Eying the wagon master outside a store, he asked.

Indicating the line of buttes to the west with a dramatic wave of his arm, the wagon master responded, "Gone, paid'em, reckon he'll come back as it pleases'em"

Gatewood's gaze had followed the direction of wagon master's hand; it now remained fixed on the vast expanse, empty expanse of the rocky slopes beyond the long stone barracks. He was uncertain. This place was both hostile and hypnotic.

As he stepped onto the parade ground to make his way toward his quarters, a gust of cold air raised a swirl of dusty grit that enveloped him. He sneezed. He sneezed again. He closed the front of his knee length duster and turned up the collar. He loosed yet another sneeze as he approached the porch of his quarters.

"Lieutenant, a dust allergy can get a man killed out here."

As the dust cleared from his line of sight, Gatewood spied a lanky figure leaning a chair back on its rear legs. He sneezed again.

"Good thing Victorio isn't close by," he observed with inaudible chuckle, his palm covered his mouth as his thumb and index finger stroked his trimmed mustache brushing it from the concave line below his nose and outward to the tip of his smile. His palm now caressed his chin fully disclosing his amusement. Gatewood's annoyance gave way to a perplexity. The figure rose and spoke.

"I take you to be Second Lieutenant Gatewood."

"If I'm not?"

"In such case, I would be mildly embarrassed and now apologizing prolifically." The smile broadened beneath the mustache.

"Well, you need be neither. However, since you have the better of me, you might consider identifying yourself."

"Ah! Well done sir," he said as the smile became an audible chuckle and he extended his hand, "Dorsey McPherson, surgeon, contracted to the Sixth Calvary."

The pair exchanged a firm handshake. Each suspected the other had increased the strength of his grip to make some obscure masculine point.

"Come, I'll acquaint you with the stylish accommodation provided officers at Fort Wingate."

Inside the structure were three wood frame beds each with its own aging mattress. McPherson patted his bed and said, "Lieutenant, you may be assured I choose the finest mattress for myself. You get your pick of the remaining pair."

He slapped a mattress. Dust flew out. He waved his hand as if to disperse it.

Gatewood sneezed. McPherson laughed.

In the officer's mess, McPherson and Gatewood moved to a plank table close to the pot-bellied wood burning stove and lingered over after dinner coffee. Cast iron pots clanging against sheet iron pans made for an irregular but vaguely rhythmic percussion accompaniment to the discussion.

The boiled beef had been comparatively tender. While tender, boiled army issue beef lacked the zesty tang of the meals of wild game he had eaten on his journey to Wingate. He again considered Tazma's wisdom, "Nuff chilies can make rawhides tastyful."

Gatewood had also considered the possibility that enough chilies could permanently damage a man's taste buds.

"So, you have been assigned a company of scouts."

Not being prone to excessive conversation, Gatewood responded, "I have."

He weighed his thoughts before adding, "Yours?"

"I have considerable liberty. Think I might choose to go a distance with you." Again his fingers stroked his trimmed mustache, his palm concealed the broad smile that broke his face as he continued, "Alchesay, Sergeant Alchesay will see to your education."

Dorsey mused, "Yes, I might just like to observe that."

Gatewood was quiet, thoughtful. Feeling the puzzlement in Dorsey's gaze, searching for the expected response which hadn't yet surfaced, he said, "You sound impressed by the Sergeant."

"Alchesay is an impressive figure of a man," he paused. "You will see."

Fingers freezing above his lips, he said, "The mess says Alchesay is far and away the most efficient of the scouts."

13

After a hesitant pause, he added, "He's White Mountain Apache as are his scouts. He tolerates us because he judges it to serve his interest. There is just little love for the Ojo Caliente or the Chiricahua. Those feuds go further back than anyone now living can recall. Make no mistake, the dislike is real enough."

Gatewood's gaze tightened as he nodded to indicate his understanding. For the first time McPherson was confronted by Gatewood's deep set steel gray eyes. He wished to glance away but thought better of it, finding no pliability in his companion's eyes.

Gatewood's gaze adjusted any first impression of frailty McPherson might have gotten when he first sighted the sneezing five foot eleven inch rail thin Second Lieutenant, fresh to his first duty station. His slender hawkish face punctuated with a roman nose of considerable character and his deep set steely eyes projected a look unyielding fiber.

"So we will be friends as long as we share a common enemy."

Gatewood seemed to be speaking of today. He first heard the concept as boy listening to his father discuss the less than faithful allies of the Confederacy. Trust based on a shared hatred is most frail.

Dorsey became thoughtful. His thumb and finger moved across his mustache. His mind stammered, seeking some fitting words. As his thoughts solidified his hand quieted and moved away from his face.

"Apaches are not horse soldiers but one will cover more desert terrain in day than a mounted soldier and leave no sign he's passed." Once the sounds left his mouth he wondered why he had given voice to such an utterance but he stumbled on, "They'll steal your horse for trade or more likely for food or just for the plain cussedness of putting you afoot."

Gatewood's gaze became more penetrating. Others found discomfort in a focus he viewed as attentiveness. It always puzzled Gatewood. He had at times utilized it to his benefit, mostly finding that it silenced conversations he had no desire to continue. It kept most men at a comfortable interpersonal distance but he found his personal demeanor to be problematic in creating more intimate relationships.

14

But then there was Georgie. She matched him strength on strength. He desired to be closer to her and to know her better. She perplexed him.

"Surgeon, you're easterner aren't you?" Gatewood's question was unexpected. Before Dorsey could respond, Gatewood finished, "It is a difficult accent to conceal from a Virginian," he smiled.

"Glad you smiled. Don't want such a disagreement with a man I'm going into the field with."

Gatewood laughed. While he considered the War to be settled business, he felt no such forgiving emotions about reconstruction. These were firmly held beliefs he chose not to share.

The men retrieved their dusters from the coat rack and moved toward the doorway.

Dorsey said, "Wrangler will be here tomorrow or the next to sell horses. Supply Sergeant does the military buying. You might want to pick your own."

A cold dusty wind greeted them as they moved on to the parade ground. Gatewood sneezed.

McPherson chuckled, gave him a healthy pat on the back and said, "You'll get used to it."

"That is your best medical advice?" Gatewood cracked a smile.

"Well Lieutenant, I have to save my best medical counsel for those above the rank of Captain." Both men shared a laugh. The surgeon considered that a shared laugh cut the north wind as well as anything.

"You can't laugh and be cold at the same time."

The horse corrals adjoined Wingate's stables at the southwest corner. Except for the rare summer day the prevailing winds carried the smell of horse mature away from the fort. A Mormon rancher from the high country to the southeast of the Navajo's sacred peaks brought some thirty head of half-broke horses to Wingate on contract.

As Gatewood first eyed the wrangler the man struck him as hefty for the job. He considered how a man could retain any excessive weight in this environment. The man's deep voice and roar of a laugh quickly convinced Gatewood the man was more pitchman than horse wrangler.

Gatewood muttered to himself, "Damn Carpetbagger."

He started to move away when a large bay caught his eye. He almost bumped into the sutler with his abrupt change of direction.

Given years of emphasis on etiquette in his home, his apology came quick and easy. The sutler nodded.

"Lieutenant, did you see something in the pen you liked."

Gatewood hesitated unsure he wanted to disclose his intent to the owner of the fort store.

Taking no offense, the sutler said, "Lieutenant, I'll not screw you over but old Holy Charley over there will. Now speak your animal and your top dollar."

"The big bay if you judge him sound. Fifty dollars."

Gatewood milled about pretending to be interested in the Corporal's process of inspecting horses. He realized that from his time buying and selling horses with his father he knew considerably more about horses than the Corporal did. Still, he just watched with a weather eye on the sutler.

The sutler examined several other animals and bought two besides the bay.

He returned to Gatewood and said, "He's a solid and sound five year old gelding. He's carrying a Babbitt brand but Charley has some paperwork for him."

Realizing the names meant nothing to Gatewood, he clarified, "Babbitt brothers have a post in the Navajo country and run cattle all the way into the pines, to the flagpole. They'd gut him if he stole from 'em." He continued with business, "Bought him for thirty-two, you owe me thirty-five. Be brushed and in your stall by nightfall."

Gatewood begin to reach for his poke. The sutler stopped him. "Come by the store tomorrow and settle up."

Gatewood extended his hand and spoke, "I'm Charles Gatewood, Lieutenant Gatewood."

The sutler smiled, "New titles just don't fix right in the mouth. Amos McCrieght." He reached for Gatewood's hand.

The hand shake completed the deal.

"Got a name for ya new mount?"

"Bob." Seeing that sutler McCrieght was waiting for more, he concluded with some emphasis, "Bob. Just Bob"

"Bob. I'll see ta Bob findin' a stall." McCrieght walked toward the pens and considered that maybe, just maybe the good Lord has blessed us with a Lieutenant that don't overly enjoy the sound of his own voice.

Gatewood contributed little to the evening conversations with McPherson. The nights were increasingly chilly and the fireplace provided a progressively welcome warmth.

"Got me a strong bay. Sutler McCrieght helped considerably."

"You don't say," the surgeon said with a little surprise to his voice.

"Surprised I found the funds for an animal?"

"Surprised McCrieght took enough of a shine to you to help at all." McPherson smiled and added, "Quiet man can be tough to know, let alone well enough to like."

"Or dislike," Gatewood said, but that was not an honest description of his motivations, and added, "I don't learn much new when I'm talking."

"Lieutenant, I'm slowly gaining a liking for you and from what I hear Alchesay is really going to like you."

They rocked, listened to the increasing quiet of Wingate, listened as the night sounds of the animals replaced the sounds of the men.

After some time, Gatewood asked, "What of McCrieght?"

"What of him?"

"He was more than helpful at the sale and at the store. Still there is a trait about the man I can't place my finger on. It -- ."

In a rare move, McPherson stopped him. "The man knows all the secrets or where the secrets are buried."

He continued, "Like with the man he calls Holy Charley. Well, I hear that he was at Meadow Mountains with John Doyle Lee's bunch."

The shrug of the shoulders and the lifting of his tightened lips communicated Gatewood had not learned of the Meadow Mountain Massacre at West Point.

So, McPherson continued, "A group of zealots, fans of the Johnny-come-lately Prophets mistook the intent of an immigrant wagon train. They slaughtered them, every man, woman and child. I hear that after most of the killing there was a brief dissent with John about three comely women, two of the men wanted to keep them as wives. It's said John declared them heretics and shot them both square in the face. Seems old John didn't tolerate a follower who disagreed with him. Then, he and Holy Charley took the three women to the river to baptize them, but the Holy Spirit drowned all three of them. Seems old John didn't tolerate no witnesses either."

He paused, "Don't know the full truth. But I think McCrieght does."

"What about Lee?" disliking his own use of the last name his revered General Robert E. Lee in such a fashion he expanded, "John Lee?"

"Know for a fact he ran a ferry over the Colorado for some years. Until he became a liability to the big church then they executed him about a year ago." He paused, "Firing squad I hear."

"Damn."

"Don't think the Utah folks can make up their mind if they want to be a church, a country, a state or a church that's a country." McPherson picked up two pieces of juniper and carefully placed them on the fire. Again, the chairs rocked.

"Think McCrieght was there?"

"No," the surgeon paused in his chair and looked at Gatewood, "No."

Feeling Gatewood's steel gray eyes piercing his thoughts, he was glad he was confident in his word. For a third time, looking at Gatewood, he said, "No. Does it matter?"

It was Gatewood's time, "Only if the U.S. Army says it does."

Dorsey released an audible nasal snort of semi-understanding, "Huhh!"

The pain in his right hip and knee awakened Gatewood before the bugler blew Reveille. As to not awaken the surgeon from his sound sleep, he quietly place two small logs and a larger one on glowing embers in the stone fireplace that covered most of the eastern wall. As he slid between the blankets, adjusting them, a fire snapped to life from the coals. He lay still trying to capture some warm beneath the blankets and against the morning cold.

His company of scouts should be arriving at Wingate today or tomorrow. That the men of his first command could rather drift in at some general time concerned him. He had seen some activity around the scouts quarters, really little more than the brush arbors in which ardent evangelists had spread their "hell fire and damnation" in rural Virginia. Freedmen, still basking in their new station in life, were converting by the droves. A fire pit in each corner made them appear none the warmer.

Restless, he quietly dressed and headed to the stable. He saddled Bob. After a solid nip on his upper arm, he mounted this spirited and half-broken animal. They rode the eastern sight line and had just topped a rise of ground. Gatewood reigned up as the notes of Reveille approached on the cold air. He turned a reluctant Bob back toward Wingate.

A young wrangler with only a home-knit scarf wrapped around his neck and tucked into his shirt to shield him against the morning chill stealthy passed a hand full of an oat and honey mixture to Gatewood. Gatewood rubbed Bob's muzzle and fed him the delicacy. Bob returned a receptive gesture.

"Time for our oats," said Dorsey as he met Gatewood on the parade ground. "I'm not joking. I believe them to be from the same supply used for the animals."

Gatewood's eyes smiled if not his mouth.

"I did not intend humor. I know that oats are not eggs, just more available."

The morning meal was in fact oats. To the surgeon's delight, Gatewood was unable to definitively state that the breakfast oats had not been obtained from a supply shared with the livestock.

The coffee was steaming and it was genuine coffee, a redeeming virtue for any meal at a frontier posting.

The sun had yet to warm the morning air as they stood outside the mess. The surgeon took a deep breath as if to enjoy the morning air and said, "Lieutenant, consider this an invitation to accompany me on my professional duties this morning."

Beginning to detach the Irish subtly to his companion, he ask, "Which would be exactly what?"

"Being the ranking medical officer, it is the day for complete sanitary inspections."

"So you are inviting me to observe you inspecting latrines?"

"Precisely."

"Surgeon, it occurs to me you are also the only medical officer here."

McPherson laughed. Gatewood enjoying his own humor, smiled.

Amos McCrieght's store on Fort Wingate was larger than most with a diversity of inventory that exceeded that found on almost any frontier outpost. The reported ethics of so many other Sutlers was taken as a personal affront by him. His wife saw that he was especially sensitive to the needs of the wives who had followed their husbands to this remote outpost. If not in his inventory, there was little he couldn't supply in his next shipment. So from food to personal needs, the sutler blended the basic merchandise with a few extravagances. Army wives only spoke well of the McCrieght Store. To be sure his pricing made an allowance for the difficulty of supplying such a remotely located business, but Amos was a man proud of his honesty. Amos understood that an honest man had no reason to be ashamed of making a fair profit.

"Good morning Lieutenant. I trust you found Bob and his quarters to be suitable."

"Superior, Mr. McCrieght. Superior," Gatewood glanced around the store and said, "Cartridges?"

McCrieght motioned as he moved toward a corner counter. "So I take it you don't have military issue?"

".45 center fires."

McCrieght's interest was aroused. "What rifle do you have?"

"A Centennial Winchester." Gatewood's feet stirred as he became self-conscious and offered, "A gift."

"An 1876 Winchester. Durable, powerful, lever never jams and rarely misfires." The pace of his speech gave away McCrieght's enthusiasm for the weapon. He continued, "I've had three on order for over a year. Then, said I had to order a case. So Hell, I just ordered'em. Hope delivery is soon."

A little embarrassed by his own fervor he asked, "Yellow boy?"

"Yes. The action is all brass." A clear pride tinted Gatewood's voice.

Although he had never heard it used for the Winchester, Gatewood assumed that the term first applied to the brass action of the Henry repeating rifle apparently was going to carry over to the Winchester's second model of lever action rifles.

"Your price?"

"Nine cents a shell. Two dollars a box of twenty four."

"Two boxes of twenty-four of the .45." He thought and added, "I assume our Armory has the .44 rim fires for S and W revolvers."

"Last I heard." Having taken something of a liking to the Lieutenant, he offered, "Ya' Apaches will have Springfield carbines. I'd ask for extra .50 caliber cartridges. Scouts aren't often long on cartridges. A box or two in ya' saddle bag can be a mighty help should a skirmish break out."

Alchesay

suppress the thought that had Michelangelo seen Alchesay first, his David would have been sculpted differently.

While travel and some weeks of the high desert winter had darkened Gatewood's complexion, his nose marked his discernibly hawkish appearance. This classic Roman structure of his face had led his classmates at West Point to call him "Scipio Africanus," later shortened to "Sip." His frame was slender and like a rawhide whip. Despite the perfect fit of the wide brimmed white field hat, it appeared a bit oversized.

It was Gatewood's gaze in which Alchesay saw something he had never encountered in a white man. The wiry Lieutenant seemed to peer into the mind of another. As if he saw deeply but did not judge, he challenged but did not threaten. Alchesay was not accustomed to being taken aback by a man. Alchesay's piercing black eyes had met their equal.

Now alone, neither man knew quite what to say. The uniqueness of the other stymied them.

Rare for him, Gatewood broke the awkward sensations of the silence, "Let's walk."

Alchesay agreed with a quick short bob of the chin.

"Officers at mess say you are the finest of our scouts," Gatewood said.

"Tazma says you're curious, that you will listen and you learn quickly."

For whatever reason, Gatewood felt some relief, "You have seen Tazma?"

"Tiswin makes talk, I listen," Alchesay said.

Gatewood did not respond. He had a total absence of knowledge of the banned alcoholic drink made from soaking corn with a dash of cactus until it sprouted, mashed in crystal spring water, boiled and then allowed to ferment as it cooled.

Unless verbalized, ignorance can be perceived as wisdom. It was such wisdom that allowed Gatewood to pass Alchesay's first subtle probative test.

They walked toward the horse pens. Gatewood decided these Apache were neither white nor Negro. He knew there must be differences. Variations must exist and such distinctions were significant to a Virginian.

Neither man was prone to idol chat. Alchesay now ask the question important to him.

"Visited the elephant?"

Gatewood was grateful for McPherson's orientation. He knew the elephant here was combat and not the fear of the great emptiness of the plains.

"No," his answer came with authority and without apology. He continued, "I'm told no other experience can prepare a soldier for the Apache."

Alchesay nodded agreement.

"You're said to have seen much of the elephant." Being taken as a statement rather than a question, Alchesay gave no response.

Then, he said, "No one knows about the elephant until it breathes on him." He thoughtfully added, "Never alike twice."

They parted. As they did Alchesay felt an odd compulsion to say, "Tazma's good tracker, wise to listen."

Like the outer layers of an onion, the barriers and prejudices that separated the two men began to peel away.

Gatewood's instruction for his first patrol seemed direct enough. Just as the land seemed straight forward, disguising its incredible complexity, so was his first outing. The patrol was to check reports of unconfirmed raids on farms along the banks of the South Verde by small parties of Apaches numbering no more than three or four warriors. Patrols from Camp Verde and Camp Apache would be moving from the west and the south. When the Verde joined the Salt River the patrol was to work east toward the new silver finds in the Gila Mountains of southwestern New Mexico.

Beyond First Sergeant Alchesay, nine White Mountain Apache scouts and two pack mules, Gatewood found that his command included a dog of questionable genetic linage. Without being ask, Alchesay said, "Dog drinks first, doesn't die we drink." As an added afterthought he explained, "Can always eat him."

Gatewood had seen worse in the days following Lincoln's war, so his response was flat. Alchesay made note.

Under Alchesay's navigation, the patrol moved south from Fort Wingate drifting slightly west. The Lieutenant was his persistently curious and observant self. Alchesay increasingly became the committed instructor.

To Gatewood, the landscape appeared to be completely resistant to retaining any form a consistency. It was high desert brush and odd shaped succulents no taller that a two feet and with barbs that seemed a misstep would place on through a man's foot.

Much of the time the cold wind, feeling to the Virginian as it were coming off snowy mountains, often distracted him, strapping his hat on tightly, he would cover his face with a large scarf in a fashion it limited his vision.

Alchesay eased alongside him and said, "Nantan must see." He added, "Hear."

Night camp brought a small cooking fire. Three jackrabbits were being prepared on nicely crafted spit. Gatewood, for the life of him, couldn't figure out when and where the rabbits were secured but seeing them skinned on the spot left no doubt it was recent.

Only after Alchesay indicated a place next to him did Gatewood sit. It was no great leap of culture for him having enjoyed rabbit or squirrel cooked over a camp fire since he was a boy. As the aroma carried by the slender but dense line of smoke in the cold thin air suggested, the simmering mesquite wood provided the meat with a unique flavor. A wrapper of issue bread was secured from a pack unloaded from the mules.

While quite undercooked compared to the rabbit of home and certainly when viewed in terms of boiled military beef, taking his lead from his companions, he laid the meat on the crusty bread. The meat shared its moisture with the bread creating a palatable result.

A bluff shielded the campsite from the wind and from a completely open view despite mesas and slot canyons. The view for some distance could be uninterrupted. There had been two tiny springs and several dry creek beds; Gatewood had seen no running water. The dog did drink first from the springs and lived.

Gatewood brushed the stones from a bed site, prepared a blanket roll and covered it with his wool field coat. Not wanting to stare but needing to watch, he saw the scouts removed their long breech clothes and transform them into blankets. They virtually wore everything they needed.

Pebbles that would go unnoticed in a week disturbed his sleep. The sky appeared immeasurable. Only the silent stirring of nocturnal prowlers infringed upon the stone silence of the night. Only prodding of the pebbles diverted him from his surroundings. Ambivalently, a serene sleep returned until stone again met bone.

Morning came and camp was speedily vacated. Breakfast was on horseback. Gatewood ate a slice of commissary issue beef. Corporal Dead Shot pulled out the largest Bowie knife Gatewood had seen, sliced a piece of jerky from a chunk. Gatewood took the meat. He chewed, found it salty but edible enough. It was dense and chewy, palatable but he found the meat to be unidentifiable. He placed a bite in the inside pocket of his long wool coat.

Third day out the country unexpectedly begin changed. The occasional clumps of tall grass sprinkled with the ever present cholla and prickly pear cactus first gave way to junipers, pinion pine and mesquite that had appeared on mesa tops and lined the walls of slot canyons. Then, as the sunset deepened in the west and the hint of a cold crisp mountain night approached, a ponderosa pine forest had engulfed them. The remnants of a recent snow covered all the shaded areas. Groves of intriguing aspens were interspersed with the pine and spruce. Unexpectedly large grassy meadows were distinct yet reminiscence of the grass lands of his native Virginia.

Without his conscious permission his mind relaxed, Georgie flooded in. He saw every detail of her face, her hair moved in the breeze as if she was there. These seconds revived and restored him. The mere snap of a branch trumpeted the return of reality.

He clung for a moment, vowed to someday share this magical place with her. He nudged Bob. They moved on.

Late in the afternoon of the fourth day, an incredibly clear lake emerged. Despite the increasingly lush meadows and steep slopes covered with the pine, spruce and aspen increased in density, Gatewood was unprepared. He had not seen such water since his train completed its passage through Missouri.

He turned to Alchesay and asked, "Sergeant, what is this place called?"

Alchesay reached for the English words, and then answered, "Lake – lake – Stoneman Lake."

Gatewood, only a final second reach for self-control prevented a gawk, gazed toward the snow capped peaks rising to the northwest.

Alchesay volunteered, "Navajo spirits live in them."

"And what is sacred to the Apache?"

"Springfield carbine."

Gatewood thought he knew better but he also knew how to accept an answer.

Trying to assume a command voice, he said, "Sergeant, I think it might be wise to water the horses and allow them to graze."

"Make camp at the boulders, Nantan," Alchesay indicated. "Grass doesn't stop a bullet."

"This is a reconnaissance patrol. Is there something you should teach me?"

"If Nantans knew, no need to look. Don't know so we look. Surprise you get – get," Alchesay thought, "Get." The word he sought came first in Spanish before he found his English, "Muerto – dead – very dead."

You reconnoiter to find out what you do not know. Gatewood was certain he must have received that instruction at the Academy. Today the lesson seemed to have more practical and immediate application. "You can get very dead."

The animals watered and grazed. A watching scout sat a silent and invisible guard in the deep grass.

Although he had hoped the bed of pine needles and grass would ease the morning pain in his joints, it did not. He sought comfort by moving to his right shoulder. He had never seen a sunrise like what blazed through the pines, highlighting the tall grassy meadow.

Canteens filled, mules packed and Bob saddled. He was becoming just a tad self-conscious Bob being the only saddled horse. Given the ease with which the scouts managed their horses, he had to remind himself that McPherson had told him they were not by nature "horse soldiers." Perhaps they were not the storied cavalry tacticians of the Great Plains, veterans spoke of the skills of Sioux, the Comanche and the Cheyenne dog soldiers with an element of reverence. Those veterans had not seen an Apache maneuver a bandy legged pony up a seemingly vertical rocky slope to the top of a butte. Gatewood found it jaw-dropping. He and Bob had hesitantly risen to the task.

Gatewood was coming to feel indebted to Bob. Bob, up and down the rocky terrain or following a game trail through the pines, kept his rider from appearing the novice he was before his command. This silent neophyte was the keenest of observers, a trait not lost on his command.

By mid-morning and still have broken no meaningful trail, the rear scout approached at full gallop, raised a finger on each hand and motioned behind the small column.

Gatewood swung off Bob, Alchesay was already beside him.

"Nantan, two ride our trail. We should watch."

All the scouts had dismounted, leading their horses into the trees, doubling back eyeing the route they had just traveled. Two scouts moved the mules and horses further out of sight. Two riders broke the horizon.

In sight it appeared one of the riders was saddled. Despite his heavy coat, the wide stripes of his uniform pants suggested military accompanied by a scout.

Gatewood and Alchesay stood and emerged from the pines. The riders reigned up. The saddled rider called, "Corporal Seger seeking Second Lieutenant Gatewood and his patrol."

A scout brought Bob and Alchesay's pony so promptly from the forest it was as if he had been prepared to do so from the onset.

"Major Evans sends his greetings and welcomes you to the Arizona Territories."

"Corporal, thank the Major for me," continuing without pause, "I know the Major did not send in search of my patrol to extend a welcome."

"No Sir. Two soldiers deserted with a six mule train hauling supplies from Fort Sumner to Fort Craig, seems about ten miles out of Craig they murdered a Second Lieutenant and two enlisted men that were with'em" Whatever response he expected from the green Second Lieutenant did not come, instead he was met with

Gatewood's penetrating eyes causing a quick turn of his head only to land on Alchesay's unforgiving face. The forest remained stone silent.

Corporal Evans who only seconds ago was completely full of himself, stammered. "Sir, it is reported they stole four mules, two carrying new Springfields and ordinance. The others carry an abundance of supply."

He went on, "General Wilcox told the Major he wanted the mules and the supplies back. The men, not so much."

"Soldier, what were my orders?" The formality of the request stiffened the soldier.

"Sir, you are to discontinue the reconnaissance patrol and attempt to intercept the deserters. Sir, Mr. Al Sieber, Chief of Scouts, suggested the deserters would follow the Rio Grande, break off due south head for the Mexican border near Cloverdale."

"You may extend my thanks to Mr. Sieber. Tell him Alchesay is my Sergeant of Scouts, a fact he should find reassuring. Now, I'm certain you'll need to be on your way back to Fort Verde."

"Yes, Sir."

As they begin to turn, the Navajo scout said, "Ya-ta-hay." Or so it sounded to Gatewood. Alchesay turned away and spit at the ground, the disgust on his face visible only to Gatewood and the Navajo.

Dead Shot kept his rifle trained on the Navajo until they departed view. While Alchesay was different by height and frame, Gatewood was beginning to realize the Apaches did not all look alike.

"Sieber makes good guesses."

"Sergeant, how can we intercept them?"

"Straight down bare mountains" Alchesay said, "Very dry, but two springs. Both on Chiricahua land." He gave a slight shrug, "Matalos."

Gatewood understood he meant no good end would come to any Chiricahua they encountered.

For the past two hours the company had moved toward a concentration of birds that first seemed to steadily hover above a sight, but now were lurching back and forth into the sky.

"Nantan, birds scared. Coyotes maybe, maybe not."

Gatewood reined Bob up. The tired parched animal resisted and Gatewood was firm. He patted his neck as he calmed. Bob had performed admirably on the parched dry march.

He motioned two scouts to the left and two to the right, Dead Shot was motioned to the point. The pack mules advanced with the party, two scouts looking to their security.

Alchesay did not express his approval by word or expression, but he approved.

As they eased atop a small rise, the breeze shifted. Dog's nose went up into the breeze, his tail went down and his ears pinned back.

Alchesay, barely audible, muttered, "Olo de la Muerte."

From Civil War battlefields of his Virginia boyhood, Gatewood knew the odor, "Dead bodies."

Alchesay nodded, "Much dead."

Dead Shot appeared, leading his pony. He signaled them forward. Giving the reins of their horses to a scout who advanced alone from the mules, Gatewood knew the scouts knew the drill.

After Dead Shot told Alchesay, the Sergeant told the Lieutenant, "Small train of settlers, four or five wagons. All look dead. Your men are here with all four mules."

A scout was left with the animals. Dead Shot was positioned to have a clear field of fire if needed. The rest then made their way down the ravine to within twenty yards of the deserter's mules. Gatewood, his hat hung on his back suspended by a leather strap around his neck, found their movement to be almost eerily silent. A virtually inaudible scuff of his boot drew a stern glance from Alchesay.

The disturbed floor of the ravine suggested several men had laid in wait until the wagons reached an ideal position. Alchesay pointed out the sign the party had left in the ground. His motions to the Lieutenant made clear his belief that the party they had sought were not far ahead.

Alchesay peered over the edge. A shoulder tap and Gatewood joined him. An area surrounding the wagons was strewn with a dozen or so bodies, men, women and children. Lost families seeking a promised land, land promised by the grossly exaggerated pamphlets circulated by land speculators about the lush valley of Gila River.

Gatewood's stomach pitted as he got a clear glimpse of the deserters. One deserter, his pants about his ankles, was between the legs of a woman spread on the rear gate of a wagon, vigorously humping her. Gatewood detected no movement from her.

"Come on! Ya ain't no idée what disease 'em 'Paches left 'n her." The man's voice sounded not of disgust but a passionate desire to be gone from the scene and on to Mexico.

Gatewood face flushed with anger. Alchesay drew that huge Bowie knife and Gatewood begin to unholster his Smith and Wesson. Alchesay's hand stopped him, pointing to his knife. Gatewood holstered the revolver and pulled his German steel Bowie shaped hunting knife. They edged from the ravine.

Turning and buttoning the fly of his army issue breeches, the deserter said, "Ain't passin' up no naked gal – not out here." As he pulled up his gallowses and started to adjust them, Alchesay knee found the rapist's back, left hand yanking the head backward as the thrust of the razor sharp knife virtually decapitated him. Blood spurted up and out as Alchesay threw him forward to the ground.

In micro-seconds Gatewood made the decision that won the respect of his patrol. Over the months and years the word would spread. His thrust was not hesitant but the density of the cartilage of the windpipe required greater pressure to finish the cut than he anticipated. Gatewood felt oddly undeterred by the spurts of warm blood that sprayed over his hand and arm. As his First Sergeant had done, he thrust the dying man forward.

He stepped back. The deserters had been dispatched. "General Wilcox wants the mules and goods back, the men not so much." He mumbled the instruction under his breath.

He expected such cruelty of a hostile, but such insensitivity from a soldier, even a deserter, angered him. The fully exposed woman was now clearly dead but she had departed recently enough that the blood was still moist and trickling from her wounds. She had not died as quickly as any legitimate Christian might have hoped. Gatewood had accepted his intermittent anger with God and his son.

Gatewood closed the woman's dress.

The pack mules were secured. A cursory search of the wagons for any overlooked food or water or water was made. None was found.

On the other hand, the deserter's pack mules were a treasure trove of supplies and water.

A brief search of the bodies for identification was conducted. Beyond some letters one of the women had tucked away none was found. The genitals had been removed from the men and tossed out with the cactus and snakes. Little other mutilation occurred. The bodies were all placed into a wagon and covered, simply a gesture. The deserters were left as they fell.

Gatewood and Alchesay stepped away from the scouts.

Gatewood asked, "Thoughts?"

Alchesay was quick to the point, "Got lucky. Cut trail with hostiles heading for Mexico." He paused, thinking and then he continued, "They will try to stay away from the miners' camp near your fort, Bayard. Got ten mules here, will want to sell them in Mexico. Maybe they will cook one, will slow them."

"Nantan, shoot deserters, might have warned Ojo Caliente we near. Don't want them know we're near." He nodded again, "We push, surprise them."

Gatewood nodded. He had understood the silent communications in the ravine.

He also noted that Alchesay's English was considerably better than he wanted any white eye to know.

Loco Lizard came from a wagon dangling two dolls by their hair.

Alchesay was very matter of fact, "Mexicans pay many pesos for young girls, more than for mules."

Gatewood felt the discovery added twinges of urgency to the pursuit. He quickly learned his feelings were not shared by any member of his command, for any Apache a female was simply property. The white man's valuing of women confused them, seeming foolish and impractical. The scouts wanted to catch the Ojo Caliente just so they could kill them.

The Lieutenant and the First Sergeant continued considering their alternatives. Alchesay had concluded that they were close to the raiding party that they had been seeking since leaving Fort Wingate some seven weeks ago. He now estimated the party had grown from eight to twelve men and were now slowed by at least thirty head of mixed livestock and at least two hostages.

Alchesay believed the raiders would avoid the small but well-armed silver town but try to fatten the animals in the meadows near the Gila River. They will briefly be slowed by caution until they passed the railroad being built along the southern stage route.

"Only the Animas Valley goes to Mexico."

Reading his Sergeant's message, he said, "So we can get ahead of them."

"Maybe and maybe wait for them near the Guadalupes, good shelter, pass to Mexico narrow."

"The girls?"

"Harmed girl of little value," Alchesay said. "No danger 'till in our sights."

The unwavering obstinate pursuit of the hostiles, warm days and bone chilling night, the stillness brought involuntary thoughts to Gatewood's mind. Settlers' made their choices, put their wives and children in harm's way as they chased their dreams. Wives who had seen their husbands slain were sexually brutalized until they died and the children taken to an uncertain fate. Gatewood mulled these things.

He opened a man's throat with his knife and felt little remorse. It surprised him, it troubled him. The man was a thief, a deserter, a man who had murdered his fellow soldiers and watched as his cohort raping a dying or dead woman. Gatewood knew he would have shot him regardless, but there was something almost satisfying about the personal nature in which he had dispatched the deserter.

Reflecting with tired body and weary mind, he considered the very simple and direct fashion the men he now commanded went about their business.

Four long days and four short nights of cold camps brought them to a place where a man could sit on a ledge in the Chiricahua foothills and look across the valley and see the Animas Mountains and everything that breathed between them.

Dog drank from the stream. Although as starkly thirsty, the scouts folded their legs and patiently watching. The dog didn't die. The men drank.

Two scouts took the exhausted, starving ponies and mules downstream to water and graze. The General's mules were unpacked for the first time since they were secured from the deserters. These scouts picked a place that those who would try to make a run for Mexico must pass.

The cold nights had been challenging for Gatewood's strangely aching joints. The days in the saddle brought no comfort. Observing the tracking and the nature of his command, fueling his insatiable curiosity distracted him more effectively than any mild dose from Dr. McPherson's bag might have done. Pain can be ignored.

A camp set and time given for dark to settle deep, sage brush fire was lit just inside the mouth of shallow cave. Gatewood knew the taste of beef cooked over a fire. He did not ask its source. He ate.

Feeling it best to not intrude upon his scouts evening meal, Gatewood always sat away giving the impression that he was lost in thoughts of his. Most often this was true. Tonight, he ate all of the beef he could and placed the remaining in his coat pocket.

Each man made his bed in his carefully selected firing position. Dead Shot positioned to extract a price for any attempt at retreating back up the valley. Gatewood and Alchesay chose the places with a clear line of fire to where a small spring jointed stream forming a fine pool of water.

Dog snuggled behind a boulder nearby.

About three in the morning, he awoke and ate the rest of the beef. For the first time since the settler's train, he was hungry. He had just settled under his blanket when he saw a figure weaving between the rocks and boulders headed toward the camp site.

He made out Poco Lizard, understanding origin of the bastardized Spanish name, talking to Alchesay.

Alchesay quickly cover the ten yards of so fast time.

"Nantan, they're here."

The point rider came in cautiously. An unwitting glance hinted at the existence of an outrider. Dead Shot motioned, Quilo, the scout with him. The silence of the dark near daybreak was broken only by the stirring of the very thirsty mule the hostile rode.

Quilo's return was unnoticed by Gatewood until a glance as day broke revealed Quilo was back in position. He knew Quilo had dispatched with the outrider or he would not have returned.

The hostile had slid from his mule. He scooped a handful from pool and drank.

Then, as if formed from the diminishing darkness, the main body appeared. The riders slid from their mounts, some ponies and some mules, all bone-dry thirsty.

One man, slow to join the others, stayed on his pony, was looking carefully back up the valley. Another man had not yet joined the others drinking but was scanning the slopes were the patrol waited for the Nantan's rifle. Alchesay's gestures were clear. He would take the mounted man and Gatewood should take the standing man.

They cautiously moved their rifles into position. Gatewood took a deep breath and squeezed the trigger of the Winchester, felt the firm recoil into his shoulder and missed his shot. He quickly levered in another cartridge, sighted the hostile now scrambling toward his mount and dropped him. Wounded, the hostile was squirming toward his pony. Before Gatewood could lever up another cartridge, a carbine shot stilled the man.

The report of Alchesay's carbine had blended with Gatewood's first shot. The now riderless pony galloped down the valley. A bullet struck the top of the rocks that protected Gatewood and made a disconcerting whistling as it ricocheted away. Gatewood rose to seek a target and drew two shots one flying stone fragment cutting his cheek. Now given exposed and sighted targets, four carbines fired.

The preliminary round was not as long as it felt. The volleys of carbine fire had been lethal but had brought no finality to the fight. There were seven bodies by and in the stream giving it slight red tint as it flowed from the bank.

Three hostiles reached the shelter of the bluff. Another found a boulder, then gathered himself and jumped to sprint for his companions. Gatewood's shot was low, but not completely off target. The sprinter's knee seemed to explode, leaving his left lower leg dangling. As he hobbled, a shot from Loco Lizard struck him solidly in the middle of his back. He fell mortally wounded. The three remaining men had scrambled to the temporary safety of the bluff and boulders lining the bank below the patrol's position.

Gatewood eased down left and Alchesay right. Dead Shot closed in from down the valley but sustained his firing angle should one sprint. Quilo appeared to move effortlessly between the boulders to the right of Alchesay, then a stone came loose and Quilo tumbled toward the ground. A shot from the bluff tore into his hip, the departing shell spewed fragments of bone and blood.

A hostile rose to get a better angle to finish him. Gatewood stood from behind his cover and laid down a distracting covering fire. As the hostile turned to return Gatewood's fire, Alchesay released a shot that struck him in the shoulder sending him lurching forward where Gatewood's shot caught him square in the chest.

With the intent of laying covering fire, Gatewood now found himself directly behind the two remaining hostiles. Two shots crashed into the rocks surrounding Gatewood. No place left to conceal him, he steadied his aim just missed the man as he tucked himself into a crevice. He was concealed from Gatewood who fired a shot to keep him pinned.

The hostile turned in the space seeking a shot at Alchesay or Quilo. The turn adequately exposed him to Dead Shot who had secured a position across the creek. Dead Shot sent the hostile straight to meet the Spirits.

The remaining hostile, assessing his position, fired at Dead Shot who seemed to present the most available target, released a screech that would grate on the ears of Satan and made a dash directly across the creek. A deafening cascade of carbine reports sounded, the bullets sent the body twisting to a running caricature and then splashing into the creek.

Alchesay shouted, "Nantan, I will secure the General's mules."

Gatewood nodded. Staying observant, he looked closely for any sign of the fate of the young girls. The scouts went about their business. They were quite efficiently scavenging the site. Tossed the mutilated bodies over mules and ponies and moved them across the meadow and into the trees. Food, guns and ammunition were premium. Gatewood walked through the site as if on a morning stroll in Virginia, acknowledging each man with a simple nod. His erect posture and easy gait concealed an increasingly queasy Second Lieutenant.

The finest of the livestock was cut out. The scouts were not cowhands and they had no desire to become ranchers. General's supplies and their own would be packed on the best of the mules. Although Fort Bayard was only a few days away, the rest would be cut loose. As much as they might dislike the Ojo Caliente band, they had no desire to secure fine mounts for the soldiers.

It was over.

Gatewood felt unsteady. He walked just upstream from the sight of the skirmish to a spot where the stream had narrowed and was splashing along creating small rapids. He brushed the top of the water and scooped several drinks from the stream. Then, he wet his 'kerchief and wiped the trickle of blood where a rock fragment nicked him from his face. Wet it again, laying it across the back of his neck as he sat down. His heart continued pounding. Areas of his blouse were soaked with sweat despite the chill of the morning air.

The elephant was clearly different from cutting the throat of an unsuspecting enemy.

He watched the water flow downstream. He could hear the sound of the shallow water rushing over the stones in the creek. A small smooth stone about the size of a silver dollar caught his eye. He squatted down and picked it up from the water. He rubbed the stone between his thumb and his fingers and then put it in his blouse pocket. He had another drink, lingering after each handful. He returned to his perch and sat. The deep breath became more of a sigh. He was settling.

Alchesay came up.

"Please sit, Sergeant." As Alchesay sat, Gatewood asked, "Quilo?"

"He is medicined, will heal."

"The girls?"

"Nantan, no sign of girls, still it was a very successful morning."

"Your thoughts on the girls?"

"Sold to whore man from mining camp, maybe Mormon buy them. Maybe already died on trip." Alchesay was thoughtful, "Never know – Incognita"

"Sergeant, I speak some Spanish but I believe you to speak impeccable English."

Alchesay paused, "I shouldn't have – I regret."

"I know your English is superior to my White Mountain Apache. Just speak your mind."

A relaxed and genuine smile was exchanged, not an easy thing for either man.

Gatewood looked at scouts now gathered at the location of the fight. He said, "The men appear tired. Do you judge this a safe enough place to rest till morning?"

"Nantan, they give all days you need, but you need no more. About a mile upstream, good place for animals, easy to defend. Rest there."

Gatewood agreed.

"Choose a scout to leave at daybreak and carry a message to Fort Bayard."

A site was established. Gatewood inventoried what seemed to belong to the U.S. Army. Dog lapped from the stream. Gatewood had not thought of the animal in days. He drew a piece of jerky from his pocket, bit off a chew and torn a piece for the dog. The dog lingered, Gatewood opened both hands showing the empty palms as he had done with his own bird dog. Dog trotted off and lay down in a shady spot.

Gatewood retrieved paper and pencil from his pouch. The precise report conserved words.

A pony was slaughtered. A couple of scouts took a quick look at Dog, considering a tasty snack before thinking better of it.

Gatewood carefully considered his place. He observed the protocol and then with the same knife that sent the deserter on his journey to eternity, he sliced a generous portion of the pony rump. Mexican beans from their own stash were prepared. With flour likely taken from the wagons and found in the goods of the hostiles, fry bread was prepared. Then, he filled his cup with creek bank coffee. Coffee along with sugar was one of the few white eye foods the Apache had embraced. He returned to his perch above the creek.

While perhaps his palate was simply adapting, he found his meal to be satisfying. His knife cut the meat and the beans were captured with help of the fry bread. It was almost luxurious.

Bellies full, the camp calmed. There was talk and even laughter, a sound he had not heard in their campsite before. It was good.

Now rifles were oiled and cleaned. Given the dust and sand, the amount of oil transferred from rag to rifle was precise. Maintenance of a scout's rifle was a required art form. A malfunction or misfire could bring deadly results. The final step involved a leather wrap placed around the rifles action. A rifle must function.

Only now did Alchesay make his way to Gatewood's place. One of the scouts accompanied him.

"Nantan, I need to speak."

Gatewood nodded. Alchesay folded his legs beneath him and sat.

"Before speaking Goso has an offer." In a quieter voice he added, "Say yes."

Goso began, "Nantan Baychendaysen" and then followed a blend of Apache and Spanish that completely lost Gatewood.

Alchesay already prepared to translate said, "Nantan Baychendaysen, Goso would be honored if you would allow him to sharpen your hunting knife. He has a fine sharpening rock...gran roca." Understanding the Spanish, the scout reached into a small pouch and withdrew the most perfect natural whetstone Gatewood had ever seen.

Gatewood responded without hesitation, "Yes, thank Goso." Though Goso's English was limited, Gatewood's tone extended acceptance of the offer and gave him considerable satisfaction. Gatewood extended his knife handle first, a trust indicator in most cultures.

"Nantan Baychendaysen." He nodded.

Gatewood observed, "The scout possesses a near perfect stone."

Alchesay said, "Be cautious with the blade when it is returned. Goso says your knife is of a fine metal, so he can place the sharpest of edges on it." "There are many sharpening stones in the mountains just to the west of us, but few so fine."

"Nantan Bayshinsin?"

"Bay-chen-Day-sen." Alchesay slowly pronounced the Apache word. He added, "Honor, Noo-tah-hah give name is to show respect or hate."

Thinking back to such grand nicknames given Confederate heroes such as "Stonewall," he said, "Then, I am truly honored."

"What does it mean?"

Alchesay hesitated. His years in the scouts had alerted him to the white man's vanity. Then, deciding to be done with it, he said, "Chief Long Nose."

To Alchesay's considerable confusion, Gatewood, with a newly emerging self-acceptance, hooted. Seeing the puzzled look, Gatewood told the short version of his nickname at West Point, he felt such identification could not have pursued him from the banks of the Hudson River to a desert land far west of the Mississippi River. But it did.

"It is hard to miss."

"Nantan, the sun reaches it first except for you big hat."

"Always Baychendaysen with Noo-tah-hah."

"New-ta-Hah?"

"Noo-tah-hah. It is us."

Alchesay could not explain that while an individual Apache might refer to himself as N'de, man, Noo-tah-hah had no meaning but it was them.

Gatewood carefully shaped his tongue, "Noo-tah-han, Baychendaysen."

"Sergeant, the girls," Alchesay stopped the inquiry and said, "Baychendaysen, I am Alchesay for you."

"Alchesay, the fate of the girls troubles me."

"No sign of hiding and escaping, much disease rides in white man's wagons. The Ojo Caliente did not have many gold pieces or new rifles." He said, "Woman keeps dolls as." He reached from the English word through Spanish, "Recuerdos – rec –," then found it, "Reminders – reminders of her children."

As it entered his mind, he spoke, "If girls fled into land, Ojo Caliente could have hunted hard, left much sign. Girl worth too much in Mexico – in silver town. Worth too much not to search hard."

Gatewood nodded and then said, "Perhaps it just troubles me that a child could be sold in Mexico or the silver camps, to be violated for the profit of another." Gatewood thought it and allowed it escape his lips, "Negro slavery is one thing, to enslave a white child quite another."

Alchesay thought of mentioning that the white man would enslave the Apache on something called a reservation. The Nantan had not yet seen San Carlos. Baychendaysen was brave, kept his own council, inquired but didn't judge. He seemed different. Alchesay was slow to convince.

Goso returned with the sharpen knife. Gatewood took the knife and shaved a small spot on his left arm. The clean cut surprised Gatewood, visibly pleasing him. Goso saw he had surpassed Baychendaysen's expectations. He nodded his head reflecting the pride of personal achievement. He left.

Alchesay changed the focus, "You met the elephant and mounted him. You have nature's gut for the elephant, like in another life you smelled his breath and liked it."

Although it was clearly a compliment, Gatewood felt uncertain. Then, he nodded and said, "I am told you are wise in such matters, that you know much of the elephant well."

"I learned about such things since I was small boy." Alchesay clarified, "I laid with the elephant before I laid with a woman."

Gatewood smiled then a chuckled. Alchesay's wit caught him off guard.

Another layer peeled away from the onions.

Three days march and almost to the Gila River, the scout returned from Fort Bayard guiding a small military detachment. Gatewood settled in on Bob and looked at the Lieutenant in charge of the detail. The Bayard Lieutenant's dress made him appear as if he were in costume. Gatewood again recognized the sound advice he had received from McPherson.

Formalities exchanged, the Bayard Lieutenant started some exchange of pleasantry but something about Gatewood's gaze and bearing stopped him short, leaving a sentence dangling.

Gatewood held his hand out and said one word, "Orders." It was not a question, it was a command.

Gatewood took the envelope and stepped away from the small group. He opened it. If he had any reaction to its contents none could detect it.

He returned, "My First Sergeant tells me that we are less than an hour from the Gila. We will camp there."

About half an hour into the ride, Gatewood with little observable effort moved away from the Lieutenant and eased alongside Alchesay. The men moved out of sight of the column.

"What was recovered from the hostiles the patrol can use?"

"One good repeating rifle, three pouches of cartridges, coffee. Knifes good."

A need to understand compelled Gatewood to ask, "Mutilated – their crotch – you cut off their dick and balls and shoved a stick in their eyes." The selective maiming was lost in Gatewood's logic.

Alchesay heard the question, "No carajo – no dick to poke at squaw next life. Eyes steal beauty around him." Anticipating a follow up question which Gatewood wasn't going to ask, "Chiricahua and Ojo Caliente cut up whites bad – hope to frighten from our land. Especially to women don't have time to sell."

It was Gatewood who reversed the focus, "Good carbines?"

"Have better now, bagged them. Need better carbines, these ain't better. Five have old breechloaders, dependable."

"The repeater?"

Alchesay produced the rifle, "No Winchester." His voice suggesting any other was make was at least somewhat inferior to the Winchester Centennial. "Yours takes big .45 and is very strong."

Gatewood closely examined the Henry Repeating Rifle that Alchesay produced before declaring it to be in excellent condition.

A glance told him Alchesay wanted more but Gatewood continued, "Uses .44 but not big powder load, one hundred yards very good. Old Spencer is more powerful but awkward, Henry is faster and good balance. The lever is quick to respond. Good brush gun. I think it's far better than a Springfield for our work."

Alchesay felt the weight and balance of the rifle, cradled it into his shoulder.

Gatewood said, "You keep it and try it. Keep all the cartridges and coffee."

He took the orders from his blouse pocket and told Alchesay, "We are to proceed to Camp Apache. Bring the General's mules. General Wilcox instructs that we may, within sound reason, resupply from the mules." He turned from directive to inquisitive, "Camp Apache?"

"Follow Gila River until we can smell it, then angle north."

"Smell the Gila?"

"River cuts alkaline ground. River stinks by San Carlos." He added, "Don't drink." He tapped his stomach, "Cramp pain, shit water."

He concluded with a hint of resentment, "Good mountain water at Camp Apache."

"Orders say to look close for hostiles escaping San Carlos."

Alchesay nodded, "Nantan Baychendaysen, San Carlos bad place. Many promises but little comes. No food, much sickness."

Baychendaysen shook his head and then ask, "Thoughts?"

"Bad agent sells many cows, much food to Mormons."

"Pick six best mules and the best ponies for us. They can carry or herd the rest to Bayard."

Alchesay understood.

"Can two hunters secure deer or elk for tonight from the mountains?" motioning pine covered hills to the east as he ask.

"Yes. But - Miners mistake scouts to be hostiles, but miners are poor shots. Little elk or deer in the bald mountains to west. What Nantan think?"

"I think I'll not risk two good scouts to fill the bellies of well fed soldiers. Cook won't know mule from elk, eat their beans and drink their coffee."

Alchesay nodded approval.

They returned to the column and eased into their places.

At the evening meal, the Bayard Lieutenant repeatedly voicing his appreciation of the tender, mesquite flavored dish that Gatewood had described as "campfire beef" cooked over an open fire. After all the social conversation he could tolerate, Gatewood excused himself and made his way toward his roost. As he walked past the scouts' fire, pleased that his White Mountains hadn't done harm to the timid Pueblos that had guided the Bayard soldiers, Alchesay rose and stopped him.

"Nantan Baychendaysen, you must eat," extending a sharpen stick with two chunks of meat. Now aware Alchesay possessed a wit about him, Gatewood paused. With Alchesay's nod of encouragement he took a bite. The meat was as sweet and moist as any he had ever encountered. It was delicious.

Only after he had eaten it both chunks, did he ask, "What is it?"

"Rattlesnake."

Baychendaysen was taken with the taste of rattlesnake meat. His expression of pleasure was genuine.

"Happy you like the snake, I like it much."

"Next time we have rattlesnake, I expect my full ration."

Daybreak came. Lieutenant Gatewood advised the Bayard Lieutenant of the necessity of the prompt departure of his patrol. The patrol was several miles gone, the Bayard column was left to collect the livestock and pack all the spoils they had collected in the hope of selling in Mexico.

The thought of all the muttering and mumbling in the camp amused Gatewood.

The patrol moved northwest, following the Gila River and taking advantage of the abundant game in the foothills. Despite Fort Thomas south of San Carlos on the Gila, this was still Chiricahua country and a path for raiders leaving the reservation, raid in Mexico, secure food and supplies, then return to their families on the reservation.

On the trip, bypassing San Carlos although as Alchesay had pointed out it was impossible to pass the increasingly unpleasant odor of the alkaline filled Gila, Gatewood began to understand that assigning Apaches to a reservation was easy. Keeping them there was altogether another matter.

Baychendaysen now ate with the patrol, accepting his education at the pace it came. He would then move to a stone venue, avoiding disrupting the conversations of the scouts. Alchesay would come for an exchange of knowledge with increasing regularity.

White Mountain Apaches trust of the white eye was slow, seeing the soldiers as a method to get where they wish to get. No question when compared to San Carlos, the White Mountain reservation was lush. Filled with natural lakes and flowing streams, timber, and high land meadows, in other words land white settlers would find most desirable. A fact not lost on Alchesay. The friendship of the white man was essential even though most unsavory.

With Baychendaysen, trust came easily. He approached a fight like an Apache. His goal was to kill the enemy, as many as possible, without losing a man. Even with camp sites, Baychendaysen quickly learned that a good escape route might prove as valuable as a sustainable defensive perimeter.

Alchesay closed this night's visit saying, "Many call us White Mountain Apache, to us – we call us Coyoteros – wolves."

He went on, "You saw Ojo Caliente fight, are billy goats – sheep."

Although Gatewood had seen their recent opponents as fighting well for a group who had been completely surprised, he kept his thought to himself.

The blanket roll was warm enough but sleeping on the ground had remained a persistent agitator of his joints and bones. His scouts seem to spring from the ground, restored and rested by their night's sleep. It was uncomfortable for Gatewood to simply sit upright. The discomfort would lessen with the movement of morning but was lingered throughout the day. He preferred to keep such things to himself, hoping his command did not notice.

Dr. Walter Reed

Dorsey McPherson and Thomas Cruse

FOUR
CAMP APACHE

IN 1869, MAJOR JOHN GREEN of the U.S. 1st Cavalry found the site for Camp Apache on the White Mountain River. He considered it to be ideally located between two warring factions of Apache, the Chiricahua and the White Mountain. He reported it to have abundant water and to be excellently wooded. He stated, "There was fine building material of pine lumber within eight miles of the site as well as limestone within a reasonable distance." An additional enticement in his report concluded, "Based on local reports the area has little to no malaria." Construction began in 1870.

The patrol's movement toward Camp Apache was uneventful. As Alchesay had stated the Gila took on an unpleasant smell that Gatewood was convinced could have become a stench had they not broken off the river trail and turned northwest.

The cool clear water of the Black Fork of the Salt River was as completely pleasant as the Gila had become unpleasant. The scouts and animals actually enjoyed an extended watering during the crossing, enjoying the shade of the willows, cottonwoods and river oaks. Unhurried, as his body acclimated to the chilly water, Gatewood tried to soak away 9 weeks of sand and the drying effects of the wind under the winter sun.

It was the first time he saw his blood soaked socks, blood that had seeped from the deep cracks in his heels. He put them on, slipped into his boots, tucked in his pants and prepared to soldier on the remaining miles to Camp Apache.

Cross the White River, colder and clearer than the Black, top a small incline on the north bank and Camp Apache emerged.

Smaller than Fort Wingate, It was of sturdy log construction well caulked with adobe. Each structure appeared to have its own stone fire place. Windows were few in both the officers' quarters and the enlisted men's barracks. Despite the tree-lined White River, there was not a single tree on the grounds. Camp Apache had some unique geographic advantages. There were steep sloping buttes near the site. The hillsides were covered with junipers and an assortment of scrub pines and cactus. The mesa tops were coated with mesquites and pines. A nearby canyon with a flowing creek had cottonwood, birch and a desert willow growing. Just to the north in the White Mountains, were large stands of ponderosa pines, easily harvested and hauled mostly downhill to the Camp.

Although technically, this land was reserved for the White Mountain Apache, the camp harvested the timber at will. The desirability of their land to the white man did escape Alchesay and other chiefs of the White Mountain Apaches. While possession of land was something of a foreign concept, they were planning to adapt and survive.

About two miles south of the camp along a small creek seasonally fed with snow melt, the column came to a halt. Baychendaysen and Alchesay talked.

"I can justify three new Springfields from the "General's Mules" but not ten."

Alchesay understood his words, but not the dilemma. He was direct, "Goso, a warrior, loyal to death. Dead Shot, use it well. Ouilo, fired his rifle after fall." He thought and added, "Baychendaysen must take something for himself."

The crate was opened and the three new owners of a Springfield rifle begin to oil and clean their prize. Each man gave his previous rifle to a man of his own choosing except Dead Shot who claimed his rifle for his son. Judging from the response of the others, it was a quite acceptable practice.

Alchesay selected a tin of sugar and opened it. The scouts sat and ate the cane sugar.

Gatewood took a can of sweet syrup peaches. Opened the can with his pocket knife, the ease surprised him. Goso took note. He ate the peaches skewering each peach with the tip of the knife. The knife tasted much since leaving Fort Wingate in Baychendaysen's pocket. At the first opportunity, Goso sharpened the pocket knife into a multipurpose weapon.

Baychendaysen had begun a journey.

The arrival of the patrol created little stir. The Coyotero scouts moved toward their corral and open quarters. Lieutenant Gatewood and First Sergeant Alchesay tied up in front of the headquarters building.

The Adjutant didn't look up until Gatewood snapped, "Corporal, Lieutenant C. B. Gatewood and First Sergeant Alchesay to report to Major Cochran."

The Adjutant snapped erect. "Yes Sir. I'll advise the Major you're here."

On returning he said, "It will be just a moment. Your mess arrived with Captain McPherson. At his request, you have been assigned the same quarters."

"That is quite acceptable," was Gatewood's response. He suppressed any overt expression might give away his pleasure to find the surgeon was here.

"Sergeant it was assumed you'd billet with your scouts. Small wikiups are allowed."

Knowing to suggest otherwise would have created a most awkward situation and that he would nonetheless be sleeping with the scouts, Alchesay nodded yes. In truth, he had no desire to sleep by any other fire.

Major Melville E. Cochran, the commanding officer at Camp Apache, took the oral reports and his expectation of a written account from Lieutenant Gatewood the next day clearly communicated.

The Major rose from behind his desk and said, "It seems you Gentlemen found a way to make an ordinary assignment quite eventful, but successful none the less." Turning to Gatewood, he said, "The Adjutant will see that the General's cargo is inventoried and forwarded to Prescott."

The formal business was concluded and respects were exchanged. "Thank you, Sir."

Again on the porch, Baychendaysen said, "Well done Sergeant." Alchesay nodded. The firm gaze passed between the men. An exchange of esteem few men are privileged to experience.

Baychendaysen said, "Soon."

Alchesay responded, "Soon."

Gatewood unhitched Bob, firmly patting his neck then rubbing it. He believed Bob had carried him through erratic weather, pushed to exhaustion with muscles tired and aching, through hunger and thirst. He got a tired nuzzle from Bob. He led Bob to the hostler.

"Lieutenant." The hostler said both acknowledging his arrival and inquiring "Lieutenant who?" without really asking.

"Second Lieutenant C. B. Gatewood." He continued, "Corporal, I have a tired animal here who served me well. Please see that he is fed, rested and ready to go again. I see there is a smith, is there a furrier as well?"

"Yes Sir. Two."

"Good, after he is rested, shoe him well."

There was something in the Lieutenant's voice that convinced Corporal O'Hara that the horse had earned the superior treatment suggested and it had best be supplied.

"Damn, the way you look its good you're bunking with two surgeons."

"It seems the sandy air has sharpened the Captain Surgeon's tongue."

Little is more welcoming between friends than the warmth of a firm handshake and an exchange of insults, insults composed of a blend of fact and fiction.

"Only a green Virginia Lieutenant could turn a five day patrol into a ten week sightseeing trip damn near into Mexico." McPherson laughed at his own humor while suppressing a strong desire to make some derogatory comment about the Confederacy.

"Can you hush long enough to show me to the bunk?" Gatewood was suddenly tired. His back seemed stiffer, the discomfort seemed more aggravating.

McPherson doffed his black field hat as if to say, "This way, Sir."

The single officers' quarter was a one room log building with a lean-to attached. Housing four, each man had a bunk, five wall pegs for hanging clothes and a lower peg for pistol belts, a small three drawer bed table and space for a trunk. The light came from two kerosene lamp suspended over a locally constructed table with four chairs in the middle of the room. Each bedside table would ultimately contain a candle. The split wood floor was a frontier luxury. The floor was starting to polish through wear but it remained a good reason not to walk around the room barefooted.

"It is newer and finer construction than our accommodations at Wingate." McPherson said as he introduced the room. He continued, "And since you have the privilege of mess with two surgeons, if needed you can set your slop jar out and it will be emptied first each morning."

Dorsey laughed. Gatewood, while he had found the extensive silences of the patrol to be quite agreeable, was contented hearing the good natured spoken English of his friend.

"So you're still the commandant of sanitation."

The room was much better than would be found on most frontier post. The large fireplace was especially impressive.

Gatewood flopped on the mattress and unfastened his braces. As he was removing his boots, McPherson noted the uncomfortable rigidity that had settled into Gatewood's back. He first supposed that was the price of weeks of sleeping wrapped in a blanket roll on rocky ground.

McPherson poured two glasses of bourbon, two fingers for himself and three fingers for the Lieutenant.

"First class Ripy Brothers. I am told it is aged in white oak kegs like those from Virginia." It was as if McPherson was saying, "Here my friend, have a drink of home."

Gatewood's first sip was not a sip, but a solid drink. The astringent taste lingered in his mouth as he took another sip. "This is truly fine bourbon."

"How was it out there?"

Gatewood paused, sipped and said, "Dorsey, I don't know yet. I have to think on it." As if each hiatus from thought brought a few words, "Your tips on the Apache and the land were immensely useful, saved me from appearing the complete fool."

The latter acknowledgement pleased McPherson.

He responded, "Knowledge only aids a man to the extent he chooses to use it."

Gatewood tossed down the remaining bourbon. Using his blanket roll as a pillow, he lay back on the bed and said, "Feels good to think about sleeping without my boots."

He found sleep quickly and deeply. He slept until Reveille awakened him.

"Walt, I want you to meet Sleeping Beauty." McPherson's Irish baritone was already sharp.

Gatewood become aware of the movement of a third man.

"Captain Walter Reed may I introduce Second Lieutenant Charles Gatewood."

Reed took a long stride, Gatewood shook the extended hand. Reed's handshake was firm, his eye contact solid. He passed Gatewood's initial criteria of trustworthiness.

Reed's hair was parted in the middle and neatly trimmed to the sided, a thick yet small mustache that added to his appearance rather than distracting. Then came the clincher, McPherson said, "I hate to say this but I now find myself surrounded by Virginians."

Reed was a born, bred and educated Virginian, the son of a Methodist Minister, who received his Medical Degree by completing the rigorous two year program at the University of Virginia. Gatewood was thoroughly impressed.

Dorsey interrupted this preliminary exchange with a reality.

"Nantan Baychendaysen, you told me Major Cochran is expecting a written report prior to lunch."

"God Damn, how – where did you get that?"

Struggling with his temptation to tweak his friend a bit more, he said, "It is the only fashion in which your scouts will refer to you. You did something that impressed the livin' Hell out of them Apaches." The temptation overwhelmed the obviously admiration he now held for his friend, "Of course, it could be they thought possessing Caesar's snout to be a sign of prominence."

Dorsey laughed and patted his friend's shoulder, Gatewood smiled and Reed looked puzzled.

Gatewood and McPherson were learning the Apache did not put a lot of stock in the white man's words. Every man was judged upon his actions.

The report was a typical Gatewood report. It was brief. Mission redirected near Stoneman Lake. As to the deserter's deaths, he wrote the deserters raping white woman at site of wagon massacre, both died, reason to believe hostiles had a small female hostage, quick pursuit of hostiles resumed, hostiles' encountered north of Cloverdale. All killed. One scout wounded. Property recovered. Weapons, animals and stores recovered from hostiles to Fort Bayard. Patrol resupplied from recovered property.

Major Cochran, noting its brevity, read the report. Lieutenant Gatewood stood.

Cochran spoke, "Lieutenant, it seems you and your scouts were quite effective." Paused as if considering his words, he motioned for the Lieutenant to sit and continued, his tone turning more informal, "Not long on taking prisoners are you?"

"No one tried to surrender." Gatewood answered.

"Deserters – Christian burial?"

"No, Sir. I judged the quick pursuit of the hostiles possibly holding a young girl to be of greater value."

The Major nodded reflecting understanding if not agreement. He then slid his chair back and stood.

"Lieutenant, it was a well executed patrol. My compliments on your command decisions to change the focus of your mission not once, but twice while in the field. It was reported you will do what a situation requires to secure a successful outcome."

Before Gatewood could bask in the praise, he found the downside of success.

"I have reason to believe you'll be back in the field within the week. I'd suggest you take advantage of the time to rest."

"Thank you, Sir."

"Lieutenant, give your First Sergeant my regards. Tell him that his performance again met the high quality I have come to expect from him."

"I will, Sir. He will be pleased."

The correct salutes came and Gatewood departed.

Just loud enough that the Adjunct could hear and spread the tale, Major Cochran said, "Just maybe God Almighty paired two men who could have hunted down Mangus himself."

The Major knew that it never hurt to let men hear a bit of praise through the humor mill of the ranks. He also knew the rumblings on San Carlos were just beginning to sound.

He retrieved his cigar from the ashtray, struck a lucifer and relit it. San Carlos was a stinking malaria infested waste land with an agency run by a completely untrustworthy profiteer. He wondered if the War Department hadn't selected the most horrid place in the Arizona Territory and put the Chiricahua on it.

"Putting a Chiricahua on a reservation is one thing, keeping a Chiricahua there is quite another task."

Gatewood took a deep breath. He no longer had the dust cough that had troubled him a Wingate. This dry air now seemed to agree with his lungs. He stretch and wished he could get it to agree with his bones. He walked toward the stable to visit Bob.

The Corporal saw him step into the stable.

"Good Day, Lieutenant. Just getting' ready to take ya horse into the exercise area."

Bob bobbed his head, pulled the Mexican handler toward Gatewood. Gatewood was almost embarrassed by how attached he had become to Bob. He gave him two sugar cubes and then a carrot that he had requisitioned from a cook. Bob nuzzled Gatewood's hand, then nestled against his shoulder.

"Lieutenant Sir, he's a tad bone sore. I'd wait a day or so 'fore taking him out."

"Thank you Corporal, I will." Gatewood lingered in the paddock area. Patting Bob and talking to him. He found the Corporal on his way out, "Corporal, you appear a man who knows his horses. You look to be a horseman with considerable experience. I suspect you have a special liniment, your own concoction."

The recognition pleased him greatly. "Truth be I do, but Calvary don't pay for it."

"How much?"

"Nickel a rub."

Gatewood gave him a dime and a nickel. "Corporal Holly, two rubs and the nickel is for caring about my horse."

The Corporal was pleased. Bob received considerable extra attention.

Gatewood felt a twinge of pain in his back and right hip. He thought Bob wasn't the only animal that returned bone sore. He considered buying a little of "Holly's Balm" for himself.

He eyed Alchesay sitting near a small fire outside a wikiup that had been reinforced by multiple occupations over time. To the white eye, the wikiup appeared a more than reasonable shelter.

"Sergeant, a moment of your time."

Alchesay had watched Baychendaysen walk across the parade ground from the corrals. He wasn't generally of the mood to move yet. He sat near the fire, legs folded beneath him, with a clear view of the parade ground, his blanket wrapped around him. While perhaps not warm, he was comfortable.

Baychendaysen's gait was stiff, appearing neither comfortable nor agile.

Alchesay got up, seemed to loosen his muscles in one flowing move, nodded and said, "Anzhoo, Nantan Baychendaysen."

Although his tongue hadn't yet gotten the hang of the greeting, Gatewood responded with something sounding like, "Anzhoo."

The men found a lean-too out of the wind but in the spring sun. Gatewood rolled a cigarette and passed the makings to Alchesay who declined.

Exhaling he said, "I understand we might go out again soon."

Alchesay nodded to the affirmative.

Realizing that nothing was being volunteered, Gatewood looked directly at him and said, "Your thoughts First Sergeant?"

"The San Carlos – rotting death. Diseases, rations, no food – Agent sell best to Mormons, give Chiricahua leavings. Chiricahua food has bugs." Alchesay thought, "Chiricahua promised long life, get long death." He stopped short of telling Baychendaysen his thoughts on agents selling the cattle to Mormons, the very Mormons who were trying to encroach on White Mountain land.

"What should this mean to me – and to you?"

"Nana, Victorio, Geronimo – with many followers will someday leave the San Carlos. Then, much – die – much death"

Gatewood accurately sensed his companion was not yet finished.

"Nantan, small parties steal cows, even hunt Coyotero game, just want to eat. Just flies on a bear." He paused and Baychendaysen waited.

Alchesay liked that a white man could wait although this was the first he remembered encountering.

"Nantan, bear will come again soon."

Baychendaysen took a tentative grasp of the situation. The Chiricahua had been put in a place that if they stayed, they would die but if they fled killing them could be justified. They were in a place that even the water carried a stench while living in the shadows of paradise. The lush ancestral home of the White Mountain Apache, land of the Coyotero, covered with game, timber, grassy meadows and mountain streams could be viewed as no less than a paradise. To view the mountains of the Coyotero, a people with whom the Chiricahua had a blood feud so old and deep only myths contained its origins. Regardless, the Coyotero would gladly help the United States military hunt down the Chiricahua. They would gladly kill to keep their ancestral land.

Alchesay had rather enjoyed sitting, watching Baychendaysen organize his thoughts. A man should think his thoughts and then choose those he wishes to speak.

"Did the Chiricahua have no ancestral lands such as the White Mountains?"

"The Chiricahua – believe all lands theirs –raid and steal from Mexicans, from everyone. Always seem to move with the seasons."

"Nomads." Gatewood mused in a half-question.

Alchesay didn't recognize the English but it didn't matter. Business was done.

The men talked. The conversation was brief as such was the disposition of both men. Alchesay inquired of Gatewood's home. Gatewood compared the land of the White Mountains they had traveled through after leaving Fort Wingate to his native Virginia. Small, eccentric comparisons of the grasses and trees were given. Other topics were saved for other days. Such men never share more than the other can completely absorb.

"Baychendaysen." Alchesay extended his arm. At first, Gatewood thought he had awkwardly missed a handshake until Alchesay hand to firm grasp of his wrist. Then, he understood and grasped the wrist.

As they parted, Gatewood thought that was better than just shaking hands. Baychendaysen could feel Alchesay in a fashion of trust, a pact of mutual assistance. Alchesay intended it to be an indication that Baychendaysen had earned an additional opportunity.

Walking toward his quarters and looking across the parade ground, he thought here I am. With two troops of the Sixth Calvary and two companies of the Twelfth Infantry under the command of Major Melville E. Cochran assigned to look over a land and a people few if any could understand. Gatewood was coming to understand this was a people who had no desire to be looked after.

He hesitated, briefly considering a visit to the Quartermaster's, but opted toward what he took to be a more pressing need. He walked back toward his bachelor's quarters.

He sharpened the tip of his pen and checked the inkwell.

17 May 1878
Camp Apache, A.T.

Dear Georgia,

I must first confess I did not know if was humanly possible to yearn for another as I have longed for you. Your last letter is now my treasure, I could hear your voice as I read your words. My mind brings forth a clear vision of you as you stood framed in the doorway of the rail station, painted in the lush lavender of your dress as it flowed over you. During my recent weeks in the field, it was a nightly image of you that made the ground upon which I slept feel soft and my blankets kept me warm. My Georgia, I do miss you so.

I judge my first patrol to have been quite successful. I could have never expected the great diversity of landscape I encountered. I rose from the cold barren landscape of Wingate into forests of ancient pines trying to pierce the sky, dotted with spruce and aspen, broken by lush grassy meadows and small natural lakes. Game exists in such abundance it is difficult to convey. I cannot help but recall my grandfather's stories of game in the Virginia of his youth.

Then, the land can rapidly transform itself into an as inhospitable an environment you can imagine. The flowing rivers in the AT would be considered mere streams in Virginia. As we descended onto the desert floor, rivers became dry, cracked beds with a pattern of erosion the only indicator that water might have rapidly coursed through during the rainy season.

As to my quarters here, I find the bachelor's mess to be superior to that of Wingate. Dr. McPherson, of whom I have written and Dr. Walter Reed, a fellow Virginian, now shares my bunk space. Both are pleasant conversationalist. It is my early conclusion that Dr. McPherson has the deportment field surgeon. Dr. Reed has just arrived.

Gatewood considered including he was impressed that neither man seemed to shirk from latrine duty. He decided that such a remark was inconsistent with the tone he wished the letter to convey.

My command is ten scouts of the White Mountain Apache tribe. There are clans within the Apache that I believe dislike each other with a similar intensity to that which divides a Richmond man from a Boston man.

I share with you alone these initial impressions. The ten are highly skilled trackers and are most efficient in battle, the untainted warrior. They are patient, maximizing every advantage before entering the fight and exceptionally proficient to the task once engaged.

He thought about telling her he believed the hostiles they might engage would have a similar bent for combat. Then, he thought better of it.

Although their skin is rather dark, I can now attest the Apache in attitude and demeanor in no way resemble the Negroes of Virginia. I cannot yet account for the dramatic difference.

He laid the pen crossway on the inkwell and got up, walking to window. He looked at the angle toward the row of married officers' quarters. Less than half of the units had curtains of unbleached muslin covering in the windows. Given the renowned durability of Cavalry wives, Gatewood took it to be a testament to the hardship of Camp Apache. He heard some wives quartered in Tucson while others remained with family.

He stepped outside. The heat was rising from the south. Camp Apache was adequately removed from San Carlos and the alkaline-laden Gila River that the odor he believed he detected was simply an olfactory hallucination.

The realization of how deeply he missed Georgie began to seep into his conscious awareness. He abruptly turned and walked back toward his quarters.

Lifting the pen and dipping into the ink, he continued his letter. The focus of his letter changed. He began describing the married officers quarters. It struck him how little exterior diversity there was to describe. Windows covered with unbleached muslin curtains, a few with lace trim, were a reliable indicator of the presence of a military spouse. He could think of no words to adequately describe these circumstances in a fashion he believed palatable to the lady he was hopeful could consider becoming a military wife. Gatewood, who prided himself on his skill with the pen, put the best face he could on the conditions. He didn't want to paint Georgie such a glamorous portrait that she would feel he had misrepresent the situation. Finally, he wrote his truth.

Dearest, as much as I desire to entice you and while I could endure the fires of Hell to be with you, I would never expect such sacrifice of you. I wish to bring you to life in a paradise but for now I am in the Arizona Territory.

This writing had rekindled Virginia in his mind and Georgie in his heart. The anguish simplified his closing, signing little more than his name.

The envelope addressed and brushed with glue from the Adjunct's glue pot, Gatewood surrender his letter.

Back in the mess, Gatewood retrieved the dollar sized smooth stone from his pocket. He rubbed the stone between his thumb and his fingers. He leaned back in this seat and relaxed. He was uncertain as to why he had pocketed the stone. In one sense it was an unremarkable stone colored various shades of brown. Nature had been the artist creating its round shape and incredibly smooth surface.

He sat the chair down and secured the stone of the table top. Dipping the pen into ink he carefully wrote on the stone the number one, below that he wrote in script April 1878. He placed it above his bunk to completely dry.

Consider it a personal talisman for a soldier.

A reliable friendship between McPherson and Gatewood was emerging. As the evenings heated, porch conversations lingered later into the evening. McPherson became one of the very few to refer to Gatewood by something of his first name, "Charlie." While those pretending to know him well called McPherson "Doc," to Gatewood and those really close to the physician, he was simply "Dorsey."

"Dorsey, that Gladstone bag of yours, what are the staples you carry?"

The question was serious.

"Let me show you." Gatewood pushed his lower lip out a bit and gave a sideways nod. The thought of a physician's tools made him oddly uncomfortable.

Flopping the black leather field bag on the table, Dorsey orderly withdraw a small set of scalpels, a folding magnifying glass, a small kit of probes and a small sewing kit with catgut sutures. He finished the row with a few forceps, tweezers and scissors. The next line contained a thermometer, syringes and needles for injections, four bags of carefully wrapped ampoules of morphine, other opiates, cocaine and an adrenalin solution. Finally, he produced several powders including aspirin, a powder derived from the bark of the yellow willow. Two leather straps for tourniquets or restraints and a small alcohol lamp were carried in his saddlebag.

He pondered a moment and produced two corked bottles, "Laudanum, all the laudanum I can beg, borrow or steal."

"I fear that good medicinal brandy has been replaced by two pints of fine frontier whiskey." He withdrew three pint bottles from his roll. "It does appear to be an efficient if not elegant replacement."

Gatewood smiled and said, "I like your medical school mathematics."

"Catch a cartridge and you'll like it considerably more."

Nana

FIVE

ON NANA'S HEEL

GATEWOOD TOOK BOB A COUPLE of carrots. He enjoyed McPherson's company and Reed was growing on him, but it was Bob he trusted with conversation about Georgie. These were eccentric exchanges in which few words were spoken. However, Gatewood was convinced Bob understood.

Alchesay walked at measured pace toward the man and horse, not speaking until he could touch Bob's flank.

"Nantan Baychendaysen, talk says maybe Kastiziden tires of San Carlos." The formal salutation unmistakably indicated a sober message was going to follow. "Might send Poco Lizard to look at the ground."

"Kastiziden?"

"Mexicans called him Nana. Most soldiers too."

"Nana."

"Old man long time with Cochise. Still quick warrior."

Gatewood thought a moment then ask, "Can we keep him on San Carlos?"

"Nantan, if going he is gone." The tone of Alchesay's voice left Gatewood with little doubt that Nana was likely on the move.

"Sergeant, your thoughts on sending Goso with Poco Lizard? If a trail is found, Goso can come to us, Poco Lizard can remain on the trail and we will find him."

A quick nod of each head concluded agreement.

71

Gatewood paused realizing they were likely ahead of military intelligence.

"Alchesay, I don't think it is wise to act as if we have knowledge of this until my commander tells us."

Gatewood hesitated and then asked, "Kastiziden? Help me understand his Chiricahua name?"

Alchesay slowly made the mental exchange to English, then spoke, "Broken Foot. As small boy leaped from high rock, break back of Mexican horse army man. Mexican muler –dead. Boy break foot."

Alchesay saw in the ice cold steel of Baychendaysen's eyes he reached to grasp the inside the mind of the man, Nana.

Gatewood sat rocking on the porch when he saw a trooper making fast time coming toward him.

"Lieutenant Gatewood, Sir. Major Cochran would have a word with you."

Gatewood knew this was not a social invitation.

Major Cochran's head was deeply buried in a territory map when the Adjutant announced the Lieutenant's arrival.

Never looking up, Cochran spoke only one word, "Sit."

He continued to scour the map.

After several minutes and with the expression of a man who had not found his answers on the map, shoved the map toward the middle of his desk and sat back.

"An old Chiricahua, Nana, has violated his oath and illegally left his assigned reservation at San Carlos." The Major was straining to sustain a distinct legalist attitude to his statement. Anger coated the emotional edges of his voice.

He audibly exhaled and moved his pen from his desk top to the Lieutenant. "It appears about twenty men are with him. It was reported that he was headed south toward Mexico." He paused when Gatewood displayed no tangible emotion rather he simply rolled his lower lip over his upper lip then moistened it with tip of his tongue.

Feeling that perhaps he had hidden too much, he continued, "Lieutenant, I want you and your command on this trail post haste. Secure what you need to sustain a relentless pursuit, take ample food and cartridges. A company of the Sixth supporting a company of the Twelfth Infantry will take the field as quickly as possible. Captain McLellan will command. I will assign a galloper to you. The column will proceed south from San Carlos until your galloper redirects them.

The Major paused, red splotches appeared on his neck, "Goddamn it, Lieutenant, I intend to make that old devil wish he'd chosen to summer on the banks of Gila. When this is over I want him to believe alkaline smells better than a dollar whore's perfume."

He arose from behind his desk, Gatewood stood.

"Just for the record Lieutenant, you stay in pursuit until they surrender or you are relieved. And off the record, I don't give a fat damn if you leave them all to cure out in the desert sun. If that is what suits you."

Gatewood didn't flinch and he didn't respond.

"Questions or requests, Lieutenant?"

"Sir, when you select a surgeon for the column, could you please consider Captain McPherson. We will be gone within the hour."

The Major nodded and then returned to Nana.

"Lieutenant Gatewood, do not underestimate the skills of this old devil. He is crafty and lethal."

Gatewood nodded acknowledging his understanding.

Salutes concluded the meeting, Gatewood's West Point proper, the Major's more of an annoyed snap.

Gatewood was no more than four steps off the porch when Alchesay fell into stride.

"Sergeant, events are as you thought."

"Nantan Baychendaysen, Nana has over day on us. Goso reports left San Carlos tracking south. Nana needs victory so boys feel as warriors, will hunt no – riesgo – no – no risk." Alchesay was working hard at his English and became impatient with himself when he couldn't get the word to come forth promptly without the Spanish assist. "South heat and nasty lizards."

Gatewood said, "We will talk on the trail." He paused to add, "Thank Goso for me."

Alchesay gave an accepting and less serious nod.

"Captain McPherson. Dorsey, you didn't hear it here, but I have requested that you accompany a column that will be leaving soon. I'll see you when you catch up to us."

Gatewood wanted to tell Dorsey to bring what was necessary to keep him and his scouts on the move. Then, realized it was just him.

Dorsey stopped him and extended a small bottle, "Charlie, I think you ought to take these ground willow bark extract powders with you."

In less than a half-hour, Second Lieutenant Charles Gatewood, First Sergeant Alchesay, nine White Mountain Apache scouts and a grainy underprepared Corporal, the galloper, left Camp Apache. Dog ran alongside the small column.

McPherson came to the porch and sat on a rocker, watching the small band depart. He thought how small the party looked and how vast the land seemed. Somehow the scene quieted him. Thoughts and questions that deepened in his mind.

His thumb and index finger met in the middle of his mustache and began a slow repetitive pattern, stroking outward. He admired Gatewood. Gatewood seemed to be a natural fit into this environment. It was difficult to string together. Contrary to all available logic, this studious gentleman son of Virginia seemed to be a natural coupling with these lethal warriors, a people harsher than their environment.

Barely out of sight and on the move, Gatewood removed his navy blue wool shirt and stuck it away. He was in his field uniform, khaki bush pants tucked into his boots and supported by his braces over his long sleeved cotton driver's undershirt. With his hand on the crown, he set his wide brimmed white hat firmly in place.

As soon as Camp Apache was behind them, Baychendaysen and Alchesay moved ahead of the group. Dog protectively followed.

Alchesay said, "Nantan Baychendaysen, Dandy Jim, not at General's Mule fight, is at point. Best tracker near to reach."

Baychendaysen understood the English and gave his approval with a quick single bob of the head.

"I think maybe pick two more and set them to the flanks. No surprise, no one dies. " Baychendaysen wanted Alchesay to know he too listened.

Alchesay nodded.

"Sergeant, My Major seems unusually annoyed by Nana leaving or by Nana."

"Major spent much time chasing Cochise and Nana across the hard mountains of the south. Never caught him, just old, tired chasing them. Maybe the Major likes Nana to have bad times at San Carlos." Alchesay hesitated then continued, "Nana will be hard to catch."

"What do you think he hopes to gain from the leaving San Carlos? Why leave?"

"Steal back the cattle the agent steals. Want food promised."

"Where does Nana think his cattle are?"

"Feeding on mountain grasses and watering from clean streams. Filling Mormon bellies."

"Like we passed at Stoneman Lake?"

Alchesay gave three turns of his head to indicate the negative. "Too high. Maybe up the Verde."

Bob gave a start. Gatewood let him jerk to the side and steadied him. Dog growled at the scrub grass.

"Alto! Alto!" Alchesay's stern command brought Dog to a point.

"Come." Dog came. It struck Baychendaysen that Dog was more multilingual than he has.

Alchesay turned to Baychendaysen. "Snake, Nantan."

He paused and added, "Maybe." Another pause. "Maybe nasty lizard."

Baychendaysen shook his head and patted Bob. They had made their way down the rattlesnake infest slopes into the Animas Valley, Bob had shied from snakes before and this was different.

He smiled and said, "Nasty lizard I suspect." In the oddest of ways Alchesay brought out the humor in him.

"If what Nana seeks is in the north, why does he go to the south?" Baychendaysen inquired.

"To number us and see who follows," came the response. "When he sees Coyotero and Nantan Baychendaysen, think go quick north."

Baychendaysen thought and then spoke, "I would try to double back behind us."

Alchesay nodded, "Split in front and double back. Three, four at a time. Poco Lizard finds us soon."

Dark fell. About an hour later, the company found Poco Lizard, sitting and waiting on a small outcropping that marked the entrance to a slot canyon.

Loco Lizard and Alchesay exchanged information in a blend of Spanish and Coyotero. Loco Lizard spoke briefly to Dandy Jim and they vanished into the canyon.

"Nantan Baychendaysen, Nana now has four horses and a mule. Will start to break into small groups. Double back soon."

Even without Apache eyes, Baychendaysen could make out the trail leading up the slot canyon. Although he had gained considerable knowledge during his earlier months out, something troubled him. Was this party so rushed they would leave sign even a Second Lieutenant could read?

Alchesay knelt examining the sign, then looked at up and said, "Nantan, two ride. Two mules, one horse – empty. I think false trail to slow us down."

Gatewood's mouth tightened and his hand supported his chin while his thumb and index finger tapped his lips. Alchesay moved to a sitting position and prepared to wait as Gatewood considered the state of affairs.

As Gatewood, sat and then broke his silence. He said, in a blend of a statement and a question, "Sergeant, I think he wants our weapons but decide not to take the risk."

Alchesay, sitting and sketching in the dust with a stick, raised his eyes till they locked with Gatewood's eyes, and then his voice took an emotionless chill Gatewood had never heard. Alchesay abruptly thrust the stick into the sand. He said as if speaking to the dust, "Matarnos muertos! – Nana want kill us dead. Then, take weapons and horses."

Then, he looked back at Baychendaysen, "No, won't take the risk."

Although the moonless night left canyon opening quite dark, he pointed the stick toward its mouth and continued "Nantan

Baychendaysen, Nana want you to chase glory into an empty canyon."

As if understanding from the tone of the voices, Dog stirred and moved closer to Alchesay. His head looked away into the darkness.

Gatewood consider the circumstance, gathered his thoughts and spoke, "Nana believes me to be a Greenhorn Lieutenant seeking glory and promotion."

Alchesay looked up, the candor and self-insight of Baychendaysen, surprised him yet it didn't. He nodded in agreement.

"If he expects me to read the sign, congratulate myself and order a charge up this canyon, where he could easily kill us and lose few of his men?"

"I dispatched the galloper about two hours ago with our position and that we had contact." His train of thought became unrelenting focused on the old Chiricahua's tactics. "Steal what is valuable to him."

"Nana needs rifles, steal first. No dead warriors." Alchesay waited just a moment so Baychendaysen understood, then said, "Steal here, find easy kills."

His English frustrated him. Baychendaysen's limited Spanish was forcing him to improve. He just wanted to tell Baychendaysen there were easier kills than ten Coyotero scouts armed to the teeth. Nana knew the scouts would track him with or without horses.

"I think he just wants to slow us down. Buy more distance for his hostiles," Baychendaysen said. "I don't think he is looking for fully armed Coyotero scouts with Cavalry nearby."

Alchesay agreed. He reached inside his hip pouch and withdrew two strips of jerky, extending one to Baychendaysen.

Gatewood was developing an affinity for the cured meat. He liked to think it was beef but his logic told it was made whatever type of meat was available. It certainly wasn't a cured ham from his native state. Nonetheless, the chewy cured meat had a distinctive flavor and stimulated the salivary glands, giving it a satisfying quality.

He sat, weighing his options. He left the Academy convinced you must understand your opposing commander. There had been no discussion of an aging, experienced Chiricahua Apache, one who had spend his youth under the tutelage of an Apache legend.

"Nana is watching us now?"

"Yes."

Baychendaysen thought a moment and said, "If you were Nana, how many men would have watching us?"

"Two."

Alchesay took the stick and drew a map of the company's position in the sandy soil, then marked the location he suspected the lookouts would be.

Baychendaysen started to look toward a position.

Alchesay flipped sand onto his hand and said a firm whisper, "No look!"

There were glances toward the positions.

"Nana's warriors?"

"South, safe but fast to here."

"As long as he thinks we might bite on the canyon, he'll stay in place."

"Yes."

"And when he realizes we are not going charging up the canyon?"

"He'll start splitting and we can try to cut him off by going west."

Baychendaysen rose from the ground and said, "Let's keep his men watching until sunrise, then convince them of the truth. We are not charging up an empty canyon."

As he started to move a hard soreness crept into his right knee and then sharpened in his hip and back. He winced. The visible display of discomfort angered him with himself. He found his canteen and the willow bark powder.

At times, the outcomes of situations are dictated not by the strategies and the skilled planning of men but rather by simple happenstance. On this morning in the mouth of slot canyon below a rim to south of Camp Apache, fate was in command. Shortly before daybreak, with a scout and the galloper leading the way, a detachment of the Sixth Cavalry arrived. Within the hour, a company of the Twelfth infantry marched into what quickly became a teaming camp site.

No mistaking the voice, "Well, I suppose one must first be fired upon to be injured." Surgeon McPherson had arrived upon the scene. "I could have slept in my bed and lanced boils and swabbed blisters."

"Surgeon, I prefer not to be shot to satisfy your perverse curiosity."

Alchesay made an almost silent intrusion into this exchange of fine sentiments. Having the Lieutenant's attention, he said, "Nana is moving."

"Yes." Gatewood looked and located Captain McLellan.

McLellan spotted Gatewood. Proper acknowledgments were exchanged, Alchesay stepped back and the Lieutenant gave his customary brief report.

"Lieutenant, Recommendations?"

"Sir, I would like to resume my pursuit of Nana immediately."

"Lieutenant, I feel my men are exhausted, especially the men of the Twelfth. We will resume the chase in the morning."

"Captain, Sir, I request your permission to take my scouts and resume tracking the hostiles as soon as possible." Gatewood was prepared to exaggerate the situation and state that his command was adequately rested from the previous evening.

"Lieutenant Gatewood, have you been able to verify that it is Nana we are pursuing?"

"Sir, Sergeant Alchesay believes it is. One of my scouts, Dandy Jim, says he saw two Chiricahua who were at San Carlos a week ago."

Captain McLellan pulled a cigar from his blouse pocket and bit off an end. After patting his pocket, he turned to his aide and asked, "Lucifer?"

The Corporal struck a match and extended it.

Gatewood agreed with whoever began to call such matches Lucifers, the burning sulfur at the match tip smelled like the "Gates to Hell" or maybe Hell just smelled like rotten eggs.

McLellan inhaled deeply and slowly released the smoke skyward. He seemed to watch the smoke to ease into the breeze. The ordinarily dour Scotsman's face relaxed.

The Captain exhaled his first full puff of cigar, "Lieutenant, we can't just let Nana leave the reservation because it pleases him, try to stay close enough to that he knows you're there."

He encouraged his lungs to make another exchange of smoke and continued, "Lieutenant Gatewood has your man offered an opinion on where Nana is headed?"

The "my man" reference caught Gatewood's ear and caused a hiccup in his pattern of thought. Finding his voice, he said, "North."

"Ah, the cool, clean air of the pine country, I don't know. Between the Mormons and Babbitt's there aren't many soft targets lying to the north. Lieutenant, it has been my experience that the Chiricahua will seek targets of opportunity where they have a distinct advantage."

McLellan exhaled a considerable volume of smoke and concluded, "I'm resting the Twelfth detachment here until we know which way the hostiles are headed. I'll see were the old buzzard is headed and catch him off guard a bit."

Rolling the cigar to the other side of his mouth, he advised, "I can send a detachment made up of eight troopers and two of the Quartermaster's men with adequate supplies to trail you. I believe if you run him to ground he will attack you."

"Captain McLellan, I do hope to be pressing the enemy, may I request that Surgeon McPherson be assigned to accompany my command?"

The Captain snorted and said, "Don't know if the Surgeon can sew closed a bullet wound but he's the finest storyteller in the mess. My column is best served if he remains with the main body."

As they moved away, Alchesay observed, "Nantan, hard to surprise an old buzzard."

Baychendaysen nodded. After several steps, he said, "Perhaps we just need to keep the old bird flying."

Alchesay nodded.

Within minutes, Dandy Jim and Goso left the encampment, each headed for separate high ground.

As Gatewood was making his way toward Dorsey, he caught a glimpse of them vanishing into the dust created by their own movements. He thought of Tazma and smiled a smile that never broke his somber countenance.

He had no more than finished an initial explanation of the Captain's decision to Dorsey than he felt Dog pawing at his boot.

Dorsey looked at the Dog and said, "Hound, you'd better be careful of the company you keep." He gestured toward the scouts continued, "That bunch will eat you." The Surgeon laughed at his own joke.

Gatewood bent to scratch Dog's head, saying, "Never listen to sounds escaping the mouth of a fool." He stiffened as he rose, but then loosened with movement.

"Stay safe Surgeon."

"You too, Nantan. You too."

"Nantan Baychendaysen." Gatewood turned. Quilo's hand was extended and holding Bob's reins. Bob was saddled and trail ready.

McPherson took his closing shot, "I thought you'd be bareback by now."

Gatewood gave a salute that contained a parting gesture.

Within what was seemingly minutes, Lieutenant Gatewood secured his well fitting wide brimmed hat on his head. His command had quickly resupplied and struck a trail to the south. Though always seeming to be a natural horseman, McPherson noted the Virginian now sat Bob in an even easier, more fluid manner.

Dog ran alongside Bob.

Dandy Jim and Goso were back within the hour, conferring with Baychendaysen and Alchesay. From their description, Nana had begun to disperse his men off the main trail until no primary path remained. Discussion concluded that Nana, given the increasingly open landscape, reformation and a trap would be difficult, too costly on such open ground, was making for the

Dragoon Mountains to the southwest or would double back and head north.

Alchesay tolerated questions because he sensed Baychendaysen sought understanding. The Dragoons were familiar ground to Nana because of his years with Cochise. Using the springs and canyons that lost Mexican or American horse soldiers in their labyrinths, he could launch raids as Cochise had. But there were now more white soldiers and they were in more places. Nana could not afford to lose men in risky raids. Even knowing the white soldiers preferred not to fight in the searing heat of the desert summer, he would seek engagements with the odds in his favor.

So, Alchesay concluded he would bend north. Cattle could be easily stolen, cattle he was certain arrived at San Carlos intended for him but left with white ranchers, especially Mormon ranchers. However, it was the Mormons that these scouts saw as encroaching of the White Mountain land that they clearly considered their territory. Baychendaysen was coming to understand that his scouts would be hesitant to interrupt a fight to protect any Mormon. Their feuds with the Chiricahua were historic. But in a very brief time they had come to dislike the Mormons even more.

"Nana will go west, stay south of the Gila, looking for wagons headed to Tucson, will raid what he finds, then turn north for the Salt where it meets the Verde."

Nantan Baychendaysen followed as best he could on his map.

"Verde, white eye farmers, aqua fria," Alchesay paused until he found the English he wanted, "Snow water." Alchesay measured his last words, "In high grass, find cows and Mormons."

Camp Verde lay between upper Verde Valley and Nana. Gatewood knew that the mission of Camp Verde was to protect the farms and ranches in the valley. The troopers may or may not be inclined to pursue a confrontation with a band of renegade Chiricahua and Warm Springs Apaches. They might feel a band hardened further by their experiences at San Carlos, might be well enough left alone.

Baychendaysen took off his hat and brushed away the dust, wiped his face, then his steel eyes honed in and he ask, "What of Camp Verde?"

"Not worry Nana now, later some." Alchesay continued, "First needs beef to send back and – get carbines. Hopes victories will bring more warriors to his fires."

Gatewood leaned forward, patted Bob on the neck and then nodded an understanding to Alchesay. He wrote a brief report on a pad, folded it and ask Alchesay to select a scout to locate the column and give the report to Captain McLellan.

Kuruk drank lightly. He filled and corked a canteen and draped it around his head. Kuruk left afoot, carbine in hand and the canteen swinging across his back, toward where they believed the Captain and the column would be.

Sensing that Nantan Baychendaysen needed clarification, he said, "Short way very uneven land, quicker on foot than on horse."

Baychendaysen was beginning to understand that there was considerable terrain that an Apache could navigate faster afoot than on horseback.

Nearing sunset on second day of a hard push to reach the Verde just north of its confluence with the Salt, the command reached the Salt River. Although he was still adjusting to the liberal use of the term river, the Salt was a most welcome sight. It was flowing and it was adequately clear. It was wet.

Kuruk appeared from a grass curtain that grew along the bank and in shallow pools along the south bank of the Salt. The grassy area was shaded by willows and cottonwoods.

Kuruk reached inside his pouch and retrieved a written message. He extended it to Alchesay and said, "Nantan McLellan sends Nantan Baychendaysen." There was an exchange in Apache between Kuruk and Alchesay.

Alchesay passed the order to Baychendaysen. As Baychendaysen read the directive his jaw tightened, squeezing the corners of his mouth downward. His gaze intensified making even a casual observer consider the possibility that the paper might spontaneously ignite.

"Sergeant, we are to remain here until the main column reaches us. We are ordered to scout the banks of the river to determine when and where the hostiles might cross."

"Yes, Sir Nantan. Kuruk reports he saw no sign of a party."

"Tell Private Kuruk well done."

Gatewood's right hand cradled his chin and his index finger tapped his lips, he spoke, "I think –," pausing to catch his tongue before continuing, "Our duty is to guide the column to the hostiles." The index finger tightened as if sealing Gatewood's mouth shut.

"Nantan Baychendaysen understands good," Alchesay hesitated to secure the correct English words but pointed to his Sergeant's stripes and to his shoulder a Lieutenant's bars would be fixed then said, "We soldiers."

Baychendaysen nodded, pursed his lips and then nodded again.

"Sergeant, secure a camp site. Let's eat well tonight. Nana might just find us. "

As if preformed by the most technically choreographed Richmond ballet, two scouts immediately took the horses downstream to water while two more scooped a handful of water in their mouths while crossing and begin to check the hills and outcroppings on the north side.

Dog had drunk first and now sat on the bank as if guarding the other animals.

Gatewood paused. He watched Dead Shot move deftly up the rocky shelf. It seemed that the wiry framed Apache were physically designed for agility, foot speed and endurance. Dead Shot's shoulder length hair seemed to snap behind him as the wide head band prevented the hair from coming across his eyes. Just as many of his contemporaries nurtured their sideburns and beards, the Apaches were proud of their hair.

The animals, now watered, grazed on blend of hardy grasses found on the flood plain of the Salt. From the tree lined river bank, Poco Lizard and Quilo had harvested three rabbits, then shortly before dusk a doe as she came to water. The fresh meat and the fleshy meat of a cactus with which Baychendaysen wasn't familiar comprised the core of the meal, but fry bread rolled in a bag of the coveted sugar converted the meal to a feast. It might have been that after a steady diet of cold camps, any warm meal would have tasted like a feast.

Dog crunched and gnawed the bones.

Quilo and Poco Lizard took some rounded stones from their pouches, stepped off a playing surface in the hard sandy surface near the tree line with a measured distance between two small holes. The stones were tossed toward holes. It seemed to Baychendaysen that the closest won. The game clearly had a gambling component to it.

Sitting with Alchesay and watching as the game unfolded, he gathered an awareness of the significance of games of chance to the Apache. Although there were four sentries station, this night was one of the most relaxed camps Baychendaysen would see while on the scout.

"The names of the men are in English, Spanish and I suppose Apache." Baychendaysen made a statement of fact. "Just doesn't make sense?"

"Hire as scout, make mark to scout, recruiter mistake name, give you name. Mexicans give some names. All know Coyotero names. I am Alchesay."

"Hmm – I – I," he shook his head. He understood, yet he did not understand. The names by which he knew most of his command were really no more than nicknames.

The light of the small fire further dimmed

The scouts converted their breechcloths into bedding. Baychendaysen spread his blanket roll. They slept just inside the tree line on the south bank of the Salt River.

The clear night sky on the desert gave the stars the illusion of being within arm's reach. The sound of the water flowing around rather large rocks relaxed Baychendaysen, he rested. He thought of Georgie.

Even the few stones that could be felt through his blanket did not disturb him.

Pain in his hip awakened him in the pre-dawn. He stirred. The hint of a sound in the tree line stilled him. A shadow moved.

Dog gave an almost silent growl. Nana's scout had indeed found them. He had come quietly and was counting their number. He hoped to leave as quietly as he had arrived.

Despite his considerable stealth, he was not silent enough to be undetected. Dead Shot allowed his passage into the camp. He never let him from slip from the sight of his Springfield.

However, as the Chiricahua was about free of the trees, Dead Shot tossed a stone into the brush behind him. The man abruptly turned and brought his rifle up to meet the challenge, but saw nothing. He relaxed and turned to resume his flight from the camp site. As he turned the butt of Dead Shot's Springfield caved in his jaw and his teeth spewed from what had been his mouth. He fell to the ground on his back. Dead Shot's rifle butt crushed his windpipe. Dying but not dead, the intruder reached for his knife. Dead Shot's foot pinned his arm to the ground. He gasped and died.

The dead hostile's belongings were checked and then he was swiftly removed from the site.

Talking to Baychendaysen, Alchesay said, "Gun not good. Had ground corn and sugar. I think settlers' wagons."

"He will need much more." Baychendaysen responded with both statement and question.

"Yes."

He took some of the yellow willow bark powder and returned to sleep.

Nantan Baychendaysen now heard sound and saw motion that Second Lieutenant Charles Bare Gatewood could have never heard.

By late afternoon, after traveling west along the Salt River valley and with Captain MeLellan at its head, the column arrived. Gatewood had washed and shaved in the cool waters of the Salt and now sat in the shade with Dog lying beside him. He did not get up until the Captain made his way toward him.

Slightly later in the afternoon, Gatewood and his scouts departed, headed northwest. No more than mile out Alchesay and Baychendaysen paused and dismounted.

Alchesay said, "Nantan, turn west, get to Verde quicker." In the gravel and sand he sketched the paths of the Salt and the Verde, drawing his case for direct westerly movement. He added a caveat, "Few ranchers, farmers on the Verde. Maybe find Nana close there."

Baychendaysen ask the questions that expanded his own knowledge base, but trusting Alchesay's familiarity with the land, Baychendaysen was already setting his compass as he agreed to the path.

The scouts spread out, hoping to cut Nana's trail, leaving Baychendaysen, Alchesay and two scouts to compose the main party.

Although moving toward sunset, the heat of the sun continued to sear through Baychendaysen's clothing with only his broad-brimmed hat saving his neck. He had tried to describe the feel of the parching desert heat, as prickly as the diversity of cactus that grew on the desert floor and on the slopes of the desert mountains surrounding the basin. He never found the words. A summer sun simply scorched and dried a man's skin. Before he left Wingate, McCrieght had recommended a balm for his lips and a soothing salve for burns, bites and cactus cuts. At first, fearing an appearance of femininity, he had been tentative about their use. After his lips had burned, cracked and bled, he sat aside any such notions. Now as he applied a thick coating of the balm, he cursed his own stupidity a delaying its use. He had disregarded the advice he had given himself on the stage to Santa Fe, "Never disregard sound local knowledge."

Taking advantage of the light of a full moon and skirting the desert mountains, the troop, all mounted made superior progress across the flatter ground. As they were nearing the Verde River, it appeared to Baychendaysen that a ghostly aberrance lay out before them. Softly glowing shafts of light, composed of varying degrees of white, swayed above the ground. The shafts swayed in a rhythmic pattern as if by the design of some primal choreographer.

As they entered the field he recognized the shafts were the brilliant moonlight reflecting from field of slender flowering cactus. It was like candles further illuminating the bright moonlit desert. The moon ducked behind a cloud, extinguishing the candles before coming again to re-light them.

Baychendaysen felt that in this unrelenting callous place he was surrounded by a soft beauty that captured all the visual arts. He bemused the contradiction.

A single repetitive thought penetrated his consciousness, "I cannot wait to show this to Georgie." He wrote her that the air of the moonlit seemed to be filled with the flickering flames of large candles that had risen from the sands of the desert itself and then separated to be left suspended above the ground.

Supper came around midnight and without dismounting. They ate some aged fry bread and jerked meat. Baychendaysen shared some rather stale Johnny-cakes that he had gotten from McPherson. He began to chew in sync with Bob's movement. He lifted his tail from the saddle and eased it back down.

He tossed Dog some Johnny-cake. It was unclear if Dog was appreciative or not, but he ate it.

The rays of the morning sun as it inched above the Superstition Mountains begin to warm his back, easing his discomfort. By mid-day as the pleasing warmth of morning gave way to a stifling heat with not a slice of shade to be found.

Nightfall found them on the banks of the Verde River. Despite its name, the water was cooler and clearer than the waters of the Salt. The flood plain had a modest covering of grass and small scrub trees. Grassy islands guided the flow of the stream.

They made cold camp and waited.

Goso reported the first sign, sign more telling than simple tracks. Quilo promptly joined him. Birds were spotted circling just before dusk.

The camp site was erased and they were on the move in minutes.

Moonlight allowed them to reach the site just before dawn. Quilo had scoured the area. Nana had left no men to spring a trap.

Poco Lizard and Dead Shot kept a firing position while the patrol moved into the site.

Nana's troop had come upon four sheepherders headed north and feeding along the Verde as they went. Alchesay and

Baychendaysen cautiously entered the sight. Baychendaysen's heart accelerated, his mouth was dried.

Alchesay halted as he came across a dry pool of blood that had no apparent connection with the bodies that lay close to the wagon. He felt searching for moisture and depth of the stain. Footprints and scuff marks indicated a warrior had been carried from the place.

They encountered similar blood sign as they approached the wagon.

Alchesay motioned for the others to check around the scene.

"Nana thought sheep, found wolves." Alchesay observed. Four sheep herders were dead, two in the wagon bed and two under it. The men had put up a fierce fight from the meager protection of the now bullet riddled wagon. Their bodies were bullet riddled but not mutilated. They lay in their blood surrounded by their spent cartridges.

"Fine fight, Nana not slice much. Stick knife there." He couldn't find the English word, so he grasp his crotch.

Alchesay handed a cartridge casing to Baychendaysen. Baychendaysen examined it and squatted to check a number of the other spent cartridges until he had checked the cartridges in the proximity of each man.

Baychendaysen said, "Likely all Henrys. I suspect Nana has them now. It doesn't look like these men left many cartridges for him."

Alchesay agreed.

He bent over and retrieved a small round red hat just protruding from under one of the men. He said, "They Basque, Nantan." He examined the men more closely before continuing, "Not Mexican, not white." He laid the red hat on the man. "Fight as cornered wolf. Take six bullets to still this one."

Baychendaysen thought of the old children's story, paraphrasing Alchesay. "Nana thought they were sheep and they turned out to be wolves."

Alchesay and Dead Shot almost smiled.

Dead Shot spoke, "Kuruk, many sheep sign." With his hands he indicated a northeastern movement of the herd.

"How do you see Nana's losses here?" Baychendaysen asked.

"Five dead. Many more wounded, maybe ten wounded."

"Damn!" Baychendaysen blurted, thinking these red hats did put up one hell of a fight. "Tough men with good rifles." He took off his hat and slapped it on his side, dust flew. He returned his hat to its place and looked toward the red hats. "Damn!"

"Sent Kuruk to fetch Captain McLellan and his column, bring them to our trail."

Sergeant Alchesay dispatched Kuruk.

"Alchesay, I calculate Nana's command to be weakened, some of his men might be questioning his leadership. Would I be correct?"

"Yes, Bay'che. I believe."

"If we fire this wagon, we might let his men they are being tracked. How will he respond?"

"Maybe will split. Send young ones toward San Carlos with the sheep and take his warriors north. Or maybe try to trick you, get our rifles."

Baychendaysen thought only a moment, "He has many wounded, he might hesitate. I want him to know we are tracking him and we do not fear him."

Alchesay said, "Nantan, we keep old bird flying."

"Yes."

Alchesay saw Baychendaysen's discerning gaze as he seemingly dissected the north horizon. The dark circles under his recessed steel gray eyes gave his examination an even more intense appearance. He patted Bob as he retrieved his binoculars and continue to scour the desert and the buttes to the north. Bob nuzzled him from behind.

Satisfied, he turned to Alchesay, "Nana will have posted a lookout on high ground?"

Alchesay acknowledged with a nod and thought his Lieutenant to be an apt pupil.

"Put the Basque warriors in their wagon and fire it."

Again Alchesay nodded agreement.

Nana's lookout spotted the thin line of smoke and reported it.

Nana arose from the boulder where he had been sitting. Under his breath cursing who or what had made a fire. The fight with the "red caps" had been difficult. He had planned on easily killing the sheepherders and stealing what they had. A fight leaving him with five dead and slowed by many wounded.

Four of the more critically wounded were now making their way toward a refuge on a tributary of the Verde.

None arrived.

Now in his late seventies, he increasing disliked any occurrence that he had not anticipated. He knew many now called him Haskenadilta, the Chiricahua word for agitated. He didn't mind, he had had many names over the years. Besides, those men were now hesitant to trouble him.

The scout he had sent to see who now followed them returned with the observation that he has suspected.

"Coyotero scouts. I think Alchesay, think white soldier who try to catch us at box canyon." He paused before delivering his other observation, "Soldier column coming from the east, very near scouts. Suspect joined by now."

Nana thought but did not share his thoughts. He liked it better when he was young and fought beside Mangas Colorados.

He considered his position for a time and then he ordered his youngest men and the three wounded still alive to accompany the sheep back to San Carlos. Nana departed toward the Verde with twelve warriors, all who had been with him in earlier fights, accompanying him.

Although exasperated with himself, he prayed for curses to be reigned on the deceased spirits of the "red caps." He could not admit he had miscalculated the fierce fashion in which the Basque would resist their death. He wished he had mutilated them but he knew they fought far too fearlessly. He knew a man could be judged by the strength of his enemies.

Nana mounted with the newly acquired Henry cradled in his arm. The now diminished party moved toward the Verde River valley.

The column, having followed the river westward, arrived at the crossing. It was a tired infantry column that announced itself with the sound of gravel slipping under their boots. The cavalry troopers appeared in some better condition. Their horses did not.

A careless trooper's mount shied as a horse abruptly stopped in front of him, causing his mount to slip in the gravel and mud base of the creek, sending the trooper head long into the cool water. He sat upright in the water, face muddy and scrapped, a soaked hat lying sideways on his head. He spewed profanities about his carelessness, and then he evolved blame to the horse. The trooper's awkward fall from his steed gave the weary foot soldiers a much needed belly laugh. To the trooper's chagrin, he slipped and fell again as he tried to rise from the creek.

Poco Lizard spotted the sheep herd headed east. From a plateau and with their binoculars, Alchesay and Baychendaysen tracked the herd.

"Young and wounded herd the sheep toward San Carlos," Baychendaysen said both making a statement and asking a question.

"Yes" Alchesay paused and scanned the procession a final time, then wiped the exterior of his glasses and returned them carefully to their case, a leather case with a large US imprinted into its side. He was still quite proud of the binoculars he confiscated from the dying Lieutenant on the upper Verde.

Baychendaysen scratched Dog.

"Warriors shameful now, but sheep will make glad women at San Carlos. Glad women make happy warriors."

Alchesay almost broke a smile. Understanding his Sergeant's effort at humor, Baychendaysen snorted a laugh. The laugh caused him to cough.

His breeches tucked into his high leather boots just below the knees, Captain Surgeon Dorsey McPherson jauntily joined the pair. He said, "That cough will kill you or get you killed."

Gatewood turned and responded, "Damn, you need to brush the sand out of your mustache."

"Now a man of your education should recognize a dust filter when you see it."

In the familiar inside out fashion, Dorsey stroked his mustache and smiled.

Taking a physician's viewpoint, McPherson thought his friend seemed rather the worse for the wear. His steely eyes now sat in even deeper shadowy circles and seem further regressed into his head, making them appear distressingly menacing and his nose more prominent.

"You look weary my friend."

Not wishing to address it, he turned away and spoke to Alchesay.

"We should keep our old bird on the fly. But we will do it with full stomachs and full canteens."

Alchesay nodded although he would rather have continued the pursuit immediately.

Baychendaysen added, "I must speak with Captain McLellan."

Alchesay nodded but he saw no value consulting a man who knew must less than he and Baychendaysen. The politics of the white man's army perplexed him. It interfered with the pragmatic Apache approach to war, kill the enemy and survive to kill more.

Lieutenant Gatewood made his report. At Captain McLellan's request he offered his suggestions.

Accompanied by six troopers from the Sixth Cavalry, the Twelfth Infantry would follow the band herding the sheep back to San Carlos. The men of the Sixth did not take kindly to the idea of being under the command of an infantry officer but they kept their displeasure among themselves.

Gatewood's patrol would track and press the point. The majority of the Sixth would be adequately close to provide immediately support. The Captain was clear that he wanted to be involved in any combat or surrender. There was little glory left to found and he intended to secure his full share of any opportunity that might remain.

Gatewood promptly found his First Sergeant and sought his council. Gatewood understood but was determined to ignore the directive if circumstances dictated. Alchesay did not understand and would be a willing co-conspirator.

McPherson again approached. Alchesay went quite. Gatewood glared at his friend.

Doing his best to address both men, the Surgeon said, "I'm to travel with you. Nantan Baychendaysen, it is in all our best interest to keep you on your feet."

He looked directly at Alchesay, "Sergeant, I can give you no reason to trust me beyond the fact Nantan Baychendaysen trusts me."

Alchesay turned his head toward Baychendaysen. Once again the penetrating gazes of the two pierced into the soul of the other. McPherson actually drew back a step. Not a word was spoken until Alchesay said, "Nantan Baychendaysen trust you. I try."

The non-verbal communication between the two men had an obvious clarity that completely eluded McPherson.

Baychendaysen's lips edged up nearing a smile, his eyes seemed less harsh, "He's iffy about you Surgeon."

McPherson understood and laughed, then said, "Nantan, you will let me know if he changes his mind and decides to cut my balls off."

Baychendaysen gave a half-nod of amusement and replied, "Should the occasion arise, I'll give your request due consideration."

Back to the business at hand, Baychendaysen spoke to Alchesay, Dorsey McPherson was the constant observer. "I think we keep the old bird on the wing."

Alchesay thought and responded, "Old bird will tire. First try to slow you and hope to kill you."

"Alchesay, when he fails to kill us, his men will be even more tired. Then, we can cut his trail."

Alchesay did not voice his approval, but he approved

"Our mules are almost packed. The moon is still bright enough. Suspect Nana has a man watching our camp," Baychendaysen said. "Let's not let the old bird find a roost for the night."

Within the hour, Quilo came with Bob, brushed and properly fed and watered. Shortly a trooper appeared with McPherson's horse. Baychendaysen laughed at his friend's frustration, not knowing if he should feel slighted or not.

They crossed the river and headed north. Dog shook the water from himself and paced alongside Bob.

There seemed little difference between the scorching days and the furnace like nights except for the night wind. Regardless of the hour, the moving air was always drying and abrasive, often full with otherwise inconsequential beads of sand. The skin darkened and toughened even when sheltered from the direct sun. Lips first became sore and then they cracked and bled. In the absence of moisture, the breeze provided little cooling to the surface of the skin.

Surgeon McPherson used some lip salve he brought in his Gladstone. He discovered it did not bring the relief as the concoction of animal fat that the Apache used. Dorsey rubbed two fingers to his lips, Dead Shot extended a pouch containing the balm. Dead Shot fancied himself something of a healer. Dorsey was curious. They would begin to exchange "healing potions." Each considered the others method to be primitive but effective.

While the Apache distained any expression of discomfort imposed by the terrain, this relentless land challenged even this vigorous breed of white man who attempted to impose his terms upon the land.

Eighteen days out Nana decided the scouts would persist in the chase, sending one warrior to continue working near the Verde with the animals while the other warriors now afoot turned uphill over terrain filled with large flatten boulders. The trail was soon lost.

Within hours the trail was regained.

Captain McLellan was notified. Smelling glory, he took an increased interest in sustaining a reasonable distance between the column and the scouts.

Nana stepped into the chilly, crystal water of Clear Creek at its confluence with the Verde River. He moved the Henry, draped over his shoulder with a leather strap, to his back. Then, he bent over, cupped his hands and captured water as it rapidly moved over the rocky stream bed. He drank and then others joined him.

A shuffling from the willows on the far bank reached his ears over the sound of the rushing water. He saw two figures emerging from the shade and shadows. He bolted upright and tried to retrieve the Henry from his back.

"Don't!"

"Alto! No Haga!"

"Anzhoo Nana," Baychendaysen said.

Alchesay followed, "Anzhoo."

Nantan Baychendaysen was seated upon a boulder, legs crossed and back slightly humped. His pants were tucked into his boots, his braces buttoned to his pants and draped over his field issue undershirt and his wide-brimmed white field hat sat at an angle exposing more of his face than usual. His Centennial Winchester was cradled on his legs. He sat as casually as if he had watched Nana take the first steps across the stones into Clear Creek.

Alchesay stood beside the seated soldier.

As Nana gauged his circumstances, Dorsey stepped from the willows about five yards downstream from Alchesay. Nana noted his beard gave him the appearance of a fierce warrior and that he held his Henry with a comfort that suggested he knew how to manage the rifle.

Nana did not find the situation to his liking but now he responded to their greeting, "Anzhoo."

He then directed his question to Alchesay, "Baychendaysen?"

Alchesay glanced to Baychendaysen before responding.

With emphasis on the first word, Alchesay said, "Nantan Baychendaysen."

While Nana was formulating a response, a buck that had not yet entered the stream broke and sprinted back toward the junipers. Quilo stepped from the junipers. The .50 caliber cartridge struck the brave squarely in the chest and drove him sideways in a twisting motion. He stilled and drifted a few feet before a shallow rapid stopped him.

Another warrior leveled his rifle but a bullet from Dead Shot's rifle tore into the man's shoulder, sending his rifle into the air and plunging him into the cold water of Clear Creek.

Suddenly everywhere the Chiricahua leader looked, he was looking down the business end of a scout's rifle.

Rifles, cartridges and other weapons were secured and placed alongside the stream. Nana remained thigh deep in the chilly waters of Clear Creek. The Henrys were shunned but two almost new Springfield carbines quickly found new ownership.

Baychendaysen promptly directed Alchesay to tell Nana that a Bluecoat Yankee would come. "Tell him the Yankee will be an asshole. An asshole is not worth dying over, he should live to fight another day."

Alchesay recognized the Apache logic Baychendaysen voiced and it pleased him. In an Apache dialect, Alchesay delivered the message. All Nootahah within ear shot stifled a laugh and relaxed.

Baychendaysen reached into his blouse pocket and retrieved his smooth stone. He rolled it in his fingers. He looked at the date inscribed with indelible ink. Whatever his thoughts, his countenance did not betray them.

Alchesay concluded with, "Nantan Baychendaysen says it is so."

The fight at Clear Creek was concluded.

Within minutes, Captain McLellan arrived at the head of the column, colors flying. He dismounted.

His voice was peeved, "Lieutenant Gatewood!"

"Sir, Nana advanced and we had no choice but to contain him until your arrival. He insisted that he will only surrender to you."

This logic made perfect sense to McLellan. His voice became pleased and his ego puffed.

The Captain swaggered into the creek. He extended his hands, demanding Nana's Henry.

Now surrounded by men of the Sixth Calvary, Nana knew what was expected. He knew the path led back to San Carlos. But for a time, he had again been free. There were other Henry rifles to be stolen.

Having a San Francisco reporter witness Nana's capitulation and hear that Nana would only surrender his rifle to him, McLellan was in a magnanimous mood. So, he adopted Lieutenant Gatewood's suggestion that the sheep be distributed at San Carlos by the Apache as a gift from the Captain and not by the agent.

Gatewood had not moved from his seat on the stone. McPherson moved closer and whispered, "Damnest thing I'd ever seen, ya surprise and capture a legendary Apache chief and let another man take the credit," then increasing the volume of his voice concluded, "and ya never lifted your fancy West Point ass off this rock."

His voice turned more sober as he noted beads of perspiration on Gatewood's upper lip and a visible discomfort he tried to rub from his hands, "Feeling?"

Gatewood's response was terse, "I hurt."

Desiring to further secure the San Francisco newsman's account, Captain McLellan ordered Gatewood and his scouts to check further up the Clear Creek. He gave the Lieutenant orders that would allow for a brief resupply at Camp Verde if required.

Now Gatewood was peeved. Every joint in his body pained and ached for a bed. Although he strained to suppress them, dreams of Georgia would intrude at the most inconvenient times. He wondered how he could have such explicit dreams of times he had never experienced. He was curious if his scouts who seemed to be capable of containing all emotion while in the field were ever troubled by such intrusive dreams. He felt he must make Georgia McCullough his wife as quickly as duty allowed.

Baychendaysen looked at his boots. He was always impressed with the width and depth of the scrapes mete out by the ever-present variety of thorns and cactus that seemed to be a constant companion in this country.

He had been in the field almost the entirety of time in the territory. Each time the food and conversation of the Camp Apache mess had begun to sound appealing, his curiosity subdued it.

Alchesay broke Gatewood's malaise. "This reconnaissance will take us to Tazma, will please him. Tazma ask of you."

"He asked if I'm still alive, or if I've managed to get myself killed yet."

An almost smile betrayed the accuracy of Baychendaysen's guess.

"Since our friends will have no immediate use for them, get a bag of the .50 calibers and a bag of the .45 rimfires for our host."

"Nantan, a fine skinning knife was in the pile. Goso would sharpen it. Tazma has use for it."

Baychendaysen felt a growing anticipation. The potential of a visit with Tazma pleased him.

Surgeon McPherson was pleased to find his friend in better spirits before the scouts departed west-north-west along the Verde. Nonetheless, he had packaged an additional quantity of willow bark powder and gave the Lieutenant a prescription instructing the sutler at Camp Verde to fill several medicine bottles with high grade medicinal whiskey.

The San Carlos residents were pleased regardless of whether it was for wool or mutton. Captain McLellan gained stature. The Agent was furious. As Nana told the tale to the Chiricahua inner circle, the stories of Alchesay and Nantan Baychendaysen grew.

Nana made every effort to sell his raid as successful. He returned with the spoils of sheep and the canvas of the "red caps" wagons. No longer able to trade for Buffalo hides to frame their wikiups, the canvas from the white man's wagons was a valuable building material.

But too many warriors had been killed by the "red caps." Losing two experienced men at Clear Creek was painful. However, at San Carlos successes were in short supply.

Victorio kept his own council, obscuring the ferocity and zeal of his vision of the future. He measured his allies as intensely as he measured his adversaries.

SIX

TAZMA'S CAMP

BEAVER CREEK FLOWED INTO THE Verde River about a day upstream from Camp Verde. The point of its departure from the Verde was unimpressive. Contrary to logic, the stream seemed to widen as it moved away from the Verde, an increasing number of large holes of water separated by swiftly running shallows creating a tranquil sound as the water hammered against the sundry stones, from boulders to pebbles, and splashed into a pool. The canyon walls grew in height. They constricted, seeming to leave barely adequate space for a couple of horses and then dramatically expanded to a width that appeared capable of accommodating a cavalry charge.

The patrol entered a narrow passage that required a cautious single file along a ledge bordered by a sheer rock face and an exposed cavern of rapidly flowing water some feet below the ledge. The closeness of the route had the potential to create claustrophobia in a man who otherwise had no such tendencies. The sounds of the rapidly flowing water gave the illusion that a man was encased on a slender tunnel of moist sand stone and water wildly racing over moss covered rock.

Suddenly, as if moving through the gates of Paradise, they found themselves in a heavily tree lined and extraordinarily lush valley. A grassy plain gradually slope up from Beaver Creek to the canyon walls.

Gatewood pulled Bob up, turned and considered the pass. As random thoughts are want to do, he contemplated that had the coastal pass at Thermopylae been this steep and restricting, the Persians would still be trying to defeat the Spartans. He smiled thinking a certain Professor of Military Tactics would be quite pleased that he made even an abstract application of such knowledge.

Dog bounded across the meadow toward the pine and spruce cabin sitting near the tree line.

A figure rose from the shadows of a covered porch, a porch floored with wear polished native stone. The figure initially acknowledged Alchesay before turning to Gatewood.

"Still 'live and got ya limbs."

"As do you it would appear."

"Gainin' bone." Tazma smiled revealing four gold teeth now covered the place the uneven, discolored teeth had occupied when last they met.

Tazma was visibly pleased with his new teeth and was eager to share his pleasure.

"Traded goods for Mexican's teeth."

Gatewood did not inquire as to where he found a competent dentist to do the work. Some years later a story reached Gatewood's ears that Tazma's teeth had continued to rot under their gold covers. Tazma, believing the dentist to have taken advantage of his good nature, found the man in Tucson and demanded satisfaction. The reluctant dentist did a more proper job with a .44 Caliber Smith and Wesson near his head. It was said that the finest dentist in Tucson left town the next morning and expressed no preference as to the direction the train might be traveling.

A fireplace appeared to cover an entire wall and was made of native stone. A large stone hearth had been laid in front of the fireplace. The fireplace drew well. The floor was compacted soil.

There were two porches floored with almost smooth stone, one that looked toward the creek and sunrise and toward the immense canyon walls and the fading sun.

Gatewood was impressed with Tazma's skills until he discovered that the hunter's wife was the accomplished stone mason.

Two smaller cabins, a half dozen or so wikiups and one hogan comprised the village. Tazma had visited in white and Mexican towns and had lived in Apache villages. He desired to recreate none of them. Except for the necessity of dealing with his Apache mother-in-law, the main cabin would have been the only structure.

Two well constructed lean-tos were attached to the main cabin. Several other less sturdy frames suggested a fluid temporary population.

"Da ya eat fish?"

Gatewood thought it to be an odd question until Tazma explained an obvious oversight.

"Nootahah don't eat it. Evil, bad luck or some such." The otherwise quite pragmatic Apache incongruously thought ill of an abundant and available food supply. The Apache Trout whose brownish yellow tinted skin gave it a ghostly appearance as it swam in the depths of a pool of water at the base of a rapid. The yellow tint was especially unsettling to the Nootahah.

It was rare that he had a dining companion who enjoyed the flavor of fish cooked while being rotated on a spit over an open campfire or grilled in a cast iron skillet he kept tuck away from just such occasions.

He emerged from the cabin with his hat in his hand. Gatewood almost didn't recognize him. His hair was balding in the front exposing a stark line between his sun toughened face and the white of his scalp.

"Pleases my woman." He said as he placed the hat on a knob of the chair back.

Gatewood nodded, thinking that was as complete an explanation as he would receive. He was wrong.

"Tiny cost. Wait'll ya taste her fish."

As was most often the case, Tazma was correct. The trout was superb.

That evening as the rest of the encampment dined on Tazma's finest beef, Gatewood and his host dined on fish fresh from the nearby mountain stream. The two men, themselves reared in quite different cultures, enjoyed the flavorful fish while those native to the land watched from a distance as if they feared the taste for the foul food might somehow be contagious.

The scouts understood that Nantan Baychendaysen was a rare invited guest into Tazma's sanctuary. Alchesay believed all concerned would profit from this casual conference.

This visit was to be different from their earlier encounters. Tazma was the curious one. He had been told yarns of the Nantan with the large nose, Baychendaysen. He had thought well of the man during their trip from Santa Fe to Fort Wingate. The tales came from the Apache view of a warrior, not from a white man's braggart sagas of reckless courage. Stories were of a cautious but lethal soldier who stacked the odds of battle in his favor to the extent possible, a man who respected his foe but did not fear him.

Gatewood was daring but never reckless. He had faced the elephant with a fearless lust.

He understood that this was not a lenient land nor was he surrounded by merciful men. Yet, through Reconstruction and the Arizona Territory, he sustained an instinctive humanity, a profound sense of integrity.

Gatewood was consummately human.

Tazma kept his origins more secretive. Although some felt he had migrated from the plains, a buffalo hunter as a boy and found the paradise of the Mogollon Rim country. He seemed to represent some convergence of the Arizona Territory. He embraced the land as only an Apache could. He had married a Mexican girl, a Chiricahua captive he courted and then purchased. She was an attractive woman with a healthy look to her, she dressed in something that blended a store bought fabric and cut in a unique personal style that was a mingling of Spanish and Navajo fashion. He never returned from a time away without cloth of some sort or another.

He embraced monogamy, permanence of one spouse. Still he understood that he could not insult a host by declining evening company. Almost in contradiction to the balance of his life, by frontier standards, Tazma deeply loved his wife and she bedded him with a great enthusiasm. He was happy on Beaver Creek.

Tazma was not a cattleman but he raised cattle. Some said he stole more than a few cattle and could be skilled with a running iron. If true, Gatewood suspected it was selective. Tazma was welcome on Babbitt land but he held no love for the Mormons.

As the beef was cooking this night, Tazma commented to Alchesay, "Mormon cow got lost."

He traded goods, often guided and hunted for freighters where the trains had not taken the routes and tracked for posses hunting outlaws. He always refused any commission that would require tracking an Apache or Navajo outlaw.

His past was as ghostly as the man himself.

They sat in the hand hewed chairs, listened to Beaver Creek and talked.

Creek bank coffee, grounds strained through cloth, and flavored with a dash of medicinal whiskey was excellent.

"Nootahah don't get my log house."

Gatewood sipped the coffee and waited.

"Nomads, steal but not thieves, just how ya live. Just don't get idee of owning nothing."

Gatewood expanded, "The land doesn't belong to anyone. So how can you steal something from a man who doesn't own it to begin with?"

"Da ya think ya can own the water in that creek?"

"No, but don't believe you do either."

Tazma smiled, something of a snort escaped him. He gave a sharp approving bob of his head.

"Nootahah not grow corn or squash."

"Cattle?"

"Maybe." Tazma considered the possibility of adaptation. "Have many wives now, didn't always. Too many have warriors died, need more sons – and daughters to have sons."

Gatewood had understood that the seemingly perpetual conflict with the white eyes had made polygamy a practical necessity. The Nootahah were a practical people.

"Squaw's property to be bought or sold," knowing the seeming contradiction continued, "but squaws can ferment more trouble than tiswin, especially a mother-in-law, pick at a man's bones like a bunch of crows." Finished talking, Tazma shook his head, his expression leaving no doubt of his confusion with these circumstances.

"Nootahah sends woman ta ya bed, best lay still. Bad insult to send away."

Tazma recognized the look of concern on his guest face. He explained, "It is honor. Woman do what woman wants. May please ya, may kept ya warm. Won't kiss your mouth like a Mexican gal." As an afterthought said, "Twan't do act facin' ya."

Looking stone serious, Tazma said, "Her mama might be at da door. Nootahah fears his mother-in-law." He flashed gold.

Desiring to change the topic, the flushing Gatewood desired to change the topic.

"Nootahah. I know that is what the Apache call themselves. What does it mean?"

"Nothing, no wise man knows, it is just a word for them."

"N'de?"

"Same. Just means them."

Not allowing the topic to drift until he had enjoyed the full measure of Gatewood's blushing discomfort, "Nantan, youse know why woman's personals called a snatch?"

Left no route to turn and having never heard the term, Gatewood shook his head no.

"When a man finds it, it snatches away his brains. Sucks his brains right out through his pecker."

Laughing at his own humor, Tazma slapped Gatewood's knee and asked, "More coffee?"

At mid-afternoon a monsoon thunderstorm rolled over the rim, lightning colored the dark sky along the rim and the thunder rolled down the canyon. The sky opened, the shroud of rain began to march across the valley until the chilly rain reached the porch. The winds and the rain carried and enhanced the fragrance of the pines.

"Be damn ifin' hot coffee don't taste best watching it rain." Tazma looked at Gatewood and continued, "Why I built porches. Rocks get a mite slippery, but ma' porch ain't muddy."

Alchesay joined the pair as the rain reached the cabin. Alchesay took a chair. Gatewood couldn't remember him ever sitting in a chair before.

The men peered at the landscape through the storm.

"Baychendaysen, white man built his God's missions long ago. The black robed men were kind, make talk of peace. Whites built churches but are a quarrelsome." Then, Alchesay made his way to the point he wanted to discuss. "I do not understand why a God of Good Spirits would allow the white man to take a land he does not respect."

Tazma intervened, "White eye builds many buildings to same God. They talk of same God but can't track his message over the rocks in some white hearts."

Alchesay accepted the incomprehensible. Baychendaysen pondered what he heard.

"Apache don't trust their own medicine teachers. Tell ya, youse can't talk Apache but Alchesay talk white and Mexican real good." Tazma reinforced his point, "Tain't no D'Ne goin' teach ya none."

Alchesay committed, "What man says means little, what he does means much."

Tazma had lured his point to the surface, "Talk don't measure a man, it don't mean as much. Nootahah ain't big talkers."

Baychendaysen spoke almost protectively, "Nootahah are doers and that's a big fat fact."

Tazma and Alchesay liked their friend more than even they had realized.

As the rain became a shower, a large vivid rainbow broke over the rim.

Children came out to play in the puddles. Children, they had to have been other places. It was here Gatewood saw children at play. It seemed oddly inconsistent with the persona of his recent life and he knew the feeling could not last. Still, the random enthusiasm of children at play brought hope.

He watched and learned.

"The Mormons do not seem to be well liked." Gatewood said. "I hear much hate and distrust." Tazma heard the question contained in the statement but didn't respond.

Gatewood followed up, "Help me here?"

"Think they see themselves in the 'tother." Tazma hesitated then continued, "Ta hear Mormons tell it, their land been stolen and they been chased till the Utah Territory is their last hope. Nootahah feel everybody trying to steal their places. White Mountains best land and Coyoteros intend to keep it, Mormons intend to take it."

He thought before he continued, "Makin' of a hell of a fight." To avoid misunderstanding, he concluded, "I'd side with Nootahah."

Gatewood considered the quarrel. He knew the indignities of Reconstruction and the exploitation of the Carpetbaggers influenced his thinking. He had seen a carpetbagger in Holy Charlie at Fort Wingate.

"I know carpetbaggers when I see them." Gatewood said. He was coming to believe the Mormons were Carpetbaggers. He would be wary. But he kept these thoughts to himself for the time being.

Tazma didn't understand the term but he understood the tone.

"Folks often get ta same spot by different paths."

There was trust between the three. Three men who on the surface were quite different were very much alike.

Gatewood made his way to the lean to on the south side of the cabin. Stopped by the corral, gave Bob a touch of sugar and rubbed his nuzzle. Bob had enjoyed the day in the meadow.

The mountain air cooled considerably after sunset. The sloped roof was solid plank with canvas flaps on each side. He bent over and opened the flap, the canvas likely removed from a wagon of some sort or another. He debated a moment and decided to trust Tazma's council on insects at this elevation. He took off his boots. He placed his Smith and Wesson in easy reach. Now he pulled the top blanket over himself and stretched. He lay back on the bed of layered blankets, gathered a deep breath and relaxed back into bed. He couldn't recall the last time he slept this far removed from the ground.

The backside flap stirred. His hand closed on the .44. Whatever the voice said, it was clearly feminine and suggested no ill-intent. His grip loosened.

The woman raised the blanket. A soft rustling sound came as she removed her garment and slid under the blanket. Then, she moved on her side until she lay next to him. He started to move away and she stilled him.

Unbuttoning his undershirt, she touched his chest. Her hand wasn't soft, but her touch was unbelievably delicate. Her fingers made an ever so light tracing across his chest. The sensation was both genuine and sensuous. She was in no rush, her fingertips sketched as if with each point she had arrived at her destination.

She laid her head on his chest, her breath was erotic. Her arm draped about his waist. Repositioning, she took his hand, guiding it along the subtle rises and falls of her breast, stopping just as his fingers contacted her nipple. Then, she let her hand relax and slide, pausing below her belly button. Bay'che's fingers, at times rather awkwardly, caressed her breast, pausing on her firm nipples as they mysteriously became hard and more sensitive to his touch. Their breathing quickened.

Unlike his very limited experience with other women, he sensed no urgency on her part. This young woman, concealed by blankets and darkness, seemed to feel no impatience to rush him toward a completion. She slightly raised her hips exposing her moist and highly sensitive province. She guided his fingers as if they were her own. He heard her instinctive gasps, her hips shuddered. She stiffened and several intense involuntarily spasms came. Both mystified, she rested her head on his chest. Her heavy breathing eased and her hand found confirmation he was fully aroused.

She unbuttoned his pants as he removed them, at times fumbling one over the other. As he finished, she positioned herself on her side with her back to him. He nestled behind her, clumsily probing. She lifted her leg, granting him open access to her. Her hand eased him inside her. The most luxurious of sensations encircled him. Her movements became rapid and rhythmic. He was lost.

Now lying on his back, the woman draped across him, a deep revitalizing sleep found him. He stirred in the cool of the early morning hours. He was alone. She had quietly left the lean to during the deepest dark of night.

He smiled and settled to sleep in the quiet solitary bed of a soldier. His smile broadened. The heady scent of the woman and their sexual intimacy lingered. It warmed the whole of him.

The pleasure of the night had overwhelmed his pain. Only now in the pre-dawn hours did the pain in his hip and shoulders return. He lingered under the blankets for a moment. Then, he took two packets of willow bark power and washed it down with two large gulps from his canteen. Such large drinks were a luxury rarely enjoyed on patrol, but they rarely camped in safety next to a stream of cold flowing water.

"Coffee's waiting," Tazma called from the adjacent porch.

The pair sat quietly, sipping their coffee.

"Had a fine night cause of ya." Tazma said expressionless. "Woman knowed love was in the air. My woman thought she was a girl 'gain. Yes, a real fine night."

Gatewood might have flushed, but he didn't mind.

Gatewood finally spoke, "You have taught me much and I thank you."

"Ya listened. I heard ya speak too." Tazma rocked and took another zip, "I feel bad winds stirring. Ya be careful out there."

Then, he added, "McCrieght fixed a short twelve gauge – 'case things get up too close." He stepped inside the cabin and produce a sawed off shotgun. "Ya might think on one."

"Cherokees had'em at Boggy Depot. Stalled Willetts and his damn Kansas Yankees out with these." Tazma rocked back in his chair, "And Willetts had cannons."

Gatewood picked up the gun, "And when shells are spent, it makes one Hell of a club."

"Nantan, startin' ta know why I like ya." Tazma flashed his golden smile.

The reconnaissance party made their way up the steep northern ascent from Beaver Creek. Baychendaysen looked back at the creek, trees now obscuring Tazma's cabin and the cluster of lodgings around it.

Alchesay stopped. "Man finds many worlds."

Gatewood carried Tazma's practical wisdom with him out of the valley. No matter how harsh, cruel and unrelenting the world might become, a sanctuary with a reliable peace and personal warmth can exist within the boundaries of an honest relationship with a woman.

A large smile, without context to the observer, broke Baychendaysen's face, as he said under his breath, "Just remove your hat at the table."

At nightfall, with a belly full of venison, he lay in a bed of pine straw, viewed stars that seemed larger and brighter than ever and listening to a the breeze through the pines sound a peaceful taps. Despite nature's efforts, his bed had never felt emptier. He ached for Georgie.

Although their skin had never touched beyond the intertwining of their fingers, he could think only of Georgie. He committed to himself that he would marry her as soon as she would have him.

Speaking to himself, he said, "If the Judge will allow her marry a lowly Second Lieutenant." His oath to himself brought him sleep.

The troop of scouts made their way southeast along the rim, pausing where the ground gave them good visibility along the trails leading in and out of the canyons below. With their binoculars they scanned the landscape, Alchesay told Baychendaysen where each useable trail departed the Verde, described in detail the landmarks that identified the path upstream. Baychendaysen listened well and made notes each night.

Baychendaysen questioned a particularly steep and narrow ascent.

His English improving by the day, Alchesay organized his answer, "Times will come when you must measure your enemy. Soldiers back off many trails. Nántan Baychendaysen should never back down a trail."

Baychendaysen caught the meaning and recited what was becoming something of standing field order humor between them, "Keep the old bird flying."

"Nantan, white eyes will always have more numbers, more rifles, more cartridges and more provisions. Nootahah hopes you are short of will."

Their eyes met with a steely firmness with which both were now comfortable.

"You think some of our officers are short the will?"

"Yes. Nantan Baychendaysen isn't short the will." It is often most difficult to measure the extent to which you can crowd a friend. Alchesay considered such before finishing, "Nantan, you live with a pain that teaches, no give up, no give in."

The observation caught Baychendaysen by surprise. Yet both knew the statement carried an unflinching truth.

Charles and Georgia Gatewood

SEVEN

GEORGIA MCCULLOUGH

"Now that you've rejoined us, you'll be pleased to know that you did not capture Nana on the Upper Verde." Gatewood smiled and McPherson laughed.

"Bay'che you should see the feather head dress a San Francisco newspaper drawer put on poor ole Nana as he stood chest deep in the Verde handing his rifle to the Captain."

The vision of Nana in the feathered bonnet of the Plains Indians brought a cackle from the room.

Walter Reed now chimed in, "Dorsey tells that Nana would have shot the Captain's balls off if you and your Sergeant hadn't been sitting on a rock and already damn near froze the poor old man's balls off, making him wait in that cold water like that. You should be ashamed."

Gatewood shook his head, "Really inhumane of us wasn't it. But I did regularly consult with my Surgeon."

"You assumed I could correctly diagnose the difference between frozen testicles and blue balls." McPherson's laughter obscured the sound of his critics.

"Lieutenant, meet our fourth and newest bunkmate. Second Lieutenant Thomas Cruse allow me introduce you to First Lieutenant Charles Gatewood, excuse me The Lieutenant Gatewood," Dorsey placed an elaborate emphasis on the word *the*.

With the intent of poking Gatewood a bit more, McPherson said, "Damn, bad enough to bunk with two Virginians, now I get another brand new West Point polished Second Lieutenant straight from Kentucky. With my luck, he'll be the only soul from his home state who finds Bourbon a vile liquid."

He stroked his mustache and the hint of a smile broke, giving away his good natured intent.

"At least he is from Kentucky and not Virginia," turning to Reed, Dorsey continued, "When I accepted a commission in the Army I thought I would find many sociable fellow Irishmen. Instead, I find myself encompassed by gentleman from our southern states.

Cruse reached opened his locker, pulled out a bottle of fine looking bourbon and sat it on the table. "Well, Captain Surgeon I have been saving this for just such an occasion. I've been told nothing will hush an Irishman like a bottle of fine whiskey."

McPherson checked bottle as if examining its ancestry, then checked its clarity in the light. He stroked his mustache in the most thoughtful of fashions before pronouncing, "It isn't Jameson's, but it appears respectable enough."

The seal was peeled and the bottle uncorked. Metal coffee cups were repurposed and a round of good Kentucky whiskey was poured.

Cruse, since it was his bottle, offered the toast, "To the men of the Sixth Cavalry and Fort Apache."

"Fort?"

McPherson chimed in, "Yes, Fort. We left for a bit they upgraded the place."

"Well, by God, I'll drink to that." Gatewood was enthused.

"Cruse old boy let me explain our comrade's excitement. The size of married housing quarters increases when a post becomes a fort. First Lieutenant's quarters are almost the size of a Captain's quarters. That is big news for an officer aspiring marriage."

"Ah." Cruse said expressing an understanding.

Gatewood was clearly pleased.

"Raise a glass to the promotion of Charles Bare Gatewood. To First Lieutenant Charles Bare Gatewood, even if he doesn't know it yet."

Suspecting more of Dorsey's humor, his response was flat. Shortly convinced by his bunk mates, he toasted his pending promotion.

The status of fort and the promotion, entitling him to acceptable frontier married officer's quarters, left only an accepted proposal of marriage separating him from Georgia. He promptly posted a letter.

Walking back from the adjunct's he acknowledged to himself that this was not the romantic summer's evening proposal he had envisioned. But it was functional and he so missed her company. At its posting, his proposal seemed oddly free of doubt. Walking toward the stable to check on Bob, passing plank and adobe buildings, he looked at the horizon. He had misgivings about the life he was offering Georgia.

He found Dorsey and Walt Reed in their new infirmary. So new that the aroma of fresh cut pine with the sap still seeping from it out-dueled the smell of alcohol and illness. He vacillated between a strong desire to confide his proposal with his friends and the twinge of concern about a rejection.

Some two weeks later, Telegraph Sergeant Will Barnes stepped a fast pace across the parade ground to personally delivered a telegram.

"Lieutenant I know you'd be wanting this post haste."

It read "Yes, yes. Letter follows. Georgia."

It seems that contrary to his fears, Georgia's father was now quite pleased to pass the responsibility for his head-strong red-headed daughter on to another man. So, the Honorable Judge McCullough arranged the prompt reply by telegram, not wanting to give the young Lieutenant the opportunity to reconsider. The line between a head-strong daughter and an ill-tempered daughter was as thin as a slender thread.

Unlike most of her female relatives and her friends, Georgia McCullough was not attracted to the stately, stable life Maryland could now offer. While she was fond of Charles Gatewood, she became infatuated with his letters. She read of places with exotic names in a land unlike any she had encountered. The Richmond newspapers even wrote that he was the most effective and daring scout in Arizona Territory. It all sounded so exciting despite the fact Gatewood had made every effort paint his letters with the brush of a harsh reality. He failed.

Georgia dreamed.

Despite her own unforgiving conclusions when she gazed into the full length mirror, she believed that Charles found her intoxicating. Dressed only in a white cotton summer night gown, Georgia viewed herself with a most critical eye. Some of her judgments had a little basis in fact, but she was tall. She was taller than most of the men in her Virginia social circle, but she had to look up into Charles' eyes. That alone melted her.

She considered her soft white Irish skin and her reddish hair to be her jewels.

As she made unhurried half-turns, she raised her gown until its height matched the length of her drawers. Though critical of her knees, she liked her legs, especially where her thighs exposed themselves from the lacy openings in her drawers. Of all her undergarments, she was most particular about her sheer, lacy drawers.

She relaxed her grip on the hem of the gown allowing it to fall back into place. The summer gown was sleeveless and the neckline dipped low. She gathered the fabric so that her breast appeared more prominently. She liked her breasts. She flirtatiously fingered the neckline of her gown, smiled at the girl in the mirror and made a giggling girlish dash for her bed.

Her head sank into her pillows, her body settled into the mattress. She couldn't suppress her delight. She was going to marry a man she could come to love.

Mrs. Lieutenant Gatewood eased herself into the shaded porch rocking chair. Logic to the contrary, she swore she could have baked bread by simply sitting it on the kitchen table. She smiled at the concept of a kitchen table. With two rooms and only one table, a table was the table.

The wagon, more correctly the half a wagon that would be assigned to a First Lieutenant, had not yet arrived from Tucson.

All such freight came north through Salt Lake to San Francisco. It would then make its way down California and over to Tucson.

When she asks, the adjunct would only commit to, "Soon, Mrs. Lt. Gatewood, Soon."

The truth was that now she had spent six weeks at Fort Apache, she was quite pleased her husband had stopped at Fort Wingate on his trip east and purchased tin cups and plates along with a cast iron skillet, stew pot and an all-purpose pan from Amos McCrieght. While the wives at Apache and Wingate had been most liberal with their advice, Charles had allowed Mrs. McCrieght to pick the necessaries. Georgia found them in place along with a lovely note of good wishes from Mrs. McCrieght.

Of course Mrs. McCrieght saw to it that Charles had a liberal supply of canned peaches. Georgia understood why he liked the peaches well enough, but she hadn't yet grasped the appeal of jerked meat.

The quarters came with a table and chairs and a bed. The Quartermaster's wife had chosen a mattress and a carpet for them. She was free to exchange them, but she didn't.

Each wife who called emphasized that when they would have to change duty stations, she would only be allowed to move one thousand pounds. They assured her of the inevitably of reassignments.

She was coming to understand her fellow wives came in two basic types. There were those who were impressed with their husband's rank and behaved as if it was their own. Then, there were those who weren't so easily impressed period. She preferred the latter from the onset.

She rocked in her chair. The quarters were not large and they belonged to the United States Army, but for right now they were the home of Lieutenant and Mrs. Charles Bare Gatewood.

"Duty, Honor, Country."

Their wedding night had been at her parent's home where they were shivareed until virtually time for their train to leave. She felt from a legal standpoint their marriage had been consummated that night. There had been many attempts that were more grasping and grabbing as various trains rocked westward through the darkness.

Even so, Georgia had decided that it would be their first intimate evening at a posting and in their bed that would bring emotional consummation to their marriage.

Once Georgia made up her mind that a thing was to be so, it would be so.

But she had yet to spend such a night with her husband.

On a long train ride almost across the United States, the young couple talked. Their words provided the basis for a unique cognitive and intimate relationship that would serve them well over their lifetime. Hopes, dreams and values were positioned in their life so that they would never be compromised even by life's most painful challenges.

Both would later conclude that the distractions from the expectations and disappointments of initial physical intimacy had profited them. The awkwardness of their sexual attempts beneath covered blankets in the seats of moving train lifted the Victorian seriousness they brought to marriage and left them more with a good humored approach to marital exchanges. They teased and they laughed.

Somewhere along the tracks her fear of being a sexual inept spouse slid away. She found reassurance in her husband's clumsy enthusiasm.

When they stepped from the train in Gallup, an escort was waiting to accompany them directly to Fort Wingate. She looked at the landscape from the window of the train since leaving Wichita. The open windows allowed smoke from the engine to fill the cars at times. There were stock yards at seemingly every stop across Kansas. Travel was not conducive to creating a unique trip for the newlyweds, but it did.

In a fashion neither of them had foreseen, Georgie McCullough and Charles Gatewood fell in love.

She disembarked the train believing she was prepared for life on a frontier outpost.

Dr. Dorsey McPherson was there to greet her. Standing on the stone platform with his hat in hand, the bridegroom presented his friend to his wife. Dorsey suppressed the temptation to reach into his repertoire of newlywed jokes, no small challenge knowing he could have his friend blushing in heartbeat.

Introductions and polite conversions exchanged, "Mrs. Lieutenant Gatewood, please excuse us for a moment."

They turned and stepped a few paces from the platform.

McPherson said, "Damn Gatewood, you have to be the luckiest son-of-bitch that ever drew a breath." Glancing back he continued, "She's lovely."

"Yes, she is," Gatewood replied. Thinking the subject best changed, he asked, "How's the latrine business?"

"Walt and I now have an Assistant to help with such matters. And the incidence of dysentery is reduced."

"Alright, Dorsey, let's hear it."

McPherson knew the chit-chat was over. "About a dozen renegades, four of them broke out of the Tuba jail and collected some friends. I understand some to be Utes and rest are Navajos, off the reservation and raiding in the San Juan Valley."

Gatewood's countenance offered no effort to conceal his questioning mind.

"This would ordinarily be commonplace. Navajo Police would manage it. But they raided the ranch house of some important Santa Fe politician." Dorsey looked down, moved the sand with his foot, continued. "Must have been one awful bloody mess. Wife and two daughters and a son. Along with three ranch hands, one a gun hand. Hell, Bay'che, said the women were raped and mutilated and left to die. Youngest girl died real slow. Parts of the wranglers were found all over the place." Emotion caused a pause, before he continued, "Boy is about eight. They took him."

"Bay'che they sat that young Momma on a stake and split her open."

"Captain McLellan said to tell you he'd like to have the boy back, the others not so much. Said you'd understand."

Gatewood's teeth clench and his eyes narrowed, he gave a steady measured nod. He understood.

Bay'che. The railroad had physically brought him back to the Arizona Territory. With the sound of his shortened Apache name, he was aware of surroundings and the expectations they bore. His emotion had traveled more slowly than his physical being.

Then, they caught up with lightening speed. The ardent bridegroom, obsessed with getting to know his wife, gave way to pragmatic officer.

"Gatewood, I have your orders from Captain McLellan. You have a squad from the Sixth under Tom Cruse and your squad of scouts. Tom's learning."

McPherson softened his voice, "I believe Captain Mac grasp what you did for him on Verde. I think he hated to pile this on you."

The surgeon hesitated then added, "He got a tad talkative when I took care of an infected tick on his right testicle, at least that's what I told Mrs. Captain McLellan it was."

What began as smiles became quiet laughter.

"Goso saddled Bob for you. I signed out cartridges for the scouts, an extra bag of one hundred for your keeping. You owe McCrieght for your Winchester cartridges," he thought a moment, "Powders and medicinal whiskey packed for you. Cruse has the rest of the necessaries on mules with him."

"Good to have you back," Dorsey said then added, "Congratulations my friend. I have two squads from the Sixth to escort your bride safely to Apache. We'll drink to your wedding when you come in."

Gatewood looked at him and said, "God save us, you're not in command are you?"

Giving his chest an exaggerated boost, he said, "Yes," a pause, "Me and two top Sergeants."

Gatewood glanced toward his wife on the platform. The locked steel eyes soften and the lines of the mouth loosen. He inhaled and released an audible exhale.

"Surgeon, it's good to see you."

He saw Alchesay at the corral and motioned him to come and meet Georgie. Alchesay waved him off.

Gatewood stepped back on the platform and to his bride.

While he was reaching for exactly the right words, Georgie ask, "How long will you be gone?"

"I'll be in the field till the assignment is done."

"I've heard that about you. Well, hurry back. I have an assignment for you." The smile was the most enticing and playful he ever encountered. The steely blue in his eyes softened.

He whispered into her ear, "Do not lose those lacy bloomers." He resisted his urge to pat her behind.

He told her of her escort to Fort Apache after a brief stop in Fort Wingate.

He gave way to his urges, took Georgie by the hand and stepped into the station and discreetly behind a screen. They kissed. It was a kiss that set the standard by which all future kisses would be measured.

Georgie squeezed his hand and in a tone reflecting both surprise and breathlessness said, "Thank you."

As they parted she heard her words bounce inside her head. "Thank you." She chastised her failure to find a better expression of her feelings. "I can't believe I said thank you."

Baychendaysen changed into his field clothes. His field shirt, his pants tucked into his boots, his broad-brimmed hat settled on his head, he made quick time for the corral.

Dog met him about half way and after a pat on the head fell into pace.

The greeting between Baychendaysen and Alchesay was warm and firm.

He stroked Bob's neck and mounted. He nodded his approval to Goso.

"Who did you send ahead?"

"Nantan, Dead Shot and Dandy Jim. Day out on us." He continued, "All Nootahah."

Baychendaysen nodded his understanding and approval, he resettled himself on Bob and said, "First Sergeant, let's go find them."

Gatewood did not look back as the squad left the corral at Gallup station.

Georgie felt the most peculiar of pride as she watched him leave. She wasn't sure about the transformation she had just observed. The kind and playful man with whom she had shared a train bench stepped off the train and solely through the reaction of others became someone different. He wasn't intimidating, but was so respected that it resembled intimidation. His straight stiff posture seemed to make him further rise from his companions.

Georgie Gatewood realized there were layers to her husband that were yet to be peeled away.

She became aware that her breasts had become uncomfortably tender. She had her usual hints over the past few days. Her woman's woes were upon her. She gathered her travel kit and found the ear of station master's wife who led her to a small bedroom. There was a night table with metal water basin and a pitcher.

"Little darlin', jar is under the bed, just leave it be when youse be done."

Alone, Georgie surveyed the room. It was some better than a lean-to but not much. The wall planks were not caulked as tightly as her Victoria modesty would have liked. A dressing screen provided her with some assurance. She flopped on the edge of the bed. Tears welled.

"Dang, Dang"! She pricked her thumb as she attempted to open a safety pin through the reticent tears.

Gathered, she stepped onto the station platform.

"Mrs. Lieutenant Gatewood, I recommend you begin your journey by spending two nights at Fort Wingate. The ladies here are eagerly awaiting any news from the east at all."

"Captain McPherson, I don't suppose there is a graceful manner to avoid it." The expression on her face convinced him of the sincerity of her question.

"I suspect not."

"Captain, from my husband's letters, I have come to know you. I'd be more comfortable if you'd call me Georgia or Georgie."

Dorsey smiled, made an exaggerated bow and said, "Georgie, I'm Dorsey but I answer to Surgeon if it fits your tongue better."

"Dorsey, I am anxious to see our Fort Apache quarters, but protocol dictates a brief stay. I do look forward to meeting Mrs. McCrieght. Charles speaks so fondly of them."

Charles. Dorsey hadn't heard Gatewood referred to Charles in years, but it rolled comfortably from her tongue.

"Still the ladies will be delighted to see you. The MacArthur's have a new baby, The Colonel and Mrs. Colonel

MacArthur, everyone calls her Pinky, had another son. Pinky was determined he would be born on the frontier but she only made it to Arsenal Barracks in Little Rock." Dorsey faltered. He didn't want to say too much to talkative wife. Relying on his judgment, he continued.

"Pinky has some unique thoughts along. From the beginning of this pregnancy, she has been convinced that this son, their third son, will become the President of the United States. She felt being born at a frontier outpost could be helpful."

Georgie's face looked questioning.

"Oh, Don't worry. Pinky is more than happy to share her vision without being asked. She'll tell you about her most special and unique baby son, President-to-be Douglas MacArthur."

"And the Colonel?" Georgie ask.

"Colonel MacArthur is a fine soldier just striving to get back to the rank of General. He was a Union General during the big war." He added, "The man's a good soldier."

Wagons loaded, the small assemblage started along the deeply rutted, dusty road to Wingate. The buggy took the lead, hoping to limit the quantity of dust and sand that would collect on their newest arrival.

Georgie was fascinated by the diversity cactus but was disillusioned that it all seemed so small and close to the ground. Dorsey assured her she would not be disappointed with the saguaro and other cactus of the lower desert.

Mostly Georgie sat quietly. Between anxiety and menstrual distress, she was uncomfortable but she sat silently. The harsh high desert landscape provided few reassurances.

"We are getting close now," Dorsey told her.

"I'm sorry I have not better company," she said.

"Are there other things I should know?"

Dorsey laughed and said, "More than you can possibly know, but not for today." "Today remember the ladies will be inquisitive, but they just want to know lady things. Ask for their help and they will embrace you."

Georgie smiled. "You're a kind man."

"Thank you."

Fort Wingate was detectable on the horizon.

EIGHT

HUNTING A MAD DOG

ON THE THIRD DAY, Dandy Jim found the squads. He and Dead Shot had cut the trail of the escapees almost on the exact path Alchesay had theorized. Staying in the mountains until a scout spotted a target of opportunity.

Dead Shot continued to track the escapees.

The squads were separated by no more than a quarter of a mile. Poco Lizard was sent with a note for Lieutenant Cruse.

"Good. Nantan Virlid must learn," Alchesay offered.

"Virlid?"

Alchesay had slipped and he now stretched for saving words, "Not Apache name, mixed words." He was trapped by his words and almost in the tone of a confession he said, "Raw Virgin Lieutenant."

Baychendaysen shook his head and smiled slightly and said, "Raw virgin. I guess we all were at one time."

Alchesay shook his head, "No, Nootahah always know, Nantan Baychendaysen knows. Nantan Cruse must watch – hear – learn."

Nantan Baychendaysen had embraced his Nootahah name. Alchesay believed Bay'che was never inflicted with the disease of vanity that infected too many white Nantans.

"And learn he will. Then, a soldier looks at him it must be Nantan Cruse."

Alchesay nodded, agreeing with the wisdom.

127

Poco Lizard returned with Nantan Cruse and directed him to Baychendaysen and Alchesay.

The conference was brief. Baychendaysen made certain that Lieutenant Cruse understood that by following Alchesay's guidance, they found themselves well positioned. They could sustain a position between the escapees and the ranches in the rivers bottoms that passed for fertile land in western New Mexico.

"We will build cook fires when we can, looking warm and well-fed while they are cold and hungry in the mountains."

Alchesay added, "They are not Nootahah. Will quick come where we wait. Don't come quick, Bay'che go kill'em. All go home."

Alchesay looked toward Baychendaysen.

Bay'che asked, "Ranch nearby?"

Alchesay nodded there was. "One – Old man, odd old man and his son." He gathered moisture in his mouth and released a contemptuous spew before saying, "Mexican woman or two. Couple of hired hands likely."

Baychendaysen rubbed Dog's head, and then his words came in a chilling murmur, "Can you make them believe we've lost their sign and have left?"

"Yes."

Bay'che turned to Cruse, "Every hour they live, the boy is less likely to live." Cruse got his first glimpse of Gatewood's gunmetal eyes. These were not the eyes of his companion at Fort Apache, they were the eyes of an unrelenting hunter of men.

Alchesay knew what Cruse didn't know. Nantan Verlid was about to shake hands with Elephant.

Suspecting McLellan had sent Lieutenant Cruse out with a number of experienced troopers in his squad, Gatewood said, "Lieutenant, see if any of your squad knows this rancher."

Quickly Cruse reported, "Lieutenant Gatewood, one of the Sergeants know them. He says they have lived along the San Juan where a creek comes in from the mountains for a number of years. Says the old man is a different sort, a tough nut and he wouldn't be leaving his land. Apaches water up the creek, keep an easy peace. He might not want to help capture the renegades."

Now Alchesay spoke, "Old man Albert. Strange man." Alchesay thought before continuing, "Rancher, trader, his women grow corn. Trades for most things – I hear for children. Treats boy like Nantan Surgeon treats woman."

He paused until Bay'che indicated he understood. "Holds no good for Dine' or Nootahah. Likes Mexicans."

As an afterthought, he added, "No rifles, no cartridges."

Bay'che squatted and stirred the dirt with a stick, "Trade for white boy with ill intent?"

Alchesay nodded. "Hear maybe."

Baychendaysen cut his eyes toward his friend, "You could speak before I sent Lieutenant Cruse on a fool's errand."

"Nantan, you have been away taking a woman. Nantan Virglid must learn to first find what scouts know."

Bay'che flopped on the boulder behind him, took off his hat and spun it on the ground covering the toe of one of his boots.

He looked directly into the face of his friend, "Damn, I hate it when you're right." Then, he finished, "No, I hate it when you let me be wrong!"

A tight-lipped smile broke his face. He shook his head. Personal oversights annoyed him.

"Do we have a scout that has traded with Mr. Albert?"

"All have passed here." Alchesay's body remained stoic but Bay'che knew his educator's ribs were clanking with laughter.

Bay'che turned to Cruse who had now rejoined them. "Tom, I want you and some of you squad to go ahead and pay Mr. Albert a visit. Take Kuruk with you. Let him believe it is a courtesy visit, that we might be seeking his assistance."

Looking to Alchesay for affirmation, "It is possible the renegades have already been there. Look closely for any sign of the boy but don't challenge the man now."

Cruse had left to collect his patrol.

Looking at Alchesay, Baychendaysen said, "I believe we will ride along behind, take Dead Shot and Goso with us."

"Sergeant O'Malley!" The squat, barrel-chested veteran of more skirmishes and patrols than most came double time.

"Sir." It snapped from his mouth with a familiarity that only time can provide.

Gatewood gave Sergeant O'Malley orders as to the manner in which he wanted the balance of the squad to follow.

Staying out of sight and using high ground to conceal them, they followed Cruse's patrol at a reasonable distance then pushed for a vantage point from which to view of the ranch house.

Bay'che spoke, "If you're interrupted by unexpected guests where would you stash a boy?"

Alchesay pointed to the tree line of a small tributary behind the ranch. "There."

Baychendaysen nodded agreement.

They make their way down the slope. A visible path led from the house to the creek and into the trees on the other side.

Nantan Cruse, three of his squad and Kuruk proceeded to the Albert's ranch house. After an initial impression that the man was unwelcoming, Cruse found the old man to be more than cooperative.

There was a light in the small bunk house about twenty yards from the ranch house.

Cruse dismounted and handed the reins to Sergeant Weldon Thomas. He spoke softly, "Things go bad in here, drop what comes out the bunk house."

As they entered the young Mexican girl was stashing a bedroll. Cruse caught a glimpse of a boy's shirt just before the blanket covered it.

In an effort to explain the inhospitable beginning, old man Albert explained he had sent his son with some cattle to Fort Wingate to sell and buy some odds items. Business done, the boy had made his way a few miles south into the Pacific and Atlantic railhead and the few tent stores that had sprung up. Dependent on the railroad paymaster for its cash flow, one of the stores, a saloon, had hung a large sign that acknowledged the paymasters last name. Over the tent's flap entrance the sign read Gallup.

"Sorry son-of-a-bitch, God damn squaw charged Junior ten cents and sent him back to me with his cock drippin'," Albert spewed. Now a month later, his son not yet recovered, Albert was still furious. "Get me nuff coal oil and I'd light that place like the Hell Hole it is."

Albert glared at his humiliated and sulking son, "That or dip Junior's wick in coal oil and light it."

Rattling on, "God Damn railroad only bring land trash and trouble."

Feeling somewhat better after verbally expunging his demons, he sat back in his chair, "Just trash and trouble – and make the trash we done got worse."

"Woman's fixing a big stew. Got cow, corn, and beans with nuff chilies to cure what ails ya."

"Mr. Albert, with your permission, the troopers will stay with you. I must report back to Lieutenant Gatewood. We hope they still have an eight year old boy with them. We want him back alive if possible," Cruse advised.

"Gatewood? Ain't that that long nosed Nantan rides with Alchesay?"

"Yes sir, but you may call him Lieutenant Gatewood."

"Well, God damn." Albert obviously considered Gatewood's presence a potentially unwelcome problem.

With the boy in tow and wrapped in a blanket, a woman sprinted from behind the ranch house. Her repeated looks back at the ranch prevented her from noticing the movement in the dense trees in front of her.

It took her two strides to cross the narrow stream of shallow water. The boy slipped on a moss covered rock mid-trickle. She straightened him and dashed for the path into the trees.

Just as she felt herself safe, with a piece of wood he had carefully chosen, Goso knocked her unconscious. He dragged her to the pool of water and tried to hold her head beneath the water. He found it too shallow so he pulled her into the trees.

Just as the woman's head touched the grass, with a hefty stone in his hand, the boy unleashed a blow with adequate fury to break her nose. The blood spurted up his arm and onto his face. As he drew back to strike again, Goso secured the boy. He held him tightly as spasms of rage grasp the boy, and then came tears that appeared to calm the boy's fury. Thinking of a crying child on a cradle board, Goso sat on the creek bank and held the boy tightly. As the boy quieted, he wiped the blood splatters from the boy's face.

Gatewood's patchwork field uniform was enough to reassure the boy they were soldiers. The boy held on to Goso and sobbed.

Dead Shot was now securely in control of the woman, roped, gagged and tied to a tree. He turned and said with a certain admiration, "Boy smash her face good."

Rifles at the ready, Alchesay, Dead Shot and Baychendaysen made their way to the ranch house.

Dead Shot stopped on a knoll that gave a clear line of fire into the possible paths of rear retreat.

Old Man Albert stepped out the door behind his visitors to see them off and was greeted by Bay'che and Alchesay.

With his best Navajo, Alchesay said, "Ya-at-eeh" It was an all-purpose Navajo greeting.

The old man started to bolt, but Bay'che's command halted him in his tracks. It wasn't the words that stopped him. It was the lethal tone of the voice that delivered them. He hesitated.

The silence was fractured by a pistol shot from behind the ranch house followed by the report of a Springfield. The stillness was brief but overwhelming. George Albert, sensing Junior's death, fired his pistol as he turned. The first shot cut a notch into the edge of Cruse's boot. The second made a whining sound as it passed his head. Cruse would never forget that sound.

Kuruk dropped Albert before he could release another shot. As he had begun his fall Gatewood's pistol fired, cracking all the bones in his shoulder. He was dead when he hit the planks.

Three ranch hands erupted from the bunk house. Cruse was framed by the light coming through the windows from the ranch house. Sergeant Thomas pulled him from the light as a pistol cartridge splintered a porch post.

Alchesay's Henry fired, followed by Cruse's pistol. The cowhands immediately stopped running, launched their guns in front of them and extended their hands upward.

Alchesay muttered into his friend's ear, "Prisoners slow us." Although Bay'che didn't respond, Alchesay knew he heard.

"May the men have Albert's now?"

"Yes, but just here." Making a motion to indicate the pelvic girdle, he continued, "When Satan sees his remains, he will know his offenses."

"Old man's dogs eat sliced dick shortly."

"Once the house is cleared, fire it."

"Prisoners slow us."

Bay'che didn't hesitate. "Take everything except their boots and start them walking to the rail head town."

Bay'che turned, "Where's the boy?"

"With Goso."

He turned his head to see the boy and Goso making their way from the darkness into the light. The pair found a seat on the porch.

The boy was holding a pocket knife and Goso was showing him how to sharpen it.

"Where the hell did he get the knife?"

"Had it in a pouch inside his boot."

Goso and the boy both spoke a broken Spanish. It was enough, that and the gift of small whet stone.

Alchesay nodded. They went to introduce themselves to the boy.

Goso did the initial introduction, "Jon-thun." The boy shook his head yes.

Bay'che extended his hand, "I am Lieutenant Gatewood and this is First Sergeant Alchesay." From habit, he started to say that he would be home soon. Then he realized the home the child had known was gone. With that realization, any thoughts Lieutenant Gatewood had of abandoning the pursuit vanished.

The boy looked at the men and said, "Jonathan Box." He extended his hand. Two men familiar with human frailty and human cruelty shook hands and hearts with a sturdy tow headed eight year old. His face reflected what they knew, the boy was unique. Jonathan Justin Box would survive and subsist.

Dog joined them.

Baychendaysen called, "Sergeant Thomas."

The Sergeant quickly appeared.

"Sergeant, Lieutenant Cruse tells me there is a fine stew pot going in the house. Please take young Mr. Box into the house and feed him." Bay'che thought and added, "Sergeant, let Dog taste it first."

133

"Yes Sir."

"And help yourself to a bowl."

"Yes Sir!"

The boy looked at the house, turned to Gatewood and said, "Please Sir, may I eat on the porch?"

Gatewood read the set in young man's jaw and said, "Yes, you may." He nodded to Sergeant Thomas.

Reading the cue, Jonathan acknowledged the permission, saying, "Thank you, Sir."

The boy grabbed Goso's arm and lead him. Dog fell into step behind the boy.

They took a seat on the edge of the porch. Goso reached the sturdy leather pouch containing what he judged to be prize knives, spoils of conflict, and an array of whet stones.

Selecting what he deemed to be an efficient sized knife, smallish by comparison and an elk skin scabbard, he said, "Jon-thun."

He handed the boy the knife. The knife was a sober gift. Goso felt the boy had need for such a knife and was glad he could give him a fine steel blade.

Jonathan agreed. Both spit on their whet stones and begin to put a finer edge on their blades. Goso's guidance came when he considered it necessary.

Dog nestled beside the boy.

Sergeant Thomas brought two large blue enameled cups of stew. The trooper glanced and offered the second cup to Goso. Goso gestured in a manner that it was clear he appreciated the kindness of the offer but left no doubt he believed the white man's stew would create stomach distress for him.

Alchesay, Bay'che and Virglid watched.

Cruse offered, "One tough kid."

"He will need to be."

"Looks like the Elephant took a bite out of your boot." Gatewood looked at Cruse's raised boot. "You did well Lieutenant Cruse."

"We hunt Dine'," Alchesay tiring quickly of any such congratulatory comments and came back to the next task.

In a rare direct sharing of such thoughts, Baychendaysen said, "Those are men who deserve to take a seat on a stake."

The Nootahah had slower, more painful ways to kill a Navajo. Alchesay suggested several alternatives.

Bay'che shook his head, feigning disbelief but he knew the truth.

They parted, refocusing on the pursuit.

As Gatewood moved toward the ranch house, a sharp pain sent him in search of a place to sit. Alchesay saw him almost go to his knees before righting himself but gave no acknowledgement. Gatewood gave no other overt hint of his pain.

As the grip of the pain relaxed, he made his way to Bob and his saddlebag. He took a prescribed dose of the "willow bark powder" and a sip of Dorsey's potent elixir.

Bay'che sat on a large stone to keep the pain from his legs and ate venison with the scouts. He drank the water secured from spring fed stream behind the house from a quart canning jar he had noticed in the house. It was a bracing change. The water from his canteens was most often warm, tasting of metal and dirt.

Lying in his blanket roll, staring skyward through the crisp fall mountain air, the stars appeared intriguingly oversized and blazing bright. He wondered if Georgie was looking into the bright night sky at Fort Apache. Sleep took him.

He awakened deep in the night. A soft scraping sound drew his eyes to the boy, outlined in the flickering light of the fading campfire and wrapped in a blanket, methodically placing an edge on his knife.

A second sip of the surgeon's syrup brought substantial relief and deep sleep.

At daybreak, four scouts departed to regain contact with the escapee's trail. Five troopers from the Sixth, under Sergeant Weldon Thomas with Goso and Kuruk scouting, left to deliver Jonathan Box to Fort Wingate.

"Dog went with the boy," Baychendaysen said to Alchesay.

"Good," was the response. Alchesay wrapped his poncho tighter against the mountain chill and said, "Might have had to eat him this winter."

Contact regained, the pursuit was intensified.

Making a situational adaptation, Baychendaysen said, "Keep jail birds in air!"

After days of pressing the escapees deeper into the San Juan Mountains, the pressure appeared to have brought a fracture.

Dead Shot came upon the escapee's cold camp. The sign at the site suggested a struggle. Alchesay interpreted the evidence as suggesting at least three of the Utes had enough of the mountains and decided to head home. It was likely that the group disagreed over what the Utes felt belonged to them. Sign read that a final settlement came with two Utes being killed in their sleep. The death of the third Ute appeared to have been more problematic. Blood sign suggested at least two wounded Navajo.

Displaying the Nootahah attitude that by dying the Ute had failed, better to flee and fight another day. An Apache would have followed the group and killed them one at a time, making them live with the appalling dread of never knowing when he might choose to kill them.

Sergeant Weldon Thomas' troop returned Jonathan Justin Box to his waiting father at Fort Wingate. The grateful father, James J. Box, opened a tab at McCrieght's store. Once dismissed, each man of the troop gulped two generous glasses of a whiskey distilled and aged to be sipped. Each soldier was rewarded with a five dollar credit with McCrieght, a credit that could not be used for the purchase of alcohol.

Sergeant Thomas delivered a written message from Lieutenant Gatewood simply stating, "Boy alive. Remain in pursuit."

Then, the Sergeant gave his full report and joined his men.

Before noon the next day, preparing to leave to catch the train in Gallup that would return them to the safety of Santa Fe, Jonathan Box walked his father to the scout's wikiup area.

A substantial gust of wind with the accompanying sand and dust partly obscured them, then with the son a stride in front of the father, the pair appear only a few yards from where Goso stared.

Jonathan stepped forward and said, "Goso, I brought my father to meet you."

Logic dictates that the successful Santa Fe politician and merchant and the White Mountain Apache, a Corporal of Scouts for the Sixth Cavalry, as they stood being introduced by the eight year old boy that stood between them felt the situation to somewhat unnatural. The boy did not.

The introductions made, James J. Box expressed his appreciation. He reached behind him and withdrew a Bowie knife, a Bowie knife made in Germany of Strassburger steel and extended his knife as a gift of appreciation. Jonathan smiled at Goso.

A rare expression crept across Goso's face. He recognized fine steel and the gift was overwhelming. He reached to his side and from just under the flap of his breech cloth unsheathed his own Bowie knife. He extended the finely craved deer antler handle toward James Box. Box now the awkward one accepted the gift.

Jonathan extended a box of McCrieght's finest cigars and said, "For Kuruk."

Jonathan Justin Box was satisfied.

Goso, pointing an open hand toward the boy, said, "Fine son Jon-thun. Care well for you when you old."

Ready to depart, James J. Box extended his hand, then paused awkwardly recognizing a social variance. Goso extended his hand. The resulting handshake was ungainly but rarely has a hand shake been more emotionally genuine.

The Boxes and Dog departed.

About the time the James and Jonathan Box's train was approaching Santa Fe, the scouts, with only the sleep that could be obtained on horseback, were pushing the Navajo escapees hard.

Just appearing from the rough terrain on foot and at a slow trot, Dandy Jim came in with intelligence. He patted Bob on the neck and reported. "Nantan Bay'che, Dine'—

Navajo police got'em.

Alchesay cut and handed Bay'che a strip of jerky. Bay'che nodded his thanks and then settled himself on Bob.

"Did they kill them?"

"No Nantan, makin' for Window Rock." Dandy Jim stopped, then spoke more. "Santa Fe soldiers jumped them. Kill all."

Obviously enjoying his moment, Dandy Jim got excited and couldn't organize his words. Alchesay translated.

"Killed them. Took two heads. Maybe bounty men. Took everything they wanted. Left a words paper pinned to Dine' Police Nantan."

"The note?"

"Were he found it."

"Tell Private Dandy Jim I am most proud of his work, tell him well done."

Dandy Jim knew enough English to be smiling when Alchesay began translating.

Bay'che slid off Bob, found a rock and sat. He took his hat between his fingers and turned it by the brim. He stood and slapped the hat against his pants as if dusting either the hat or the broadcloth pants. His face was expressionless, but his eyes released an unrelenting white heat.

Cruse was confused. Alchesay understood the frustration of what his friend viewed as unfinished business.

Alchesay said, "Enemies you kill. Enemies you punish. Enemies you punish until they die." His eyes scanned Cruse to know if he needed to say more. He did not.

Dandy Jim lingered. Alchesay stepped aside and Dandy Jim conveyed an opinion. Alchesay nodded understanding, his body language indicated agreement. Now feeling that his report was complete, Dandy Jim left.

Bay'che look asked the question.

"Dandy Jim saw Goshe Loco, Crazy Dog, mad dog. Breed. Padre Mexican. Crazy, mean – outlaw. Crazy. Not with dead." He hesitated wanting to be certain he had communicated the pure evil he believed Loco Goshe to represent.

"Dandy Jim see fast trail of one man, three ponies headed to high timber. Never catch him this time now."

"The headless ones?"

Pointing to his own left bicep Alchesay said, "Padre bit him bad. Say has mark of teeth here." "Destripar," Alchesay stopped, found his English, "Goshe Loco gutted his father."

"How could this crazy man escape?"

"Evil came for Evil's son."

Gatewood knew that the explanation made perfect sense to Alchesay. The logic eluded him. Perhaps Alchesay thought the man to be the Devil's spawn.

His own thoughts dragged him back to the evil he had seen during the war with the North. From the uncomplicated slaughter of several men along a fence row, from soldiers drawing lots and lining up to assault women and girls, to the burning the crops and homes and to his personal shame that he watched from hiding fearful of discovery. If he thought too much about it, guilt overwhelmed him. Most often he repressed these thoughts from his conscious mind.

Nantan Baychendaysen thought, unlike on his very first outing, a child had been recovered. In the darker recesses of his mind, he knew they had gotten lucky. Lucky that the renegade Navajo knew an old pedophile, a perverted man who would pay a premium in trade for young white boys. The Arizona Territory was a better place with coyote's feasting on old man Albert's remains.

Accepting his dissatisfaction, he stood up and said, "Alright, let's go to Fort Apache." He repeated the mantra under his breath, "Duty, Honor, Country."

Cruse chuckled and said, "The Lieutenant has a bride to bed." Alchesay shook his head in mock puzzlement.

NINE

THE UNIQUE LIFE OF THE MILITARY WIFE

MOST OF THE OFFICER'S WIVES at Fort Apache were reared in the east. They married for the love of a man and an irresistible attraction to a romantic notion of adventure. Many would candidly say they wished to escape the life of their mothers and their sisters. This life would transform them from ladies who could not remove a dead mouse from a room into women who could sweep large spiders from their quarters with a broom and crunch the head of nosy coyote with a cast iron skillet. Their sense of femininity evolved but was not lost. They gathered in social circles speaking of fashion, recipes that might make frontier cuisine more cultured and child-rearing in such an undomesticated land. They spoke of softness in the harshest of places.

Holiday dances and concerts were organized with the music provided by the Company band. The women reached for a cultured style of life in the most coarse and remorseless of places. Through the collective efforts of the wives, culture took root and then flourished.

Georgie sat in the rocker on the front porch of Unit 102. She was rubbing yet another lotion into her skin, but freckling now seemed to be inevitable as was the dryness of her sensitive Irish skin. During her first week at the post, her neck and face had gotten crispy red sunburn. Dr. Reed and Mrs. Sergeant Wilson cut the thick leaves from a cactus looking plant with a spine protruding from the end. The leaf was sliced and by squeezing the leaves a cooling pulp was extracted. The pulp worked magically on the sunburn.

Nothing in her visions had prepared her for the loneliness of Fort Apache. The other wives were available and supportive of the new bride. However, they had households to operate. She enjoyed the perk of inexpensive laundry lady. Cooking was entirely new different venture. Most meat was boiled or cooked over an open fire. It rarely tasted as the meat with which she was familiar.

This despite the fact that a nice heard of cattle was kept tended nearby and fed with good hay brought in by the White Mountain Apache. This was a rare contract between the military and the Apache under which the Apache actually profited.

The fireplace heated effectively and drew well. Fireplace was as important a household cooking aid as was the wood cook stove.

Vegetable gardens regularly watered and with the extended growing seasons, thrived. If the sandy soil was adequately turned, potatoes, turnips and carrots grew well, tomatoes and a variety of peppers flourished.

Given the available ingredients and the modes of cooking, soup and stews were popular and common. Georgie quickly became adept at making stew made of meat, chili peppers, beans and tomatoes. The locals called it Chili Con Carne, Georgie just called it Chili.

Although the wood cook stoves were the newest the Cavalry had to offer, preparing food was a challenge. The wood was most often pine or cedar. It burned quickly and hot. It was so inconsistent that Mrs. Captain McLellan spoke fondly of cooking with buffalo chips while on prairie duty. She would speak in glowing terms of the even heat for baking anything from bread to cakes that the chips produced compared to the territory wood. Georgie picked up the knack for making both corn and flour tortillas. The fact that her husband heaped high praise on the chili and tortillas influenced her creativity.

However, the wood was oddly plentiful. Wagon loads were brought in each day from the mountainsides by a wood detail. The wood box behind each unit was filled regularly.

The fort well water, although flavored with desert salts, was tolerable. A water wagon regularly hauled in spring water from upstream on the White River and from two tributaries coming out of the White Mountains.

A family latrine was behind each building. Two enamel pots of decent size and with sturdy handles were placed under the beds. Sat to the side of the home, the Fort Sanitary Detail saw to their collection each morning shortly after Reveille.

A warm water bath was every bit the occasional luxury that one would suspect it to be. She knew that during the scorching hot days of the long desert summer small groups of the wives would arrange an escort to a beautiful sheltered pool of water up the White River.

Adapting to the climate, the clothing was considerable less formal than Virginia. What Georgie would come to consider a loose fitting house dress with ties to keep the hint some feminine shape were the most common. Full aprons were worn most of the time and certainly for most household tasks.

It was the company of other wives that made the adjustment to Army life tolerable. Georgie felt twinges of envy toward the wives whose husband's assignments kept them on the Post, rarely requiring field duty. Then, she slowly observed that many of these men were the most directive and controlling of their wives. They intruded on the daily operating routine of the household.

Sharing her wisdom only with herself, she thought, "There are husbands who are best loved when they are gone." Georgie flashed her impish Irish smile.

In a rapid change to melancholy, she missed her husband. A dust devil blew across the parade ground toward the horse pens. These were not the gentle whirlwinds of her Virginia girlhood. She went inside.

She jumped as a lizard dashed across the floor and scurried into a crack. In Virginia she might have been frightened by a dead mouse, now she was hearing of women crowning coyotes with iron skillets.

She jerked her shawl from the chair and wrapped it around her shoulders, opening the door and closing it with a moderate bang. Inappropriate or not, she intended to make straight away from Dorsey and Walter's quarters.

A Corporal knocked on the door just before she opened it.

"Mrs. Lieutenant Gatewood, Captain McLellan sends his best regards and asked me to advise you that Lieutenant Gatewood and his scouts should be little more than a day away."

Excitement somewhat muted her previous concerns.

"Thank you, Corporal. Please convey my thanks to the Captain."

"Yes Ma'am."

Georgie again sat in the rocker. Dorsey, with his confident measured gait, walked toward her.

He removed his hat in an exaggerated display of good manners and said, "May I join you, Ma'am?"

"Captain, please come and sit."

Dorsey eased his way into a rocking chair. He pulled a cigar from his jacket pocket, held it up and made a non-verbal request to smoke.

"Dorsey, of course you may."

Georgie sensed that this was more than a simple social call to check on her well-being. She pulled her shawl tighter around her.

"I understand that the Nantan will be in soon."

"Yes."

McPherson outlined the customary protocol for the arrival of soldiers from the field when a platoon of scouts was involved.

When he paused, she looked directly at him and said, "Dorsey, tell me of my husband."

Her unwavering gaze made him pause, then he answered, "Georgie, your husband will not have slept in a bed since last you slept with him. A blanket doesn't soften the rocks much. His "aches and pains" might be bad."

He looked away. Georgie said, "Apparently my husband is many things. Tell me."

Dorsey weighted her query.

"Of the two years of so he has been here, he has spent almost all his time in the field with his company of scouts. They have chased renegades of all stripes across this merciless, callous and unforgiving land. This place will not tolerate weakness in a man," he thought before going on. "He has seen brutality, butchery and cruelty beyond what can be imagined. Yet, he has the strength of will to keep his moral compass aligned."

"His mind stays firm although his body betrays him at times."

Georgie had not flinched. Dorsey thought that perhaps Gatewood had married a woman who could endure him.

"Surgeon, I care greatly for this man. I listen to the wives and their husbands. It is my opinion that he needs me. "

Dorsey nodded. She called him Surgeon with the same respectful ring that her husband used and that pleased him.

Reaching into his Gladstone, he retrieved several packets of the yellow willow bark powder and handed them to her and said, "These help him, but they seem to trouble his stomach considerably. I've come to believe mostly because he doesn't eat much food with them. Some in the east are referring to it as aspirin powders now."

"I try to get him to eat some hardtack regular with the powder. Company, St. Joseph, around St. Joe started putting a pinch of baking soda in their hardtack, Mormons brought out here. Seem to be better. Call'em crackers." He paused to see how Georgie was taking the information, then said, "It would be a great help to him if you made them and blessed them."

Georgie pondered, "Of course, there are always canned peaches."

They both smiled.

He stopped again, looked at her and explained, "He won't eat much different than his men and I swear they can go two days on a small desert lizard." Inserting an over-sight, he added, "Georgie, he genuinely likes his men. He understands them and he does not judge them for being who they are."

Dorsey strongly suspected the sips of the special elixir on an empty stomach weren't soothing to the stomach lining. He made a mental note to give random thought on the matter.

With his thumb and index finger, Dorsey smoothed his mustache and continued, "Anyway, Georgie, sleep and good basic food helps him considerably. I hope he will talk to you until sleep takes him for a long while."

He drew in a deep breath and released it, "Your husband and his scouts chase marauding Apaches who can made Sherman's foraging hordes seem like amateurs."

This was a comparison a daughter of the South grasped.

"Sometimes what a man sees out there is slow to leave him."

Georgie measured her words and said, "A wife worth her salt can keep a man's mind off pain and fear." They were her father's words, but now she had use of them. "Anticipation followed by appreciation."

Georgie Gatewood rose, reassured, and said, "Surgeon, you are our friend and I thank you."

Walter Reed was sitting at the table playing a game of solitary. Dorsey stomped his boots and dusted off his hat.

"Reed, did you ever consider that military history might note that our greatest achievement was that we kept Lieutenant Charles B. Gatewood on his feet and in the field?"

After the giving the suggestion mock consideration, he responded, "I'd consider that to be a distinct possibility."

They chuckled.

"I think I'll have Emilie join me. The quarters are decent enough. I miss her greatly."

Dorsey stroked his mustache and said, "Well damn if I don't think Gatewood has let loose some mysterious disease on us, an epidemic of loneliness. It must be the fragrance only a female can unleash."

"Yes, I would consider that to one component. But mostly I just miss my wife."

"Reed, you're nothing more than a randy ram." McPherson had his wide Irish chuckle.

Within the week, Emilie Lawrence Reed, now eighteen years old, boarded a train in Richmond and headed west to God only knew what and where. When this striking petite beauty married Dr. Walter Reed, who graduated from the University of Virginia as a Medical Doctor the age of nineteen and then promptly graduated with a second degree from Bellevue in New York City, had envisioned herself as the wife of a city physician. Now after a month together before he departed to Arizona, she just wanted to be with her husband. There was plenty of time for financial success after he had satisfied this adventurous spirit that lurked inside him.

Nightfall brought Gatewood's command into Fort Apache.

Animals settled and men dismissed, Gatewood made a cursory report and proceeded across the parade ground.

Someone barked, "Lieutenant!"

Having secured Gatewood's attention McPherson inquired, "Care to stop by for a drink before you go home?"

Gatewood shook his head no and doffed his hat toward Dorsey and continued striding toward 102. Dorsey stroked his mustache, his hand marginally disguising his broad smile.

The new husband didn't know what to expect on his first homecoming. A fleeting thought born of his insecurity came. I hope she didn't change her mind and leave. He chastised his foolish thought.

He stopped on the porch. He had already dusted himself off. He held his hat in his hand and knocked on the door. Now he really felt foolish.

As the door opened, Georgie stood framed in the lamp light. The open door caused the candles to flicker, adding to an accidentally exotic fantasy. Her hair gave the illusion of glistening in the backlight of the quarters, the breeze made the loose fitting emerald green housedress tied above her waist line wave and cling to her body. A vision that no amount of deliberate effort could have created emerged.

Her intent had been to look well for her husband, to let him know at a glance she had adapted to life in the arid air of their new home. Instead, she mesmerized him.

Gatewood stood in the doorway of his own quarters feeling completely inept and enchanted.

"Charles, you can come in. It is your home."

Still feeling awkward and heavy footed, he stepped inside.

She took her open hand and made a circle on his chest.

"Isn't there a custom about a soldier kissing his wife upon his return?"

They laughed.

Charles Gatewood enjoyed the sense of warmth that came over him.

"God, Georgie you are an enchanting vision."

The welcome home kiss lingered.

He became aware of the smell of beef stew and corn bread.

"Georgie, the stew smells tasty."

"Well, I'd hope so after you've been on a diet of lizard and jerky."

Charles laughed. This marriage thing could really grow on him. He liked to laugh.

He went to wash up. The luxury of a wash cloth and a small towel refreshed him. He washed his hands and splashed water on his face with great enthusiasm. He turned to Georgie and said, "That makes you feel as clean as this territory will let you feel."

She busied herself with the meal and he sat at the table. They continued to visit.

Their conversation pattern began to establish itself. Georgie talked. She told him of the funny stories and conveyed the necessary information. It came in a scattered blend to which even Georgie didn't understand the blueprint. But it worked.

She talked Charles in from the field and into their home.

"The stew is wonderful." Holding up a soda hardtack, broken into irregular chips, he asked, "These really blend well with the stew. What do you call them?"

"Crackers."

The main room was lit by two kerosene lamps, one was a White Owl lamp given to Georgia by her favorite aunt as a wedding gift. The soft glow that poured through the white milk glass globes provided a pleasing illusion of fashion to Unit 102 in Officer's Row at Fort Apache. The brighter light came from clear lamp placed near the doorway leading to the bedroom.

She reached into a drawer by her dishes and withdrew a leather pouch and placed it on the table. "Charles, your scouts left us a gift at the train at Wingate. Dorsey suggested we open the draw string together."

"Georgie, the Apache do not give white eyes gifts. This is rare. So, whatever it is, be proud of it."

Georgie laughed, saying "I peeked."

She slid out four knifes, of varying sizes, from a slender boning knife to a large Bowie knife. There was a bone handled knife about the size of a paring knife that she would find extraordinarily useful over the years. And a perfectly round whet stone, an easy fit into a woman's hand.

"Woman, those will be the sharpest knifes you'll ever own."

Alchesay would tell that Goso's two wives and the mother-in-law of the eldest had helped select each knife from his cache. He placed an incredible edge on each knife so that Bay'che's woman could properly prepare his food. Kuruk found a suitable pouch with a draw string. Each of the original scouts pulled the pouch shut. Alchesay delivered pouch to Captain Surgeon McPherson to give to Mrs. Lieutenant Gatewood when they were on the trail from Wingate.

Goso's knifes and a cast iron skillet from Mrs. McCrieght were the two items Georgie would use all her life.

During the scalding heat of the long summers, bedding was placed on the porches of the officer's quarters. The families slept in the slightly more temperate night air. The clear bright night air gave the couple laying on their mattress a luxurious view of the night sky, large shining moonrises and stars appeared with crystal clarity.

In deference to modesty, every couple slept under a nice sheet. The quality of the cotton sheet became one of the few status symbols on the desert outpost.

Charles and Georgia were avid porch sleepers. They only slept inside when an ill-wind of weather required it. The McPherson's were next door in 103. They were often on the porch, and although about twenty-five feet separated the units, at times the couples would lie in bed and converse. Gatewood was always the first asleep, but often a flash of pain followed by a stinging muscle spasm would startle him to complete consciousness. After a few weeks, Georgia was not even awakened by the neuromuscular responses.

Dorsey's snoring on the other hand could awaken porch sleepers several units away. Legend had it that disturbed coyotes and that wolves begin to howl in a more menacing fashion. Gatewood and Cruse fueled the tale.

It was considered poor post etiquette to notice when a couple quietly went inside to enjoy each other's company in a more friendly fashion. Outpost life on the frontier shined a spotlight on the fractures in Victorian modesty and morality. For enamored young newlyweds, in a survival based environment, more flexible customs evolved.

In the early morning hours, the lightening cracked along the mesa to the southwest, a wood rattling thunder rolled as if sliding down slope to engulf the fort. Georgie and Charles felt the air cool and then smelled the rain well before it reached them. They spooned.

Georgie snuggled tighter to him. Arousal encompassed her, Charles embraced her. Charles hand found her breast under the sheet and through her nightshirt. Her nipples quickly firmed as his fingers probed to sustain contact. Each time his fingers slipped away she tingled and wanted to him to swiftly find his way back.

She lifted her hips and raised the nightshirt; certain he could find his way through the baggy legs of her bloomers. In her memories, he found her special place and easily entered just as the heaviest rain began to pour. The wind carried the rain in such a way the porch remained dry. She did not.

She was convinced she climaxed as a bolt of lightning put the large rain drops on brief display. The speed with which her pleasure came surprised him but brought him completely into the moment. He gently joined her. Thunder shook the porch.

Georgie and Charles lay together, somehow gradually becoming closer, a feat which did not seem possible moments ago. Both snuggled closer, fearful if they moved away the moment would forever escape them.

He slipped from her and lay high on her inner thigh. She felt an extraordinarily warm moist erotic awareness of herself. She soaked in the overwhelming sensations of her femininity. She felt luxurious.

Dorsey began to snore. Georgie and Charles giggled and snuggled.

They were not certain how long they lay in that fashion. They awoke to the smell of rain, Charles lying on his back and Georgie with her head on his chest and a leg across his legs. He stroked her hair as she pressed against his chest and deeply inhaled him.

She thought such times should last forever but she knew they didn't. She was just grateful they existed at all and that she had been allowed to discover them.

As days and weeks past, he would gradually speak more about his life in the field. He rarely talked of the violence or the isolation. Within a few months she had become his closest confidant. She grasped his feelings about the Apache. He could explain his beliefs that the agents were the primary source of the discontent, yet he never downplayed that the Apache were nomadic warriors, a pure and pragmatic warrior culture, which had no real permanent residence.

TEN

GERONIMO VISIT ON THE GILA

As with most mornings at Fort Apache, Gatewood was making his way toward the scouts' billet. Alchesay unfolded his legs and stood erect, then took a couple of steps toward him. The men veered away from any ears, finding a distance that insured a more private conversation.

"Nantan Bay'che, Geronimo has asked maybe you come talk him."

"Why?"

"Want to scout you." Alchesay gave a quick satisfied nod, please at his wisdom and wit.

Bay'che just shook his head.

"Tazma tell him, I tell him, your word has trust. Keep word. Keep your word."

"What do you think?"

"He Nootahah. He Chiricahua." Alchesay measured before adding, "Wants to measure Bay'che."

"A get to know your enemy talk?"

"No. Curious about Bay'che. Nootahah trust Bay'che. Bay'che like Nootahah. For him to see. Scout some maybe."

Bay'che thought, moving his index finger along his chin. He moved a rock with the toe of his boot. Looking at Alchesay, he said, "I believe this should be a visit, not a meeting."

Bay'che could see that his friend was puzzled. He gave some thought and said, "I go for me, not for soldier business."

Believing he still had not made himself clear, he tried again. "I can go visit a friend of my friend."

"He is not my friend. He is not my enemy. He is Geronimo," Alchesay's eyes emphasized his point.

Bay'che responded, "Then, I will visit this man who is not now our enemy."

"That is good, Bay'che. Dead Shot and Goso will go along."

Bay'che nodded and then inquired, "Did you hear from Tazma?"

"That he sent two elk rumps and a bear hide to the mother of his son's wife. Tazma not come to San Carlos. Still never long at Wingate or Verde."

"Then, we must go see him when we can."

They turned and begin to walk toward the scouts' encampment.

"Alchesay, I am your friend and you are my friend."

Alchesay nodded in agreement.

They took about ten more steps and Alchesay said, "Geronimo's English talk is good. Want you to hear his stories, most truth. Want all to know why he is mad." Then, he added, "Bay'che, best you not see what tiswin you see."

"I do not see tiswin well."

Dead Shot and Goso accompanied him on what appeared to the casual observer to be a routine show of military presence. The smell of Gila River had not improved but his nose was no longer as sensitive to it.

There was nothing to distinguish one wikiup from another, the Apache found no status in the size of a wikiup. Gatewood could not tell Geronimo's wikiup from any other wikiup in San Carlos. Although it was one of about dozen located east of the main encampment, it gave no hint of the status of the family it housed. The Apache were unaccustomed to the concept of permanent dwellings.

A rack of beef strips hung near Geronimo's wikiup. The meat was salted and the rack rotated to the sun to cure the beef and keep the green flies from lingering too long. He knew the process but still he liked the jerky on the trail.

Although just a short time ago Gatewood could not have distinguished them by the subtle differences in their dress, he now knew several Nootahah, some Mescalero and Chiricahua, shuffled near the wikiup.

Gatewood reined in Bob. Goso slid off his mount and took the reins. Gatewood paused and patted Bob's neck. He believed the action conveyed the casual attitude with which he approached the visit.

Two men stood by the entrance. He recognized the short, squat Nana. Now slightly older and carrying a walking stick, but his appearance left Gatewood with no doubt this old man could still rally dangerous group to his side.

The men stood gazing at each other. Catching Gatewood by surprise, Nana spoke, "Baychendaysen, you move like your bones grow hard."

"You, Nana, move better than when I saw you last."

"Not so cold and wet today."

"I hope we do not fight again."

Nana nodded, an adequate greeting had been exchanged. Both suspected they would be enemies again, just not today.

A woman emerged and held open the flap of the wikiup.

Entry required him to bend his knees and stoop at the waist. The loss of bright sunshine made him wince, blinking for vision. His host simply waited for his orientation to return. The smell was pungent but not completely unpleasant.

As his vision cleared, a vague figure motioned for him to sit.

"Nantan Baychendaysen, I am Goyathlay. I am happy you came to visit."

"I thank Goyathlay for inviting me to his wikiup." Bay'che responded, his tongue faltering with the unfamiliar Nootahah word.

"My Mexican name is easier for white to say, call me Geronimo."

Bay'che replied, "I will. I will also work at your Nootahah name."

His vision now sharpening, Bay'che could now see his host with reasonable clarity. Geronimo had the broad thick chest and wide face common to the Chiricahua. The thick, course black hair

157

hung to near his shoulders but was held from his face by a traditional red head band. His broad face drew greater attention to the narrow set of his eyes. Years of exposure to the sun and wind had begun to weather his face, causing deep lines that emphasized the natural contour.

He sat with his legs crossed beneath him. His breechcloth was white but stained by the dust that had adhered to the grease left on the fabric by many meals. Leggings protected his calf up to his knees.

Bay'che sat, folding his legs as best he could. As always, he sat with his back in the most upright position he could sustain.

After the slightly awkward cross-cultural greetings, both men became more at ease.

Bay'che got a glimpse of the barrel of a Winchester protruding from under a blanket beside Geronimo. He judged it to be bait which he would not take. He knew most men on the San Carlos had weapons of some kind.

Alchesay was right. Geronimo wanted to tell his story.

"I was born alongside a creek in a canyon far from here. The water was fresh and clean. The ground grew food well. My mother grew corn and melons, beans and pumpkins in a straight row." He painted a picture of agriculture and trade in a time of peace with the Mexican towns.

This was the first mention Bay'che had heard of any form of agriculture in the Apache culture. He suspected if the soil was tilled it was done by the women. Bay'che doubted that the Apache had ever lived peacefully. The rifts between the Nootahah bands were commonplace. Disagreements between Chiricahua and the White Mountain tribes seem to have a perpetual life of their own.

"We went to trade, made camp at Kaskiyeh, Mexicans call Casa Grande. We had gone into the town to trade. The Mexicans from a another town slipped in killed the eight warriors left to guard the camp, then butchered the women and children except for a few who escaped into the hills. On our way back to our camp, we came on two women sent to search for us. They told us of the betrayal."

"I arrived to find my wife and mother used and killed. My three children were dead. All of our supplies and weapons were stolen. Bay'che, the camp was littered with the bodies of our families."

"Our leader, Mangus Colorado, counting eighty warriors left, most with limited weapons and surrounded by Mexican soldiers, we must flee for Arizona and the safety of the stronghold in the Dragoons."

Bay'che knew the name and he felt Mangus would be considered a better warrior than a trader.

"I had no one left to mourn me if I was killed. I wanted revenge on the Mexicans. We prepared for war until the next summer. When Mangus and Cochise judged the time to right, we went forward. None of us had horses. Each man wore moccasins and a breech cloth and carried a knap bag with three days of supplies and ammunition, we traveled light. The cloth could be spread over us when we slept. We stayed to the mountain ranges to keep our path hidden."

"I guided us into Mexico, staying away from small towns until we came to the city that killed us. We camped and eight men from the town came out to talk with us."

Geronimo paused knowing that not all white men understood what followed. He measured Bay'che and continued.

"We killed them all but one, the one was hurt but alive enough, tied their scalps to his high saddle horn sent him to town as our messenger. The messenger only saw about one-third of our warriors. As we hoped they sent for their Army, two companies of cavalry and two companies of infantry came after a day passed. They came to quickly defeat a small party but found one of equal size, well-armed and well-hidden."

"I saw the cavalry as the soldiers who killed my people at Kaskiyeh. I told this to our chieftains. I was given the honor of directing the battle. I took the vengeance I vowed on my father's grave."

"I chose those who lost families at Kaskiyeh. We stayed in the camp and their cavalry attacked us there. Throughout this fight, I saw my wife, my mother and my children with every battle stroke I took. We fought fiercely. Killing horses and men, braves being killed until it appeared we were defeated. Then, we sprinted. They chased us as we led them toward our braves massed in the timber."

"A Captain swung his saber at me twice just missing me, teasing me with death, he was sure he could kill me when he wished. I reached the timber, grabbed a spear from a brave. He had slowed his horse approaching the timber, I turned and ran toward him. My spear point went into his chest, knocking him from this horse. I raised his saber and sliced into his face many times."

As Geronimo described it, a fierce Apache war-cry echoed through the timber as the braves poured over the stunned soldiers who now realized they were ensnared. The Nootahah trap slapped closed.

"We trapped them all and struck from the timber and closed the escape to the river." Geronimo seemed rather inflamed, a rising blood lust, by his own telling of the tale.

"Their blood soaked my moccasins as I walked through the field of dead Mexicans. Fresh hot blood was splashed on me as the Mexican remains were butchered into a sight that would raise the fear in bravest Mexican soldier."

"Baychendaysen, I could not bring back my loved ones, but I could rejoice in this revenge. I still rejoice in this revenge."

"Killing Americans does not bring the same pleasure that killing Mexican soldiers does. At times, I killed Americans to kill more Mexicans."

Geronimo seemed to relax, feeling his message had been heard. Baychendaysen has listened and heard.

"Talk of your home."

Bay'che said, "I was born in Virginia. My home is as far away as yours is near. It is covered grass and trees and large rivers. It was a nice land."

Geronimo said, "It seems a soft land. But Baychendaysen grew hard."

"Many battles in our big war were fought near me. I saw the hard side of many men. Like you, I saw much death as a boy." He paused, seeking a connection, "Somewhat like you, when my father was off to the war, my mother taught me. She was soft and kind, but she knew a man must grow hard.

"You went to the soldier school when a man. Nootahah is born into a warrior school." He changed his focus and asked, "Green land empty when your ancestors arrive?"

Gatewood knew the truth but he chose to avoid it. He said, "It was with us long before my father's time, I must ask if the land had ancestors before my ancestors came to the land." Realizing that he had been baited, he corrected himself, "I do know many years ago there were tribes living there."

"Baychendaysen, you know the agent here cheats us, steals our beef, steals our supplies, and gives it to his friends."

"I do."

"And I know he does not work for the soldiers, but for someone else." Geronimo selected his words, "But soldiers have to protect him."

Bay'che wanted to not doubt here, "Soldiers do as we are ordered to do. Unlike Nootahah, we cannot refuse. Honor binds us to our orders."

"But you found a way for Nana's sheep."

"I did. I did because I could."

"If I steal a Mexican's cow, what business is of the soldiers?"

Gatewood was quizzical. He was grateful Geronimo continued without a reply, "But if I sell it to a Mormon, it becomes the Mormon's cow."

"Geronimo has presented me puzzle without an answer. But it does seem that in the end, the Mexican is one without a cow," Gatewood stated.

Geronimo liked the answer. Almost by accident, Gatewood has given his host the correct answer.

Both men now more comfortable with the other, their conversation expanded, then concluded.

"Baychendaysen, you may always come in safety to my camp. You will be welcomed." Geronimo wanted to be clear, "Someday I may have to kill you in battle, but if we live at day's end, come to my camp. We will eat and talk."

They stepped outside the wikiup. Gatewood's spine cracked as he straightened to full upright. Geronimo laughed.

The men grasp right wrists.

"Baychendaysen."

"Go-ya-ath –a - athey," Bay'che stumbled over the name. He pinched his lips upward and gave a sharp nod, then said, "Geronimo."

It was a meeting that resolved nothing but both men left the better for it.

Alchesay was waiting on a boulder behind the corral. His presence asked the questions.

"We talked. As you told me, he told his story. I know he hates Mexicans more than he hates Americans. And he likes all eight of his wives."

Alchesay said, "I will hear if you did as well as you believe." The usually stoic Alchesay was pleased with his friend.

"I think I'll suggest to Captain Crawford that a patrol down through the northern Dragoons would be good. See if there is much coming in or going out down there. What do you think?"

"Good time to pass that way. Chiricahua will see us, be a good thing. Big sign leading in or out, maybe not such a good thing."

"Talk with Geronimo was good, but something is stirring in the San Carlos. The pot hasn't started to bubble yet, but there is fire under the pan."

After a few paces, Gatewood asked, "Geronimo's Nootahah name, Go-away, what does it mean?"

He knew that such "white man's questions" amusing, but he was curious.

"Goyathlay, means man who yawns."

"Well be damned!"

Captain Emmett Crawford approved two squads of scouts for the reconnaissance patrol.

Crawford said, "Mid-October there was killing down in Tombstone. Earps and a card-shark friend of theirs shot several of that bunch been rustling cattle. Then, an Earp was ambushed. Now, them Earps are chasing them cowhands all over down there. Both sides are claiming the law's with'em. Last heard "Injun Charlie" and some Ringo fellow were killed in the Dragoons."

"Now, Lieutenant, I don't give a fat damn which bunch is right. I think they are all crooked as a sidewinder's trail. The

United States Sixth Cavalry does not want involved in a civil dispute."

"Yes, Sir." Lieutenant Gatewood understood.

Surgeon Dorsey McPherson prepared a medication pouch.

Georgie had accepted that her husband's duty was unlike any other duty. She was coming to believe that the Cavalry was taking advantage of his unique skills. From her prospective, Tom Cruise and the newly arrived Augustus Blocksom were good soldiers and good men. She knew that the mutual trust between her husband and the White Mountain Apaches could not be taught. She knew Charles genuinely liked his scouts and that Alchesay was as loyal a friend as he could have.

Georgie was utterly devoted to Charles. When he was not in the field, their evenings together were extraordinary. He made her feel that he could not wait to be home with her, to hear her stories. He enjoyed her conversations and valued her opinions and her observations. He wanted to hear of her days and her dreams.

Late fall mornings with Georgie nestled beside him were superb.

Dorsey McPherson, Contract Surgeon Sixth Cavalry

ELEVEN

PETONE AND MCPHERSON

THE FALL OF 1881 HAD seen many days that the air was filled with dust. There had been significant variations in the temperature. Many of the men were coughing and hacking.

Shortly after midnight, Alchesay stepped heavily onto the porch. Gatewood stirred and sat upright. Realizing they had a visitor, Georgie tucked the blankets tighter around her.

"Alchesay?"

"Come, Petone bad sick."

"Petone has never scouted with us."

"No, but he has helped us."

Gatewood knew Petone had helped them with intelligence. He was just pure Nootahah and he would never work for anyone. If a struggle broke out, Gatewood did not know whose side he would take.

"Bay'che he does not believe in our medicine men. But the sound he makes to get a breath is bad."

"My friend, what do you want me to do? I know no medicine."

"You have a pouch that cures your pain some. Magic powders might cure Petone."

Bay'che thought, "I don't think so. Let me wake our surgeons."

Bay'che could see the reservations on Alchesay's face.

167

"They have ridden with us. They will guide us."

They eased several units down and awake Dorsey.

"Dorsey, Alchesay is with me. Our friend, Petone, is very ill. Alchesay came to us."

Dorsey slowly pulled his braces over his undershirt as he listened to Alchesay's descriptions of Petone's symptoms and then he asked, "Where is he now?"

Alchesay explained that Petone had been brought on travois and was just off the Fort property.

With a raised and firm voice, McPherson said, "Blessed Mary! Let's go before you kill him getting him help."

McPherson was out the door. He stopped when he realized it didn't know which direction he was going.

Gatewood couldn't stifle his laugh.

McPherson said, "May the Good Lord have sent you to me for latrine duty."

Alchesay took the lead. The travois was just over the rise. Two men stood by the horse.

Petone was fully in the grasp of pneumonia. He was burning with the fever, but sheltered from the wind. He was covered with a blanket and laid between two bear skins.

The threesome gathered. Dorsey said, "I can't help the man out here. I can't bring him into the hospital unit."

After limited discussion, there wasn't a great deal to talk about, the men agreed.

Alchesay tried to stir Petone. "If you agree, we will take you into the scouts' camp. The Captain Surgeon will try to make the sickness leave you."

Petone made some motion with his hand.

McPherson said, "That's good enough for me."

With enough darkness remaining, they moved him into a Wikiup on the edge of the encampment. The air was stale and stuffy. Alchesay waved to move the air, then left. He returned within minutes with enough men to cover the cracks with blankets and canvas, converting the hut into a sick room.

A small fire began to create a draw of air out the roof.

Water was boiled over the fire.

Soon, over the patient's moderate objections, a mixture honey with a bit of kerosene was being swallowed. A woolen rag soaked in camphor and menthol was placed on his chest. After consulting with Reed, large doses of the yellow willow bark powder were administered.

The air smelled of white man's medicine giving Petone the hope of cure.

A military physician treating a civilian on the military grounds was a very grey issue. Petone's presence was a closely guarded secret. McPherson visited his patient only after dark had fallen hard. The scouts prepared a thin but quite nourishing broth from the beef meat ration and traditional herbs.

Given her southern and Irish roots, Georgie could not stand the thought of such an ill man being deprived of the curative properties of chicken broth to be followed with a chicken soup filled with tiny potato chunks as he progressed.

She was convinced that drinking hot liquids was necessary. Petone disliked the taste of the white man's coffee. Georgie taught Kuruk to brew a green tea and add a touch of honey. In the beginning, Petone tolerated it. Then, he came to crave it.

Petone was a large man and a fierce warrior even by Apache standards. Dandy Jim swore he had seen him rip apart a company of Mexican Regulars with a pistol and Bowie knife. Dandy Jim had been known to exaggerate but nonetheless Petone was a warrior of considerable reputation and proficiency.

The illness would leave Petone. He remained the unusual tea sipping Apache.

After eight days, Petone was recovered.

Petone sat outside the wikiup. While he still was reaching for his strength to return, he was grateful that the pain in his chest had left him. He was grateful to his physician.

He sat with Alchesay and Dead Shot while he waited for the physician. Dorsey and Gatewood came walking toward the shelter. The men rose as they approached.

Petone began talking immediately.

"Surgeon, you defeated sickness that gripped me. Thank you. I have no your coin to pay you." He looked at Alchesay to be certain he had said it correctly. Alchesay nodded.

"Do you have enemy? I kill him. He die quick, he die long time, but he die."

A rare event occurred, McPherson was completely flabbergasted.

The proposal of payment was so direct and amiable that it almost concealed its fatal nature. It was Dorsey's turn to stare toward Alchesay who only nodded, confirming the authenticity of the offer.

Alchesay said, "Accept it."

Gatewood listened. Watching a friend who at times was a tad full of himself caught on the horns of a cultural and moral dilemma had its pleasing aspects. But he gave no visible sign of such.

Dorsey stammered. He knew this was a serious payment being offered by a serious man.

Dorsey said, "I have no enemy I wish dead at this time. May I accept your payment and use it at a future time?"

Petone looked puzzled, but Alchesay translated McPherson's words.

"Sergeant, please tell Petone that his method of payment pleases me."

Alchesay again translated and Petone's chest expanded, he was pleased his offer had been accepted and his debt could be paid.

"And Sergeant, tell Petone I consider it a most generous payment. It will give me great comfort to know vengeance awaits my enemy."

Petone responded in Nootahah. Alchesay translated, "He says it is small thing for saving him from the grip of his disease."

Alchesay struggled with the final part, "He wishes good things for the red faced soup woman." He shook his head, "He is grateful to her."

Continuing Alchesay said, "Nantan Bay'che that is high praise for a woman by a Nootahah."

The pair stepped into the infirmary where Reed was watching over some troopers suffering from dysentery.

"Reed, you're not going to believe this one!"

Dorsey McPherson would never again receive a fee payment that would make him so animated.

The three men shared a round of medicinal bourbon and shared the potential exaggerations for the use of the Petone payment. There was no shortage of suggestions.

Then, Gatewood went home to Georgie.

Reed went home to Emilie.

McPherson went home and wrote a letter to Ida Deland proposing a prompt marriage.

Dorsey McPherson married Ida Deland. Mrs. Surgeon McPherson was soon busily making Officers Quarters 103 habitable.

Victorio

TWELVE

VICTORIO'S REVENGE

IT SEEMED THAT PEACE WAS never intended to be anything other than a temporary state with the Apaches. Peace was always tenuous where the Apache felt the agents managing the reservation were thieves and robbers, constantly misappropriating funds and goods into their own pockets. Selling half an allotment to beef to local ranchers was common practice.

When a Nootahah is wronged, vengeance is justified.

Word reached Victorio that a Judge in Silver City, New Mexico had issued a warrant for his arrest and was hiring men to enforce it. It wasn't true but that made no difference. Victorio needed little prodding from his fellow leaders, Nana and Tomas, to break from the San Carlos Reservation. Within a month the people of the territories were in a state of fear, demanding that the Army run Victorio to ground and provide protection for them.

The fall night still carried the hot breath of a San Carlos summer as Victorio led a party of about two hundred braves, women and children off the reservation. The party slid west of Fort Apache, following the dry washes and staying beneath the skyline, avoided detection.

At daylight, they turned and headed northeast for Ojo Caliente. Taking a route that paralleled the military route between Fort Wingate and Fort Apache, they made for a site Nana judged to have ample water and easy to defend. The Zuni Pueblos offered no immediate threat and certainly would not betray their presence to the soldiers.

Victoria's plan was to use this as base for conducting a variety of raids collecting weapons, food and animals. Then, with adequate stores, they would make due south to Mexico through the Animas Valley.

Almost to Ojo Caliente, two of Tomas' scouts sighted what appeared to be a small patrol from Ninth Cavalry operating out of Fort Bayard. Tomas' followed the patrol back to the column.

From a ridge some five hundred yards away, Tomas', through his binoculars, found himself surveying a supply train headed south. He sent for Victorio.

Victorio did not like the idea of changing what he considered to be a well-conceived plan but to decline the opportunity to take an army supply train seemed foolhardy.

Victorio had over forty warriors who had seen considerable combat as well as a dozen or so inexperienced but highly motivated boys.

Victorio, Nana and Tomas sat. Tomas wanted to strike immediately but fearful reinforcements would arrive. Nana argued with the need to secure every weapon and animal available.

Victorio stirred the coals of the fire with a stick.

"Tomas, do white soldiers ever reinforce a supply train?"

Tomas responded, "No. But three chiefs never leave the stink hole reservation together before."

Nana added, "They are in no hurry, so sense no danger."

Victorio recognized the times were new. There were more white soldiers and the Nootahah grew fewer and more desperate.

"We will wait for them where the canyons open to go toward Ojo Caliente. It is a good place for us and a bad place for them."

Nana added, "Secure the pack animals while white soldiers are confused."

"I want no soldiers to escape and report where we are. We must find their scouts and kill them."

Victorio estimated twenty-five mounted men with pack train.

The plan was simple enough. The ground was in their favor. There was no warning from their scouts who had died quietly.

As the last of the lead Cavalry emerged from the narrowest part of the canyon, the Chiricahua cut the party in half. Leaving the pack train trapped in the canyon and cavalry cut off from them.

The Cavalry regrouped more quickly than Victorio or Nana had anticipated. But it made no difference. As they rushed back toward the men and animals trapped in the canyon, they were literally in a four way cross fire, bullets torn into them from every direction.

They fought their way to the steepest wall and dismounted. Hoping their attackers didn't want to kill their horses, they laid their horses down as shields. There was a brief lull in the skirmish as the Apaches made their way up the canyon sides to secure a better firing angle. Then, with almost disciplined volley fire, they killed every living thing in the defensive perimeter within minutes.

During that brief pause, Sergeant David Washington left in command of the forward group, dispatched a two pair of couriers, one toward Camp Thomas and one toward Fort Bayard. Taking the Apache by surprise, he and his troopers charged back into the canyon in an effort to relieve the trapped men. The ensuing struggle was brief but intense. The dispatch riders left under the cover of the charge.

The Chiricahua turned their focus to the group they believed they had cut off and secured in the front only to find them charging down the canyon toward them. When in solid rifle range, the charging cavalry suddenly reigned up dismounted and kneeled. Three times the reports of Springfields discharged in a measured precise volley fire rang up the canyon walls and descended. As the Apaches over-ran the positions, pistol shots killed over half of their mounts.

Sergeant Washington gravely wounded but still erect with pistol in hand amidst his men. The first Apache paused, startled at the sight of the dark black face of the soldier. The Sergeant dropped the man where he stood. He saw no benefit in allowing the Apache to dictate the place and pace of his own death. He was born a slave and felt the whip but he would die a soldier, a free man. Sergeant Washington placed the pistol in his mouth, smiled and squeezed the trigger.

Victorio watched the Sergeant fall backward and turned to Nana, "Waste a good warrior."

Nana replied, "Nootahah would have used the bullet on an enemy."

Victorio saw it differently. He turned to Lonely Bird and instructed, "No one shall touch him before I do."

Lonely Bird nodded and dashed toward the mound where the Sergeant had fallen and took a position standing over the body.

Victorio and Tomas moved through the battle field. All ammunition and weapons were being collected. With a large stick he carried at times, Tomas flicked the cap off of dead black cavalry man.

The black soldiers troubled Victorio. He knew there were more whites all over the white man's land. If there were as many black soldiers as white soldiers the days of the Nootahah would be even shorter. The thought troubled him.

He was angry that they charged and did not make a break for open country. The move had surprised him.

Six Nootahah braves were killed in a fight he believed he should have lost none.

Then, Nana appeared, moving at an excited pace. The group had received an unexpected windfall. The pack animals carried more than food and basic supplies. There were three cases of new Springfields and a considerable number of cartridges. The heavens had smiled on them.

Nana smiled and said, "Mucho sugar."

Tomas walked through the dead troopers. He was most curious about these black men. He thought most Americans looked pretty much the same. These with the blacken hide were clearly different. He would take his stick and adjust the bodies for a different angle. They had fought well and died well enough for foolish men. They chose to die when they might have lived to fight again.

The soldiers were staked and mutilated. Sergeant Washington was staked alone on the mound surrounded by his men. Although the back of his head was gone, his face was left unmarred.

It was at this point that Victorio realized that two cavalrymen had escaped.

Maybe cowards but Victorio did not think so. His logic said they were headed for the nearest fort. The Nantans would soon know of the fight at Ojo Caliente and would surmise his plan. Their good fortune prompted a change in plans.

They could no longer winter at Ojo Caliente. Every soldier in the territory would soon be chasing them now. But it was no longer necessary to gather arms and livestock one small ranch or wagon train at a time. They had more than their necessary supplies. They would make directly for Mexico down the Animas Valley.

Tomas kicked about a large lizard that had been disemboweled during the fire fight, struck by Springfield cartridge. He was never one to trust good fortune.

Nana and Victorio were of like mind. They had gained valuable rifles and supplies, but they lost six experienced braves.

And they lost a winter of wives, warmth, food and relative safety, a winter of rest and recovery that could cleanse San Carlos from a warrior's soul.

Victorio looked toward the west.

He said to Nana, "I have vision. A dark bird whispered to Alchesay and he told the Long Nosed Nantan. Already they hunt us."

Nana nodded, "Most will tire and turn back. Alchesay will never lose a trail for long. Baychendaysen will not turn back."

Victorio said, "Maybe soldiers will get in their way."

"Or maybe we will kill them," Nana concluded.

An exhausted private and a telegraph detachment found each other about fifteen miles outside Fort Bayard. A skilled wireman was quickly up a pole and the telegraph wires hummed with the news of the fight at Ojo Caliente.

Major Albert Morrow, in command of the Ninth Cavalry stationed at Fort Bayard, based on his Civil War experience, assumed that the renegades would try to winter in the pueblo country. He marked a route that would keep them out of the mountains so as to not get caught up in the winter snows. It was his intent to catch them in a winter camp, lulling like a fat bear.

He ordered two companies of the Ninth Cavalry into the field. Captain Charles Beyer was in command of one company, Morrow the other. In all about two hundred men with six officers and thirty six scouts took the field.

A West Point classmate of Gatewood's, Lieutenant Mathias Day was in command of two platoons, one of black cavalrymen and one of scouts.

By reaching the Ojo Caliente region quickly and surprising the Chiricahua renegades Morrow planned on a short campaign.

Captain Curwen McLellan, a stern soldier prone to display his intense Scottish heritage in a grim fashion, was in command at Fort Apache.

When the wire of the Major Morrow's plan reached him, McLellan snorted loud enough every clerk in the outer office heard him. This veteran of years of campaigning in the southwest was not in mood for such foolishness. But a Major is a Major.

He seemed to burst out his door and said in loud voice, seeming to be directed at no one in particular, "Get me Gatewood, Blocksom and Cruse. Have Gatewood bring that Sergeant of his. Now!!"

Four men answered at the same time and almost stumbling over each other trying to stand. McLellan slammed the door behind him.

The Captain had calmed some by the time the Lieutenants and Sergeant Alchesay were assembled. His map of the territories was spread on his table. He held a slender stick of polished red mesquite wood about a foot long that he used as a pointer.

"Old Vic caught a supply train moving from Wingate to Bayard near Ojo Caliente. Only two couriers survived."

Gatewood wasn't certain that either the map or the pointer would survive. McLellan quickly laid out the Major's plan.

In the mood to waste little time, he addressed Alchesay, "Sergeant, what do you believe Victorio will do."

"He will not winter and wait for the soldiers to come."

"We agree. Now what do you believe he will do?"

"Trade some animals for supply with Zuni, with White Eye traders."

McLellan nodded. His countenance softened, he said, "Continue Sergeant."

"Start as big trail, split off many times, small parties raid some. Don't have to carry much food. Got many rifles from supply train, but need all the cartridges and rifles he can get. Hopes more warriors will hear of victories and join him."

Alchesay leaned forward, looked at the map he couldn't read, "All will rejoin in Las Animas Valley, near Animas Canyon. Then, make fast run to Mexico."

McLellan tugged lightly at his Scottish second chin and surveyed the map. Then, he turned and inquired, "Lieutenant Gatewood?"

"When we find him, we have to latch on to him and stay," Gatewood responded, "Lieutenant Cruse and I have discussed the logic of a small mobile supply once contact is made."

"It might just pose an attractive target."

"It might. Lieutenant Cruse will have to balance himself between us and the main body."

"I'll wire General Willcox for approvals." Captain McLellan hesitated and then added, "Lieutenant, I suspect the General will want a Company of the Sixth to be with you or nearby. Lieutenant Cruse can work a supply train, even resupply, from there. You just assume he is under your command."

Gatewood understood.

McLellan continued, "Don't let the Company slow you down. Re-route them if necessary."

"Sir, you're permission for Surgeon McPherson to accompany the party."

"That order will be issued."

McLellan turned and faced the four but was clearly addressing Gatewood, "You find Old Vic, you grab him by the nuts and you tear'em off." McLellan paused and said, "Kill him. I want him dead."

"In the field by daybreak, Quartermaster will work all night if necessary. Sutler will supply any ammunition that Quartermaster doesn't have."

Dismissed, they had just made the doorway when McLellan called, "Lieutenant Gatewood, a moment."

Then, turning to Alchesay asked, "What is the name the scouts call Victorio's men?"

"Chihennes"

"Chihennes?"

Gatewood knew Alchesay had no intention of providing a definition, so he stepped in, "I'm not certain, Sir. I believe it is close to 'son of a female wolf' or perhaps 'son of a bitch'. But I'm not certain."

Just inside the office door, McLellan said, "Lieutenant, there are two glory hounds at Bayard. I know I was guilty myself up on the Verde and I've regretted it since. I'm telling you, if you get the chance at any of the three chiefs, you kill them."

McLellan felt he did not want to know the thoughts concealed behind hard steel of Gatewood's eyes.

A brisk wind was blowing from the southeast when they stepped out of Command Post. The air carried more than just a hint of the smell of the Gila River.

"That place does have an odor to itself," Blocksom observed. He was just making anxious conversation.

Gatewood didn't respond.

Blocksom was able, but the least experienced of the group. He knew they would be in pursuit of the most dangerous and deadly of the Apache war chiefs. He also suspected that Gatewood would have rather had Cruse in charge of the second company of scouts.

Lieutenant Gatewood and Sergeant Alchesay disturbed him.

No one answered him.

Gatewood and Alchesay had a brief conversation. Alchesay headed for the scouts area.

At four in morning, Georgie woke him. The aroma of coffee met him. Eggs, ham and a large jug of fresh water sat on the table. He devoured the meal while he and Georgie made small talk. A ritual they both enjoyed.

Georgie had quickly washed her face with a wet cloth and squeezed color into her cheeks.

She took him by the hand and stepped back toward the bedroom. She said, "I know we have but a minute. Let's not waste it."

She discarded her robe and removed her night shirt revealing her bare breasts and the loose legged bloomers that he found so eye-catching. She lay down on the bed, partially covered herself with the blanket, holding it open for him.

"Charles, look at me," Georgia words were gentle yet firm. "I'll not have you deep in the Miembres remembering some whimpering wife in a doorway. That is not who I am."

The motion of her hand moved the leg of the cotton eyelet bloomer in a fashion that in the dark of the morning its motion promised much but visually revealed little, it created a captivating illusion. She smiled at her husband and whispered, "I won't keep you long love."

Georgie had discovered an essential eroticism in her that made fulfilling such a promise easy. There were times to linger without the hint of a hurry. At other times, the circumstances did not lend themselves to a leisurely pace. She was finding that she exercised a level of control she never expected. Her capacity to please her husband delighted her.

A hug lingered inside the doorway. Charles said, "I will remember how warm you feel, your voice. Your fragrance lingers for days." He sought the words he wanted but they were just beyond his reach. It pleased her that he tried.

Georgie smiled her broadest smile, "That other thing isn't bad either is it?"

"That other thing is absolutely splendid."

Georgie desperately wanted to hold him, to not let go, but instead she said, "I'll be here waiting for you."

The door closed. Georgie got a cup, poured some coffee and sat down. She took a sip and then took a deep breath reaching for composure. It escaped her.

The tears streamed down her face and sobs poured from her heart. She prayed to God to watch over him.

Mid-morning of the fourth day, a courier from Captain McLellan caught up them.

McLellan's communication, while not surprising, required a change of plan.

"Corporal Goso, ask Lieutenant Blocksom to join us."

Blocksom, Alchesay, McPherson, Cruse and Gatewood gathered. Bay'che spoke, "Well, gentleman it seems that Captain Beyer of the Ninth out Bayard sighted a handful of Nana's Chihennes just near Animas Creek. It seems he believed his company hadn't been sighted, so watched through their glasses as the Chihennes went up a canyon. Then, Captain Beyer took his company into the canyon. Going to give the Chihennes a surprise."

"Well now seems Old Vic knew exactly what he was doing and Beyer got ambushed. Heavy fire from both canyon walls, reports say they never saw who was firing at them. By the time the Ninth got regrouped, they couldn't find a Chihenne in the canyon."

"Now, General Morrow has a battalion of the Ninth with two companies of scouts in the field. Communication says they are headed due east toward the site of the fight."

In a question really directed at Alchesay, Bay'che asked, "Gentlemen, may I have your thoughts?"

Alchesay responded, "A raiding party. Nana smart with canyon traps. Victorio will not be happy with Nana's attack. Force him to gather and push south fast. I say main party still split. All be south of Las Animas by now."

Blocksom, with a little doubt to his voice, ask, "Sergeant, you believe raiding party could tree a company of the Ninth Cavalry?"

"Yes," Alchesay's glare discouraged Blocksom questioning further in such a vein.

"Captain McLellan says General Willcox is going to take the field with a battalion of three companies. He would like guidance from scouts already the field."

Nantan Bay'che stopped, but no one offered. So he said, "I think Alchesay is correct. I suggest they follow a path south passing Fort Thomas on the east and be certain that Old Vic isn't making for any of the strongholds in the Dragoons. We will send a courier when we make contact."

Alchesay responded with a sharp positive nod.

"Alchesay, is there a route through the Miembres?"

"No, Nantan, part way, can blaze a trail. Rough mountains. Slow but quicker than going around."

"Cruse's mules can make it?"

"Yes, few have to lead horses, scouts on foot." All the scouts were already on foot.

"Glad Bob won't miss anything." Bay'che patted Bob.

Alchesay never understood the White Eyes attachment to their horses. Alchesay knew any good ride could quickly become a good meal.

Bay'che found a rock to sit on while he wrote his response to Captain McLellan. He cursed the sharp pain made it difficult for him rise from his seat. It shot down his spine and made him feel unsteady on his right foot.

The ever observant Alchesay said, "Nantan Bay'che I glad Bob going."

Bay'che gave a derisive snort. Alchesay was pleased with his effort at humor.

Dorsey showed up in minutes.

"Alchesay has become a talkative Nootahah."

"He likes you old boy, but he's got killing Chiricahua on the brain."

After four grinding days, they emerged on northwest side of the Animas Canyon. Scouting pairs were quickly deployed. Kuruk and Dandy Jim returned within the hour. They had cut clear sign suggesting that the main party of Chihennes, not yet completely regrouped, had moved out that morning.

Nantan Baychendaysen had made the decision to cut loose the pack mules, leaving them with Cruse to follow their trail, when the sky turned black, darkening the afternoon. Lightening cracked illuminating the mountains they had just descended. The clouds opened up and rain began to pour.

The wind-driven rain was cold and stung as it struck bare skin.

Baychendaysen had faced monsoon rains, a few hours in length, before. From the beginning, this was different and he knew it.

"Can Nootahah move in this rain?"

Alchesay replied, "Victorio and Nana don't know we are here. So, they will keep ammunitions and food dry as can. Find high caves in walls. Water will run big and fast. Dry creeks get full."

"This rain will wash away the trail."

"Yes," Alchesay confirmed, then added, "New trail be easy to find."

Quilo located a place where the tree line made its way upward between two sharp stone bluffs. The soaked soldiers guided the mules high into the tree. Rudimentary shelters were prepared for the mules and the packs removed.

Most of the bread and all of tobacco was lost, but mostly the tarps had held the rain at bay.

The scouts found shelter in slips of caves carved into the walls of the red stone buffs. These proved to dry enough, fire pits dug under trees whose trucks were at the slot openings and the branches would scatter the smoke. Fires of cured wood with the bark peeled, produced limited smoke, the boughs further dispersing the smoke. Bay'che was surprised at the amount of semi-dry wood that could be found in crevices and elongated caves along the bluffs.

A staked tarp concealed whatever limited flame might have flickered above the side wall of the fire pit.

As secure as the fires were made, the thought of a wayward ember giving away their presence to some group of Chihennes stragglers troubled Bay'che. Then, McPherson stepped out to urinate and, despite Alchesay's warnings as to how slick the red stone could become when wet, as he was relieving himself, Dorsey's feet shot from under him and sent him scooting on his seat several yards down the slope.

When Bay'che couldn't see the camp site as he and Dandy Jim retrieved the fallen surgeon. Bay'che ceased worrying about being spotted.

Dorsey was wet and the seat of his pants was stained by the red soil. Having not completed his business when his footing left him, he was convinced he had wet himself during the fall but he was so soaked he couldn't tell for sure. He considered taking off his blouse and pants, but realized everyone was soaked. He found a space near one of the fires. He wished his friends had made bigger fires. He just felt foolish.

Bay'che sat down beside him and folded his legs. Redirecting McPherson's attention to the storm, he said, "Dorsey, have you ever in your life seen a storm like this one."

"No, I haven't," both men peered into the wall of darkness and awaited the next explosion of lightening to illuminate the sky.

Only the colossal bolts of lightning, unlike anything Bay'che and Dorsey had seen, appeared capable of piercing the otherwise ostensibly impenetrable wall of water. At times the thunder sounded as if it was rolling down the valley and other claps felt as if they had shaken the trees down to the base of their roots.

Bay'che was fascinated with the wild raw power of this strong and relentless storm.

"Surgeon, I don't think I've ever seen a storm like this. It has staying power like a big strong storm blowing in off the ocean," he said. "Just doesn't have the winds."

Turning his attention to McPherson he asked, "How you making it?"

"I didn't break any bones, but the soreness is setting in. Fall bruised the hell out of my pride." Dorsey found confession to somewhat good for the soul.

"Those concoctions you mix for me might be helpful with the soreness."

"Already down a swig of my Gatewood Special and some willow powder," McPherson went on, "Stuff is tougher on a man's stomach than I'd thought."

"Have my aches and pains and it won't matter." Bay'che realized he had disclosed more than he intended, he offered, "Try one of Georgie's chips."

Dorsey declined.

Bay'che's pain had come over him earlier like a chill. He had taken a dose of the special elixir and a wrapper of willow bark powder. He opened his oil paper lined pouch and pulled out a couple of Georgie's homemade crackers. While the soda made him belch on occasion as she was refining her recipe, they brought considerable stomach relief. A cracker chip or two served as a reminder of his wife. He was grateful. He had drink of medicinal whiskey.

He spread his blanket roll. Shortly, he started to warm some. The pain would be gone for a few hours. He slept.

The dense driving rain gained intensity just before morning. If there was a sunrise no one could see it. By mid-morning it was gone. The lightening and the sounds of thunder were replaced the sounds of rushing water. Every fingerling was overflowing, from dry rivulet bed to stream to river were all gushing with water.

Dry creek beds that two days before Bay'che believed had not seen water since The Great Flood were overflowing, the force of the water rolling large stones along with it.

Faster than the rain fell, the ground reclaimed its water. Only the tell-tale high flow remaining in the Animas River remained to tell the story of the potent storm.

The scouts with Cruse's pack train in close tow, found the combining trail they had been hoping for late in the afternoon near deep canyon.

"Bay'che, they make camp on Cuchillo Negro, next canyon," Alchesay noted, "Good water holes near canyon walls make for many camp sites. All lead to Cuchillo Negro."

"Cuchill Neegro?" Bay'che inquired.

"Black Knife"

"Black Knife Creek, Black Knife Canyon."

Alchesay again gave that sharp single nod of the head.

"Bay'che, we want to fight here. Not let them get to Skeleton Canyon. It becomes wide and narrow – over and over – many ambushes, many escapes."

"Then, we will fight here."

Bay'che and Alchesay explained the situation to Blocksom.

A large Chihennes campsite was located about midway up the canyon. The assault was immediate and took those in the campsite by surprise. With weapons and cartridge bags in hand, the Chihennes darted through the scrubs, the mesquite and ironwood trees, heading for cover on the slopes of the canyon.

After the initial charge into the campsite, the scouts had control of the campsite. It was their intent to hold the campsite with Blocksom's platoon while Bay'che and Alchesay routed more from the mountain side.

General Morrow, arriving at the site as the initial battle was engaged, was to seal the canyon and sear the canyon walls.

The attack on the camp was well executed. But Victorio and Nana's scouts had spotted Morrow's column and prepared for an ambush for them.

Victorio and Nana with their warriors strategically deployed along canyon walls, with clear fields of fire at the two best water holes, were waiting for Morrow when Bay'che's scouts attack. At first, they thought they had been out maneuvered. But when his men from the camp made their way up the canyon walls and swore they saw "the Big Nose Lieutenant and Alchesay" in the firefight. Victorio quickly surmised what had happened.

"How?" Victorio asked.

"I don't know. We know when they left San Carlos, they could not be here."

"You think men didn't see what they saw?"

Nana stopped, puzzled. "Big Nose not Nootahah, maybe Alchesay lead." He didn't finish his sentence.

The two men sat and watched as Morrow advanced into the canyon. Old Vic and Nana lifted their field glasses to their eyes and surveyed the troops. They silently watched as the troopers made their way into the canyon. Then a look of satisfaction crossed Victorio's face.

"Leaving horses and loaded mules outside Cuchillo Negro."

Dark fell and Bay'che's scouts began their work. They moved silently in and out of the rocks, frequently frozen listening for the slightest rustle of a tree or scrub brush, metal will glisten or make a different sound. Goso swore he could hear a knife being removed from a belt. As much time as Goso spent sharpening and polishing knifes, rubbing them with various hides, few doubted him.

Bay'che never knew were they carried them until this night, but a bow and arrows seemed to materialize in Kuruk and Quilo hands.

They organized into four groups of two. Each group had a marksman to cover the silent killer as they approached their pray. McPherson, Bay'che, Dead Shot, and Dandy Jim were the marksman. They began to sweep the northern slope of the Cuchillo Negro.

Moving laterally across the steep slope for over three hundred yards, not so much as a single lookout was found. Alchesay was perplexed.

"Either gone or waiting for daybreak," Bay'che offered.

"Not gone yet. Where are Bayard soldiers?" was Alchesay's reply.

It was obvious to both that the other was concerned.

The party made their way back down the canyon to the recent Nootahah camp.

By then, both had gathered their thoughts.

"Nantan, Victorio and Nana wait for light."

"Where should we wait?"

"There is a good side canyon, good distance from trail in Cuchillo Negro. Spring water hole. Can't get ambushed there."

Bay'che offered, "We don't have enough for Old Vic to hunt, he's after a bigger bear."

Bay'che knew no one in camp would challenge the comings and goings of a Captain, so he turned to Dorsey and said,"Captain McPherson, I'm going to ask you to go fetch Lieutenant Cruse and his scouts for me. Bring Sergeant Weldon Thomas if he's there and available, he should already be with Cruse. Dorsey, Dead Shot's going walk along with you to keep you company."

Alchesay motioned Dead Shot.

Alchesay sat next to Bay'che, "If he is inviting attack, will keep Cruse?"

"I think so."

McPherson returned within the hour. "Some Major or the other says General Morrow is keeping Lieutenant Cruse and his men for now."

"Dead Shot, what did you see?"

Dead Shot answered in Nootahah for clarity.

Alchesay translated, "Three clusters, largest is troops up canyon, smaller in middle, animals back outside Cuchillo Negro."

Bay'che completed the thought, "General thinks Old Vic would rather kill soldiers than steal horses and loaded mules. I think he's got it backwards."

Alchesay responded with his familiar sharp nod of agreement and said, "Mules don't shoot back much."

Then, he completed their thoughts, "Chiricahua can kill a few soldiers, steal horses and guns, then kill more soldiers on his way to Mexico."

"Then, he can kill Mexicans."

Bay'che was far too accustomed to being in the field alone, just he and his scouts. The situation frustrated him, the pain in his spine and joints had intensified as evening fell and brought its chill.

McPherson knew his friend as well as any man except Alchesay. Bay'che turned to them and said, "Well, crap! I guess we will just try to make those animals as expensive for Old Vic as we can."

Alchesay and Bay'che were both resigned to what tomorrow would likely bring.

Bay'che moved to make out his bed roll.

Since he treated Petone, Alchesay had felt McPherson merited a degree of respect and trust, "Bay'che needs to sleep without hurt."

"Alchesay observes well."

Bay'che slept well and awoke before light with the aid of a cup of cold spring water to his face.

"Jerky?" Alchesay asked as he extended the strips of meat.

Bay'che pulled a strip of the chewy meat.

McPherson, only able to think of green flies, declined. Dorsey found pleasure in the adrenalin rush of the fight and the telling of the stories after it was done. He never understood the seeming calm of his companions. They just sat in virtual silence, chewed their jerky, listening for any telltale sound.

Alchesay stood and stepped away to relieve himself.

As he returned to his seat on the ledge, a series of rifle shots came for near the site of Morrow's smaller camp. The shots from the camp became more organized as the soldiers understood what was happening, and then the sounds of the rifle fire took on more of an indistinguishable roar.

Bay'che's command moved toward the gunfire. Within a hundred yards, they knew that although their camp was between Morrow's large camp and his smaller camp, their site had not been detected. Using the heavy mesquite as cover, they made their way unnoticed.

They paused watching the movement on the slopes below them. Bay'che and Alchesay had their glasses on the action. Alchesay having seen enough, using a clean spot on his blouse, spit on the lens and cleaned the glass before putting it away.

They dropped behind a boulder.

Bay'che said, "Old Vic is about to cut off the animals from help."

Alchesay's concise nod stated his agreement.

Alchesay added, "Best shots keeping big camp pinned. Path back to small camp is narrow."

Alchesay offered, "Will take animals, pack mules and good horses, scatter the rest. Will keep soldiers pinned, maybe kill many soldiers in small camp without losing a Chihenne."

Bay'che thought. Alchesay never interrupted his thinking.

"Small camp defending itself well enough but – If we kill enough Chihennes, get the pressure off the small camp."

"Nana will council leave, kill the few that chase, fight some more another day. They have killed soldiers and captured goods, will be a good day."

"Well, then let's get about killing Chihennes."

Bay'che's scouts eased into firing positions that allowed them to shoot down slope into any exposed Chihenne.

Bay'che beaded the signal shot. The recoil of the Winchester shoved into his shoulder. He saw the Chihenne drop as he was levering in another cartridge. McPherson dropped his target.

The reverberation of the added rifles off the canyon walls created the illusion that Chihennes were surrounded. Such great noise confined in a canyon can disorient the most experienced combatants.

While was always to be a war of attrition and Victorio knew he had to expend his men wisely. From just below the canyon top, he unleashed a surge of rifle fire toward the scouts' positions. Bay'che found himself on the wrong side of a boulder.

The first rounds struck the boulders that shielded the scouts, whistling as they ricocheted off the stone.

As the bullets continued to whistle and Bay'che hadn't moved, he said, "By damn, they are everywhere!!"

From the other side of the boulder, Dorsey yelled, "Help if you'd get your ass on the side they ain't shooting at!!"

Bay'che busted around the boulder out of breathe. He wiped the sweat of anxiety from his upper lip.

"I almost got myself shot to hell."

"You should shoot that way." Dorsey smiled.

Now with the covering fire, the Chihenne scurried up the slope, dodging from boulder to boulder. If nothing else on rough terrain, the Nootahah were quick and agile making them very difficult to hit on the move and with covering fire coming in to your position.

For a moment, Dead Shot and Kuruk got an open field of fire. Both hit the same fleeing Chihenne. He didn't move. Then, he unexpectedly wiggled behind an outcropping.

Kuruk stood and spewed a rare phrasing of English, "God damn shit bitch!"

The bullet whistled past him so close that his recoil sent him spinning to the ground. He sat immobilized by his anger.

Dead Shot's muffled laughter rang out of character for the situation.

A voice shouted over the hill, "Anzhoo, Kuruk!"

Kuruk response was in Nootahah, but it only increased Dead Shot's laughter.

The fight on the north slope was done.

Morrow brought the larger camp and ordered both camps to move to mouth of the canyon.

"Gatewood, Charles Gatewood!"

Bay'che looked to see his friend and classmate, Mathias Day. The handshake was warm.

193

"My negroes fought well. I'm damn proud of them."

"Yes, they died hard."

"Well, if you'd graduated at the bottom of the class like me, you could have commanded some "Buffalo Soldiers" too." They parted with "Catch you tonight." Day hesitated, looked at his friend and said, "You know you're a damn legend out here."

Bay'che just shook his head and said, "I hear you got it in a crack for dragging a wounded trooper out of the fight."

"Captain wanted to leave him." Day checked to see who was in earshot. "Captain said to leave him, just a nigger. I suppose just didn't hear him say that. See you when we finish this business."

Day saw the impatient men waiting for Gatewood.

"Good to see you, Sip."

A random thought slid through Bay'che's mind, "Good friend from another life."

Bay'che saw Blocksom walking his way.

Bay'che motioned for Goso. "Go find Cruse. He was with the stock. I need him and I want to know he's alive."

Turning to Blocksom who was now with them, "Tell me," Bay'che said.

"General Morrow came in took command. I ask permission to join you and some Captain declined. He used us to search the south slope. Never even saw a track."

"Sounds like right idea on the wrong slope."

The sound of a detail loading bodies onto a nearby wagon distracted him, he glanced that way. He took a second look. Almost all the dead were Negro soldiers. He stored the observation for a later time.

He turned to Alchesay, "What is Victorio thinking?"

"That he lost warriors he could not afford to lose and got supplies he will need if more join him. He will tell stories of a great victory over the Bayard General at Cuchillo Negro. Still makes to Mexico."

"How will he go to Mexico?"

"Doesn't think soldiers will follow fast. Maybe trade many animals before reaching Mexico. Cloverdale has traders."

"Captain McLellan should be close to us now."

Alchesay sharply nodded agreement, "Need to lose Bayard soldiers."

Cruse joined the group, visibly pleased to be rejoined with the group.

McPherson's query came first "Any wounded that need my attention?"

"I've got five wounded. A Ninth surgeon worked on them. I've got two men I'd be a lot more comfortable if you'd check out for me in a bit."

McPherson knew the skills of some Cavalry Surgeons was lacking, especially contract surgeons like he was. Cruse's reply gave him validation.

"How did you fare Tom?" Bay'che's voice reflected some concern.

Cruse looked about to see who might hear his response before answering. "I got left with a short platoon, sixteen men and one really good scout, Lizard Eyes. The first fire we heard came from the soldiers here. I realized how exposed we were, barricaded a knoll, got as many of the loaded pack mules as we could behind it and defended ourselves. With my glasses I had a view of this fight. Old Vic had them pinned and was just shredding them. Never gave them a target for return fire."

Cruse thought a minute and again checked the terrain. He continued, his anger thinly veiled, "Some Bayard asshole hung them Negro troopers out as targets. Guess he thought Vic would come charging in like the Comanche or the Sioux, didn't know Apaches. Seems he thought the large camp could come to the rescue. Found everybody pinned down."

"Gatewood, your scouts did most all the killing. We killed two Chihennes, just because they got greedy. Maybe wounded another one."

He took a deep breath, as if saving the worst for last, and reluctantly confessed, "They got away with Bob."

Gatewood visibly felt a sense of loss. Horse had carried his aching body places no mount should be asked to carry a man. Sugar and a soothing salve carefully rubbed into his legs where cactus barbs had penetrated the leather leggings that covered his legs above his hoofs. Gatewood mumbled something no one understood, but it sounded more prayerful than angry.

He turned back to Cruse and said, "The Negroes got put out to suffer the bulk of this." It wasn't a question, it was his conclusion. He took out his small note pad, stepped over to a wagon and counted. Then, he wrote, "Dead, twelve black, one white."

On another page, he wrote, "Hot trail, pursuing hostiles." He signed it, torn it out and gave it a Sergeant from the Ninth.

"Tom, have a good judge cut me out a mule and saddle him. Take the pack mules with what we need to stay out a bit." Then, Bay'che turned to Alchesay and said, "Let's go find a hot trail."

Cruse paused as if he had something to say and couldn't find the words.

Bay'che said, "Come on, Tom. You did well or we wouldn't have a mule to cut out."

Surgeon McPherson delivered a good Irish slap to his back and said, "I'll go with you and see if those men are treated right and won't slow us."

The report of a fifty caliber rang out from the wall. And then another. Occasionally a volley would rise from the canyon floor.

Bay'che looked at Alchesay and McPherson.

"Chihennes take shot and move," Alchesay observed. "Shoot, move, hide, shoot again."

"How many Chihennes on the slope?" McPherson asked

"Most five. Old Vic moving." Alchesay guess was likely on the dime. He turned to Bay'che. "Nantan Baychendaysen want scouts out?"

"Yes Sergeant, scouts out. I'd like to find that hot trail by nightfall."

Now alone, Bay'che looked at Alchesay and said like a student reporting, "Kill your enemy and save yourself."

He gave a sharp nod of agreement. "Bayard General not know. Dark soldiers fight hard and die."

Bay'che thought about the Negroes. They did fight hard. Yet, they get no respect and get the shit details. While his general opinion of Negroes hadn't changed, he did believe they were used as bait to make some General a hero.

The mule sat just fine. It was not Bob.

Kuruk found the hot trail before nightfall.

"We will keep them on the move. Let's get them tired and thirsty."

Alchesay added his thoughts, "Nantan. Victorio, Nana not want to lose even one warrior. Doesn't want to big fight."

"Does he want to kill white eyes on his trip to Mexico?" Bay'che asked with a touch of sarcasm.

"Yes. Want all the winter food he can steal."

Making a rare entry into the talk, Dorsey said, "And he'll steal everything he thinks will help him steal more."

Alchesay agreed.

"I think Old Vic will do what he wants to do. I don't want to lose a man either," Bay'che stirred the ground a piece of red mesquite wood. "Our job is to find him and stay with him."

They tracked Victorio and Nana. The Chihennes split into smaller groups, doubled back, split again and then like an accordion folded back into larger group. Nantan Bay'che had no doubt he had the finest collection of trackers that would ever be assembled. Bay'che remained the apt pupil. He listened and inquired without insisting to be shown. He knew his skills would never compare to those of his men, but he wanted to become the most adept tracker he could be.

It was understood he didn't want to be Nootahah but he genuinely enjoyed their company and appreciated their skills. He was ethnically pliable, knowing the importance of a person's ways.

After the War for Southern Independence was lost, despite an effort by the Union, attitudes reminded unchanged. To the extent possible, the culture was salvaged. Tradition was stored and preserved for another time. Its righteousness emphasized.

Perhaps, most important to his men, he didn't want change them. The Nootahah care little about words and promises, actions are meaningful.

Captain Curwen B. McLellan's two companies of the Sixth Cavalry sustained a practical contact while following a straight line down the Animas Valley toward Cloverdale. There was water and adequate grass. They would surge close to Lieutenant

Gatewood's scouts who were staying tight on the Chihennes as skill and the rugged mountains to the east of the valley permitted.

Blocksom and his scouts scoured the mountains to the west.

For the next thirty eight days and as many nights, Bay'che sat the animal he only called "Mule." The pursuit was grueling and grinding on a man, physically and mentally. At times his pain almost overwhelmed him. If it clouded his judgment, he never lost track of the primary goal pursuit.

Victorio was going deeper and higher into the barren mountains to the east, searching for a place that Bay'che would be unwillingly to risk following him.

There was the occasional exchange harassing fire. No one ever hit anything.

Deep in stony, boulder filled mountains within an hour they crossed the headwaters of the Gila River flowing west and the Mimbres River flowing south toward several silver mining camps. Neither river was more than three feet in width. They were identifiable only because of the intimate knowledge of the White Mountain scouts.

Victorio kept raiding parties out. Having no desire to engage the cavalry or their scouts, they searched for easier prey. A party under Tomas picked up the trail a group of four wagons headed toward down slope into the Animas Valley. Tomas' party ambushed the train as the wagon brakes were being applied slowing down their decent into the valley.

Tomas quickly received a return fire he hadn't expected. A train of what he thought was immigrants was wagons of frontier merchants, aspiring saloon keepers toting considerable gambling equipment and a wagon of seven brothel hardened women headed for promise of a life in the new towns springing up in the region of a recent silver boom.

Quite unexpectedly Tomas found himself significantly out-numbered by a force that had superior weapons. The exchange was brief. Tomas withdrew with two Chihennes wounded and grateful none had been killed. The whole situation left him quite baffled.

The group of hardscrabble entrepreneurs had their share of assassins and ex-soldiers in their assembly. These lethal ladies could kill you a rifle or with small hide-out pistol.

Within hours, the business folk came upon Blocksom and three of his scouts. They immediately took up pursuit of Tomas.

Blocksom knew the vicinity of Gatewood and Cruse. He had two Coyotero scouts with him, Itzachu and Hides Foot. He had learned to take advantage of their guidance and intercepted Tomas' party at Gable Springs.

Still rather confused by the events of the prior day, Tomas stumbled into the ambush. The sudden burst of fire sent him scurrying back down the path he came only to encounter the fire of four carbines. The lead horse hesitated, a hesitation that cost Tomas the lives of three men before the remaining eight could fight their way free of the trap.

Tomas made straight to rejoin Victorio.

Victorio had believed he was too high and deep into rugged country for soldiers to follow him. They just wouldn't have the grit to follow him into such harsh terrain. He had rested well the past two nights as they inched their way south.

A night scout awakened Victorio. Victorio woke Nana and the three moved over the stones and along the top of an escarpment high above a canyon floor.

Daylight eased its way into the base of the canyon. The scout pointed to a group of willows and scrub oak near a water hole.

The two men took out their glasses and scoured the tree line. A skinny man with a wide brimmed hat bent down, appearing to fill his canteens. Two blue coated Nootahah joined him.

Victorio's face flushed.

"It is Baychendaysen and Alchesay." Victorio was furious. The men casually moved around the camp.

Nana responded, "Not only are they here, they know we are watching them."

"We turn and they are there. I can not kill white eyes this way."

Tomas' raiders returned. The report only darkened Victorio's mood.

The Chihennes made their way deeper into the stones and crossed the divide.

Bay'che followed until Alchesay convinced him Victorio was in strange territory and would have return to the Animas to trade the considerable quantity of goods that had been amassed.

Bay'che thought, rolling his round stone in his hand, before saying, "Time to get in front of Old Vic and not behind him."

Alchesay's swift single nod confirmed their agreement.

"We go to see Magruder."

Cruse joined, "Met Magruder a couple of times passing through Bayard. He knows a lot if he trusts you."

This time it was Bay'che who gave a nod of agreement. He would be happy to get back to a warmer elevation. His spine was chronically painful, his joints hurt and the sensation in his feet was dulled. But he would never have suggested to Alchesay that they knew where Victorio was headed and they pull off the trail.

Beyond the proximity of their headwaters, the Mimbres River and the Gila River had little else in common. Bay'che was startled by the Mimbres.

As the river made its way due south, grassy plains became more frequent and more varied than even those along the Verde. The trees were more diverse, deeper and denser. While not a deep river, the water was crystal clear, even in four foot deep water you could see the rocky bottom as if looking through a glass window.

At a rather leisurely pace, the company made its way down the Mimbres River to Georgetown and John Magruder, some thirty miles east of Fort Bayard.

Bayard was built to protect the stage route and Georgetown sat on the route.

John Magruder and his brother, George, had founded a lumber mill, harvesting the timber from around the Mimbres River. George was killed in a milling accident. Their small settlement was named Georgetown in his memory.

When silver was found in the area, the population of Georgetown and nearby Silver City exploded. Silver City was ambitious and embraced the growth, while Magruder didn't want too many people ruining the unspoiled land where he and his brother had chosen to live their lives. He owned and operated the Mimbres Mining and Milling Company. John Magruder kept his thumb on Georgetown.

Over the years he had kept a good relationship with the Apache. His relationship with the military at Fort Bayard became tenuous when the Negro soldiers were stationed there.

Still, Magruder made it his business to know what was going on in his part of the territory.

They found John Magruder at the lumber mill. He always found the lumber business to be more honest work than mining silver. He wore the overalls of a woodworker.

John was a bull of man, about five feet, six inches tall with broad shoulders yet a barrel chest. He had the arms and hands of a blacksmith. On second glance, Gatewood decided that he might be capable of out pulling a bull.

Magruder knew Alchesay and recalled Cruse. While he gave no hint of it, he knew Gatewood by reputation. However, it was McPherson with his Gladstone he was pleased to see.

"I have two men with big sores on their butts and a kid with a boil in his crotch. I was going open'em up but – well, Doc you're here now and better your tools than my pocket knife."

Dorsey's voice carried no hesitation, "I'll check them all. And anyone else you might be concerned about."

"You can use my office up there. I'll send'em to you."

A Mexican who looked to be a cross between a valet, a body guard and an assassin and hadn't let Magruder from his sight relaxed. John sent him to assist McPherson in finding the office and to fetch the workers. Gladstone in hand, McPherson followed the Mexican up the hill to Magruder's offices.

Magruder kept a cluster of chairs on a wooden deck by the water. They walked down next to Mimbres and sat. Taking a deep breath, Gatewood felt as though he was in as lush and as relaxing a place he'd been since he sat on Tazma's front porch.

"Mr. Magruder, this is a fine porch."

"Thank ya. Get's washed down river along but I just built it back."

Alchesay sat on a boulder next to the deck. Magruder saw to it that Alchesay knew he was welcome on the deck. Alchesay simply preferred large stones to chairs. The three men angled their chairs so that the conversation was open all four.

With an excess of sawdust and access to cold mountain nights, John had an ice house. He kept some classic ale, brewed and bottled on the premises, deeply chilled by dropping a basket in the Mimbres. If he took to you, you were offered ale. Indians and abstainers were offered a flavored drink similarly chilled.

It didn't take long to pass out the ale and place a vanilla tasting drink in Alchesay's hand, a drink that Alchesay preferred to the ale.

John Magruder was the most eclectic of men. Done with the necessary exchange of information, including two sightings of Victorio's band moving along the route Alchesay had forecast.

Magruder asked, "Some wagons of gamblers and whores came through Silver City, bragging they'd laid a whippin' Old Vic in a gun fight although he had them outnumbered."

Alchesay smiled, the others laughed. Cruse responded, "Tomas had nine good men, took the wagons to be settlers and they did surprise him bit. But I can say that account was grossly exaggerated."

"He will trade for only one piece of goods," Alchesay contributed, "He trade for books." He pointed to the small stack of books on the table beside John's chair.

A copy of *Moby Dick* and *The Adventures of Tom Sawyer* sat on top of Tolstoy and Dostoevsky.

"I do have many books and I cherish them. I have these here because I read what the day feels like." Magruder slowed then continued, "And I'm not proud to say I will trade for the right book." John's English changed from rather loose to very correct.

"I have a broker in Philadelphia who is on the lookout for a Kilmarnock Edition of Bobby Burns. I adore the lad."

Cruse, an avid reader and eager for such a conversation asked, "How do you believe Dostoevsky would view the settlement of the American west?"

"I have considered it. When you have much time, come and we will discuss Crime and Punishment, the morality of a man's theft of what he believes himself to be entitled. I would enjoy an evening of literary discussion."

Gatewood joined, bringing the morality of Tom Sawyer into the conversation.

For the two Lieutenants, the hour flight into the realms of literature was a luxurious respite from the harsh reality of soldiering. It exercised parts of their brains that had not had the cobwebs dusted off for some time.

The only interruption came when McPherson joined the group.

"All fixed Doc?"

"Repaired not healed yet. Soap and water and they'll be fine."

"Anything we can reasonably do to keep'em away?"

"Beyond the soap and water, I'd not give them breakfast until they'd had a nice portion of oats. That seems to help."

Dorsey didn't share that he had told the young boy with the sores on his groin to stop taking excessive pleasures with himself.

The men stayed as long as they could justify on the porch next to the Mimbres River.

Gatewood stood and said, "John, we must have another meeting of Mimbres River Literary Society soon. You can teach me much."

Cruse simply said, "Mr. Magruder you are an impressive scholar of the printed word. Thank you." Magruder's handshake was crushing.

"Gentleman, don't wait for Victorio to bring you this way for another visit. My door is always open."

In the rarest of occurrences, Alchesay accepted Magruder's extended hand and gave the firm handshake and said, "You are good man. Can't talk of pleasure and feel pain."

John Magruder walked up as far as the mill with them. He watched them leave.

He turned to his lumber foreman and said, "Poor old Vic. I'd hate to hell to have that pair on my tail. Kin to a cow swishing its tail at flies. Ya swoosh it here and fly lands over there. Get ta be a damn annoyance."

Gatewood turned and took a good look at the porch and the river. He couldn't wait to tell Georgie of John Magruder and his porch.

Victorio was making for Mexico. He would stay wide to the east of Silver City still believing there was some Judge with warrant after him and intent on hanging him. Also, it was just too close to Fort Bayard for him.

From Magruder's insights, there was the new railroad town on Southern Pacific, Lordsburg but the type of traders Victorio needed weren't there. The whores and gambler's are there. It was attracting cattle workers, rustlers and variety of other thieves.

Cloverdale was the logical spot. Trade and be in Mexico in two days.

"Victorio will send most straight to Mexico and wait across the river."

"We need to get him before he gets to Cloverdale. Where do you think?"

"If not Cloverdale near," Alchesay allowed.

So down the Mimbres Mountains, up the Animas Mountains and down toward the valley, they came the shortest but also the driest route. Cruse struggled to keep his pack mules on pace. Blocksom was scouting their eastern flank.

Nantan Bay'che's pain hobbled him for three days before it passed. It did not slow the scouts. He refused an increase in McPherson's elixir feeling that it dulled his senses.

Once in the western foothills of the Animas Mountains, the pace increased. The scrub forest gave and adequate cover. Periodically, a sizable outcropping would provide a first-rate observation point. With their glasses, they were able to scan the entire valley.

On the third day, a survey revealed Captain McLellan's two companies making their way down the valley. The scouts, tired but disappointed they had not made contact with any Victorio or any of his Chihennes. Everyman felt they were lurking somewhere just to the east of them, likely not far from Blocksom and his men.

"Lieutenant Gatewood, good to see you and you look like all bloody hell," came McLellan's greeting.

"Thank you, Sir," Gatewood responded. Both men shook their heads.

"Lieutenant Cruse, you on the other hand appear quite sound."

"Thank you, Sir," Cruse responded having read Gatewood's cue.

"Gentlemen, let's have coffee and a conversation."

McPherson came into view. "Is Dr. Reed with you Sir?"

"No, not by his choice, but he was needed at Fort Apache. Some illness is loose down at Fort Thomas, I felt it best he stay."

"Thank you, Sir."

"Doctor, you may join us."

Overhearing Reed's whereabouts, Dorsey thought he'd rather be here than dealing with an infirmary filled with soldiers and the squirts. Out here he could shoot back, poor old Reed couldn't even shoot the whiners who didn't "suffer sickness well."

Field chairs and coffee felt like a seat in the Founder's Club in Richmond.

McLellan glanced at the threesome. These men were exhausted in a fashion he had rarely seen, yet stood combat ready.

"First, a job well done. It now seems that Victorio's men had killed a number of rancher's families and sheepherders before you took up his trail."

"Once you kept near him, it seems he missed a number of opportunities. Let me say you prevented it from being much worse than it could have been."

"General Owen has written up a standoff at Black Knife Canyon. Most other officers have written it up much differently. There is the feeling that perhaps someone led the command into a trap, got a lot of Negro members of the Tenth killed. A large amount of the stock was reported to have wandered off."

The last statement seemed to be a question.

Cruse answered the question he heard, "Captain Sir, I was in command of the stock. We were sheltered some stock, the rest was headed off by Chihennes. My men fought admirably. I believe stealing stock and supplies was the goal of their mission."

"They stole Bob!" a clearly still agitated Gatewood inserted.

"I'm sorry to hear that, Lieutenant. He appeared a fine animal."

Gatewood was now embarrassed by his sharp selfish tone.

"The reports are that your scouts cleared the Chihennes from their firing positions. Several wrote of how well coordinated the sweep was. Regardless, everyone concurs that when the fire was relieved the fight turned," McLellan continued.

"How did your men get in position to scour that canyon side?"

"Sergeant Alchesay suggested a camp site near a spring at the base of the canyon. No one could see us from above and we were beyond the boundaries of the main camp and the secondary camp. I agreed with his recommendation."

McLellan's voice was serious as he asked, "So, no ranking officer placed you the position with combat instructions?"

Gatewood didn't waver, "Only if they say they did Sir."

McPherson enthusiastically stroked his mustache and his smile spread. There were times he just really admired his friend.

"Gatewood, the troopers below report there was a hell of fight on those slopes."

"I'd call it that, Sir." Gatewood paused then said, "Surgeon McPherson fought as well as any man on the slope."

"Include Dr. McPherson combat in your report," then he added, "There will be an officer's mess shortly."

When he saw Gatewood stiffen, he concluded, "Don't get your bowels in a roar Gatewood, your platoon has been provided the makings of an Apache wedding."

"Well done gentlemen, well done."

As the men walked away, McPherson, talking to Cruse, said, "Notice how our friend's stones have grown rather large."

Cruse chuckled.

"Captain Mac hasn't figured out we couldn't catch Victorio if we wanted to unless he made a huge mistake." McPherson continued.

"Better chance of catching smoke in the desert wind," was Gatewood's conclusion.

Alchesay heard the last as he joined the group, "Bay'che know old bird can't fly forever."

"Bay'che doesn't walk so well but he rides a mule just fine," Cruse said.

"Big hat scares birds," Alchesay finished.

They laughed.

The next morning a courier from Lieutenant Blocksom arrived. Solid sign indicated that Victorio now headed west.

Before he was within smelling distance of Animas Valley, Victorio and Nana realized they were nearly trapped. Two Companies from Fort Bayard were along the river and three platoons from Fort Thomas were near Cloverdale, and two companies from Fort Apache were closing in.

Victorio was certain that Alchesay and the Long Nose were trying to align him in their rifle sights. Despite his distrust of the Mexicans, he would trade in Mexico. Old Vic was tired but he wasn't going back to San Carlos, back to the terrible stench and the diseases that corroded a man's body and soul.

Nana took about fifteen warriors and ambushed a platoon of the Ninth Cavalry along the lower valley. Through his glasses he saw an officer with Springfield repeater. He wanted that rifle.

Nana's ambush sprung clean, they killed three troopers, turned and quickly fled north. The platoon dashed behind him following right into the rifle sights of five waiting Chihennes. The platoon lost six more members including a Lieutenant with Springfield lever action repeater.

Nana's raiders rode north. Three miles up valley they fired an abandoned log farm house. The Ninth Cavalry closed on the smoke. They knew they had been had when they reached the smoldering cabin.

All of Victorio's party crossed into Mexico. Nana taking advantage of a rock escarpment was also making fast time toward Mexico.

Dandy Jim and Quilo reported the skirmish.

Captain McLellan sounded Officer's Call. Gatewood asked Alchesay to stay within hailing distance. Gatewood was moving quick paced, happy he had taken a good dose of willow powder.

Alchesay suddenly stopped him, "Victorio escaping into Mexico right now."

Gatewood got McLellan's attention. "Captain, my Sergeant believes this is a feint and Old Vic is headed into Mexico right now."

McLellan decisiveness further changed Gatewood's view of man he first met up the Verde River. "Take that personal platoon of yours and go check. Do it now!"

His eyes found McPherson and ask without a word if he wanted to join them. Dorsey fell in beside Gatewood and quietly said, "Of course, who wouldn't want another week on a hot trail with cold meals." Both men smiled and nodded.

Victorio was long into to Mexico by the time Gatewood gave up the chase knowing he too was further into Mexico that treaty allowed.

But Nana was not.

Still in Mexico, Bay'che's troop stopped at a water hole. They water and rested the animals, left a trail away from the water into the rocks, then moved to a vantage point above the water. They ate a bite in a cold camp.

Dead Shot slid quietly into the camp. He said he had sighted six warriors. He believed it was a splinter from a raiding party.

Augustus Blocksom and his scouts were on this track and moving up the valley. Augustus also didn't know he was no longer in the United States. But he did know he was on the trail of a number of Chihennes bucks.

The Chihennes stopped just short of the water hole and sent one man to check the security of the situation. The main party was waiting when Blocksom. Not having an unobstructed observation point, Bay'che was never certain who surprised who but chaos followed. There was a rapid exchange of rifle fire and then both parties limped for cover. The Chihennes took off into the cactus and rock.

A dust cloud suggested Mexican Cavalry about three miles away and closing.

Bay'che turned to Alchesay and said, "Let's go home." They gathered up Blocksom and did.

Shortly, they heard gunfire from the vicinity of the water hole. They didn't know who won the firefight. Given Mexican Cavalry and six Chihennes a draw struck Bay'che as a fair result.

By the time the Company reached Fort Apache, Gatewood's pain was crippling. His steps were painful and awkward.

Reed and McPherson were directed, "Get him on his feet before some bronco decides it is a good time to jump the reservation."

The directions they got from the military paled in comparison to the dressing down they received from Georgie.

Alchesay and the scouts passed the time as best they could. Nootahah and idle time are not a natural blend.

Kuruk carved an oak staff, gave it repeated rubbings with grease of animal fat. He carefully carved three deep "claw marks" into the ball like grip on the staff. He tempered it over the fire.

Bay'che was grateful. He found the claw markings a decoration that gave the appearance of strength as well as increasing his grip.

"Tell me about the markings?"

Alchesay responded, "Kuruk Nootahah for bear."

Alchesay's English was progressively better but he was still reluctant to disclose even the slightest piece of the Nootahah language his only white eye friend.

Bay'che looked at Kuruk and held the staff with both hands over his head. "Bear club will make Nantan Bay'che strong when he must be strong." Bay'che again showed Alchesay the claw marks in the fashion one shows off something in which he has considerable pride. Kuruk was pleased.

In a few months reports of Victorio's death began to circulate. The first account to arrive at Fort Apache said he was killed in a trap laid by the Mexican Army. After a successful trading exchange, many of the Chihennes drank tainted tequila. As they writhed in the pain, vomiting, they were shot by Mexican Regulars.

Alchesay doubted that tale, rather he accepted what the Coyotero considered to be the truth. Two Mimbres scouts hired by the Mexican Army and promised a substantial bonus, made their way into Victorio's camp waited in the scrubs and brush near his wikiup. When Old Vic came out in the wee hours to relieve himself, they shot him in the back from less than twenty yards away.

Nana's Chihennes caught them within the hour. Nana promised them their lives if they led them to the men who hired them. Not that they believed he would not kill them, but it kept them alive with the hope of an escape or a rescue. The assassins accepted.

Two Mexican officers and their escorts were captured and secreted from their camp. Nana took them back north. It is said the fortunate one died after three days. Legend has it that the Chihennes randomly sliced pieces and removed organs in sections, scattering the men all over the Paseo del Notre country of Texas and New Mexico. Perhaps they can still be heard as the winds whine over the canyons of great bend in the Rio Grande River.

In the spring, the New York Times confirmed Victorio's death but the details remained vague.

THIRTEEN
BLOODY CIBICUE CREEK

WITH DORSEY MCPHERSON'S ENCOURAGEMENT and at Walter Reed's insistence, First Lieutenant Charles Bare Gatewood took a medical leave to be examined and treated in his native Virginia. The prospect of an extended visit where physicians with more resources might examine her husband pleased Georgie.

All the White Mountain Scouts, including Alchesay, did not re-enlist. They opted to spend the summer in the cooler mountains with their wives.

Although the Arizona Territory was a quiet as it had been since Gatewood had been in the country, Alchesay was unsettled. In their final visit before Bay'che departed for Virginia Alchesay said, "Tell Nantan Virglid to not scout up the Salt or the Black River, leave to Wingate soldiers."

Gatewood inquired more directly until he was convinced that his friend just had a bad feeling about the temperament around the reservation and even among many of his own White Mountain people.

"Will not let white eye agents and Mormons steal from us so long. Wives bellies rumble too much. Happy Bay'che be gone. Happy Alchesay go hunt, eat good. Go see McCrieght, buy good cloth for wives."

"Hear buying officers will not buy horse like Bob for you."

"Said he wasn't Government property, I'll just ride a good government mule from here on."

"Not right!" Clearly having been practicing, Alchesay said, "Assholes!"

Bay'che laughed. "I will only ride high quality US Government mules from now on."

Gatewood relayed the information to Cruse. He was likely to draw any meaty assignment that came up in Gatewood's absence.

The heads up didn't enter Cruse's mind again until he begin recruiting replacement scouts. No White Mountain Apaches answered the recruitment call. A group of twelve Western Apache formed the core of the platoon he was able to enlist.

Cruse was uncomfortable. His men were compliant but none the less discontented. He wasn't certain how this new group felt about him but he did not trust them. A second enlistment campaign produced another platoon but they were equally unenthused and inexperienced.

Dorsey and Reed were supportive but he now had instincts with the Apache that they did not have. Plus, they were overrun with malaria and dysentery among the Apaches at San Carlos.

Discontentment and distrust were the prevailing emotions along the Gila River the summer of 1881. An abnormally hot summer was rapidly bringing a sinister sizzle to this frail, dysfunctional community.

For the Apache, hope whispered down from the cooler climates to the north. The words flowed like an undercurrent out of Cibicue Creek and down to the Black River into the Salt. The current carried the promise to rid the country of the white eye and bring back all of the Nootahah the white eye had killed, a resurrection.

Just up Cibicue Creek, the Nootahah Medicine Man Nock-ay-det-klinne made medicine. He preached the message. The spirits told him that all dead Nootahah could return when the white eyes had been driven from the land. Prophecies of great victories were abundant. A war so violent no white would remain on Apache land, so cruel that every white would fear to return. Both of his wives led fertility dances that promised lushness in the wikiups and rich Mexican villages to raid.

His youngest wife, Ela, a rail thin twelve to thirteen year old girl, had a disturbed look to her. Her songs reflected her belief and her passion about her husband's message. She had a disconnection with the real world that might trouble white eyes but most Nootahah saw as a gift from the spirits. Her name meant "earth" and she incorporated the earth, the dust, into her dances and chants.

Nock-ay-det-klinne preached the gospel of annihilation and resurrection. The Nootahah understood annihilation. An ample supply of tiswin and peyote was making the concept of resurrection more palatable.

He offered victories. She offered a rebirth of the Nootahah fertility. The believers came, the curious came, and their camp grew. The shroud of mystery and zeal brought intrigue.

Dorsey knocked on Cruse's door. Cruse opened the door. A distracted McPherson was looking across the parade ground at nothing in particular.

"Dorsey?"

"Tom, you trust your new scouts?"

There was no indecision in his answer, "No."

"General Carr is going to issue an officer's call shortly."

Cruse waited.

"Be careful out there, Tom."

McPherson said, "I'm going to go have a stiff shot of the good stuff."

He sat on the porch with a small glass of the good stuff as the officer's scurried for Coronel Eugene Asa Carr's office.

All assembled, Coronel Carr produced a telegram. "I want each of you gentlemen to read the orders." Carr stood silently as the paper made its way from officer to officer.

Back in his hands, he read the closing aloud, "You are ordered to capture or kill Noch-ay-del-Klinne."

Gatewood received a telegram ordering his immediate return to the Arizona Territory before the news of the Cibicue Creek Massacre reached the eastern newspapers. Although he strongly encouraged Georgie to stay out her visit, she adamantly declined.

After a discussion, she glared at him and said, "Charles, you are not leaving me here alone with my family!"

There was no further dialogue on the matter.

The Gatewood's returned to Fort Apache. Georgie stepped on the spiders and a single scorpion as she began sweeping the dust from the floor and out the door. Ida McPherson and Emilie Reed quickly appeared, cleaning gear in hand.

By mid-day, rugs and bedding had been beaten, plates washed clean.

Georgie made a large pot of tea. The ladies could now enjoy the news from Virginia, fashion held the forefront. Despite the social isolation and the inherently uncomfortable climate, they made every effort to appear in a stylish fashion. The Arizona Territory demanded that lotions and creams occupy a major role in personal upkeep, therefore in feminine conversation.

Fearful that Georgie would conceive in such a foreign, primitive place, her sisters had given her a discreetly wrapped going away gift, a supply of the new more durable rubber sheath covers for her husband and for her the latest in womb veils. Georgie shared these latest advances with Ida and Emilie.

Gatewood reported. After being briefed, he made straight away for Tom Cruse.

"Tom, what the hell happened out there?"

"Glad to see you too."

Gatewood hesitated, shook his head and smiled. "Sorry Tom, I just felt I had a man who would tell me the truth, without the whitewash and thinking about his next promotion."

Cruse tightened his lips into a knowing smile and said, "I really am glad to see you."

Cruse when inside and brought out two glasses of good bourbon. "I don't think I can tell you all this without a stiff drink or two."

"I've had those times, Tom." Thinking deeper, Gatewood repeated it, "I've had those times." Gatewood eased himself into the rocking chair. He looked out over the parade grounds and thought, "Good to be home."

"Western Apache Medicine Man, Nock-ay-det-Klinne, was preaching about the spirits giving all the land back to the Apache and raising the dead warriors if they could run the white eyes from the territory. Old man Thompson, Abraham James, Pendley and some other settler's in the Oak Creek area were rightly concerned and made a big stink with the right folks in Prescott. Fort Verde was just writing reports confirming the situation was serious and getting worse."

Gatewood nodded.

"Fair to say it was getting bad fast. Finally, General Wilcox ordered Carr to go capture or kill the medicine man. Washing his butt, Carr passed the order around at an officer's call. But good thing he did, Court of Inquiry came quick and the General's memory was faded."

Cruse took a moment to group, and then he continued, "The Coronel asked if I trusted my scouts and told him the truth, that I didn't."

He looked directly at Gatewood and said, "Bay'che, I'm not you but I'm not a miserable recruiter either. Everyone understood why your men had returned home, most had been in the field since you got here. Things just never had a good smell to them."

Gatewood couldn't restrain his response, "You mean it reeked like the Gila passing through San Carlos."

"Yes, that bad."

"The Coronel was prudent and sent an invitation to the medicine man to come into Fort Apache for a conversation. The Medicine Man answered that he had too many sick people to heal to come at the time." Cruse stopped and took the first sip of his bourbon.

"I'll tell you this affair has just made all bourbon taste the same."

"Cruse I never knew you to drink a drop."

"I hadn't. My daddy told me a soldier would have times he couldn't sleep without a drink. This is one of those times."

"I've had them myself, Tom. And I always hope each one is the last one."

"I swear, I was born during the December blizzard of 1857 in Kentucky. I thought I was going to die on the hottest August day."

The men sat and rocked for several minutes. Gatewood retrieved his round stone from his buttoned shirt pocket. In a fashion so unthinking it appeared automatic, the stone moved its way around his fingers.

"Do you suppose Magruder is sitting out on his porch?"

"I would be if I was him."

Cruse continued, "Carr did only thing he could do. He ordered us into the field to bring the Medicine Man in, to kill anyone who tried to interfere. I said we didn't need the scouts. The Medicine Man was sitting all comfortable on Cibicue Creek just waiting for us. Carr felt we needed the scouts to track them if they decided to run. Bay'che, I could have tracked a camp that size but the Medicine Man would have broken off and the scouts I had couldn't have tracked him.

"I'm convinced they tried to lead us into an ambush when we were three days up the Verde Trail, tried to convince us that there was a shorter route along the north side of the Verde. A patrol from Fort Verde spooked the ambush."

"Carr never believed they were leading us away from the Verde Trail, but they were." Gatewood sensed that his friend was seeking non-existent answers, searching for small clues he should have seen.

"There are days we are just no better than our scouts make us," Gatewood said hoping Cruse understood. The path of offering understanding to another man is frail trail.

"Mose was the best of the scouts I had. Carr sent Mose ahead into the Medicine Man's camp." Cruse shook his head and said, "Can you believe it? He wanted Mose to reassure the Medicine Man that a large column closing on his camp meant him no evil intent. We were there to give him two choices, surrender or die."

"I followed with the rest of my scouts and the point of the main column was about a mile behind us. Sergeant Mose came back to Carr and told him that Noch-ay-del-Klinne was too exhausted from the previous night's dancing that he couldn't meet Carr on the trail. He said he would wait for the Coronel at his camp."

The former abstainer took another sip of a whiskey. Gatewood joined him. "Tom, you didn't lie. This is good bourbon."

A strained but well-intended smile cracked Cruse's face, "A motivated drinker can learn the difference quickly."

"Well, Coronel Carr ordered us up the creek and into the camp. First Apache I encountered was that renegade Sanchez. He tried to block my path. I ordered him out of the way. He was slow and defiant but he moved. I stared him down but I swear I wanted to tell him to go to Hell and add some thumbnail sketches of his ancestors. But I held the ground. Several others made a run at us, reining up short and backing away."

"Mose led us to a wikiup with more canvas than most, actually more of lean-to than a wikiup. The Medicine Man sat on a pile of Navajo blankets."

"He was the lightest colored Apache I ever saw, almost pale white, a really small man. He looked almost sickly but he wasn't. Bay'che he had one of the most unusual faces I've ever seen, still can't quite put my finger on it."

"Carr arrived. He addressed Noch-ay-del-Klinne properly but he had an interpreter I didn't know. Swear to God the Medicine Man looked like an ancient priest in his tabernacle. He had a couple of wives, but this young one was spooky, all skinny and covered with dust. Bay'che, she just had a wild look out of her eyes like she was seeing things I couldn't see."

"Anyway, Carr issued his ultimatum. I could actually feel the tension rise. The Medicine Man said he couldn't come now, saying soldiers should leave and he would come to the fort in three or four days."

"Carr told him no, that he came with him now."

"Sergeant Mose quickly moved beside Noch-ay-del-Klinne. Whatever he said, it seemed to calm the renegades. The Medicine Man stood up, Carr sent Sergeant McDonald to take assist Mose with him. One on each side they moved the Medicine Man out of his tabernacle."

"He had sent the young wife to get his pony and some other things. She was very slow getting back. She did some odd little dance as she brought the pony. Just damn weird. I could see more and more Apaches coming into view, stripped down to breech cloths and cartridge belts. I did see several Apaches across the creek who just seemed to be curious observers, one of them was Dandy Jim."

He tilted by the glass and drained the last of the whiskey.

"Just crossed the creek and all hell broke loose." He looked at the arm of the chair through the empty glass. He took the bottle and poured two more fingers.

"I know for certain Sanchez fired the first shot. Dandy Jim shot Captain Hentig, killed him dead out. Sergeant McDonald immediately fired and dropped the Medicine Man. He just hit the ground and never moved. Weird little wife sprawled out over him and began the death chant. Mose and McDonald both put shots in her before her moans could compound the circumstances. She must have ended up with six bullets in her. Mose jumped next to me for protection for both sides, don't blame him. Then, McDonald got hit in his leg. Mose reacted fast enough to keep McDonald on his feet and moving. There were times Mose had both sides shooting at him."

"The Apache had every vantage point and were firing. We were scrambling for decent cover and returning fire. I never heard anything like the noise. The noise blocked my thoughts, bullets whined and ricocheted all around."

Cruse stopped, looked up the barren bluffs to the east but Gatewood didn't think he saw them; he was looking into an elusive place in his own mind. Sounding like a sinner in the confessional, he said, "Gatewood, I was scared all to Hell. Don't know how I kept my wits about me, never heard such a noise. We were completely surrounded!"

"Did you know a bullet makes different sound when it cracks bone and buries in a man's guts?" Cruse took a sip and finished, "It does. Two different sounds."

Gatewood knew the sounds but he sat silently. He held his stone between his thumb and his forefinger, appearing to be carefully examining both sides. Alchesay always contended Bay'che preserved each memory of the land and the people in that stone. Maybe he was right.

"We fought our way back across the creek and formed a solid perimeter. I sat Sergeant Mose near the Coronel, told him to protect Coronel Carr. I figured Mose had been shot at plenty for one day."

"It was only now that I found the scouts had turned and fired on our troopers, killed five or six men. Sergeant Mose, Sergeant

McDonald and I had fought back to back for almost two hours, slugging our way from the tabernacle, across the creek to Carr's perimeter."

"Bay'che, I've never seen an Apache with tears. Mose heard as I heard about our betrayal by the scouts. I do believe Mose was profoundly hurt. God bless Coronel Carr, he took a couple of steps, shook Mose's hand and praised his actions that day."

"The Medicine Man was still lying near the creek. Carr placed sharp shooters with clean lines of fire to the body. Every Apache that tried to retrieve him was killed. Bay'che we killed three squaws who tried to recover his body.

"As dark fell, the firing became sporadic. Fewer targets presented themselves. By morning, all the Apache were gone."

"Sixty-eight white men went go to Cibicue Creek, forty-seven of us left. We buried the dead as best we could. Troopers in one grave and Apache in another, put the Medicine Man on bottom."

"When we started back down the Black River, Mose and I took the point.

"Last week Carr sent two platoons to more properly bury our dead. They had all been dug up and severely mutilated. It was impossible to conduct the individual burials, so they dug a really deep grave and reburied our men. They assembled some type of stone monument. It will last a while. The Apache graves weren't bothered, didn't dig up the Medicine Man's remains."

Cruse quieted. Gatewood said, "They died when they could have stolen your animals and lived to fight another fight. The Nootahah don't build monuments to dead heroes."

Cruse drew a deep breath and continued, "General Wilcox ordered a sweeping round up of the present and former scouts. Alchesay was even arrested. Held him, he was north at Fort Wingate trying to make some kind of business deal providing hay. Let him go, let all your men go except Dandy Jim and Dead Shot. I saw Dandy Jim at Cibicue, didn't see Dead Shot."

"Where are they now?"

"They were taken to Fort Grant and both hanged."

The blood drained from Gatewood face, then filled with the flush of anger. "God damn, God damn – God Damn! Wilcox order it?"

"Yes. Willcox has been replaced. General George Crook is now in command."

"Are you telling me that Willcox had Alchesay put in jail?"

"I'm not defending Willcox, but the paranoia was so rampant every Apache scout was a viewed as a traitor. Dandy Jim's curiosity got him in the wrong place. I'd wager that he was the only one of your scouts that was at Cibicue Creek."

Cruse paused, not liking the feeling he was justifying orders he found profoundly disagreeable, and then said, "Gatewood, I think had it not been for Alchesay's level head the peaks could have blown off the White Mountains."

Gatewood gave the first hint he might have known some of the story saying, "That and the manner in which you and Sergeant Mose handled the retreat down the Black. It might have been a lot worse except for Sergeant Mose."

Cruse smiled, his voice sounding somehow relieved, "Yes, and I'm getting an undeserved medal."

"That my friend is the Sixth Cavalry we know and love."

They touched glasses and took a drink.

"I heard Geronimo is out again."

"Yes, got more followers from Cibicue Creek, word is he is ripping across northern Mexico."

As random thoughts tend to drift in and out of the mind, Cruse shared, "Bay'che you need to see the waterfalls up Cibicue Creek and the Black River. They are stunning."

Gatewood agreed and smiled, said, "Well, Tom you picked a hell of time to bring Bea out here."

"I am anxious for her to get here. She'll arrive in Tucson next week."

"Tom, from what you tell me of Bea, I guarantee your life will better."

Suddenly solemn, sounding doubtful, Tom said, "How long does it take to get over something like Cibicue Creek?"

Gatewood response was dead serious, "Never and not as long as you think."

Cruse shook his head, "Never and not as long as I think."

"Going to 102 Tom, if I was you I'd start cleaning this place up before your bride arrives."

Charles B. Gatewood

FOURTEEN

MILITARY COMMANDANT

GENERAL GEORGE CROOK TOOK command in September of 1882.

He immediately chose his subordinates carefully. He selected Lieutenant Charles B. Gatewood as Military Commandant of the White Mountain Reservation and picked Captain Emmett Crawford for the similar position at San Carlos. He assigned Lieutenant Britton Davis, new to Arizona to assist Crawford at San Carlos.

Most of the Sixth and Third Cavalry considered Gatewood to be the perfect man for the job.

As fate would ordain, Phillip Wilcox became the new agent at San Carlos. As qualified as Gatewood was, Wilcox was completely ignorant of the Apache. He undermined every effort Crawford would make to improve the circumstances at San Carlos. Wilcox was interested in power and profit.

Georgie, now five months into her confinement with their first child, was thrilled that her husband's new assignment would limit his time in the field. She had always felt Charles would be a marvelous father if he were home. She was pleased.

His new duties were largely administrative and included functioning as the Judge of the only court on the reservation.

This was not Crook's first assignment in the territory. Ten years previously he served here. The Chiricahua had given him a Nootahah name, Nantan Lupan, the grey wolf.

General Crook felt that for position of Military Commandant to successfully manage the reservation matters and Apache disputes it would be necessary that the Apache understood that the Commandant spoke for him. When the Commandant spoke, it was if the words came for Nantan Lupan himself.

He ordered all males that could carry a weapon to assemble at the San Carlos Agency and meet the new department commander, though some remembered him from ten years earlier. He wanted to introduce the Commandant and explain their power.

He also wanted a census of men capable of carrying weapon, their tribe and their band. They would be given a small brass tag with a letter to designate the band and a number determining now many men in each band. The true purpose was to make a quick and easy identification of male missing from either reservation possible.

"Sweet, there is something about it that I just don't like. It is a little like one might have treated a slave before we lost the war."

Georgie looked up from checking her stew pot, a little puzzled and said, "I didn't know you had great trouble with slaves."

He responded, "The Apache are not slaves."

Running what he had just uttered through his mind, he added, "Georgie, I think we could eventually kill every Apache, but I don't think we could ever make slaves of them."

The room was quiet. Georgie had become skilled at knowing how to listen to the silence between her husband's verbalization of his thoughts.

"I don't know, Georgie. I'll do it, but I just don't like it."

Georgie poured them each a cup of coffee and they moved to the porch. September afternoons are still hot at Fort Apache. "Stew will ready on time."

Georgie took his hand and placed it on her stomach. "Junior has been very active this afternoon." She knew that to feel their child kick was the sure way to lift her husband's mood. A strong kick could make Charles Gatewood grin and almost giggle. It was so out of character for her husband that a giggle would escape her mouth. They were both elated with the pending birth, a birth still some four months away.

After they had rocked a bit, Charles said, "Sorry Sweet, I shouldn't have brought it past our front door."

"Of course you should have. The General has ordered you to hang tags on men you respect. Some are your friends, it has to feel amiss." She abruptly changed the topic, "Oh, feel here."

Gatewood laughed as the child unleashed a stiff leg thrust.

"Georgie, I am very optimistic that this position will finally open the door to promotions. I know the Apache and they know me. It is as if the job was made for me."

Georgie took his hand and gently gripped it.

On the last morning of September and well into the count, the White Mountain Apache arrived. Clouds of dust announced their location, then on the north mesa men on horseback appeared, first in formation falling into a skirmish line.

They were now embracing the white eye calling them Coyotero. They considered themselves wolves or wolf-men and all other men to be sheep. It was conceded by all that the Chiricahua and Coyotero were the finest warriors among the Nootahah.

In the morning sun, they looked like fine warriors.

Dorsey McPherson was standing next Gatewood. He was there to provide any medical services that might be required.

Dorsey said, "Now that is damn fine cavalry for born foot soldiers."

"Yes, they are."

Their rifles glistened in the morning sun. Each man wore one or two belts of ammunition. Then, in single file they made their way down the butte, reforming into a skirmish line at the base. They rode toward the camp.

Nantan Bay'che, as the Military Commandant of the White Mountain Apache, walked out to greet them. He stopped and motioned for Surgeon McPherson to join him.

"Look who is out front."

Dorsey squinted and then recognized Alchesay. Still straight as arrow, as graceful and he was powerful.

"Anzhoo, Alchesay."

"Anzhoo, Baychendaysen. Your nose has grown since I saw you last."

Bay'che touched the brim of his hat and asked, "Think I need a bigger brim to keep it out of the sun."

They laughed, visibly pleased to see each other.

"Anzhoo, Surgeon, I polite to you. Petone with me and you still hold his chit."

"Alchesay, I am very pleased to see you look well. You killing food or stealing it these days?"

"Depends, Surgeon, depends."

Dorsey informed him, "The people relying on San Carlos rations are not so well nourished."

"Bay'che make treat us fair now," Alchesay exaggerated his sarcastic tone. His voice becoming sober, "New agent another stealer."

His straight-forwardness surprised no one.

The three men clearly enjoyed the irony of their new circumstances.

"Do you have men who need treated?"

"Yes, after census counts us and Nantan Lupan speaks."

The formalities and the informalities went well. Alchesay was more pragmatic about the executions of Dandy Jim and Dead Shot than Bay'che had anticipated. It did ease his conscious some for being away during the events.

"If Nantan Lupan's orders hold, come spring, bring your woman to see our mountains," Alchesay said and then added, "Bay'che, you keep skinny so wolves won't eat you, too bony."

"Not all that look like sheep are sheep."

The Coyotero, newly counted and given tags, left.

Watching them disappear over the crest of the mesa, Dorsey said, "Maybe this time we will get peace or at least the killing stops."

Gatewood looked at the cloud of dust settle below the mesa, turned to Dorsey and reminded him, "It is one thing to put an Apache on his reservation and quite another to keep him there."

Lieutenant Gatewood quickly found that the role of the Military Commandant was Judge and broker and a single member legislature and Chief of Police. He understood the White Mountain Apache at war. He had to learn to settle the social and marital disputes on the fly. His police force consisted of fifty handpicked scouts who were accountable only to him. He made laws as they were needed.

Nantan Bay'che quickly realized that there were a disproportionate number of domestic matters coming to his court. He sought out an old Coyotero named Sanchez, but commonly called Iron Tooth, to consult. Iron Tooth was good man who enjoyed being in the court each time it convened. His dour, frowning face belied how much he enjoyed being a thorn in Gatewood's judicial side.

While Gatewood would be reading a decision, he would sternly rise and walk stiffly from the courtroom as if expressing some profound disapproval.

Iron Tooth's private counsel was quite helpful. "Look to the mother-in-law." Such conflicts are always between the man and his mother-in-law. A loud mother-in-law can create considerable strife for a husband.

Gatewood observed that each wife who came with a complaint had her mother by her side steering the ship. In this society of plural marriage, the mother-in-law was going to be certain that her daughter got her fair share from the other wives.

Gatewood and Crook agreed on how a reservation should be run. Gatewood seemed headed up the military ladder. Gatewood's career seemed on the rise until he began to protect women's rights and Indian rights.

However, the first problem that he had to solve was the fact that there was no reliable translation from Nootahah to English; it had to come from Apache to Spanish to English. A Military Commandant needed reliable interpreters.

Gatewood found two men who could not have been more different in their personalities. He first hired Severiano. As boy he was captured by the Apache in a raid into Sonora. He was reared with the Coyotero and married a Coyotero squaw. By this time, he had spent thirty years with the Nootahah. While he on occasion visited his relatives in Mexico he always returned to the tribe. Most considered him smart and daring, but capable of carrying a grudge as long as any Nootahah.

Then, he found "Old Jack" Conley. This hyperactive old Texan made everyone aware his parents were Irish. He had worked as a cowboy, mail rider and a guide. His pride and joy was a .36 Caliber, cap and ball, Navy Colt Revolver which he kept in perfect working order.

Severiano was reckless and "Old Jack" possessed an unswerving devotion to simplistic predictability.

While they possessed little valuing of grammar, both were capable in the three languages.

With the court prepared to function, Gatewood made his first administrative announcements. First, the males would be expected to take a fair share of the plowing and hoeing of the cornfields. Women were not longer required to turn all their earning over to their husbands. Second, the beating of women without significant aggravation shall cease. Third, the unwarranted abuse of women and children, especially in matters regarding their sex, shall be prohibited.

Initially, husbands who were accustomed to gambling and drinking away the family earnings filed numerous complaints with the Court. Gatewood's rulings, several of which placed the complaining male in the jail for a few weeks, convinced the bucks that for the time the law had changed. Gradually, women with their mothers at their sides, began to file complains of their own. The concept that women were allowed such access to the Court distressed many of the bucks. The sight of badly battered and bleeding women brought the policemen to the side of Gatewood's Court. The policemen began to arrest those they saw as lazy malcontents.

Many were found guilty and there was no appeal from Gatewood's court on strictly Apache matters.

Even Nana was coming to believe that only peace and order could protect the Nootahah from total annihilation. Peace and order meant change.

When one of Nana's sons beat his wife excessively, crippled with arthritis and left with limited vision, Nana grabbed his by his ear and walked him to the calaboose. Then, although Court was not in session, he found Bay'che's office and demanded to see him. Hearing the voices in the entry room, Gatewood came out of his office.

"Anzhoo, Nana."

"Anzhoo, Nantan Baychendaysen."

Gesturing with his open palm, Bay'che directed Nana into his office.

"I am very pleased to see you again." Bay'che stopped short of acknowledging his positive feelings toward the old warrior.

"I you to." Nana's voice carried his age. "Walk son to your calaboose."

Bay'che nodded that he understood.

"He beat wife too much. You maybe keep four days?"

Nana was Chiricahua, technically under the purview of Lieutenant Brittan Davis. However, Gatewood acted in the fashion he considered expedient and had the paper drafted.

Bay'che was encouraged. Nana despite his age, was as agile on horseback any of the younger leaders and this new system had only moderately muted his capacity for cruelty. Nana understood the fight could no longer be won.

"I never trap you. You always there first."

"Nana, I chased you and Victorio all over the territory. Like chasing smoke on a windy day."

Nana, who expressions had mostly soured with age, was visibly pleased. Then, he added, "Stand in cold water time. I didn't know you fight like Coyotero, I learn. Now I know."

The papers were ready, four days in the jail. Nana waited. He glanced at the gavel.

Nantan Baychendaysen saw the glance, picked up the gavel and banged it on the paper three times. He said, "It is done."

Nana responded, "Good."

He called for his orderly and said, "Please show Nantan Nana out."

He looked at the old man. His look was returned. Appreciation and respect were communicated without the exchange of a single word. Gatewood was impressed that the old renegade, a man who had long proven himself to be a crafty and a cruel opponent, was making an effort at upholding the new laws.

Britain Davis enjoyed the good laugh when the papers arrived.

Gatewood's original expectation had been that the court would hear many cases of thief and assault. He was surprised when domestic cases dominated the docket. He quickly arrived at the conclusion there was no one meaner and more vindictive than a Nootahah mother-in-law. The women could wield gossip as proficiently as a brave could slice with a bowie knife.

Because of his understanding of the lengthy history of some of these feuds, often the quarrels arose from events that occurred when the men were off raiding.

By late fall of 1882, Georgia pregnancy was quite visible. After considerable discussion and despite her husband's concerns, it was clear Georgie was going to deliver her baby in Unit 102 at Fort Apache.

Mrs. Sergeant Weldon Thomas was considered to be a highly skilled mid-wife and carried the endorsement of both Walter and Dorsey. Walter agreed that come Georgie's time, he would always be nearby. Walter's medical education had made him quite familiar with pregnancy and delivery. Dorsey, on the other hand, was a skilled army surgeon.

Ida McPherson, Bea Cruse and Emilie Reed, Georgia's almost daily companions for tea or coffee, were clearly not going be far removed from any activity.

The truth is that every woman on the post would be available to assist. Such was the way of childbirth on a frontier post. An infant's cry brought humanity into an often inhumane place.

In early October Ms. Thomas came for tea and a visit with Ms. Lieutenant Gatewood. Georgie Gatewood and Nancy Thomas became fast friends.

It took Nancy an hour to instruct Georgie as to the body changes in the final months before the birth. They laughed about naïve husbands and discussed the management of intimacy during these final months.

"Now your man will not cease to be a man because you are becoming a mother. A resourceful woman can manage both nicely." Nancy watched her face, gauging her needed response, "Do you consider yourself a sexually resourceful lady?"

"I consider myself resourceful but intimately naïve."

"Well, let me made a few helpful suggestions. Having a baby and husband you are going to need to be informed and practical." Mrs. Sergeant Wilson chuckled and said, "Oh lady the stories I could tell."

Georgie experienced some difficult times, but the final months were easier than she had expected. She was so very pleased with her husband. He rubbed out her back pains like it was the task for which he was born. His hands could relax her shoulders in an instant. Both were astounded at the changes in her body and remained enthralled with the increasing movement of their child.

The birth was rapid. Dorsey had prepared a mild dose of chloroform. If Reed reached for it, Mrs. Thomas would wave him off, saying, "This sweet child don't have need of that."

There were a number of times that Georgie started to tell Mrs. Thomas she thought she was wrong. Each time Georgie, in fear she might be judged less a woman by her Fort Apache peers, endured.

Mr. Thomas was more than proficient. Reed could not praise her enough. Dorsey sat on the porch with Gatewood and took sips of whiskey to keep the anxious father-to-be from coming unwound.

"Hell, you weren't this nervous when you got caught on the wrong side of the rock at Black Knife."

Now make no mistakes, Dorsey was enjoying his friend's impatient anxiety.

Charles B. Gatewood, Jr. was born on January 4, 1883.

A small wooden cradle joined the Gatewoods, the Reeds and the McPhersons on the front porch. They looked forward to the stories from the day in court or in infirmary. Now, tales of Junior's day completed the evening.

Georgia enjoyed having her husband home almost every evening. Charles adored his wife, he was so proud of her. She did not know how many times he would brush aside her hair and softly kiss her neck. He worshiped the child, talking and whispering to him, telling her what their son was saying.

"You are an annoyingly good father." Georgie often told him.

Mrs. Thomas came to check on Georgie and Junior. Georgie was a wonderful mother.

"Don't become so busy loving Junior that you forget you are also a wife," Mrs. Thomas said.

Georgie started to offer some rationalizations but immediately recognized the experienced mid-wife and consultant would not be accepting any of them.

She had become so enthralled with her infant son she had even been letting the welcome home kisses slide by.

"Do you have concerns about conceiving another one?" Ms. Thomas asked.

"No."

"Are you taking measures or do you trust such outcomes to the Good Lord?"

"We will take measures." Georgie was glad she did not inquire as to the exact nature of the measures. Her sister had brought a supply of the new rubber penis shields. Georgie had not told Charles yet.

"Good, I do believe you are likely safe as long as you are nursing that handsome boy." Mrs. Thomas reached into cradle and tickled Junior under his chin. He giggled.

"You might be a touch sore when you resume married life. I brought a small gift that will help you," She said as she handed Georgia a small jar of petroleum jelly. "Just a dab on your entrance will help. Tell that handsome Lieutenant not to get to wound up and that will help too." She smiled at Georgia as she had with many young mothers in most Forts west of the Mississippi River.

That night she found that Charles was more concerned about her pain than she was. The tenderness of her breast disturbed their established foreplay. The dab worked well. His penetration was so timid that he hardly entered her. When he did not proceed beyond that point, she encouraged him with little success.

"Charles, I will not break."

"Are you sure?"

She thrust her hips consuming more of him than was her intention, but after an initial tinge of discomfort she was fine. She relaxed, feeling a primary element of her femininity had been restored.

He started to move, but she held him in place for a just a bit longer.

Georgie whispered, "I have missed you my love."

Charles could only make some soft satisfied sound.

They loved cuddling after sex.

Then, in February of 1884, word reached Gatewood that Captain Crawford had granted a number of Chiricahua permission to locate up Turkey Creek on the White Mountain Reservation. The Coyoteros were outraged as they were not consulted and had they been they would have never agreed to the relocation onto White Mountain land.

Gatewood complained to Crook, who hardly listened to Gatewood's arguments. Crook simply replied, "It seems the best way to keep the Chiricahuas on the reservation."

Gatewood snapped, "So we are going to anger the tribe that has been the most loyal to us, has provided dependable scouts and leaders. There will be a trouble."

Crook's face hardened, "Lieutenant Gatewood, if that happens they will be killing each other and not whites. The decision is made." Before Gatewood could respond, Crook dismissed him.

As spring came, the Chiricahua moved. The original approved small band grew to over five hundred. Geronimo, Naiche and Mangus were with them.

As the volume grew, rather than seizing control and reducing the size of the party, Crook simply assigned Lieutenant Brittan Davis to accompany them as their military agent.

Turkey Creek had pine trees and crystal clear running water. Mule Deer and Elk, as well as a number tasty smaller animals, were bountiful. The summer was very mild with afternoon monsoon rains.

Gatewood wrote several letters to General Crook expressing his concern about intent of the Chiricahua.

Alchesay and the other White Mountain leaders were furious. The very thought of Chiricahua residing on White Mountain land was intolerable.

During August 1884, Gatewood was approached by F. M. Zuck about constructing a stage station on the White Mountain

Reservation between Holbrook and Fort Apache. Zuck already possessed a number of government contracts for mail delivery. Gatewood examined the concept, determined that the stage passed through the proposed building site at midnight and was not necessary.

Zuck appealed to General Crook. Crook overruled his Military Commandant and granted permission for the station.

By September, Zuck requested that Gatewood set the price to be paid to the White Mountain Apaches for cutting and hauling hay. Gatewood told him he had to negotiate directly with the tribe. Zuck vehemently opposed formal recognition of a tribal government and he viewed this as a step in that direction.

Gatewood did not bend. Zuck and his partner, Joseph Kay, met with Pedro and his sons. Kay was a well-liked Mormon trader with a flawless reputation. Satisfied, Gatewood attended and brought Conley and Severiano to interpret.

An arrangement was reached. All agreed it seemed fair.

That evening over dinner, he told Georgie, "I felt everyone worked in good faith. Then, as I was leaving the courtroom, I saw Zuck and Kay visiting with Holy Charlie. I met Holy Charlie when I first arrived at Fort Wingate. I do not trust the man."

"Perhaps it was just a chance meeting." Georgie said.

"It seemed a serious conversation."

At the end of the first season the White Mountain Apache filed a suit against Zuck and Kay alleging the hay contract had been violated.

Gatewood kept jurisdiction before the Military Commandant's Court although it would have been easy to pass the case to the Territorial Court. The evidence was clear that Zuck and Kay were attempting to pay the tribe about ten percent of the agreed upon price. In fact, they harvested more hay than agreed and had sold a considerable amount of the hay to the Army at a price higher than anticipated.

Old Jack Conley and Severiano were interpreters for the Court. As was his custom, Old Jack next to Gatewood's table. This case brought on a case of fidgets worse than his usual motion.

He took his soft rags and cleaned and polished on his Navy Colt while listening carefully to the testimony and interpreting it.

The trail went on and the court room filled with White Mountain Apaches. Many more were milling around outside the building, word as to the progress of the proceedings would be passed on by those standing next to the open windows.

"Georgie, we have drawn quite a gathering. It would make a brush arbor revivalist back home proud. Many I recognize, many I don't."

"Who do you know?"

"Alchesay, Goso, Poco, and Quilo are inside. Oh, Petone was there today."

A glint hit Georgie's eyes, "Charles, I would like to send some him some tea."

He smiled and hugged his wife. He turned to Junior and said, "Your mommy likes rascals." Charles loved his wife.

Petone's stone face fractured with pleasure when he received the tea. "Mrs. Honorable Bay'che my friend." He was proud of his tea and her remembrance.

After three days of trial, Gatewood ruled in favor of the White Mountain Apache.

Kay abruptly leaped from the table and angrily voicing his objections toward the bench. He wasn't objecting to the correctness of the ruling but that it was purely racial.

Old Jack saw this as a hostile move. Kay had not gotten his objections out before he was looking down the barrel of Old Jack's Colt. Gatewood's gavel and Old Jack's common sense quickly calmed the situation but not before Kay, to his great embarrassment, wet his pants.

Order restored, Gatewood took his seat, got a deep breath and thought "Oh, Georgie is going to love this."

"The Court will be advised of our intention to file an appeal to the Territorial Court."

Gatewood noted the intent and banged his gavel. The courtroom cleared of red-faced businessmen who never dreamed losing a case to an Indian was possible and of jubilant, optimistic White Mountain Apaches.

FIFTEEN

GOODBYE TO TURKEY CREEK

ON MAY 17, 1885, THE CHIRICAHUA broke away from Turkey Creek. Geronimo, Naiche and Mangus were believed to be at the core of the outbreak, they were all three missing.

General Crook assigned two companies of the Fourth Cavalry posted at Wingate and Lieutenant Jim Parker's A Troop of the Sixth Cavalry from Apache in pursuit. He placed Captain Allen Smith of the Fourth in command.

Crook reluctantly gave full authority to Gatewood to quickly assemble a group of White Mountain scouts and pursuit of the renegades. Gatewood quickly found and contracted Alchesay. Goso, Kuruk, Poco Lizard and Quilo contracted. Sergeant Mose at Fort Apache volunteered and gathered Dark Moon and Slippery Knife.

Surgeon Dorsey McPherson, over the strong objections of his wife, joined the party. He started to create some explanation about it being his job, but then he just blurted, "The chase is addictive. The elephant is addictive."

Unintentionally overhearing the next door departure, Georgie stepped on the porch of 103.

Ida looked at her and asked, "Georgie, what in the Hell is he talking about."

Georgie retrieved a handkerchief from her front dress pocket and handed it to Ida. Ida wiped her eyes. Then, Georgie answered, "My mother told me that a man had questions that could only be answered when he was young. If the questions are left unanswered, they fester in doubt and they will become vinegary old men."

"All men?"

"Ida, I don't believe so. But I believe it true for the men we chose to be our husbands." Bea Cruse joined them. She was approaching four months pregnant, the most poorly kept secret at Fort Apache.

From the porch, they could see the scouts milling about the scout quarters.

The lead scout command departed.

Ida asked, "How do you do this?"

Georgie responded, "I send him off with a kiss any man would want to come home to. Then I pray often until he is back at our door."

Bea said, "Pray all the time. I get angry with Tom, angry with God but I get most angry with me."

They watched the dust until the wind carried the last grains from sight. Georgie stood up and said, "Ida, what I don't know is how wives live in Tucson or Prescott. I know I belong here."

Charles Junior, napping on pallet on the front porch, stirred and sat up. Georgie said, "Ahh, there is my sweet little man."

Knowing they must move quickly to have any hope of find the path of the hostiles escape route, they made quick time toward the area of Alchesay's projected path. Bay'che knew Geronimo had his escape route well planned. He would be reluctant to alter it unless forced.

However, Captain Smith had been instructed to proceed cautiously during the first night, fearing that haste would bring him into an ambush. Days past and Smith continued to proceed at a measured pace. Bay'che often found his command closer to the hostiles than to Captain Smith's command.

Some of Smith's officers began to feel that Smith was in no hurry to find the hostiles. Smith became concerned that about the distance between his column and his most skilled scouts. He ordered them back closer.

Aware of the proximity of the White Mountain scouts, Geronimo and Naiche did as the Nootahah had done since times of legends, they begin to split off into small groups and blend into the landscape.

After four hard days, near Devil's River, smaller canyon with ample water and with the walls of the Mogollon Rim towering above them. Smith called a halt to rest and regroup.

Alchesay eased up to Gatewood and McPherson. Lieutenant Parker from the Sixth joined them.

Gatewood and Alchesay had their glasses out and were scouring the canyon walls, looking for anything that might be the least out of place.

"What do you think?" Parker inquired.

McPherson always available with an opinion offered, "I think we are traveling awful slow. I'm certain somebody has a reason."

Smith and Lieutenant Lockett approached.

Captain Smith issued orders, "Lieutenant Gatewood, take your men and reconnoiter deeper into the canyon. Lieutenant Parker, you are in charge for while. Lockett and I are going to take a bath in the creek." And they left.

Alchesay took Goso and Kuruk up into the canyon with him.

Dorsey asked, "Sergeant, when you're up stream just a bit will you and your friends take a big piss in the water."

They never turned around but they received the message.

Gatewood removed his hat and gave it spinning toss under a nearby tree. He followed the hat and sat down. He took the round stone from his front pocket and began to seek its wisdom.

Parker and McPherson followed him.

"I guess there is no glory in catching hostiles until they have had a chance to make a big dust up or two."

The trio went quiet.

The canteen filled with fresh cool stream water tasted exquisite. It did not taste of stale mud and dust, it tasted of water. Gatewood washed down the last bit of Georgie's soda cracker and was preparing to chew some jerky.

The reports of rifles rang from the upper reaches of the canyon walls, firing straight down into the men camped along the west bank and into the pack train. Parker seemed to explode upright. A voice yelled, "Gather the herd."

An angry Parker bolted downhill and shouted louder, "Fuck the herd, get your rifles!" "Find cover and return fire!" He stumbled and rolled several yards and bounced to his feet in the creek. He squared and levered three quick shots toward a puff of smoke. Then, Parker snatched a trooper who was wondering as if he was confused and tripped him making him fall into to Devil's Creek. The cold water brought the man to his senses and Parker's boot sent him sailing toward the bank to cover.

Those closer heard Parker said, "Get a rifle and start shooting at the smoke or by damn I'll start firing at you." The trooper responded.

In the middle of a fifty foot wide canyon, Parker's words rallied his command into the fight, bouncing among his men between reports of rifles.

Bay'che whipped out his glasses and began to scan the rim. From his angle telltale rifle smoke gave away the positions of the hostiles. The most intense fire was coming from behind the rock outcroppings just under the rim before the canyon became a sheer vertical cliff.

Bay'che turned to Alchesay saying, "Same set as Black Knife. This time we are not going to let them vanish in the smoke."

Alchesay gave that curt nod of agreement.

"I only see two paths back to the rim from where they are," he said, handing Alchesay his glasses. "You see?"

After a prudent scan, Alchesay handed the glasses back and said, "Two paths."

"We'll take McPherson and Mose with us, send Quilo with a note to Lieutenant Parker to fire everything he's got when our scouts start firing on their positions up canyon and above the hostiles."

"Bay'che, Sergeant Mose can command the scouts here. We take Kuruk."

"Yes." Bay'che knew it had only to do with perception. Mose needed to regain the full respect he deserved, wiping away lingering doubts from Cibicue Creek.

In his note, he directly referred to Sergeant Mose's scouts.

The four made their way up to the rim, found a spot they could quickly move into the cover of thick junipers and scrub brush. They carefully worked into the rocks and larger junipers just off the hostiles' campsite. Alchesay gauged eight to ten warriors, a raiding party since there were no women or children.

Using the time they topped the rim as his guide, Mose and his men started to fire on the position and close ground. Then, better than could ever be hoped for, Parker's troopers unleashed a volley of fire. The organized fire of sixty troopers sent rock fragments and bullet ricochets all over the hostiles. Parker then sent ten troopers across the stream, up canyon and ten more across stream and down canyon, so the hostiles could see them. He then let loose another round of volley fire.

Parker's ploy sent the hostiles scrambling for the rim. Mose stood up and shot the first man into the clear and then kneeled behind the cover of the rocks and watched the man roll off the ledge.

Four men topped the rim, rolled out the fire from below. One sprinted toward the horses, McPherson's first shot took his leg from under him, Kuruk's shot tore his shoulder away. Two hostiles seeing Kuruk's smoke rushed him, Bay'che hit one in the chest and Alchesay gut shot the second. The remaining three surrendered.

"Prisoners can't slow us down this trip."

"Let Mose take them in."

Desiring no more surprises, Alchesay, Bay'che and McPherson found a spot on the rim and surveyed the canyon with their glasses.

Dorsey saw Captain Smith and Lieutenant Lockett coming out of the willows. They had been cut off or maybe just chose to miss the fight.

"Assholes!" Alchesay was enjoying his newly acquired term of disrespect.

The firefight at Devil's River Canyon concluded more satisfactorily than Black Knife had.

"Damn!" Gatewood stirred and grunted to suppress any more natural sound of pain.

Gatewood's companions realized he couldn't get up from his seat on the rim. He rolled over, got a knee under him and was placing his Winchester as a brace when Alchesay extended his hand. Gatewood hesitated. Then, he took the aid.

His first movements were awkward and stiff. With each step he took, his movement improved. The pain did not leave.

Dorsey knew his friend was being overtaken by the pain in his joints.

When reports were written, Smith and Lockett omitted the fact that they were not directly involved in the firefight. Lockett did submit that he was cut off from the company by hostiles although no one else saw hostiles in the canyon floor. Neither wrote that they concluded the fight smelling of soap.

Gatewood and McPherson were direct, stating they saw the pair coming from upstream after the clash was concluded. All the others simply made no note of seeing them during the battle.

All commended Lieutenant Parker and Lieutenant Gatewood. Most made note of Sergeant Mose and his performance.

Captain Allen Smith decided that this was going to a long, drawn out campaign. He communicated this to General Crook. Crook was prone to constant, grinding pursuit. This suited him just fine. He did not want to be hasty and read in the eastern newspapers of Crook's Massacre or any other such thing.

When a writer suggested that once again Lieutenant C. B. Gatewood and his scouts had conceived and executed the master plan for victory at Devil's Canyon as the firefight grew toward a major battle, old competitive resentments reared their ugly head.

The disgruntled Crook assigned Gatewood to return to Fort Apache and recruit two hundred Apache scouts for the upcoming campaign. While Crook believed Gatewood's hay decision was correct, he just didn't need the misery it created. Further he needed the support of the locals, not their anger and distrust. If Easterners make Gatewood a hero, it could become even more problematic.

Knowing Geronimo was long into Mexico by now, Gatewood was sent home. Alchesay, Kuruk and the others who were volunteers and not enlisted at the time returned to Fort Apache. Surgeon McPherson simply accompanied them.

A week later Gatewood received orders. He was to remain at Fort Apache in his role as Military Commandant as well as administrator of the reservation. At a date in the near future, he was to report to Fort Whipple, near the Territorial Capital of Prescott, and would be on the staff of General Crook. The absence of any mention of promotion or the intent to promote made the purpose clear to Gatewood.

The formal message included a handwritten note from General Crook stating that the Arizona Territorial Court had overturned his ruling in the Zuck-Kay matter. Stating his concern for Gatewood's safety and that of his family, he thought the transfer to be expedient. However, he valued his unmatched knowledge of the Apache and did not want to transfer him from the territory. Quarters above his rank of First Lieutenant would be reserved for his family. In the meanwhile, Crook recommended that Gatewood insure his safety and that of his family to the extent possible.

Kuruk's bear claw walking stick became Gatewood's constant companion. After much practice and Georgie's assistance in their quarters, he assured himself of getting up with ease and no telltale wobbles. The bear claw stick became a plaything he enjoyed. Georgie exaggerated the extent of her irritation when he would reach out and lift the tail of her dress.

Thomas Cruse and Augustus Blocksom were placed in command of the scouts.

By the fall of 1885, Crook was convinced that Geronimo was deep in Mexico. He constructed something of a picket line near the border, stationing troops with scouts at every identified source of water. He realized that the border was far too vast to really be effective but it played with the locals. The local newspapers were constantly criticizing the troops and especially their commanders. Crook felt he needed time and Geronimo would make a mistake.

Geronimo was equally convinced that for his band to survive and prosper the family unit had to be restored. Especially, the women and children had rescued and brought to Mexico.

On September 22, 1885, Geronimo acted.

Walter Reed, headed home for lunch, stopped to visit the Military Commandant.

"Well, I hear Old Geronimo slipped in and stole one of his wives and their daughter night before last."

"I'm betting he's just started. He came for his wives and kids, will make a sweep of Coyotero land. The General has authorized a company of Coyoteros to protect the Mogollon District," Gatewood advised. "I recommended Tom command."

"Keep that new daddy safe and sound."

When Tom Cruse heard the news, he was grateful for the decision he and Bea had made. Bea returned to Owensburg, Kentucky to have their child. Fred Taylor Cruse was born in February, 1886. The wives of Fort Apache waited with anticipation for his spring time arrival. These ladies were skilled at waiting, busying themselves as the time passed.

"Seems most of the Coyotero bucks are already scouts."

"Yes." Gatewood paused, "Too many small bands are just women and children with old men to watch over them." He thought more, "Geronimo not here to kill, he is here to capture. But Ulzana and maybe Naiche are here to capture, kill and steal. Ulzana killed everything in his path in the Florida Mountains over in New Mexico a few months ago."

Itzachu now aged but once great hunter and warrior had been charged with overseeing a small village of some eight women and their children. Itzachu had no sons of his own. His son-in-laws were scouting for the white eye soldiers. His daughters and his one grandson were in the village.

He had his bow and a fifty caliber Sharps that was as old as he was. The powerful buffalo rifle had to be cocked and the trigger squeezed three times before it would fire. He had been hunting all day without success. Such a lack of success will tire the ego of an old man.

He topped the ridge that afforded an overlook of the village. His heart sank and his empty belly filled with angry. Three young women, roped together, stood in the midst of mutilated bodies. A large fire was burning in the center of the village.

His arrival could not have come at a more unfortunate time. A buck took a stone in one hand and crushed the face of his grandson and flung the limp boy into the fire. He witnessed the brutal destruction of the prize of his life, his last surviving blood relative, his only grandson.

A cold rage overwhelmed him. He found a firing angle, slid behind the rock, took several deep breaths to calm the shaking his wrath brought. Then he steadied the Sharps, sighting the man who had murdered his grandson. On the third squeeze of the trigger, the shell exploded. The old buffalo gun struck the hostile square in the heart, blowing a gaping hole in the man's back as it exited.

The raiders were staggered. A fifty caliber Sharps can destroy a man in a fashion that creates panic. The momentary confusion gave Itzachu time to reload, sight the man who seemed to be in charge and with three more squeezes of his trigger the head of young buck exploded.

By the time the hostiles figured out that they only faced one man, Itzachu had disappeared. The hostiles gathered up the three young girls and quickly left.

The old man made his way to McCrieght's by morning. He told his story. He showed McCrieght his Sharps and begged for ammunition and new spring lock. The trigger on his rifle was repaired. McCrieght gave him a new belt full of ammunition. The McCrieghts gave him some traveling food, hardtack and tortillas. He filled his canteens from the horse trough. He took his knife and placed an "x" notch on each bullet increasing its damage on impact.

He settled on his horse, an animal as aged as its rider, and extended his rifle to the sky. He said, "Watch over me until I have my revenge." He left headed southeast.

McCrieght sent Gatewood a note advising of the man and the incident. He concluded that the hostiles had made an assassin from an aged grandfather.

To the extent legend can be relied upon, Itzachu did become an assassin. He was highly skilled tracker and the tales of a periodic ambush of a Chiricahua, blown apart by a single cartridge from a big rifle. The stories made their way to Gatewood, Alchesay or McCrieght. Gatewood would observe, "The Assassin exploded another Chiricahua."

The likely exaggerated stories filtered into Fort Apache and were told on the front porches of 102 and 103. Always different yet much the same, one hostile killed with a single shot from a buffalo gun. It would occur at the most improbable of times in the most unlikely of places. The Assassin was never seen.

Then, the old man just vanished. No one ever claimed to have killed him or even heard of his death. Itzachu was just gone.

By November, Crook informed Gatewood he was to turn over management of the White Mountain Apaches to Lieutenant Lockett. The transfer was abrupt and unexpected by most, but a move Gatewood had expected was coming. The transformation occurred smoothly.

The move was not made before Gatewood, acting as Judge, fined a white man for allowing his cattle to destroy a Coyotero corn crop and gaze in his hay meadow. To most it seemed outrageous to even consider fining a white man, to Gatewood it seemed just.

The Coyoteros and the Chiricahua agreed.

Although most thought such a move without a promotion in rank was odd, most did view him as a "Crook Man." The truth was that Crook and Gatewood had regular harsh exchanges concerning the quality of life provided the Apaches. Crook was prickly at any questioning of his management of the territory. Crook was an ambitious man. He wanted to be the supreme leader of the United States Military. Only General Nelson Miles had the credentials and the ambition to challenge him.

Crook knew Gatewood had no peer in his knowledge of the Apache and he was a proven military commandant. Crook found his knowledge to be invaluable at times. Gatewood believe he was in a position to advance.

However, the Zuck-Kay matter continued to haunt Gatewood. The territorial papers labeled him as commanding a band of savages who were allowed to arrest peaceable citizens and cast them into jail.

Crook was perpetually angry with Gatewood but he did not feel he could afford to lose him. Gatewood was an anomaly he could not explain. This Lieutenant with a stern moral sense of right and wrong, yet given the pragmatism of combat he was a stone cold killer. Crook was coming to understand neither was the complete truth. He reassigned Gatewood to Fort Apache.

Zuck continued to file various and numerous criminal complaints against Gatewood in different jurisdictions. Crook washed his hands of the whole matter. Finally, a combination of a lost election, anger of the cost to the territory to pursue Zuck and Kay's personal issues rose and the assignment of a widely respected Judge brought a stop to the matter.

As a matter for local and military politics, the Zuck-Gatewood case was never settled. Gatewood's refusal to apologize to Zuck as General Crook requested would haunt him the rest of his career.

Geronimo's intrusion and the repeated raids across the border, the Department of the Army's confidence in Crook waned.

On April 2, 1886, General Nelson Appleton Miles replaced Crook. Crook's program of using Indians to fight Indians was set aside. Miles was intent on amassing troops and hounding the hostile Apache relentlessly. There were only two acceptable outcomes, unconditional surrender or total annihilation.

Miles established his headquarters in Albuquerque. In quick order he had six thousand troops on the border. Following a hastily negotiation, Miles was sending patrols across the border and deep into the Mexican wilderness refuges of the Apaches.

At Miles insistence, Congress authorized a twenty-five thousand dollar reward for Geronimo, killed or captured.

Gatewood was ordered to Fort Wingate to recruit and train two hundred Navajo scouts. Miles, a Massachusetts man, viewed Gatewood as a Virginian, both "Crook Man" and "Crook's outcast" and too empathic toward Apache rights, a man Miles just needed to keep away from the conflict but keep close for now. He just didn't know what to do with him. Miles knew this; he did not intend to fail. He would keep any man who might prove useful nearby.

"Ah, Mr. McCrieght, I'll have an officer's whiskey."

"Well, Lieutenant Gatewood, how did your men drill today?"

"Tolerable. I believe they might track well if their rifles would arrive. For now they drill with genuine US Army issue sticks, but the sticks don't shoot real straight."

They both laughed.

"Have ya heard from that lovely Irish thing ya tricked into marrying ya?"

Georgie was very pregnant when he left her at Fort Stanton. Gatewood answered, "Her sister, Nannie, is staying with her. Georgie's last letter said she was well. She said the ladies of Stanton and her sister were suffocating her with care and kindness. Still, she pines for Mrs. Sergeant Thomas."

Mrs. McCrieght interrupted with enthusiasm, "What a wonderful mid-wife that woman is!" Then, she added, "Just a truly gentle woman."

"Guess ya heard the new man sent about fifty Chiricahua prisoners to Florida day 'fore yesterday?"

"Yes, Nana and Josanie were among them." Gatewood advised, adding, "I suspect they are just the first."

As their visit was concluding, Mrs. McCrieght said, "Charles, do not worry about Georgie. Army wives have been having their babies with their men away since there has been an army."

She smiled, almost giggled and finished, "Charles, your presence is only required for the conception. We can pretty much do the rest without you."

Her husband laughed and swatted her leg.

Gatewood rose, steadying himself with the chair. He had become expert at concealing the grimace that often came after being seated. He swung his bear claw stick as if he never needed it and said, "I enjoyed the whiskey and as always I enjoyed the conversation."

Gatewood walked back across the parade ground toward the officer's mess. His pain dulled his appetite but he would eat. Then, take the prescribed dose of Dorsey's brew and a couple of slips of willow bark powder. Eastern physicians had tried to give him considerable opium tonics but they never set well with him.

Dorsey's creative concoctions were the most effective. Those things and some good Tennessee sipping whiskey on occasion brought sleep.

He acquired a little more of a taste for the broiled meat, whatever its origin. But tonight he really would like to have rattlesnake cooked on a spit by Poco Lizard.

On April 13, 1886, Hugh McCullough Gatewood was born to Georgia and Charles Gatewood in Fort Stanton, New Mexico. A telegram from his sister-in-law announced the birth.

Boy – stop – Both well – stop. Nannie.

In two weeks, a melancholy took full grasp of him. Gatewood was a lonely man and made his feelings clear. "I can find no pleasure in going to bed alone and waking up alone."

Gatewood felt he seen his last combat assignment, was struggling to make financial ends meet on a First Lieutenant's pay. He requested a leave to go visit his family in Fort Stanton. The leave was granted.

He left his Navajo scouts well drilled and unarmed. They would never be armed or sent into the field.

Charles Junior returned to Frostburg, Maryland with Nannie, so that Georgie could care for Hugh's needs and regain her own health.

Fort Stanton had a sense of permanency to it. The officer's quarters had four room of nice size. The sanitary facilities offered privacy and even cleanliness rarely found on frontier posting. It was close to the pines and was in perhaps the only cool spot in southern New Mexico during the summer months.

He saw Georgie and feared the worst. The birth had been exceptionally difficult. Hugh was healthy but frail. Georgie was pale, having lost considerable blood during the delivery. Confusing to Charles, her skin seemed so loose in places, yet she looked so thin.

"Oh my God, Georgie, I did not know," his voice softened and he shook his head in disbelief.

"Charles, I am so happy you're here. I've felt so alone. It has been worst time of my life without my very best friend. I've missed you, I've missed you."

His arms engulfed her. The bear claw stick clattered on the floor as he dropped it. They hugged. Both a little embarrassed by the tears that swelled and wet the others cheek. They became lost in the embrace.

Neither could tell you how long the embrace lasted. It seemed forever, shutting out the rest of the world, yet it felt that it ended far too soon.

"Come see your son." It was as if she unexpectedly felt the world be right again. She took his hand, waiting for him to retrieve his stick and they walked to the cradle.

Holding the tiny infant touched his soul in a fashion only fatherhood had been able to touch him. "Georgie, my Georgie, what a wondrous gift you have given us."

He rocked his son and talked to his wife. Her fingers found his shoulders when she passed. Her words were not as significant as the sound of her voice. Charles was felt at home, he soaked.

Georgie's recovery would still be slow and arduous but they were together. Georgie knew she was improving, slowly regaining her strength. Soreness was no longer attacking her every movement. Her sadness subsided.

The kisses exchanged with her husband now had a soft gentleness to them. To awaken next to her husband, feeling placid warmth as the scent of the pines drifted through the open window secured her. As she dozed in the early mornings, Charles always had enjoyed kissing her neck. While she never understood it, but she knew he found something very pleasant in the bouquet of morning.

After about a week, she awoke to find him aroused yet quite asleep. She whispered, "Soon, my love, very soon." She did not move away from him. She found an odd reassurance that somehow she had aroused her sleeping husband. A smile came followed by a deep sigh. She snuggled close to him. She dozed.

A package from with a return address in Georgetown, New Mexico written over an original Philadelphia return address arrived. The contents had been closely examined and it appeared one copy had been removed. The package contained a gift for Hugh, a copy of Mark Twain's recently published <u>The Adventures of Huckleberry Finn</u>. The note was to the point.

To Baby Gatewood,

I believe every child should have a fine book to mark their birth. Throughout your life you will hold this book and remember those who mattered to you.

Congratulations,

John Magruder

P.S. Tell your parents I extend my invitation to accompany you on some future visit to Georgetown.

Tears came to the corners of Georgie's eyes. She blinked and closed her eyes, fighting them away.

"It is comforting to know there is a person here who holds books in such high esteem, a person who thinks about the continuity of literature and life. It is a special gift."

"And he has a wonderful porch," Charles added. He put his arm around his wife and kissed her forehead.

"Lieutenant Gatewood, I love you."

Captain Henry Lawton

SIXTEEN

FIND GERONIMO

JUST AFTER THE INDEPENDENCE DAY celebration at Fort Stanton, General Miles summoned Gatewood to his headquarters in Albuquerque.

"What do you suppose he wants of you?" Georgie asked.

"Well, I know it is not because he desires my company." Charles smiled.

"You just come back here. Hugh and I appreciate you greatly." Georgie grew serious, "Charles, I hope he does not ask you to take on a long campaign."

"Georgie, I feel out of touch. I don't know what to expect."

In the six years since the arrival of the rails of the Atchison, Topeka and the Santa Fe, the railroad effectively putting an end to the almost half century dependence on the Santa Fe Trail as the major pathway for freight transportation. Albuquerque had grown into a center of commerce since its establishment in 1701. Now it boomed.

Miles stated that he preferred being closer to the conflict than Fort Whipple. He also favored Albuquerque's lifestyle, offering a suite of rooms in a fine hotel, nice steakhouses and quality entertainment.

On July 13, 1886, Gatewood presented himself at General Miles offices.

Gatewood was impressed with the fine leather furniture, leather chairs that allowed a man to sink into them. It had been some time since he had seen such luxury.

"Well, well, Lieutenant Gatewood. Come in and have a seat."

Miles offered him a cigar, he declined and the General fired one up.

"Lieutenant Gatewood, take off your jacket," he was in the midst of removing his as he spoke. The two men sat in two large chairs that afforded a view of the main street of Albuquerque. They sat eye to eye and only a few feet between them.

"Lieutenant, I wish to be straight with about this. I know you supported Crook's plan of solving the Apache problem. I also know that you got into a fight in a bar in Prescott because you spoke out in support of my approach. I was never unaware of these things. When you took that Bowie knife of yours and pinned his hand to the bar, I could have been quite punitive. But I felt the Zuck matter was punitive enough."

Miles thought a moment, drew a large puff of the cigar and tapped the ashes into a large ashtray.

"Now if you'd used that Bowie knife on that man instead of defending my Apache strategy, I'd been more grateful. Zuck and that Mormon friend of his, Kay, are stealing the White Mountain Apache blind. On the other hand, I still do not understand why you refused to sign the papers that allowed me use enlisted men to keep up my home in Prescott. Now perhaps I enjoy my comforts too much, but I felt you were being unnecessarily abrasive about the situation. Let me restate that. You can just be one pig headed son-of-a-bitch."

There was a knock at the door.

"Yes."

"General, your special order is here."

"Excellent, bring it in."

An aged Sergeant with three rockers on his arm came through in the door. He reached inside the poke he was carrying and retrieved a bottle of whiskey.

"Two bottles of fine Tennessee sipping whiskey Sir," he said and smiled.

"Pour us two glasses but first sample it and see if it is what the dealer said."

He poured a small sip. General Miles said, "Sergeant, now get enough of a taste that you are certain."

"Yes Sir."

Drinks served, the Sergeant left the two men alone in the room again. Miles watched the Sergeant slowly depart.

Miles voice lost the informative authoritarian tone it had carried as he said, "Sergeant Stetson has been with me since Antietam." He stopped. He had volunteered all the personal information he cared to acknowledge.

"Lieutenant Gatewood, I understand you are a man who appreciates fine Tennessee whiskey."

"I am Sir. Thank you."

Miles extended the glass and toasted, "To the venture you do not yet know about."

"That Sir is fine Tennessee whiskey."

"Lieutenant, Geronimo and Naiche are in Mexico. I want you to carry an offer of terms to Geronimo. You will have little latitude to negotiate. President Cleveland is unbending about this. It is to unconditional surrender. They have his word they will not be executed for any past crime. It is most likely the leaders and their families will be sent to Florida for two years."

Miles took another sip and wished Gatewood was not so comfortable with silence.

Miles voice became more personal, more direct, "Gatewood, you are by far the best qualified man for this task. You would not have been my first choice. But Crawford got himself killed in Mexico and Britton Davis resigned his commission. So, by default I have to send the best man."

Gatewood broke his silence, "Sir, it sounds as if you are asking me to deliver an ultimatum to men who do not receive such demands well."

"Yes," General Miles paused and then continued, "I believe the message must be delivered accurately by a man they trust, a man whose council they will believe."

"What if they reject the ultimatum?"

"My order is clear. There will not be another offer. We are to hunt them into extinction."

Gatewood's thumb and right index finger found the corners of his mouth. He made a thoughtful movement as if pulling his mouth tighter.

"May I ask the General for another taste of his fine Tennessee whiskey?"

"My pleasure and I think I will join you."

They drank. The General offered his congratulations on the birth of his son. They spoke of children and families.

"General, it seemed as if I received a direct order, but may I say I accept," Gatewood said. "I'll need the best interpreter I can find and two or three good scouts."

"I hired two scouts, Kateah and Martine."

"I know Kateah, he was with Britton Davis and is a good tracker. Martine, I only know he is Kateah's good friend. I'd like to find George Wratten to interpret."

"You'll stage out of Fort Bowie. I'll see that Mr. Wratten is there. What else might you need?"

"The best riding mule in the territory."

Miles laughed. Maybe it was the Tennessee whiskey or maybe he genuinely liked Gatewood. "Son, in the field with your scouts, you have no peer, you're a superb administrator, and you can be a colossal pain in my ass."

Gatewood laughed. "I thank you for the former. And I know you're correct about the latter."

Miles stepped to his desk and signed two pieces of paper. He returned to his seat.

"These are you orders for this mission. The second sheet appoints you as my Aide-de-Camp upon your return."

Finally, Gatewood had his ladder to climb the ranks.

In a stroke of good fortune, George Wratten was in Albuquerque. Wratten had worked at the San Carlos trading post during Gatewood's tenure as Military Commandant of the White Mountain Reservation. He had made every effort to learn the Apache language, both the White Mountain dialect and the Chiricahua dialect. Alchesay claimed Wratten spoke and understood their language better than any other white man.

He now worked for the Army as an interpreter.

Gatewood explained the mission to Wratten to which Wratten responded, "It seems ta me ya been sent on a fool's errand."

"I know that. But I know fool's like us are the only one's who have a chance to succeed," Gatewood said.

"Ya still carry ya lucky rock?"

"Yes."

"That does make me feel some better," George said, "I'll travel to Bowie with ya. Ya still riding mules."

"Yes. Leaving tomorrow."

Gatewood spent the evening in Old Albuquerque's nicest hotel. He didn't want to tangle with the smells of stock yards near the newer buildings.

He sat at a hotel desk and wrote Georgie a three page letter. It was sent by courier the next day with General Miles correspondence to Fort Stanton. The Adjutant personally delivered the letter to Georgie.

The letter bared the soul of the man Georgie had married. His dreams, his fears, his ambitions but mostly importantly his passions, his love for Georgie and their children were written with a scratchy hotel pen on three sheets of paper. She never allowed that letter to read by another and it was never far from her.

A friend noted that even the Declaration of Independence was not so well guarded nor so treasured.

Fort Bowie

Fort Bowie sat on a piece of flat desert ground in far southeastern Arizona, encircled by rocky barren mountains. In many ways it appeared a military installation in a setting difficult to defend and vulnerable to siege. In another war, in another era, it probably was precisely that but Apache was not prone to siege warfare.

Fort Bowie in July was torturously hot. The mountains to the west blocked the sun earlier in the evening allowing some relief, but relief is a relative term. The night time temperatures rarely dropped into the eighties.

George Wratten and Lieutenant Gatewood had renewed their acquaintance on the trip from Albuquerque. Wratten encouraged Gatewood to talk to familiarize himself with Gatewood's manners of speech. Exact interpretation with the correct inflection was going to be critical if this mission was to succeed.

"George, I hadn't been in the territory long when I ask if you ever got use to the heat. The answer I got was no but a man could get use to being hot."

"Lieutenant, I've never lived anywhere but here. I know I'd rather have summer duty up in the pine trees and rain storms."

Gatewood laughed. If nothing else, the heat had been easy on his pains.

Martine and Kateah, who had scouted with Britton Davis, arrived two days before them. The men had been boyhood friends and both had relatives with the hostiles.

Frank Huston with three pack mules joined the small party as the packer. Just before they left "Old Tex" Whaley, a local rancher, was hired as a courier and to help with the good riding mules. Everyone had a good mule and two extras were secured.

To the extent possible, Gatewood outfitted the men to appear as a peace commission and not a war party. While they sought to deliver a peace offer to Geronimo and Naiche, there were many other groups ranging from bandits to Mexican irregulars to hard case men seeking the lucrative reward on Geronimo's head.

While it is likely he would rather have had his Coyotero scouts, he was now satisfied with his small party. General Miles orders stated that he was to secure an escort of twenty-five troopers from the garrison at Cloverdale on the Mexican Border. Gatewood strongly felt that a party of that size could never approach Geronimo's camp to talk. He hoped to manipulate his way around the order.

Gatewood and his five men arrived on a bluff near Cloverdale on July 18. Gatewood stopped and dismounted. Through his glasses he assessed Cloverdale. The corral contained no more than ten broken down old cavalry horses and a few mule teams. Cloverdale had declined considerably since he passed through last.

"Well, I'll be. I think I know that officer!" A rather surprised Gatewood continued, "George we might just have some good fun here."

Gatewood's group eased their way down into Cloverdale.

With all the dignity and pomp a man can muster for the task, Gatewood dismounted his mule.

"I'm seeking Captain John Stretch. I have direct orders for him from General Nelson Appleton Miles," Gatewood spoke with all the authority he could muster.

A surprised Corporal leaped to his feet and saying, "Yes, Sir. I find him immediately."

George whispered, "I believe the Corporal thinks you are the damned General himself." Holding no abiding love for the military, Old Tex was really enjoying the act.

Captain Stretch appeared from the shaded area of an abandoned building.

Gatewood adjusted the brim of his hat, further shading his face.

Captain Stretch shaded his eyes from the bright sun with his right hand, trying to see the officer he was walking toward. Before he could get a clear view, Gatewood distracted his eyes by extending the paper and saying, "Captain, your orders directly from General Miles."

Stretch read the orders, looked back at Gatewood. He said, "Screw you, Gatewood. I don't have twenty five men who can walk to the edge of town."

A good natured laughter broke out between the men. Gatewood placed his arm around Stretch and introduced him to his five men.

"Captain John Stretch was the most practical instructor I had a West Point. And just as importantly, he sat the finest table on the banks of the Hudson River."

Stretch's rotund frame belied the man's pugilistic skills. On closer inspection, his two hands appeared as two cured Virginia hams attached to ends of his muscular arms. As a young man he had been most formidable prize fighter. The man loved fine food, fine whiskey and a fist fight.

"Lieutenant, tonight we will eat well."

Of all the unknowns of the New Mexico territory, how John Stretch placed a spread of beefsteak so tender it could be cut with a fork, boiled corn left on the cob and boiled red potatoes with hot dinner breads baked in the brick oven of an abandoned café on a table in Cloverdale, New Mexico places among the great mysteries.

The sun had set, lamps were lit. While George Wratten joined this officer's mess along with two Lieutenants from Stretch's company.

"Gentlemen, your may have your choice of Kentucky whiskey or Tennessee whiskey."

Stretch's tales of his years as an instructor and prize fighter provided the after dinner entertainment. The laughter was as full bodied as the whiskey.

Gatewood and Stretch knew there was no way twenty five men of the Tenth U.S. Infantry could benefit Gatewood. They also agreed that Stretch didn't have twenty five men fit for duty.

Gatewood left at daybreak leaving Captain John Stretch's company to guard the border crossing at Cloverdale.

Gatewood's group headed south for the Sierra Madres. He would quickly come to believe the Sierra Madres was the most harsh, sinister and intolerant land he had encountered. The land would punish even the smallest error in judgment.

On July 21, Gatewood and his men reached Carretas, Mexico. For the past week, Gatewood's body began to again betray him. He simply made no mention of it. He suspected George had noticed his difficulty walking and that he was using his bear claw staff for stability on uneven surfaces more often. Every joint in his body ached. He felt the pain biting into his alertness and it distressed him. McPherson's elixir helped but not as it once did.

At Carretas, Lieutenant James Parker was waiting on him. Parker was to have placed the small mission on Geronimo's trail.

"Lieutenant Gatewood?"

"Yes. Lieutenant Parker I'd guess."

"Yes."

"I have to inform you that we lost Geronimo's trail. The heavy rains of two weeks ago have washed away his tracks and we have not been able to find the new track."

"Parker, would you have me return to General Miles and simply tell him there is no trail."

"No. If General Miles wants you placed on a trail, I will find a trail and put you on it."

Gatewood didn't respond. His eyes had sunken further and the skin surrounding them had darkened. The steel blue grey eyes were more pronounced. Parker knew that Gatewood intended to play no more word games.

Parker said, "Let's sit." The men settled into to chairs on the porch of a general store.

"Lieutenant Gatewood, first I'll find you a track. I'll offer you all of my command as escort if necessary."

Gatewood was rather surprised by what seemed a rapid change of positions.

Parker continued, "Let me tell you, Captain Henry Lawton is not in favor of your being here. He sees it as he has his orders to capture or kill Geronimo, Naiche and their band. He doesn't hear where treating for peace is in his orders."

"Parker, do you want me to order you to go find a trail?"

"No. I just want you to know how this all stands. My orders are to find you a trail."

Gatewood leaned back and observed, "Well, I suppose there is no glory for the ambitious in leading the folks to a peace treaty." Gatewood considered the situation and added, "Guess there is no glory for a soldier in making peace."

Parker responded, "I suppose Captain Lawton would like to be remembered as the man who ran Geronimo to ground. Man might just make a career from that."

Gatewood didn't respond.

Parker said, "I understand you know Geronimo."

"Yes. We have met."

"Will he surrender?"

"Only if he knows he can't win."

"Can he win?"

"No."

"We will have a trail soon."

Gatewood got six days of badly needed recovery time. His joints had calmed, the swelling had subsided and the dysentery had run its course. The abundance of well water seemed to heal his bladder discomfort which had made even riding his mule challenging. Resting in the hot, dry climate seemed to ease his pain.

Lieutenant Parker reported, "Gatewood, I think we have you a trail. If not it will take you near Captain Lawton's camp."

Gatewood felt Parker had more to say. He waited.

Parker said, "I will escort you as far as I can. If we find Lawton before we find the hostiles, I will follow Lawton's orders. So, I am yours until Lawton says differently."

As the party wound its way deeper into the Sierra Madres the terrain became more complicated. The boulders and cliffs became more formidable and irregular. The party climbed westward, until they intersected with the Rio Bavispe.

The Rio Bavispe reminded Gatewood of Clear Creek near Tazma's settlement and other clear water streams feeding the upper Verde River. The water was much warmer but still it raced over shallow rapids and a rocky creek bed.

No travel anywhere in the Sierra Madres was easy, but this was the easiest six days of the trip. The convoluted topography limited travel to daylight hours. The campsites were conducive for Gatewood to sleep. A bed made over rocks that had been heated during the day to the extent they were hot to the touch relaxed his aching joints. The sound of water flowing over rocks brought tranquility. It was an easy six days.

Following the water, they arrived at Captain Lawton's camp near the junction of the Rio Aros and the Rio Bavispe, some two hundred and fifty miles south of the established border with Mexico.

Captain Lawton's greeting was more cordial than Gatewood expected, but they were divided in the exact manner Parker had predicted.

Lawton had sat up a tent, a covering open on all sides, for a command post. With the help of Kuruk's walking stick, Gatewood was able to conceal his pain as he dismounted and walked toward the tent.

Lawton said, "Lieutenant, this weather is killing my bones too. Come in and take a load off."

Gatewood forced something of a laugh, "Thank you Sir."

"Coffee?"

"Please." Gatewood spotted a water barrel covered in burlap, it would be wet with stream water and the rapid evaporation from the dry air cooled the contents of the barrel. "And some of that cool water if I might."

"Certainly."

Lawton's aide quickly reappeared with both.

"Lieutenant, what brings you to this paradise in the Sierra Madre?"

Although he knew Lawton was aware, he reached inside his open blouse and withdrew his orders. He handed them to the Captain.

"Lieutenant, I'd say this puts our missions at odds with each other."

"The end result we seek is the same, no more bronco Apaches killing and stealing in the territories."

Lawton agreed. Then, he added, "But my orders are to kill Geronimo or any other Apache on sight, yours to treat peace."

"I'm quite uncertain Geronimo will agree to the terms of an unconditional surrender and be hauled off to Florida."

"Hell of deal General Miles sent you to offer the man."

Formalities faded. Coffee was shared. The water was cool.

Lawton asked, "How are you scouts?"

"Not the White Mountain scouts I had, but Martine and Kateah are skilled and they have relatives with the hostiles. With a reasonable direction, they'll get me close enough to talk to Geronimo or to get me killed. George Wratten is an exceptional interpreter, only man I know who can take English right into Apache. He knows Geronimo too. Frank has brought our mules across rough country in fine shape. Old Tex is the courier. It would be helpful to have two couriers. One courier just isn't enough."

"So you think your scouts can track them if I can tell them about where to look?"

"Yes."

"Gatewood, you don't know my scouts."

"No Sir, I don't. But you inquired about my scouts and I do know them."

The two men sat.

"Gatewood, eat with me tonight. Perhaps Lieutenant Parker and your interpreter might like to join us. We'll talk some more."

"Thank you Sir. I'm certain Mr. Wratten will be pleased to join us."

Gatewood found Martine and Kateah. All five of Gatewood's party was in the shade of something resembling a willow grove. The air had grown still and felt hot. Gatewood took a couple of steps toward a thermometer. He read it then walked over to his men.

"Say one hundred and seventeen on the thermometer, in the shade."

George said, "Early August, likely the rainy season will hear soon."

Old Tex said, "Hell man, even Texas don't get this hot."

"Don't have no rainy season either," Frank Huston responded. "Not that a Texan would know."

"Been takin' to ya damn mules to long, now ya thinkin' like'em," was Old Tex's rejoinder. "What say ya George?"

"I think the mescal hasn't left much brain in either of you." The group was in a good humor.

Looking directly at Martine and Kateah, Gatewood said, "I told the Captain that if you had a trail you could track it."

Both scouts nodded their heads. Kateah spoke, "But monsoon come soon."

The sky over the western mountains darkened and then it darkened again. Gatewood thought he had seen black skies over the Mogollon Rim but this was as black he hadn't seen.

Martine said, "We should sleep on high ground." Kateah seconded the suggestion.

Just before nightfall, large bolts of lightning followed by deafening claps of thunder. The thunder seemed to shake everything in the canyon. In the dim light of pre-dark, the line of rain could be seen making its way from the mountain peaks. The rain approached in steady tantalizing wall. It rolled in, first the wind and then the sky opened and the water poured.

Gatewood's half dozen were increasing grateful they had made their camp on much higher ground. Rivulets begin to flow down the canyon walls, each cutting its own small gulley filled with water rushing toward the Rio Aras.

The morning sky broke clear but the pattern of the murky sky turning to lightening and the thunder followed by another heavy rain that lasted until shortly after midnight. In the pitch black night, you could hear the water gushing down the river, rolling boulders made the most ominous and unfamiliar of sounds.

Daybreak revealed a wild running river where a short time ago a clear mountain stream had ambled along a bed of gravel.

Gatewood's mules were secure and supplies relatively dry. Frank Huston's knowledge and instincts would make some hard days ahead more tolerable.

Beneath the tarp, Gatewood had an unhurried visit with Kateah and Martine.

"If we just struck out on our own, what are the chances we can find Geronimo on our own?"

Martine spoke up first, "Rain will have washed any tracks, they travel they leave sign. Find faster with two hundred eyes rather than eight eyes."

Kateah said, "Has made good camp, wait until monsoons and horrible hot pass."

Gatewood reached back to an early lesson, "He won't want to raid near his camp, so he'll send braves or maybe squaws to Mexican village to trade."

Gatewood had made a question sound like a statement but George heard the question and answered, "It makes Chiricahua sense. Plus looking at the men here, I'd say Geronimo and Naiche's men are hungry, wounded and exhausted. Need a rest." George stopped to consider his own words.

Gatewood looked at the soldiers. Their shirts were threadbare and ragged, the canvas pants were patched. Hats ranged from straw sombreros to cavalry issued floppy brimmed hats. There was little uniform left to identify them.

The extreme heat closed in after the rain, the sun scorched every exposed inch and the wind carried heat like it had just been released from a blast furnace in an Allegheny iron mill. The food became rancid.

The storms gave Lawton and Gatewood time to devise an agreement that more resembled an agreement to disagree. In principle, they agreed that General Miles had sent two men into the field with conflicting orders. Surgeon Leonard Wood was Lawton's second in command. He sat in on most of the discussions.

Lawton said, "I do not know why General Miles sent us on such opposite missions. I only know he did. I do consider my orders to have come from President Cleveland."

Gatewood countered, "Lawton, you know as well as I do General Miles has made up his mind. He wants Geronimo's unconditional surrender."

In basic agreement, the discussion was ended. Surgeon Wood said, "I would like to speak with Lieutenant Gatewood concerning another matter."

The two took quick shelter in Wood's tent, next to a sizeable medical shelter.

"Lieutenant, Walt Reed tells me you might be need of some medical assistance now. If you're not, your appearance fooled the hell right of me. How long have you not been able to stand straight?"

"Gets better, field is tough. Yes, my knees and ankles are painful. Dorsey McPherson prepares a tonic of God only knows what, but it helps a lot. Not as much as it used to but it helps a lot."

Wood carefully examined Gatewood's limbs and spine.

"God damn man, you are eaten up with what ever kind of rheumatism has taken hold of you. You're joints are full of some kind of inflammation but I don't know what kind."

"Reed and McPherson tell me that and some doctors they sent me to see in Virginia. Nobody seems to know what to do for it."

"I hate to tell you, but I'm like the rest of them," Wood said obviously befuddled. "Tell you what I am able to do, I can spare two bottles of strong brandy mixed with some medicinal powders for you. Good big swigs before you try to rest. The willow bark powder is now in tablets, call it aspirin, take four tablets when you need them. They will set better with food."

Then, almost as the Gatewood group had prophesied, one of Lawton's Mexican spies reported that several squaws known to be with Geronimo's band were seen leaving the village of Fronteras, the northeast of Lawton's present site.

Lawton and Gatewood agreed that Gatewood would make a forced march overnight toward Fronteras. Using the wagon trails that weren't washed out reasonable time could be made during the night, avoiding the oppression that came with daylight. Even during darkest early morning hours, the temperature remained in the nineties.

Gatewood's party of five added six troopers hand picked by Lieutenant Parker and left immediately. They pushed hard that night and into the next day. Men and mules were exhausted when they found shade along the Rio Moctezuma.

Gatewood's soreness was continually increasing. Every joint seemed to be racked with pain. Wood's concoction was effective but seemed to drown his senses limiting the quantity he was willing to take.

Speaking to George Wratten, Gatewood said, "I calculate we are about twenty miles out of Fronteras. We'll rest and travel by dark and be in Fronteras before day break."

"Huston, your mules got us here." Gatewood knew were the credit belonged for the condition of the mules. He recalled

Napoleon being quoted, "An army marches on its stomach." The success of a forced march in the Sierra Madres depended on the quality of its mules.

Martine and Kateah found the squaws track. The trail was hot and led toward the Bavispe valley. Gatewood dispatched Old Tex to find Parker who was some ten miles behind them. Parker sent off a courier to find Captain Lawton's command, some sixty miles away.

George cut a white standard from substantial piece of flour sack he had been saving since they departed the Aras River.

Martine and Kateah trail left the Rio Moctezuma and crossed to the Bavispe valley. The scouts stopped as they saw the hot trail leading into a canyon. The canyon visibly narrowed at the entrance. They guessed the canyon would widen behind the slot entrance that was visible at a distance. As they drew closer they saw a pair of worn canvas pants draped over a nearby bush.

Within fifteen minutes, Gatewood and the rest of the party arrived.

Kateah said, "Only live in that canyon if Geronimo wants." For Kateah, it was statement of fact.

Looking at Gatewood, Martine said, "Go more only if you lead."

Gatewood looked at Martine. The canyon could conceal a large open area favored by Apaches on the run. However, Gatewood eyes saw no tracks other than the squaws. His gut didn't feel a hiding place beyond the slot opening.

"You and I will go," Gatewood said to Martine. Martine wasn't thrilled.

"George, if this turns sour, you get these men back with Parker."

"Here, time to fly the flour sack. All know you want to talk," Wratten said as he finished tying the flag to a short pole with three rawhide strips. "Sir, permission to

accompany ya as standard bearer."

Gatewood nodded. George elevated another notch on Gatewood's belt.

Martine picked up the squaws track, now six pack animals were visible, and followed the path directly into the slot.

Gatewood took the lead as they entered. His Winchester remained in its scabbard despite his desire to have it more readily available. His eyes scanned just below the rim, a favored place for crossfire. His mouth dried, every nerve was controlled but hyper-alert. But no one could mistake their mission.

The canyon opened but only about twenty yards wide. The three reminded spaced, but George replaced Gatewood on the point, the white flour sack standard flying in the breeze.

Geronimo took his good field glasses from his pouch and surveyed the party at considerable distance.

He turned to Naiche and asked, "What fool stay on our scent like hungry wolf? I know Coyoteros are on their land."

Naiche observed, "Too few for a war party."

The scouts were only working about three hundred yards ahead of the party of ten men. They moved like soldiers in columns of two but they did not appear as soldiers.

"Squaws leave crooked trail, yet there they are."

The trackers pulled up, dismounted and started to walk their mules. The man in front of the right dismounted, leaned against his mule and steadied himself. His walking gait was pained.

"Baychendaysen!" "Baychendaysen never stop never."

Naiche acknowledged the likelihood. Then, he said, "Find out who else is with him."

They sent two men to get a closer observation and they returned to their camp.

"Martine and Kateah scout, both have cousins with us. Nootahah talker 'Rat-ton rides next to Baychendaysen."

Geronimo thought, and then Naiche said, "Bring talker, you want to talk."

Geronimo shrugged his shoulders.

Naiche and Geronimo didn't know why Baychendaysen came. They were curious. They were hopeful.

Geronimo's camp was in a very high rocky position in the Teres Mountains just in the bend of the Bavispe River. Gatewood established a camp about three miles away near a cane break just off the river.

The river had cleared somewhat from the recent rains but was still muddy. Canteens were filled with the clearest possible water, the woolen coverings were soaked and the evaporation in the extremely dry air cooled the water inside the canteen. While carrying a slightly muddy taste, the cool river water was fine.

Look outs were posted by both camps in a fashion making the both camps easily aware of the presence of the other.

Martine and Kateah were sent to approach the Apache camp. The pair approached the camp site, Naiche, Geronimo and a half dozen braves met them.

"Anzhoo." Greetings seemed rather simultaneous.

Kateah said, "Baychendaysen brings a message from General Miles. He wishes to talk the message with you."

Naiche responded, "We knew from the size of your party you were not here to fight. Tell Baychendaysen he may come to my camp without concern."

Geronimo added, "Baychendaysen has been told he is always welcome in my camp."

Baychendaysen begin to move up the mountain the next morning. An unarmed Chiricahua met them. He restated Geronimo and Naiche messages from the previous day. He then said Geronimo recommended that they meet and discuss the matters where the river bends and there is grass, water, and shade. Geronimo said Lawton who was closing on Parker's camp site must remain there. "Lawton come no closer while we talk."

All were acceptable and reasonable terms.

The party made its way to the bend in the river. It was indeed quite grassy and shady.

Unexpectedly, armed Chiricahuas appeared on the slopes around them. They began to move down toward them. Everyone's anxiety level shot up, except for Bay'che. He knew these people on an individual basis. He ordered releasing the horses to graze to carry on and continue with preparation for a meal.

At one minute they seemed completely surrounded. The next minute the Chiricahuas were finding places to put their rifles and spread blankets in the shade.

Geronimo was the last to arrive. He just appeared in the canebrake and twenty feet from where Bay'che was sitting. He laid down his Winchester rifle. He walked to Bay'che.

Geronimo said, "Anzhoo, Baychendaysen."

"Anzhoo, Geronimo."

"Soon I try to teach you say my name."

"And I will again try to learn"

Both smiled.

They shook hands. In a distinctive sense, the men were pleased to see each other.

"Your eyes are finding the back of your head," Geronimo said. "I worry about you health."

Bay'che said, "I envy you yours. You seem to be well." He paused and said, "As to my eyes, I know if seek you I'd best grow eyes in the back of my head."

The stifled laughs gave way from the Chiricahuas who understood adequate English.

Naiche joined them.

"We are tired, too many braves dead, too many women and children ill," he said.

"I know."

"Do you have whiskey? We drank much mescal the squaws brought."

"No, I don't but I wouldn't give it to you if I did." Baychendaysen replied, "You should be cautious, the Mexicans will poison the mescal to kill you."

Geronimo responded, "Mexican drink from each bottle before squaw pack it."

Baychendaysen's lips tightened as he nodded in approval.

Geronimo was surrounded by armed bucks while Bay'che and his men went about the duties of peace emissaries.

There was one common mess prepared. Neither group had a great deal of food.

Bay'che group had flour, bacon and coffee while the Chiricahuas had some jerked horse meat and mescal cakes. Most importantly for this gathering, Bay'che had fifteen pounds of dry tobacco and cigarette papers.

They sat, ate, smoked and spoke in a most friendly fashion.

Sitting in a circle, the gathering commenced.

On Baychendaysen's cue, George Wratten joined the circle.

"I believe you know Mr. George Wratten. I ask him to help me understand Nootahah. I can talk to you as we just spoke, but what we have to say is too important for a misunderstood word to bring a misunderstanding. The message is not long but it is very important to the future of the Chiricahua, to so many of the Nootahah.

Baychendaysen continued speaking, "I will read you the message from General Miles. I am to read it exactly as it is written, speaking every word on the paper."

Baychendaysen slowly turned looking at each man, lingering with Geronimo and Naiche.

As serious and restrained as a man can be, Baychendaysen read the statement and then paused. George translated into the dialect. Since the pair had rehearsed it many times, it had a natural flow.

"Surrender and you will be sent to join the rest of your people in Florida, there to wait the decision of the President of the United States as to your final disposition. You will not be executed for your past acts. Accept these terms or fight it out to the bitter end."

Every man listened, watching Baychendaysen's every movement. Eyes often locked. The last sentenced translated, a stone silence fell around the circle.

Geronimo sat on the log next to Baychendaysen. He moved as close as he could get. Bay'che could feel Geronimo's revolver against his hip.

Geronimo whispered, "Sure you don't have any whiskey?"

Suspecting the hangover symptoms to be genuine, Baychendaysen quietly answered, "No, but I'd give you a sip if I did."

The stunned hush remained. The terms were harsh.

Geronimo's focus moved from Baychendaysen to Wratten to the group.

"Last evening we sat in council and made medicine. This war grows old. Our children have known no safety. Our women are barren. We are tired and with many wounds."

Baychendaysen understood the message but George translated.

"We were happy to see a man we trust come to talk in peace. We would leave the warpath if we are allowed to return to the reservation, take up the farms we held when we left, get same rations and supplies we need to farm. We are given exemptions from punishment for what we have done."

Baychendaysen knew he could end it all by agreeing to those terms. He knew he could not.

He said, "I cannot change what General Miles has sent me to say." Baychendaysen turned to Geronimo, fixed a good lock on his eyes and said, "I know you have not met him. I believe none of you have met him. I do know that many of you know me and I tell you that General Miles intends to keep his word."

Baychendaysen waited for George to translate and then he continued, "General Miles promises that this will be your last chance to surrender. General Miles promises that if you do not surrender the war will continue until you are all killed or captured. He promises that the captured will not be offered terms this liberal."

Naiche bristled. Baychendaysen stared at him in a peculiar fashion that was firm yet understanding. Naiche shoulders drooped, an involuntary response for such a proud man and such a fierce warrior.

For the next hour or so, Geronimo told the story of the Chiricahua and the white eyes. He emphasized the betrayals, injustices, and theft. He spoke of the harsh treatment from the Indian Agents. Baychendaysen had heard Geronimo cite the legitimate grievances beginning in his wikiup on San Carlos. Then, he made a compelling argument that the Nootahah were the first settlers of the Southwest. Bay'che was intrigued.

Geronimo concluded, "We can give up more to survive in our country. We can not give up all."

Geronimo stood. He placed his hand on Baychendaysen's shoulder and nodded. Bay'che nodded.

The Chiricahua milled about for a few moments and then gathered for a private council on the other side of the canebrake. Gatewood walked with his bear paw stick, trying to relieve the soreness from sitting on the log so long. Feeling he needed his full wits about him this day, he did not seek relief in the brew Leonard Wood had prepared.

George walked with him, steadying a couple of times as rocks rolled and turned his feet quicker than he could regain his balance.

"Do you think they will take the offer?" George asked.

"A proud man can foolishly choose to die. The Apache has always believed in living to fight another fight." Gatewood took a deep breath and said, "I like many of these men. They are Apache. I hope they choose to live."

They walked downstream a bit more, "The Coyoteros were fortune to have Alchesay. He knew how to win and keep the prize Coyotero land. He will lead them long and well."

George said, "I wish I could have made one scout with Alchesay and Baychendaysen just to say I did."

He smiled and patted George on the back and said, "Thank you, George. I hope today the Chiricahua choose life."

The Chiricahua conference finished about noon. Everyone had coffee and ate what was left for morning.

After lunch the circle reformed. Geronimo started, "We do not want to give all our land to white eyes that came from the east to steal it. We will give up all of it except for our reservation. Take us to our reservation or fight."

Geronimo issued his ultimatum.

Gatewood knew he couldn't comply and he didn't have the authority change Miles Ultimatum of surrender or die. He knew he couldn't fight or escape.

Then unexpectedly Naiche, who had said little to this point stood and said, "If we keep warring or not, your party is safe as long as you do not start the fight. You came as our friend not as our enemy. You can leave in peace when we are done."

"Naiche, I came hoping no more friends died. I do not know what I would do if faced with your position. I hope we both see many more days."

Wratten translated. He recognized that Gatewood had woven traditional Apache wisdom of living to fight another day in the response. He was impressed.

Baychendaysen realized that he had to make them believe that the reservation was no longer a desirable option. He decided to take a liberty with the truth, a truth he believed might have in fact happen by now, a pending truth that would become a truth but was not yet a truth. He found humor in his attempt to justify his exaggeration.

"The reservation is not as you recall it. All the Chiricahua were to be moved to Florida." He turned to Naiche, "Your mother and your daughter were to be among to the first to be moved."

Squaring up on the log, he said, "Go to Florida and you may join them. At San Carlos you will be living side by side with the Coyoteros." The Coyoteros and the Chiricahua were time-honored enemies.

Geronimo snapped to and looked Baychendaysen squarely in the eye. "Do you tell the truth?"

Bay'che responded, "I do not use Mexican tricks. I have been told they were moving to Holbrook to the train station. I have not been told they were loaded in the train cars. It is General Miles intention to remove them and I know General Miles."

Naiche asked, "How could this General Miles capture them and remove them without someone getting away to tell us."

"Naiche, I do not know. It came as a surprise to me also. But it does seem to have been done. It is hard to say how such crafty things are done. Perhaps others helped so that they might remain in the Arizona Territory."

Geronimo said, "We must discuss this."

Naiche clearly agreed.

The Chiricahua moved to the other side of the cane brake.

Gatewood turned to Wratten and said, "George, see that Kateah understands."

George understood and Kateah, who owed his very life to General Crook, understood the importance of this misstatement. He also knew that could well be truth by the time they returned.

When Kateah's cousin approached him later, he simply said, "I have heard it to be so, if not by now, soon."

Gatewood, Wratten, Old Tex and Frank Huston sat along the river. Every effort was made to appear relaxed. They ate and smoked, drank warm muddy water from the river.

Gatewood took the smooth worn stone from his pocket. He turned the stone in his fingers and considered the Apache situation.

In the late afternoon, the group re-assembled. Geronimo announced that they would not surrender on those terms. He asked Baychendaysen if he could go present those terms to General Miles.

"I do not know where General Miles is, but mostly it would do no good. General Miles has made up his mind as to what he would do. He told me when he sent me to offer you a way to join your families and friends," Baychendaysen hesitated as if reluctant to restate the option of failing to surrender. "He is determined. It is surrender or a fight to the end."

Further, Gatewood knew but would not admit that the days of hard riding, if he could find General Miles, would bring on the sickness and render him unfit for service for some time.

Naiche and Geronimo conferred. Naiche said, "We shall talk more, all night talk and we will find a beef and eat well tonight"

"I will not talk all night. Our matter is far too important to make an error from the dullness not sleeping would bring to all of us. There is no beef to be found near here. I will send to a message to the small group who accompanies me to send a pack mule. We can a feast of mule, beans and flat bread."

They agreed. The afternoon would be spent talking and then they would eat well into the night.

The circle smoked and talked. Then, Geronimo started to ask pointed questions about General Miles.

"I know Crook well. I could talk surrender with him. What kind of man is this that will not talk?"

"General Crook was removed because he was seen by the Washington President as being too willing to talk. The President sent a man who would follow the letter of his terms. I have told you those terms. Surrender or fight to the end."

There was a silence.

Then, Geronimo continued asking about General Miles age, his height, his weight, color of his eyes and his hair.

Is his voice pleasant to listen to? Does he talk much or does he talk little? Does he look you in the eyes or down at the ground or does he look toward the clouds? Does he have many friends among his own people? Do his men like him? Has he fought other tribes?

Short answers were not acceptable. Baychendaysen did his best to answer each inquiry as truthfully as possible, without exaggeration.

Geronimo concluded, "This General Miles must be a good man, the Great Washington Father sent him and he sent you all this distance to us." Geronimo looked deeply into Baychendaysen's eyes, as steely blue as ever, and said, "You know us well and you chose to come this long hard way to us at a time your health hides from you."

"We will take the night with ourselves and the medicine men to look into the future."

It was agreed they would return to the cane brake in the morning.

Naiche stood with Geronimo and asked Baychendaysen, "Stay for a moment."

Wratten looked at Gatewood and Gatewood motioned him to leave them.

Alone, Geronimo said, "We want your advice. Consider yourself one of us and not a white eye. Remember what has been said here. As an Apache, what would you advise us to do in these circumstances? Should we surrender or should we fight it out?"

The request was unexpected. Baychendaysen remembered his mission. "I would trust General Miles and take him at his word. Good or bad, he will keep his word."

Baychendaysen did not want to understate the situation. He continued, "General Miles is bringing in more troops by railroad every day. There will soon be more white eye soldiers in Mexico and the territories than I can count."

"As I came to know you, I have always been a friend." He felt an odd regret. He knew these men are Chiricahuas. They were born and bred nomadic raiders, pure warriors. "If I thought it was best, I would advise you fight it out. I know it is a fight you do not have the numbers to win."

Baychendaysen took a deep breath, felt an increasing soberness as he spoke, "I must council peace on the only terms offered."

Geronimo and Naiche had listened solemnly. They felt somber.

"Baychendaysen, you have spoken a truth. We will go back to the mountain stronghold. We will again council and ask our medicine men to again look into the future. We must see if your truth is our truth. I will let you know in the morning."

The handshakes had a firm warm grip. They were grips that be exchanged only between friends in serious times.

Gatewood mounted his mule and joined his party who waited just downstream. There was little conversation on the three mile ride back to our camp.

Captain Lawton had arrived in Gatewood's camp with Lieutenant Parker and about forty of Parker's men.

Mexican beans with some meat of some sort laced with a substantial dose of peppers, scooped from the tin with flour tortillas were tasty enough. Gatewood provided an oral report to Lawton over their dinner.

"Can we trust them," Lawton asked.

"As much as they can trust us," Gatewood responded.

The men sipped coffee and talked of other things and other times.

While his body was unusually stiff and he was getting little support from a swollen left ankle, his pain had moderated. A dose of Leonard Wood's brandy mix brought a deep early sleep.

He awakened about three in the morning, the pain in his hips and right knee had gotten more intense. He took a small dose of Wood's brandy, laid back and looked into the night sky. It was a wet moon yielding bright stars across the sky. He listened to the running water, thought about what might need to be said the coming day. Then, he rested.

Shortly after the morning meal, a small party of Apaches approached the camp.

"Baychendaysen," they called until they saw him.

"Anzhoo," Baychendaysen called to them. George Wratten was now by his side, Martine quickly joined as they walked toward the party.

"Anzhoo," the bucks replied.

"Anzhoo Baychendaysen," called Geronimo as he stepped to the front of the group.

The Apaches unsaddled their horses and laid their weapons on the saddles.

Geronimo came forward, still wearing his pistol under his coat, and begin to shake hands.

"Baychendaysen, say again the terms you were to declare"

"Surrender and you will be sent to join the rest of your people in Florida, there to wait the decision of the President of the United States as to your final disposition. You will not be executed for your past deeds. Accept these terms or fight it out to the bitter end."

"Again, tell me of this General Miles."

Baychendaysen repeated his answers to Geronimo's lengthy earlier inquiries as best he could.

Geronimo grasped Baychendaysen's hand. "If the American commander here will accompany us and protect us from the Mexicans and other American troops, we will meet this General Miles in the America and surrender to him there. Baychendaysen's men will stay with us and will sleep us at night. We will not surrender our weapons until we can surrender them to General Miles."

Given the land to cross, the number of Mexican and American soldiers in the field seeking Geronimo, Naiche and their band this was a most reasonable request.

"I can agree to this. Captain Lawton must agree for his men to accompany us," Baychendaysen said. This time Baychendaysen reached for Geronimo's hand and said, "This will be hard for you, but I am happy you choose to live."

"Captain Lawson, this is Geronimo of the Chiricahua."

"Geronimo, Captain Henry Lawson of the United States Army."

"Geronimo, sit and eat"

Captain Lawson agreed to all of Geronimo's terms.

Lawson said, "Now we smoke. I assure you Lieutenant Gatewood brought enough tobacco to conference with everyone in Mexico."

Captain Lawson was not a smoker. Gatewood rolled him one in the brown, stiff paper.

Geronimo rolled a cigarette as neatly as any frontiersman. He chuckled as Lawson did his best to manage the cigarette. At first perturbed, Lawson's humor found him and he burst out laughing as he almost burnt a hole in his canvas pants.

"Men, I believe smoking and laughing seal a deal better than only smoking alone."

As much as Gatewood had struggled to accept Lawson back on the Rio Arro, he liked the smiling man with a smoldering hole in his pants much better.

The men talked. It was decided a meeting at Skeleton Canyon, about sixty miles southeast of Fort Bowie.

The balance of Geronimo's party, about forty men, women and children, moved down near the camp site. Food was short until Lawton's pack train found it way to us, having meandered off the trail.

On the morning of August 28, 1886, Lawton's command broke camp and began their march toward Skeleton Canyon. As they passed the cane brakes Gatewood realized that to conference with Geronimo and Naiche he had followed a path south down the east side of the Sierra Madre Occidentals and then back north along the west side. He now started his trek back with sixty miles of the place he crossed the border into Mexico.

Gatewood and George Wratten traveled with the Chiricahua as had been agreed. Geronimo and Naiche had agreed to peace but everyone in the whole of Lawton's troop knew there was a number of people, Mexican and American who would accept nothing less than Geronimo's death.

Gatewood would later hear that there was even a plot among some of officers in Lawton's command but they made the mistake of approaching Leonard Wood who promptly but a halt to the plan.

Two days into the march what seemed the most unlikely of events begin to unfold. The troop had just halted to go into camp when an upset Mexican commander suddenly appeared with about two hundred infantry.

Captain Lawton sent an officer out to explain the situation to the Mexican commander. Their conversation was visibly animated.

Lawton's emissary returned and said, "The man says we stole his reward. He had invested much Mescal in these Apaches, get them drunk and kill them. It seems he believes Lieutenant Gatewood got to his drunken Apaches before he could. Now he says we are on his territory and he is going to take our prisoners from us."

Captain Lawton beckoned to Gatewood and Parker. He apprised them of the situation.

"Well, Lieutenant Gatewood it appears you have stolen this Mexican's prisoners."

Lawton voice was sounded quite serious until he said, "Do you wish to give them back and apologize?"

Lawton's dry wit had captured another victim.

Lawton's actual plan surprised Gatewood even more. "Lieutenant, take a squad of Parker's men, your men and the soon-to-be prisoners and make a run for the border. I will stand off the Mexicans. We will fight if we have to. I'll keep Martine to help track you.

When told of the situation and the solution, Geronimo and Naiche were surprised. The squaws were saddled and packed within a heartbeat. With their future prisoners, they made a dash for the border, through brush and uneven terrain. The troop maintained a ten mile pace. It took just over two hours for the party to cross well into United States territory.

Within another hour Leonard Wood caught up them. Wood enjoyed relaying the story of Captain Lawton convincing the Mexican Commander that Geronimo had surrendered in the United States. Lawton's order was for us to keep moving further away from the border, make camp at nightfall.

Lawton and his men joined them before noon the next day.

Gatewood pulled George away from the group. He said, "Tomorrow we should enter Guadalupe Canyon, it is the only water for some eight to ten mile. Naiche is concerned because they killed a number of Lawton's troopers there in the spring. Just keep a weather eye."

Wratten nodded and added, "Both camps are tense."

Gatewood nodded and said, "Let's just be very careful."

George nodded.

The tension continued to mount. Leonard Wood again came to Gatewood expressing his concern of a plot to kill all the Apaches.

"I'll talk to the Captain. I think its time and better me than you. You have to stay in this command."

Wood agreed.

Gatewood made his way to Lawton and expressed the concern.

"I would hope it was not true. However, the Apache have been our enemies for many years now. We have hated them and feared them. We have killed them and they have killed us. We have buried the butchered remains of families, of children."

Lawton's felt his emotions spiraling and he managed to stop.

Lawton's voice more controlled, he continued, "Lieutenant, I detest those savage beasts I've vowed to protect. But if I protect them, get them to General Miles no one else has to die."

"Gatewood, I had heard many stories of you before I met you in Mexico. I didn't understand you then and I only understand you a little better now. I do know this, if I ever have to send a man into Hell to retrieve wronged soul, it is you I would send."

There was a reflective silence between the two men.

"We didn't get off to the best of starts on the Rio Aras did we?" Gatewood mused.

Lawton smiled, "We both had our orders." The Captain wanted to ask Gatewood about enduring pain but didn't, maybe another day. "Lieutenant, what should the Captain do?"

"Sleep in our camp with us."

Lawton released a deep guttural grunt, nodded his head and said, "Of course."

Before dinner, most every man in camp saw Captain Henry W. Lawton toss his bedroll over his shoulder and carry it into the almost prisoners camp.

He shook hands with Naiche and his young wife, with Geronimo and said, "I decided I'd join you for dinner as well."

There were disgruntled soldiers, but not murderous plot was unleashed, foiled by food and good night's sleep.

On September 2, 1886, they arrived at Skeleton Canyon. A number of regulars were already camped in the canyon and more were arriving. There were enough troopers to concern Geronimo, so he sought out Baychendaysen.

The Apaches made camp deeper into the canyon, not far from where a spring fed on stream and joined a second stream. The spring water was cold and crystal clear.

Geronimo found a roost on a rocky ledge that gave him a view of the San Bernardino Valley spreading out below.

Baychendaysen surveyed the campsite and said, "I don't believe even Coyote, the trickster, could surprise you here."

"I am old and have grown weary of surprises."

Baychendaysen gave an understanding nod of agreement.

"It is a private camp and every one can cleanse themselves, even the women and children."

Wratten stepped up and said, "Lawton is coming up."

Baychendaysen nodded, watched as the one small party moved up stream. "It took me a while to understand how clean the Nootahah are with themselves."

Wratten responded, "It is a religious thing with them. I learned some about it while I was trading at San Carlos."

Gatewood said, "You should spend a few summer months with the Navajo. I didn't know the human body could smell so bad." Gatewood thought a bit, "The inside of a hogan was god awful."

Lawton walked up and Gatewood said, "Captain, we're discussing the relative hygiene between the Apache and the Navajo. Do you believe there is military paper there?"

"Lieutenant, you have obviously been in the sun too long. I'd suggest that cottonwood shade as a remedy." He pointed to a cottonwood tree near the stream.

Lawton and Gatewood took advantage of every opportunity to talk. Lawton was increasingly interested in sharing their viewpoints as to the nature of man.

This day Lawton finally ask, "Gatewood, help me understand the Apache at war."

"Apaches? The Apache is a warrior. War, raiding and plundering and the chase are their chief occupations. It is their profession and their recreation. War – they do want to do the greatest damage to the enemy with the least possible risk. They will work to create situations where the odds are in their favor. Kill your enemy, steal his goods and save yourself to fight another day. When being chased, they will separate and reassemble."

"Another thing you need to know. An Apache never forgives a betrayal. When I was Military Commandant for the Coyoteros I found feuds going back two hundred years or more."

On the morning of September 3, 1886, there had been considerable activity in the main camp. Couriers were coming and going at an unusual pace.

In the early afternoon, Geronimo loudly called, "Bay'che." He motioned for him to come to the perch.

Baychendaysen and Wratten scrambled up the slope and into the perch. A stabbing cramping pain pulled Bay'che down and he eased his way back to the bottom. Wratten through Geronimo's field glasses saw General Miles contingent making its way toward the canyon.

"Lieutenant, it is General Miles and he has brought a damn parade with him."

The parade turned out mostly to be newspaper men and photographers.

Geronimo immediately sought the conference with General Miles. Miles was no less eager than Geronimo to get the surrender concluded. Naiche was found and hustled along to the gathering site.

General Miles told his aides, "As many trees and as much shade as possible."

This brought some objection from the photographers, a compromise was reached.

Geronimo and Naiche sat on a log in a shady creek bed while Miles sat on log positioned up the bank, across but above the

Apache chiefs. Gatewood and Wratten were seated behind and on each side of Geronimo.

It was not the conference Geronimo had hoped would occur.

Miles simply restated the ultimatum. Then, ask Geronimo and Naiche to state their decision. Geronimo turned to Gatewood and said in Apache, "Tell him I will surrender."

Despite the fact he knew Gatewood was very proficient in basic Apache, Miles abruptly said, "I would prefer Mr. Wratten interpret for us."

George looked at Gatewood and spoke in an almost inaudible Apache, "Not a friend I'd say."

It was clear that General Miles had no intention of sharing whatever glory there was in the surrender of Geronimo. He especially did not intend to share any with Lieutenant Gatewood.

The surrender was simple and direct and unconditional.

Miles stood up and ordered, "These two will proceed post-haste with my party back to Fort Bowie." He pointed to Geronimo and Naiche. "The other prisoners will follow with the main body."

Miles introduced Captain Lawton to the gathered press as the commander in charge of Geronimo's capture. He introduced Martine and Kateah as the scouts who had located Geronimo's camp site.

"General, I understood Lieutenant Charles Gatewood was in charge of a special tactical group you sent to find Geronimo and that Lieutenant Gatewood conducted the negotiations in Mexico." The reporter from the San Francisco Chronicle was informed and had a basic dislike for General Miles. He took pleasure in finding Miles self-aggrandizing statements to be less than candid. The reporter smiled.

"I will clarify Lieutenant Gatewood's role in this mission at a future time."

The reporter from the Tucson Citizen looked at Geronimo and asked, "I understand that Lieutenant Gatewood is the only American who could have approached your camp and lived."

Planning to cut off any questions to the prisoners, the General said, "No questions --."

Before he finished Geronimo said, "Yes, only Gatewood." This was the only time Gatewood ever heard Geronimo use his name.

The conference was ended.

Miles aide, Alden Smith, later saw the several reporters gathered around Martine and Kateah. They were visibly talkative and enjoying these seemingly important men listening to their descriptions.

When brought to General Miles attention, he broke up the conference and chastised the reporters for conducting unauthorized interviews.

Geronimo knew he had gone from feared enemy to defeated enemy. He turned and said to Baychendaysen, "You told me the truth."

Geronimo was hustled away.

Naiche and Hoazinne

SEVENTEEN

FADE TO BLACK

On September 4, 1886, Captain Henry Lawton and Assistant Surgeon Leonard Wood were among those assigned to accompany the surrendered Chiricahua prisoners to Fort Marion, Florida. George Wratten was going to serve as an interpreter. Geronimo, now forty seven years old and his wife Shegha as well as Naiche, now thirty-five, and his seventeen year old wife, Haozinne, were on the manifest.

There were four unexpected late additions to the roster of prisoners. Kateah and Martine and their wives were deported to Florida.

Gatewood received an unsigned note from General Miles to that effect. He dressed and dashed to the Adjunct's office, bursting through the door.

"Sergeant, there must be a mistake here. May I...."

The Sergeant allowed him to go no further. He pointed to the newspapers on the table. The San Francisco Chronicle, the Tucson Citizen and a number of other papers had written detailed articles on Geronimo's surrender. They minimized General Miles role and emphasized Lieutenant Gatewood and Captain Lawton's role. Martine and Kateah were cited as eyewitness sources.

After guiding him on the quick tour through the Chronicle article, he said, "It is speculated these had much to do with the General's decision."

"Sergeant, thank you. I apologize for my initial conduct."

"Lieutenant, this came for you."

Gatewood took the envelope and left.

Conceding to his pain, Gatewood sat in a chair on the Adjunct's porch and opened the envelope.

"Good morning, Lieutenant Gatewood." Old Tex said.

"Good morning, Tex. Where are you headed?"

"Drawn my money and headed to Globe. Wednesday is nickel night at that fancy whorehouse they got down there."

Gatewood would have laughed had he not seen the serious intent on Tex face.

"Well, Tex after our trip to Mexico I do believe you have earned some leave time."

"Now Lieutenant ya take care of ya self."

Gatewood opened the envelope. Miles had kept his word. He appointed First Lieutenant C. B. Gatewood, Sixth Cavalry, as the aide-de-camp to the Brigadier General commanding. The possibility of promotion and a positive career move lifted his spirits. Georgie would like the assignment at Fort Whipple, near Prescott in the Arizona Territory. He considered it to be the most moderate of the diverse Arizona climates.

He so missed Georgie, Little Charles and Hugh.

But little changed, a Celebration Ball was scheduled for Tucson. Gatewood was to be one of the primary honorees. At the last moment, General Miles assigned his aide-de-camp to remain in the offices so that any necessary business could be handled. Although Miles found himself making some awkward explanations as to Gatewood's absence, he found it preferable to Gatewood's presence.

Gatewood was still a member of Sixth Cavalry surrounded by men of the Fourth Cavalry. He was still viewed as a "Crook Man." All of his friends from Fort Apache were scattered now. Again, he found himself isolated.

He rocked, reluctant to admit it but the excursion into Mexico in pursuit of Geronimo had broken his health. He would never fully recover.

There are things in life from which recovery seems impossible, the wound leaves scars so deep into the heart that the ache feels as if it will never leave. On October 6, 1886, six month old Hugh McCullough Gatewood died of an unexplained illness. Carrying Georgia's maiden name, he had been known as "Little Mac." While he had been lethargic for several days, it was like he just died.

Georgie had taken him to one of the Fort Stanton surgeons. She blamed what she felt was negligence on the part of the physician for Little Mac's death.

Gatewood made the trip from Fort Bowie to Fort Stanton as rapidly as possible. It is impossible to know which had the deepest need for the other. They held each other for the longest of times. It was if they believed holding each other in a long forceful grasp could heal their pain. They clung to each other, time was irrelevant. They would only have to deal with the reality when they let go of each other. So, each clung to the other.

An early cold snap moved through the mountains of southern New Mexico. Charles built a fire in the fire place. He started to bring the rockers in from the porch but the pain made him falter. Together he and Georgie carried the rockers inside. They covered themselves with a large quilt, she snuggled against him.

Georgie, at her own pace, told him of everything that had happened. He listened. At some time late in the conversation, he said, "Love, I do not know where you found the strength to manage it. I do not believe I could have been so strong."

"Mostly I took my advice from you. You didn't know I was asking but somehow you always answered me from wherever you happened to be. Also, it let me know you were safe if not well."

Charles didn't respond because he didn't know how to respond. Georgie's voice gave a tangible aspect to an otherwise mystical belief.

"Charles, I now know that when you are gone, you are still here. I do not know how but I know you are."

Charles thought on it while Georgie slept. Certainly, they had spent hours talking. It was their favorite pastime. Perhaps, you can come to know someone so well that you will never not know them, never not have them with you. He did not know.

The next morning Georgie ask, "Do you want to see his grave?"

"Yes."

"I buried him with his book from Mr. Magruder. I wrote all the family names inside it and sealed it as very best I could." Georgie looked at Charles, "I want him to know who his people are."

"You did well, my love."

Charles did not want his young son buried in the southwest. He would talk with Georgie about that at another time.

Gatewood had taken many long treks in his career, but moving Georgia to Fort Whipple was one of the longest treks in his life. Leaving Little Mac buried at Fort Stanton was agonizing.

Traveling with a company of Sixth Cavalry headed to Fort Verde, accompanying four other families changing post, they took the southern route, through Lordsburg and Tucson before turning north to Fort Whipple was the best route. The desert route north from Tucson was pleasant. The saguaro cactus was majestic. Then, they climbed out of the valley toward Whipple and the Territorial Capitol of Prescott, into the pines and soft drifting snow.

They were assigned quarters befitting his position.

"God, Reed did you hear Gatewood's got his ass in a crack with Miles."

"Dorsey, I think everyone in the Fourth and the Sixth have heard about it."

"I hear Miles was trying to pay his personal servants by listing them as packers and getting them paid with government checks," Reed said.

"I guess they were packing his steaks and drinks to him. Guess that isn't the kind of packers the government pays," Dorsey smiled.

"Any way it seems the papers made their way up to Gatewood and he refused to sign them. Actually, wrote that it seemed signing them would be fraud and against the law."

Now Dorsey was laughing, "The man has stones in his pants bigger than that rock he carries in his shirt pocket."

Reed answered, "He is stubborn as any mule he ever rode if he thinks he's right and if it is wrong it is wrong." Reed continued, "Anyway I heard Miles turned blood red when he was told. He ordered Gatewood to sign the papers and Gatewood told him he could not order him to knowingly break the law."

"I'm going to assume the servants didn't get paid by the government."

"They didn't and I hear Miles is hunting every way possible to get even with Gatewood. Bay'che does have a way of pissing people off. And the General can be a petty jealous man."

Dorsey said, "Funny, in the field Gatewood would bend any rule to get the man he was after. Put him in an orderly civilized world and he wants the rules and regulations followed all the way."

Reed chuckled, "Right now, Miles is satisfying himself by declining every transfer that Gatewood submits."

McPherson laughed, "Like you said, he is a petty jealous little boy all dressed up in his soldier suit."

Reed joined the laughter and said, "The General does like to dress up in his finery."

Dorsey continued, "I'll bet that is getting close to submitting an application a day. He's a member of the Sixth Cavalry trapped in the Fourth Cavalry. I'd say he's really cork screwed himself on this one." Dorsey changed the subject, "Is his health any better?"

Reed replied, "No, it is almost completely broken. I hear he can hardly move without that staff Kuruk made him."

"Suppose we could work around and get him a medical leave?"

"We could try."

Again, Gatewood's unyielding sense of morality had gotten him isolated and professionally alone. Those who knew him best, his friends from Fort Apache and Fort Wingate were now scattered across the country. Regardless of their current postings, there was a regular exchange of letters.

On the personal front, the marriage of Charles and Georgie Gatewood was the envy of every wife at Fort Whipple and Fort Verde.

Given the more peaceful times, Georgie, Charles and Junior were able to frequently take extended horseback rides around the country side. The Verde River Valley was filled with unnamed side canyon with beautiful clear flowing streams.

They would travel Crook's Trail to Fort Verde. The stagecoach station at town of Camp Verde was located at the southern tip of a u-shaped adobe structure. They would rent a room. Each room had a door that opened into the patio that filled the u-shaped center. During the day, they explored some ancient ruins to the northwest or traveled further northwest to view the extraordinarily striking red rock formations. In the evening, they lounged in the U

Other times, Georgie would spread a quilt in the shade while Charles taught Junior how to fish. Nannie had been thoughtful enough to bring two fly rods when she returned Junior. The two males fished, Georgie rested and read.

In the midst of the u-shaped structure were tables and lounge chairs under elm and locust trees. They would talk, always including Junior in the conversation, until he went to sleep. Then, Georgie would carry him to bed as Charles relocated chairs near their room.

As a family, they swam and bathed in the cool water and great privacy of the streams.

On a lovely early fall night in 1889, they were sitting in the U and enjoying glimpses of the stars.

Georgie's head rested against his arm. She sat up a bit and whispered to him, "Love, I know you have a man's needs and you have been too long without my full company."

Without hesitation she continued, "I believe we should try to have another baby."

Hugh's loss would never leave them, but they found the path back toward life.

Georgie was shortly with child.

Charles' illness was becoming increasingly unrelenting.

Within the year Gatewood received notice he had been granted an extended medical leave of absence to seek treatment.

Charles B. Gatewood, Georgia McCullough Gatewood and Charles B. Gatewood, Jr. boarded the east bound train in Flagstaff. Georgia sister, Nannie, had come to help the pregnant Georgie move and was traveling with them.

Georgie was pleased they were returning to Frostburg. She did not want to have another child attended to by Army Surgeons. She felt a twinge of guilt as the thought passed because she felt Walter and Dorsey should not be painted with the same brush as the others she knew.

The rhythmic clank of the rails, each cycle moving them closer to Maryland, to Frostburg, brought them a sense of finality. The long trip across country gave them time to discuss the past, the present and the future.

As they left Kansas, the rails cut a path through the dense oak forest of the Missouri Ozarks. It was enough like the eastern foothills of the Appalachian Mountains around Frostburg, Georgie found them visually pleasing.

When she could contain herself no longer, she said, "Look Charles, a land with water, grass and trees. The country side is green, not the everlasting browns of sand and rock."

Charles leaned against her to peer out the window. The setting western sun highlighted the divergent but complimentary hues of the countryside.

"This land looks calmer, more at peace with itself," Georgie observed.

"Georgie, I brought you to such a cold and unforgiving land. I wanted you with me so desperately, to share my life. I couldn't even imagine now hard a life it would be for you." His voice carried tones of regret and apology.

The landscape darken, the lamps in the coach were being lit.

Georgie realized her husband had misunderstood her remark.

"Charles, Charles." She paused. "You didn't just give me a life in the territories, you rescued me. I was never like the other girls in Frostburg. Charles. We shared a glorious, immense journey together." She took a deep sigh, "Oh, what an adventure we lived! We knew great joys and felt horrible losses and together we survived."

She reached out and touched his hand, "I know great love and passionate romance. Very few women will ever even glimpse what I have had. What tales we will have to tell our children and our grandchildren!"

Georgie has so much more she wanted to say but you are only allowed to say so much, even to your husband. She knew she had been tested and found to be worthy.

In the dimly lit coach, Charles took her hand tightly.

He whispered in her ear, "I love you Georgia McCullough."

She squeezed his hand and they listened to the rails.

The conductor checked their tickets and handed them blanket.

Charles spread the blanket over their laps.

They never returned to Arizona, but it never really left them.

Emily Natalie Gatewood was born on July 28, 1890 in Frostburg, Maryland.

In April 1891, the military officially acknowledged his role in the end of last Apache War.

"In the year, 1886, First Lieutenant Charles B. Gatewood, 6th Cavalry, commanding Chiricahua Indian scouts: For bravery in boldly and alone riding into Geronimo's camp of hostile Apache Indians in Arizona and demanding their surrender."

In December of 1890, Gatewood's regiment was ordered to the Dakotas. His health had only continued its steady decline. The period of the Sioux Ghost Dance had concluded, so he had been hopeful of some other assignment.

General Crook's unexpected death in early 1890 and the appointment of General Miles as his replacement gave Gatewood some concern. The Commander of the Army west of the Mississippi River had considerable power.

Gatewood had most recently applied for a position at West Point and as a recruiting officer. He was given neither position and ordered to return to frontier duty. The Johnson County War was raging in Wyoming. Gatewood was assigned to Fort McKinney.

Despite an extreme winter, the fighting increased. The large ranchers hired a literal army of gunmen and they were sent to wipe out the small ranchers. The army stepped in just in time to prevent a complete massacre. The hired killers were taken to Fort McKinney.

On May 18, 1892, a number of small ranchers set fire to the portion of the fort were the gunmen were being held. The fire was spread quickly. The entire fort was at risk.

In an effort to save the remainder of the fort, Gatewood led several men inside a building with kegs of gunpowder. The men stacked the kegs against the wall as the fire progressed. Gatewood intended to build an explosive wall designed to explode and blow out the fire. Gatewood ordered the men out as he continued to construct the wall. Two remained with him.

Just as they completed setting up the explosive wall, a section of the roof fell in and bits of burning wood began to drop around the three.

Gatewood refused to quit. He almost had the barrier constructed when the flames reached it. As he hobbled toward the door the explosion threw him into the door frame. Two of his men dragged him outside before the flames could reach him.

The wall exploded and successfully put out the fire. Gatewood lay on his back, put his arm around the staff Kuruk had craved, seeming to hug it and watched the fire extinguish itself. The balance of the fort was saved.

Gatewood lived. His injuries were severe and crippling. His left arm, hip and shoulder never healed properly. Routine movements brought pain.

From his hospital bed, Gatewood again applied for promotion to Captain. He was evaluated at Fort Custer, Montana in October of 1892. He was pronounced "Permanently Disqualified" to perform the duties of a Captain of Cavalry.

He returned to Frostburg and his family.

Charles Bare Gatewood was placed in an inactive position that allowed him to remain on the payroll. He was now the longest serving Lieutenant. As senior Lieutenant he believed it was just a matter of time until he was made Captain.

The promotion never came.

The love affair between Georgie and Charles Gatewood never withered, but rather flourished despite the circumstances. The hobbled Charles, supported by Kuruk's staff and the hand of the durable upright Georgie, they would slowly walk paths through the woods to the west of Georgie's family home. The couple would enter the forest and vanish from view.

They had three routes, each route taking them to place they could sit and watch a running stream. Charles had to stop frequently, to rest and gather his strength and wind. They talked and held hands. He still adored Georgie's soft Irish skin.

Neighbors with whom they shared the woods would hear their laughter.

Charles and Georgie never forgot the wispy warmth of a gentle lingering kiss.

Today Charles and Georgia Gatewood, Walter and Emilee Reed, Thomas and Bea Cruse are buried in Arlington National Cemetery. Dorsey and Ida McPherson are buried in nearby Rock Creek Cemetery in Washington, D.C.

Alchesay is buried on the Fort Apache Indian Reservation in Whiteriver, Arizona. Geronimo is buried in the Beef Creek Apache Cemetery at Fort Sill near Lawton, Oklahoma.

CPSIA information can be obtained at www.ICGtesting.com
Printed in the USA
LVOW06s0241190714

395088LV00005B/582/P